ONLY MINE

Recent Titles by Elizabeth Lowell from Severn House

ONLY HIS
ONLY MINE

ENCHANTED
FORBIDDEN
FORGET ME NOT
UNTAMED
A WOMAN WITHOUT LIES

ONLY MINE

Elizabeth Lowell

This title first published in Great Britain 2007 by
SEVERN HOUSE PUBLISHERS LTD of
9–15 High Street, Sutton, Surrey SM1 1DF,
by arrangement with Avon Books,
an imprint of HarperCollins Publishers.
This first hardcover edition published in the USA 2007 by
SEVERN HOUSE PUBLISHERS INC of
595 Madison Avenue, New York, N.Y. 10022.

British Library Cataloguing in Publication Data

Lowell, Elizabeth, 1944-
    Only mine
    1.   Frontier and pioneer life - West (U.S.) - Fiction
    2.   Love stories
    I.   Title
    813.5'4 [F]

    ISBN-13: 978-0-7278-6465-9

All Severn House titles are printed on acid-free paper.

Printed and bound in Great Britain by
MPG Books Ltd., Bodmin, Cornwall.

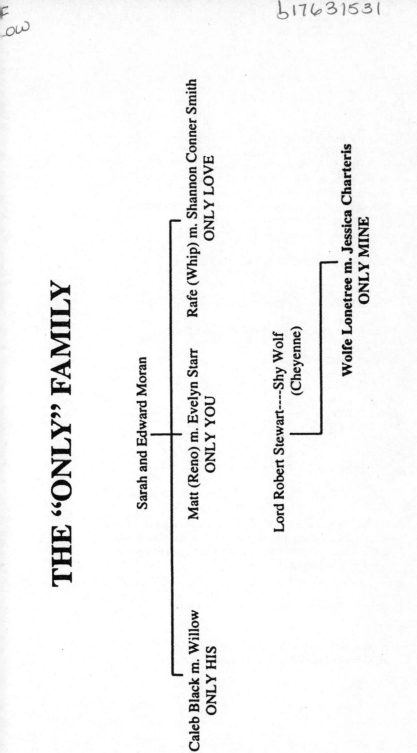

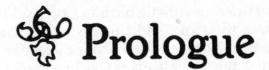 # Prologue

London 1867

"Marry you, elf?" Wolfe Lonetree laughed aloud as he twirled her across the dance floor. "Don't be ridiculous. What would a halfbreed mustang hunter do with an English aristocrat?"

"I'm Scots, not English," Jessica Charteris said automatically.

"I know." Wolfe smiled the way he used to years before, when he had tweaked her long braids to tease her. "You still rise to the bait just like a hungry trout."

Concealing the urgency and fear that lay beneath her flirtatious exterior, Jessica tilted back her head and smiled up at Wolfe.

"It would be a perfect union," she said coaxingly. "You have no need of heirs because you have neither lands nor titles to pass on. I have neither need of money nor desire for the marriage bed. We both enjoy silence and conversation together. We like to ride, to hunt, and to read in front of a fire. What more could be asked of a marriage?"

1

Wolfe's delighted laughter drew more than one glance from the titled lords and ladies who graced Jessica's twentieth birthday party. Wolfe ignored both the looks and the aristocratic company. The man they called the viscount's savage had learned long ago that his place was in America, not in England with its titles and cold disdain of his illegitimate birth.

"Marry you."

As Wolfe repeated the words again he shook his head, delighting in the company of the sprite whose hair was an auburn so deep that only direct sunlight revealed its hidden fire.

"Ah, elf, I've missed your quickness and mischief. I've laughed more in the few minutes I've been here than in the years without you. I'll tell Lord Robert to bring you with him on his next hunting trip. Or perhaps your future husband is a sportsman. Lord Gore, is that his name? I have yet to meet your fiancé. Is he here tonight?"

Fear made Jessica miss a step in the smooth waltz. Wolfe caught her and set her right with the same casual grace as he did everything.

"Forgive me," he murmured. "I'm clumsy tonight."

"You're like a great dark cat, and you know it as well as I. It was my clumsiness, not yours."

Though Jessica's voice was light, Wolfe sensed something just beneath her glittering surface. He watched her with dark eyes as they waltzed, hardly able to credit what he was seeing. Gone was the thin child with ice-blue eyes, burning red hair, and quick laughter. In her place was a stunning young woman who had an uncomfortable effect on his senses, an effect he had refused to acknowledge for years.

"A clumsy elf?" Wolfe asked. "Not possible, little one. Like a marriage between a halfbreed bastard and the Lady Jessica Charteris." He grinned, showing strong white teeth against the darkness of his skin. "What a lively mind you have. I must compliment you on your wit."

Jessica stumbled again, and again was caught by the easy strength of the man who was holding her within the civilized confines of the waltz. Yet even on the dance floor, Wolfe's power was apparent. She had always thought of his strength as a refuge, even when she hadn't been able to see him for years on end. She had lived on her memories, on the knowledge that there was one place on earth of refuge for her. Believing that had kept her from panic when her guardian insisted on the marriage to Lord Gore.

But now Wolfe's refuge no longer seemed available to Jessica, leaving her fighting for her life. Alone.

Dear God, what will I do? Wolfe must agree to the marriage! How can I convince him?

"Your fingers are cold, Jessi." Wolfe frowned. "You're trembling. Are you ill?"

The concern in Wolfe's expression and voice gave Jessica hope once more. He did care for her. She could see it in his unusual eyes, neither black nor yet blue, the color of deep twilight or sapphires in candlelight. She smiled with relief, not knowing how her smile lit her delicate face.

" 'Tis but excitement at seeing you, Wolfe. When you didn't answer Lady Victoria's letter, I was afraid you had forgotten me."

"How could I forget the redheaded elf who plagued me by sewing my sleeves shut so neatly that the stitches didn't show? The elf who switched salt for sugar and laughed with such delight at the faces I made? The elf who hid in a haystack during a storm until I found her and promised to hold the thunder at bay?"

"Which you did quite well." Unwittingly, Jessica moved closer to Wolfe as she had in the past, seeking the reassuring warmth of his body, the shelter of his strength. "Quite well indeed."

"A matter of timing rather than control over the elements," Wolfe said dryly, easing Jessica away from his body. "The storm was spent."

"I called you Talks Back To Thunder for weeks afterward."

"And I called you Hay Maiden."

Jessica's silver laughter drew approving glances from nearby dancers.

"Your laugh would make a stone smile," Wolfe said.

"I have missed you, my Lord Wolfe. Surely you did not have to absent yourself for so long. The duchess' heart healed within the half-year. You could have returned."

"I'm not a lord. I'm the viscount's savage, the bastard son of a Cheyenne woman and Lord Robert Stewart, Viscount of—"

Jessica's small hand covered Wolfe's mouth, cutting off his words. The gesture was as old as her understanding that his lack of legitimate birth laid him open to the same caustic thrusts from the English aristocracy that Jessica's commoner mother and titled Scots father did.

"I won't have you belittle my very best friend," Jessica said firmly. "Elves have magical abilities. You are *my* Lord Wolfe. If you will save me from the ice storm outside, I will save you from the lecherous duchesses inside."

Smiling, Wolfe looked over Jessica's carefully coiffed head to the black night beyond Lord Stewart's windows. Sleet gleamed dully with reflected light.

"You're right," he said. "It's storming. It wasn't when I stepped off the ship."

"I always know when it's storming," Jessica said. "I used to watch the storms rake across the firth and count the seconds until they reached the house."

Wolfe sensed rather than felt her repressed shudder. His eyes narrowed as he looked down at the young woman who clung just a bit too tightly to him. Yet she wasn't putting out any of the signals of a woman looking for a lover.

"Were you always afraid of storms?" he asked.

"I don't remember."

The lack of music in Jessica's voice startled Wolfe. He had forgotten that she spoke rarely, if ever, of the nine years before the Earl of Glenshire died and she became the ward of a distant cousin whom she had never met.

"Odd that you don't remember."

"Do you remember your boyhood among the Cheyenne?"

"The smell of a certain kind of wood smoke, the leap of a campfire against the night, chants and dances meant to call spirits . . . yes, I remember."

"I bow to your superior memory." Jessica smiled and glanced up through her lashes as she had been schooled to do by Lady Victoria. "Could we dance farther from the garden window? The draft is quite cool."

Wolfe glanced at the graceful curve of Jessica's neck and shoulders and the more intimate curves of breasts whose upper swell was barely sheathed in ice-blue silk. A smooth gold locket lay in the shadowed cleft between her breasts. He had given her that bit of jewelry just before he went to America to remove the Stewart family from the cuckolded duke's wrath. Wolfe wondered if she carried her fiancé's picture in the locket.

Then Jessica took a breath and Wolfe's eyes moved from the gold jewelry to the fine skin beneath it. It reminded him of warm cream. The scent of her was a rose garden beneath a summer sun, and her mouth was a pink bud from that same garden. She rested in his arms as lightly as a sigh.

She was a child eleven years younger than he was, and she was making him burn.

"If you're chilly, Lady Jessica, next time wear a gown that covers more of your flesh."

The coolness in Wolfe's voice startled Jessica. He called her Lady Jessica only when he was angry with her. Perplexed, she looked down at the modest décolletage of her gown. No other woman in the room was so well-covered.

"What are you talking about, Wolfe? Lady Victoria was quite put out by the lines of my gown."

"A rare show of good sense on her part," he retorted.

Jessica laughed. "You mistook me. She wanted the neckline lowered, the waist drawn tight, and a much greater girth of crinoline. I preferred the French fashion, which lacks all those bothersome crinolines."

Wolfe remembered Jessica running toward him when she first spotted him across the room. He had seen quite clearly the feminine curve of hip and thigh beneath the filmy cloth. It had been an unwelcome reminder that his elf was grown... and soon to become a lord's wife.

"I didn't want a huge weight of petticoats or pearls or diamonds," Jessica continued. "Lady Victoria thought the dress and the jewelry too plain. She said I looked like a stick fetched by one of the hounds."

"A stick," muttered Wolfe, looking at the velvet shadow that lay between Jessica's young breasts. "Your guardian is in need of spectacles."

If another man had looked at Jessica in that way, she would have found an excuse to end the dance. But Wolfe was different. He was a man with no title, no need for heirs; he was not looking for a brood sow for his get.

Wind bellowed and hail scattered like shot across the glass. Shuddering with a fear whose source she remembered only in dreams and forgot before waking, Jessica tried to get closer to Wolfe. Even the reduced skirts of her modern ball gown prevented it. She stumbled for a third time, and again was caught by hands that were both powerful and gentle.

Around her the final strains of the waltz swirled, wrapping the room in music. It was almost midnight.

So little time left.

"Jessi, you're shaking. What's wrong? I thought you outgrew your fear of storms when you were ten."

"Only because I knew you would protect me."

"You survived quite well while I was gone," Wolfe said dryly.

"Only because I knew you would come back. And you did." Jessica looked up at Wolfe with a plea that was all the greater for its lack of artifice. "You must marry me, Wolfe Lonetree. Without you, I am lost."

At first he thought she was teasing him again; then he realized that she meant every word. Automatically, he executed a graceful turn and released Jessica as the music ceased. She clung to his hand as she had at the end of their first dance only a few minutes before.

"Elf, you must let go of me," Wolfe said quietly, looking down into the face that had become so unexpectedly, dangerously beautiful to him. "I'm not a lord and you are no longer a child. You are a lady of the realm whose engagement will soon be announced. One dance with the viscount's savage will be tolerated. Two will elicit comments. Three will cause a scandal. We have danced twice. We will not do so again."

"Wolfe," she whispered.

It was too late. He bowed over her hand and turned away.

With eyes darkened by fear, Jessica watched Wolfe walk away. No matter how great the crush of people, he was easy to find. It was not his height, though he was taller than many men. Nor was it his looks, though he was undoubtedly handsome with his straight black hair, dark skin, and remote indigo eyes. What set Wolfe apart was his way of moving, a combination of strength and unconscious grace. He was a man thoroughly at home within his body in the way a hunting cat is at home within its own body.

Jessica needed that masculine strength, that self-assurance. The prospect of Wolfe's return was all that had kept her from screaming as the net of circumstance and custom had drawn more tightly around her each day. Somehow she had to make Wolfe understand her need. She had made no joke when she proposed marriage to him. Far from it.

She had never been more serious in all her twenty years.

A gust of wind moaned outside Lord Robert Stewart's London house and rattled windowpanes. Winter was coming to an end but spring had not yet fully arrived, and now the seasons were fighting for supremacy, shaking the puny stone cities of man in their battle. Jessica's heart squeezed with fear as the wind's voice became a sustained, soulless howling that threatened her composure. Automatically, her hand went to the locket that held Wolfe's likeness inside.

I'm safe. Wolfe won't let me be hurt. I'm safe. Whatever stalks the storms can't get to me.

The feel of the locket and the silent litany had soothed Jessica during the years when Wolfe had been exiled to America. Now he had come back . . . yet she felt more alone than she had ever felt since he had plucked her from her fragrant hiding place in the hay and held the storm at bay by calling to the thunder in the words of his Cheyenne mother.

Jessica laced her fingers together, concealing their trembling, but there was nothing she could do to conceal the pallor of her skin or the bleak desperation in her eyes.

"Come, is that a face with which to celebrate your birthday and your engagement to be married?" Lady Victoria asked in a voice that was as gentle as her eyes were shrewd.

"I want never to marry."

Victoria sighed and caught one of Jessica's cold hands between her own. "I know, sweet, I know. I kept your wishes in mind when I chose your husband. You will not be burdened by Lord Gore for long. He is old and overfond of port. In a handful of years he will die. Then you will be a wealthy widow with your whole life in front of you." She smiled thinly. "If you wish to be as scandalous as a French duchess, you may."

"I would die before I let a man rut upon me."

Rueful laughter was Victoria's only reply. "Ah, Jessica. You should have been born to a staunch Catholic family and sent to a nunnery, but you were not. You are the only offspring of a Scots Protestant highland lass and a lowland earl. The title and lands passed elsewhere, leaving you no wealth of your own. You must marry. Lord Gore, whatever his drawbacks as a gentleman, has enough wealth to keep the Queen herself in luxury."

"So you have told me. Often."

"In the hope that someday you will listen," retorted Victoria.

"In America slaves have been freed. Would that we in England treated our women so tenderly!"

A soft hand closed around Jessica's chin. "Stubborn little Scots lass," Victoria said. "But in this I am more stubborn even than you. You have enjoyed the perquisites of aristocracy. A common woman your age would have been tumbled and set to breeding years ago by the first lout who got beneath her skirts."

Jessica's mouth flattened.

"You were protected by my second husband and raised as gently as though you were a child of his own loins," Victoria continued, her voice cool and relentless. "You were educated in managing a great house and a great fortune. Despite that dreadful American maid whom you imitate, you were taught to speak proper English and to be a proper lady. Now you must repay the generosity of your upbringing by producing an heir who will forever bind together the fortunes of the Viscount's family and the wealth of Baronet Gore's shipping empire."

Long auburn lashes swept down, concealing the revulsion in Jessica's eyes. "My lady, please—"

"No," the older woman interrupted. "I have heard your pleas for much too long. I have spoiled you, but that is at an end. Your engagement to Lord Gore will be announced at midnight. You will marry within the month. If the old drunkard can coax his staff into readiness, you will produce an heir within a year and your duty will be fulfilled. Then you may live as you please."

"Oh, Lady Jessica," Betsy said unhappily, "I don't think you should go to Mr. Lonetree's rooms."

Jessica pushed away from the vanity where Betsy had been at work undoing her mistress' elaborate jewelled coiffure and brushing out the long, silky hair. Normally, the ritual soothed Jessica, but tonight it had made her impatient. She began pacing the room like a caged cat. As she moved, the lacy peignoir which she wore while attending to her toilet billowed and rustled in pale shades of blue.

"There's no choice."

"But—"

"I won't hear any more," Jessica interrupted sharply. "You are forever telling me how women in America have more freedom in the choosing of their husbands and the living of their lives. If I must marry, I will choose my husband and live my life as it pleases me."

"You aren't American."

"I shall be." Jessica tied the peignoir's robe around her waist with a firm yank. "American men don't have titles or great wealth, so they don't need heirs. I won't have to endure revolting marital duties or ruinous pregnancies with an American husband."

Hesitantly, Betsy said, "American men do like a warm bed, my lady."

"Then they can sleep with hounds."

"Oh dear. I fear I've led you astray. Just because American men aren't titled doesn't mean that—"

"No more arguing," Jessica interrupted, putting her hands over her ears.

For a moment she stood very still, fighting the fear that threatened to choke her. The feel of Lord Gore's sweating palms closing over her hand was too fresh, as was the memory of the lechery in his bloodshot eyes. The thought of those same hands touching her in the marriage bed made bile climb in Jessica's throat.

A nightmare prowled just beneath her awareness, chilling her even as it strengthened her determination. She lowered her hands, straightened her spine, and headed for the door.

"My lady," the maid began.

"Sweet Betsy, do shut up." Jessica smiled at her maid with trembling lips. "Wish me well. If I succeed, you'll get that trip to America I promised you three years ago."

Jessica opened the door and stepped into the hall. Betsy's low sound of distress was cut off by the soft thump of the closing door. Gathering the flyaway layers of silk in her hands, Jessica hurried toward the wing of the house where Wolfe's rooms were. Fragrant oil lamps burned in stone niches in the hall, for Lord Robert was a great lover of tradition in the home. The illumination was dim, but that didn't worry Jessica. She knew every alcove and corner of the great house.

Flinching when she passed windows where the storm beat in merciless demands for entrance, Jessica hurried through the huge stone house. She didn't expect anyone else to be about, for she had waited until even the servants had gone to bed. She did avoid the library, however, for she knew the lord often gamed there until dawn with his friends.

Jessica hurried down another hall and ran lightly up a stairway. Just as she gained the top, she overran Lord Gore, who was considerably under the weather from port.

"Dear God," she said, righting herself frantically.

Gore staggered, then caught himself by grabbing Jessica. Though drunk, he wasn't beyond telling the difference between male and female flesh. Nor was he weak. When Jessica tried to twist free of him, his hands tightened. One hand dug into her breast. The other bruised her shoulder.

"Damn, but 'tis my little lady." Gore's eyes narrowed as he dragged himself erect and focused on the silk and lace confection Jessica wore. "Very fetching, sweet. I'd not hoped to find you so eager for the marriage bed. Had I known, I'd have put less port under my hatches and got under yours sooner."

"Let go of me!"

Gore ignored Jessica, intent only on getting closer to the soft, fragrant creature who was finally within his grasp. Part of Jessica's peignoir ripped in her struggles to be free. He stared at her exposed breasts and tried to understand his good fortune at having found a fiancée who was so eager for him she sought out his rooms while the house slept.

"Just look at those bubbies, by God," he said heavily. "Lord Stewart drove a mean bargain for you, but it was worth it to the ha'penny."

Gore bent down to Jessica's breasts, staggered, and ended up shoving her against the wall with a force that knocked her breathless. That was the only thing that kept her from crying out in pain as his teeth closed over one breast. Grunting with growing excitement, he ignored her struggles as he flattened her against the wall and fumbled to undo his pants. Desperately, Jessica remembered what Wolfe had taught her just before they parted four years ago. With a silent prayer she brought one knee up hard between Gore's legs. Instantly, his hands fell away and he staggered backward.

Clutching her ruined peignoir around her body, her hair streaming like dark fire behind her, Jessica fled to Wolfe's room. The door opened easily beneath her shaking hands.

Wolfe came out of the canopy bed in a single flowing movement. He had just enough time to recognize Jessica and drop his knife on the bedside table before she threw herself at his chest. Her arms locked around his bare waist and she shook as wildly as she had when he had found her huddled within a haystack.

Automatically, Wolfe lifted Jessica onto the bed and sat holding her close, trying to soothe her. A few feet away the storm beat mindlessly against stone and glass.

"Gently, little one," Wolfe murmured. "You're safe with me. The storm can't get you now. You're safe. Here, I'll light the lamp so that you can see. The storm is out there and you're in here."

Wolfe leaned over, lit the lamp one-handed, and resettled Jessica in his lap.

"There, elf. Is that better? You can see that you're safe, can't you? You can see . . . sweet Jesus Christ!"

Wolfe fell silent, unable to speak. Jessica's breasts were bared and shockingly beautiful despite the bright drops of blood and blue-black bruises forming on her skin.

From somewhere in the house, raised voices could be heard. Wolfe barely noticed. The realization that a man had broken Jessica's soft skin with his teeth and bruised her delicate flesh with his fingers enraged Wolfe.

"What bloody bastard did this to you?" he asked savagely.

"Lord G-G—" Jessica took a long, shuddering breath and tried to still the shaking of her body so that she could speak. "Lord Gore."

Very carefully, Wolfe pulled the torn ends of Jessica's peignoir in place, covering her breasts. "Hush, elf." He kissed her hair gently. "Hush, little one. You're safe. I won't let him hurt you again."

"P-promise?"

"Yes."

Jessica let out a broken sigh. For a few moments there was no sound but that of the wind and Jessica's slowly calming breathing.

Gore burst into the room through the open door. His face was sweaty and he was somewhat less drunk than he had been, for pain could temporarily sober a man.

"You need a taste of the rod, you little baggage," Gore said coldly, stalking toward the bed, "and you shall have it. Get your arse out of that savage's bed."

Wolfe put Jessica aside and stood up in a single motion. For the first time she realized that Wolfe was naked from the waist up—and from the waist down, as well. Lamplight ran over his body, outlining the power that ran through him like leashed lightning.

"I take it you're the bastard who mauled my Jessi?" Wolfe asked in a soft voice.

Jessica forgot Wolfe's nakedness as his voice sank into her. She had never heard that tone from him. She shivered and realized that Wolfe could kill . . . and he would, to defend her.

Before Gore could answer, Lady Victoria came rushing into the room, followed by a distraught Betsy.

"I'm sorry," Betsy said, looking at Jessica. "I just couldn't let you come to Mr. Lonetree's room. The man has a wicked reputation with the ladies."

"Fully earned, from the look of it," Victoria said dryly, her gray eyes taking in Gore's fury, Jessica's deshabille, and Wolfe's nakedness. "Do cover yourself, Wolfe."

Wolfe ignored Victoria. His hand snaked out and fastened around Gore's throat. From the hallway came the babble of excited voices. Lord Robert Stewart's was foremost.

"My dear lady, would you mind explaining what in the devil is—*Wolfe!* Good Christ, man!"

Robert slammed the bedroom door behind him, but the damage was already done; five lords of the realm had gotten a look into Wolfe's bedroom. The scandal would be all over London by dawn.

Grimly, Lord Robert turned back to the five people who remained in the room. "Release Lord Gore."

"I don't think so," Wolfe said evenly. "The man attacked Jessi."

"You are a liar as well as a bastard," Gore said.

He would have said more, but Wolfe's hand had contracted. Powerful fingers shut down Gore's carotid arteries, rendering him unconscious with brutal efficiency. Reluctantly, Wolfe opened his hand and let Gore fall heavily to the floor.

"Dear God, Wolfe. You have killed him!" Victoria said in a horrified voice.

"In America I would have. Unfortunately, I'm not in America."

"You shall be soon," Robert said. "Damn! You have a gift for scandal, son."

"It doesn't come from my mother's side," Wolfe said coolly. "Scandal is a civilized notion."

He turned back to see if Jessica was over her fright. He saw her eyes widen as her glance went down his body. She turned scarlet and looked away so quickly she almost lost her balance.

Calmly, Wolfe went to the dresser and pulled out a nightshirt. He hated the things, but he didn't want to distress Jessica any further.

Gore began snoring. Robert spared him an irritated glance before he turned his attention to Jessica. He meant to make his voice kind, but he was too angry at losing his son again to be anything but blunt.

"Is Wolfe your paramour?"

The question brought back Gore's drunken onslaught. Jessica went pale, then flushed with a force that made her feel dizzy. She put her burning face in her hands and shuddered, fighting for control, wondering if she was caught ·in one of her nightmares where the wind screamed with a woman's voice and dawn was an eternity away.

"I can't—Lord Robert—I—" Jessica said desperately, trying to make him understand that she couldn't marry Gore. "Dear God. You have been so kind to me. I'm sorry."

Her voice broke and she trembled. Her distress astonished both Stewarts, for Jessica had never shown anything but composure, even when she was a newly orphaned child.

"What Jessi is trying to say," Wolfe said coolly as he buttoned the shirt, "is that we aren't lovers."

"But you would have been, if Betsy had not come to me," Victoria said. "You have wanted Jessica since her fifteenth summer."

Even as Wolfe opened his mouth to deny it, he knew it was true. The sudden realization that he had wanted Jessica for years made it impossible to speak.

"Wolfe..." Victoria sighed wearily. "If you could not keep your cock in your breeches out of respect for your father, the least you could do is limit your attentions to married women and whores."

"Enough, wife," Robert said. "Wolfe is my son. He knows his duty."

"Which is?" Wolfe asked quietly.

"You seduced Lady Jessica. You shall marry her."

"There has been no seduction. Gore mauled her, she ran to my room in hysterics, and Gore followed. A minute later, Lady Victoria arrived."

"Jessica?" Robert asked sharply. "If you are a virgin still, the engagement can be saved. Lord Gore is quite keen on you."

Jessica held out her hands to Wolfe and whispered, "You promised . . ."

There was a shocked silence followed by Wolfe's curt command. "Leave me with Jessica for a moment. And take that drunken swine with you."

When Victoria started to protest, Robert simply grabbed Gore's feet and dragged the man into the hall. Gore didn't awaken. Victoria stepped over him. Betsy hurried after her employers. The door closed firmly. Before Wolfe could speak, Jessica sank to her knees in front of him.

"Please, Wolfe. I beg of you. Marry me. Don't let that man have me."

"Are you a virgin?" Wolfe asked tightly.

Jessica's head snapped up. "Good God, yes! I can't bear being touched by a man. It makes my stomach heave."

"Then why were you coming to my room dressed—or rather, undressed—as you are?"

"It was what I was wearing when I realized I had to talk to you," she said, perplexed. She held out her hand to him in silent plea. Despite the rigid control she exerted on her voice, her fingers trembled. "I came to ask you to save me from Lord Gore."

"Consider yourself saved. No matter what my father thinks, I doubt that Gore will have you after tonight."

"But another man might. Victoria will contract another marriage for me."

For a moment Wolfe said nothing. He hated the thought of another man having Jessica, but there was nothing to be done for it. Even if the Stewarts permitted Wolfe to marry her, the match would be a disaster for him. No matter how much Jessica's body tempted Wolfe, he knew she simply was all wrong as a wife for him.

"Finding a suitable husband for you is Lady Victoria's duty," Wolfe said tightly.

"*No.* I will lie beneath the ground before I lie beneath a man."

Wolfe's eyes narrowed at the certainty in Jessica's voice. She would sooner die than couple with a man.

Any man.

"But you want me to marry you," he said neutrally.

A smile trembled on Jessica's lips. "You would never touch me like that. Men marry because they must have heirs. Women marry because they want wealth. You have no need of an heir and I have no need of wealth."

A dangerous stillness came over Wolfe as Jessica's words sank into him. "Even a bastard has . . . needs."

"What does bastardy have to do with it?" she asked with exasperation.

For a few taut moments, Wolfe said nothing. Then his breath rushed out in a soundless sigh as he understood that Jessica had meant no insult to him by assuming that a bastard wouldn't want to couple with his wife; she simply didn't realize that men wanted more than heirs from a marriage.

"Dear Wolfe," Jessica said softly, touching the sleeve of his nightshirt. "Do marry me. We are good friends. We would have such fun living in America, hunting and fishing and eating by the campfire."

"My God, you really mean that," he said, stunned by the magnitude of her misunderstanding of what marriage was.

"Oh, yes." She smiled as the cage of fear loosened around her heart. "I have never enjoyed being with anyone so much as you, my Lord Wolfe. Now we can be together again. What could be better?"

He said something profane, then ran his hand wearily through his black hair. "Did you set me up, Jessi? Did you send your maid to fetch Lady Victoria as a witness while you ran to my room looking like a girl on the way to her lover?"

Jessica shook her head vigorously. The motion made lamplight twist and run through her long hair like streamers of fire.

"No. I didn't plan this." She drew in a long, ragged breath. "But now that it has happened, I will swear on my mother's grave that we have lain together. Then you'll have to marry me. Then I'll be free."

"What of me? What of my freedom?"

Jessica looked up at Wolfe with clear, brilliant eyes. "I've thought of that, too. I won't ask anything of you. You will be free to come or go as you please. If you want a shooting companion, I'll hunt with you. If you want to travel alone, I won't complain. If you want a special fly to lure trout, I'll tie it for you."

"Jessi—"

She talked right over Wolfe. "If you want my conversation, I'll be there. If you want silence, I'll leave the room. I'll see that your house is well run and that only food you like is served. And when dinner is over I'll warm your brandy glass in my hands until fragrance fills the crystal globe and then I will give it to you and we will sit together and no storms will ever come inside . . ."

The silence stretched and shimmered like a candle flame pulled by wind. Finally, Wolfe turned his back to Jessica because he couldn't trust himself to look at her any longer and not lose his temper in a way that he had never done with any living creature.

"Jessi," he said finally, softly. "The life you're describing is the life of an English lord and lady. I'm not a lord. My wife will live in America. She won't live the life of an aristocratic lady."

"I love America. I've been sick with longing to see the tall grass and great buffalo again. I've missed the endless sky. Betsy has taught me American ways. When I'm with her, you can hear my British accent hardly at all. I've worked very hard at being American," Jessica said earnestly. "I knew you wouldn't want to live in England."

Wolfe spun around. "You *did* trap me!"

Jessica bent her head and looked at her tightly laced hands. "No, my Lord Wolfe. When I understood that Victoria meant to see me married, I tried to imagine belonging to a man. And I simply couldn't imagine belonging to any other man but you, so I had to learn how to belong to you. I've thought about this quite a lot, you see."

When Wolfe said nothing, she looked up at him again, her eyes luminous, pleading. "I don't want to disappoint Lord Robert. I don't want to lie to Lady Victoria. I don't want to trap you into marriage."

"But you will."

"Only if I must."

Wolfe said something shocking under his breath, but the words were lost in the sustained howling of the wind. Trembling despite her determination and straight spine, Jessica waited.

When Wolfe finally moved, it was so suddenly that she flinched. He went to the bedroom door, jerked it open, and was confronted by two pairs of anxious eyes. Betsy and the sleeping Gore had disappeared. Glancing from Wolfe's shuttered expression to Jessica's desperate composure, the Stewarts came into the bedroom and closed the heavy door behind them.

"Well?" Robert demanded.

"Lady Jessica is prepared to swear I've had her," Wolfe said coldly. "I haven't."

Robert looked at Jessica. "Is that true?"

"I will marry Wolfe," she said in a low voice, "or I will marry no man at all."

"Bloody hell," muttered the lord. He looked at Wolfe. "What are we to do?"

"Just what you've always done—give the spoiled little aristocrat what she wants."

"You will marry her?"

"After a fashion," Wolfe drawled. "Lady Jessica has some girlish romantic fancy about living in the West."

"Hardly a fancy," Jessica said. "I've been beyond the Mississippi. I know what awaits me."

"Like hell you do," Wolfe said. "You think it's going to be one long hunting holiday. It won't be. I can't afford such things, and even if I could, I wouldn't."

Victoria looked from her stubborn ward to the savage planes of Wolfe's face. She smiled and then began laughing softly. "Ah, Wolfe, your mind is as quick and sharp as a rapier. But Jessica is also quick, and as stubborn as Scots granite."

Wolfe grunted. "I'm a hell of a lot harder than stone. Lady Jessica will soon realize that marriage to me isn't some long hunting expedition complete with china, silver, and enough servants to curry the buffalo before they're shot. If she lasts until we reach my home at the edge of the Rockies I'll be surprised."

Jessica's back became even straighter as she heard the rage and derision in Wolfe's voice. The look he slanted at her out of his dark eyes was no kinder.

"When she gets over her foolishness," Wolfe said curtly, turning back to Victoria, "I'll have the marriage annulled and return her to you the same way she came to me—completely untouched."

"Oh, I hope not *completely*," Victoria said with amusement. "Teach the stubborn little nun not to fear a man. Then you will both be free."

Wolfe turned his back on Victoria and looked at Jessica with cold indigo eyes. "It's not too late to stop this farce, my lady. You'll soon tire of being the common wife of a common man."

"I shall not tire of being your wife." It was a vow, and Jessica said it as such.

"Yes, you shall," Wolfe said.

And that, too, was a vow.

1

"**D**o be reasonable, my Lord Wolfe. It wasn't my idea to dismiss Betsy and the footmen."

"I'm not your lord. I'm a bastard, remember?"

"I find my memory improving with each moment," Jessica said under her breath. "Ouch! That pinched."

"Then stop wiggling like a worm on a hook. There are twenty buttons left and they're as small as peas. Damnation. What silly idiot made a dress that a woman has to be helped into?"

And out of.

That was the worst of it. Wolfe knew the time would come eventually when he would have to undo each of the glittering jet buttons, and each undoing would reveal more warm, fragrant skin and fine lace lingerie. She was an elf who barely came up to his breastbone, but she was bringing him to his knees with raw desire. Her back was supple and elegant as a dancer's, graceful as a flame; and like a flame she burned him.

"I'm sorry," Jessica whispered unhappily as Wolfe's words scorched her ears. "I had hoped . . ."

"Stop whispering, damn it. If you have something to say, say it and damn all this aristocratic foolishness about talking so softly a man has to bend double to hear you."

"I thought that you would be glad to see me," Jessica said with great clarity. "Until this morning, I've not seen you once in the months since we exchanged vows. You haven't asked me how my voyage was, nor about the train trip across the United States, nor—"

"You said you wouldn't complain if I left you alone," Wolfe interrupted curtly. "Are you complaining, Lady Jessica?"

Jessica fought against a wave of unhappiness. This wasn't how she had imagined her reunion with Wolfe. She had been looking forward to riding over the Great American Desert with him on eager blooded horses. She had been looking forward to long days of comfortable silence and lively conversation, to nighttime fires beneath the blazingly clear American sky. But most of all, she had looked forward to seeing Wolfe.

"When your letter came asking me to meet you here," she said, "I thought you had gotten over your pique."

"Pique. Now there's a mincing, aristocratic kind of word." His fingers fumbled and touched warm flesh. With a savage curse he jerked his fingers back. "You don't know me very well, *lady*. I wasn't piqued. I was bloody furious. I will remain that way until you grow up, agree to an annulment, and return to England where you belong."

"Nor do you know me very well. You thought

I would give up and beg for an annulment at the prospect of traveling alone to America."

Wolfe grunted. That had been precisely his thought. But Jessica had surprised him. She had arranged for her own passage and that of her maid, hired two footmen with the small inheritance that had come at her marriage, and crossed the Atlantic alone.

"I doubt that you'll find traveling with me as pleasant as you found being alone. Not that you were truly alone, my lady. Your entourage took care of your every need. Damn it, can't you even keep your hair out of the way?" he asked roughly as a long, silken tendril of hair slid from her grasp and over his finger.

Jessica's arms were weary from holding her hair on top of her head, but all she said as she gathered up the fugitive lock was, "A maid and two footmen aren't an entourage."

"In America they are. An American woman does for herself and for her man as well."

"Betsy said she worked in a household that had twelve servants."

"Betsy must have worked for a carpetbagger."

Jessica blinked. "I don't think so. The man sold stocks, not rugs."

Wolfe tried not to let humor blunt his anger. He wasn't completely successful. "A carpetbagger is a kind of thief," he said carefully.

"So is a rug merchant."

Wolfe made a muffled sound.

"You're laughing, aren't you?" Delight and relief were in Jessica's voice and in her face when she looked over her shoulder at him. "You see? It won't be so bad, being married to me."

The line of Wolfe's mouth flattened once more.

All he could see from where he stood was a badly buttoned dress and the graceful curve of a woman's neck. But Jessica wasn't a woman. Not really. She was a cold, spoiled little English aristocrat, the precise kind of woman he had detested since he had been old enough to understand that the glittering ladies of privilege didn't want him as a man; they wanted only to know what rutting with a savage was like.

"Wolfe?" Jessica whispered, searching the face that had once again become that of a stranger.

"Turn around. If I don't get this bloody thing done up, we'll miss the stage."

"But I'm not dressed for the theater."

"Theater?" Belatedly Wolfe understood. "Stage*coach*. Not that you're dressed for that, either. Those crinolines will take up half the bench."

"Stagecoach?"

"Yes, my lady," Wolfe said mockingly. "A means of conveyance having four wheels, a driver, horses—"

"Oh, do hush up. I know what a stagecoach is," Jessica interrupted. "I was just surprised. We went by horseback and carriage before."

"You were a proper little aristocrat then. Now you're a plain old American wife. When you get tired of it, you know the way out."

Wolfe reached for another button. A gold chain gleamed just beneath his fingers. He remembered giving the chain and locket to her. It was a symbol of a time that would never come again, a time when he and his redheaded hoyden had been free simply to enjoy one another.

Except for an occasional low curse, Wolfe silently finished fastening the maddening jet buttons on Jessica's day dress.

"There," he said with relief as he stepped away. "Where are your trunks?"

"My trunks?" she asked absently, wanting to groan with the relief of no longer having to hold the heavy, slippery mass of her hair over her head.

"You must have packed your clothes in something. Where are your trunks?"

"Trunks."

"Lady Jessica, if I had wanted a parrot I would have become a sea captain. Where are your damned trunks?"

"I don't know," she admitted. "The footmen attended to them after Betsy unpacked."

Wolfe raked a big hand through his hair and tried not to notice the picture Jessica made with her ice-blue day dress peeking through the muted fire of her unbound hair.

"Bloody. Useless. *Lady.*"

"Swearing at me won't help," she said stiffly.

"Don't bet on it."

Wolfe stalked out of the hotel room and slammed the door behind himself.

Jessica barely had enough time to hide her unhappiness beneath a serene expression before Wolfe reappeared with a trunk balanced on each shoulder. Behind him were two rough-looking strangers who were little older than boys. Each carried two empty trunks. The young men dumped their cargo and stared with great interest at the fashionably dressed woman whose loose hair tumbled in shimmering waves to her hips.

"Thank you," Wolfe said to the young men as they set down the trunks.

"My pleasure," said the younger one. "We heard a real English lady was in town. Never thought we'd get a chance to see one."

"Actually, I'm Scots."

The youth smiled. "Either way, you're pretty as a kitten in a velvet box. If you need any help getting the trunks to the stage, just holler. We'll come running."

Jessica flushed at the young man's open admiration. "That's very kind of you."

Wolfe grunted and gave the youths a look that sent them out of the room in a hurry. The bold one turned back and tipped his hat to Jessica just before he shut the door.

"Bind up your hair," Wolfe said coldly. "Even in America, a woman doesn't let anyone but her family see her with her hair tumbling to her hips."

Without a word, Jessica went to the small dressing table and picked up one of the brushes Betsy had set out before she left. Drawn despite himself to the implied intimacy of her unbound hair flowing around her hips, Wolfe watched from the corner of his eye as Jessica began brushing.

After a few minutes it became apparent that Jessica wasn't happy with the brush. She kept shifting it in her grip, trying to figure out the best way to tame her seething, silky hair and make it behave as Betsy had. Twice, Jessica dropped the brush. The third time the brush fell, Wolfe picked it up, ran his fingertips over the ivory handle, and looked at Jessica curiously.

"It's smooth, but not slippery," he said, handing it to her.

"Thank you." Jessica looked at the baffling tool that seemed to do nothing more than make her hair leap and crackle with electricity. "I don't understand what's wrong. It worked well enough for Betsy."

"It worked well enough for..." Wolfe's voice died.

"You're right. There seems to be a parrot loose in this room," she said blandly.

"My God! You don't even know how to dress your own hair."

"Of course not. That was Betsy's job, and quite good at it she was." Jessica looked at Wolfe cautiously. There was a stunned expression on his face. "I take it that American women complete their toilet unassisted?"

"My God."

"Ah, then it's a religious custom." Jessica sighed. "Very well, if every Betsy and Abigail here can do it, so can I. Give me the brush, please."

Wolfe was too staggered to resist. Numbly he watched as Jessica brought the brush down through her hair with great determination and no finesse. The too-rapid stroke caused another surge of static electricity. Her hair crackled and fanned out, tangling with buttons and clinging to whatever it touched.

One of the things her hair touched was Wolfe's hand. Fine strands wrapped around his skin and clung like a lover. The sensation was indescribably silky. His heartbeat doubled. With a curse he snatched his hand back, accidentally yanking her hair in the process.

Jessica's breath came in with a startled sound as her eyes watered. "That wasn't necessary."

"I didn't do it on purpose. Your hair attacked me."

"Attacked you?"

"You have a point. We must do something about that blasted parrot."

She turned and saw her hair wrapped around

his wrist and tangled in the button on his cuff. "Are the teeth very sharp?"

"What?"

"Betsy warned me about my hair's unruly appetite for buttons," Jessica said gravely, "but she said nothing about flesh. I hope your wound isn't serious."

Wolfe's shoulders moved as he tried to stifle laughter at Jessica's solemn teasing. He snickered as he picked individual strands of hair from the button.

"Perhaps I'd better do that," she offered. "If you startle the red ones, they bite quite savagely."

Wolfe gave up and laughed aloud, knowing as he did so that he was a fool but unable to do anything about it at the moment. Of all the people he had ever known, only Jessica was able to make him laugh so easily.

"Damn it, elf . . ."

Jessica smiled and touched Wolfe's hand. The light caress made his hand jerk, but he said nothing. When the last silky strand of hair was freed from his clothing, he went to the table and poured clean water over his hands from the ewer. Shaking off loose drops, he went back to Jessica.

"Stand still."

Slowly, he smoothed his damp hands over her hair from her crown to her hips. Soon her hair was lying in obedient waves.

"Give me the brush," Wolfe said.

His voice was low, almost hoarse, and his eyes were nearly black. He dampened the brush slightly, then returned to work on Jessica's hair. Unlike her maid, he stood in front of her rather than in back as he brushed her hair.

"Wolfe?"

"Hmm?"

"My maids stand behind me."

"Too many buttons. Don't want to tempt the beastly appetites."

Jessica looked up at Wolfe, curious about the velvety roughness of his voice. Her breath caught as she realized she was standing closer to Wolfe than she had when they waltzed on the night of her twentieth birthday. With other men, she hadn't liked being close, but with Wolfe she had resented the decorum of the waltz that had prevented her from burrowing closer to Wolfe's strength.

The pulse in his neck beat strongly, intriguing her. If she stood on tiptoe and leaned forward just a bit, or if she lifted her hand, she would be able to feel his heartbeat.

"Did that hurt?" he asked.

"Hurt?"

"Little redheaded parrot," he murmured. He gathered a handful of hair, lifted it well away from Jessica's breasts, and brushed slowly all the way to the ends as he talked. "When you made that odd little sound, I thought I had hurt you again."

She shook her head slowly, sending the cool silk of her loose hair over Wolfe's hands. "No. I was just thinking."

"What were you thinking?"

"I've never noticed the pulse beating in your neck before. Once I noticed it, I thought of touching it, of feeling the very movement of your life beneath my fingertips . . ."

Wolfe's hand jerked at the sudden surge of his heart. The motion brought him very close to touching her breasts. He stopped brushing her hair.

"Dangerous thoughts, Jessi."

"Why?"

"Because it makes a man want to let you touch the life in him."

"Why is that dangerous?"

Wolfe looked down into Jessica's clear eyes and knew that she hadn't the faintest idea how much her words might arouse a man.

Teach the stubborn little nun not to fear a man's touch. Then you'll both be free.

Wolfe wondered if Jessica was teasing him solemnly once more, as she had about the ferocity of her silky, unbound hair. Slowly, he decided that she wasn't teasing him. She truly didn't know what he was talking about. The extent of her innocence astonished him. The aristocratic ladies he had known in England acquired new lovers the way a gambler acquired new cards—frequently and unemotionally.

"Have you ever touched a man like that, feeling his very life?" Wolfe asked, lifting the brush once more.

"No."

"Why not, if it intrigues you so?"

"I never noticed it before now. And if I had, I would have done nothing."

"Why?"

"I would have to stand quite close to a man to touch him like that," Jessica said. "The thought appalls."

"You're standing quite close to me. I'm a man."

"Ah, but you're my very own Lord Wolfe. When the storm had me in its teeth, you snatched me close and held the thunder at bay. When other children teased me savagely about my common blood, you came and put an end to it. You taught me to shoot and to ride and to fish. And no matter how I teased you, you were never cruel to your elf."

"Very few men are cruel to elves."

A delicate shiver of pleasure moved over Jessica's skin as Wolfe resumed brushing her hair.

"You're shivering. Would you like a wrap?"

"It was pleasure, not a cold draft that made me shiver."

Again, Wolfe's hand hesitated as the meaning underlying Jessica's words sent a shaft of desire through him.

"Did Lady Victoria teach you to flirt like this?" he asked curiously.

"Flirting consists of feints and sighs and lies. I am merely telling the truth. It never felt this good when Betsy brushed my hair."

There was a time of silence broken only by the whisper of soft bristles through Jessica's hair. Finally, Wolfe put the brush aside, turned her until her back was to him, and divided the dark red mass of her hair into three equal lots. The touch of his hands on her nape made her shiver again.

"It's a pity we're all wrong for each other as man and wife," Wolfe said quietly as he wove her hair into a single thick braid. "There is passion in you, Jessi."

Abruptly, Jessica's body became rigid. "I think not," she said distinctly. "The thought of lying with a man makes my stomach twist."

"Why?"

The quiet question startled Jessica. "Would you like a man doing that to you?" she demanded.

"A man?" Wolfe laughed. "No, not a man. But a woman . . . ah, that's a different thing entirely."

"Only for a man," she retorted. "He is strong enough to say yes or no as it pleases him. When it's finally finished, he doesn't lie weeping on the bed. Nor does he scream in agony months later, as what he put in the woman's body tears her apart trying to get out!"

"Someone has filled your head with nonsense. It's not like that."

"Not for a man, certainly."

"Nor for a woman."

"From what great font of wisdom do you draw this conclusion?" Jessica asked sardonically. "Have you attended a woman in childbed?"

"Of course not. Neither have you. Hand me the light blue ribbon."

"Ah, but I have," she retorted, grabbing the ribbon and holding it over her shoulder.

"What? I can't imagine Victoria permitting that."

"It was before I went to live with her."

Wolfe's hands paused. He took the ribbon and began wrapping it around the tail of the single braid he had woven.

"You were only nine when Lady Victoria became your guardian. What was a girl so young doing at a birthing?"

Jessica shrugged. "I was the first born. My mother had many pregnancies before cholera took her."

"You never told me you had brothers and sisters."

"I don't." An involuntary shudder moved over Jessica as memories tried to surface, memories she had banished to her nightmares years ago.

"Jessi," Wolfe said. He touched the curve of her neck with a gentle fingertip. "A young girl doesn't always understand what she's seeing, especially when it comes to the mystery of sex or birth. But if it was all so terrible, no woman would bear more than one babe."

"Not willingly, no. Have you noticed, my Lord Wolfe, that men are considerably stronger than women, and considerably more interested in rutting?" Abruptly Jessica's hands swept up and down her own arms, rubbing warmth into skin that was cold. "You're right. It's cool in here. I wonder where Betsy put my Chinese shawl. Do you see it, Wolfe?"

For the space of a breath there was no answer. Then Wolfe sighed and accepted the change of subject. "I'll get it for you as soon as I finish braiding your hair."

Jessica turned and looked over her shoulder at Wolfe. She smiled at him with lips that were too pale. "Thank you, my lord."

"I'm not your lord." The protest was automatic, but not angry. He had seen the gratitude in her eyes, and the fear that lay beneath it.

"Then thank you, my husband."

"I'm not that, either. A wife lies with her husband. Or are you planning to pursue the vows of the Scottish marriage ceremony we took?"

"What?"

" 'With my body I thee worship,' " Wolfe quoted softly. "Are you planning to worship me, wife?"

Jessica turned away quickly, but not so quickly that Wolfe missed the horror in her eyes. Knowing that he repelled her as a man made anger twist as deeply in Wolfe as desire. The knowledge that he now had a weapon with which to force Jessica into an annulment should have pleased him, but it did not.

"What if I demanded my husbandly rights?"

She flinched, but said instantly, "You would not."

"You sound very certain."

"You didn't want our marriage. If you rut on me, you can't cry annulment."

Wolfe's mouth turned down in a bitter curl. "You're right, Lady Jessica. I will never *rut* on you. I don't want to be saddled for life with a creature so spoiled and useless she can't even comb her own hair."

He tied off the ribbon with a few abrupt motions.

"Wolfe, I—"

"Start packing your clothes," he interrupted curtly. With grim pleasure, he saw Jessica's look of surprise and uncertainty. "Don't know how to pack? What a surprise. You had better learn quickly, Lady Jessica. The stage leaves in an hour. You will be on it, with or without your six trunks."

She looked at the armoires and wardrobes that had been brought into the suite of rooms in order to hold all her clothes. Then she looked at the locked trunks. It seemed impossible that so much clothing had come from so little packing space.

"It took Betsy the better part of a week to pack when we left," Jessica said faintly.

Wolfe ran a measuring eye over the armoires and wardrobes. "That's because you brought too much. Sort out what you'll need for a month. Leave the rest here."

"Are we planning to come back here so quickly?"

"Not we. You. You'll be back as soon as you get it through your stubborn Scots skull that you don't want to be an American wife married to a halfbreed commoner."

Jessica's head came up. "I remember other vows, Wolfe Lonetree. Whither thou goest, I will go.

Whither thou lodgest, I will lodge. Thy people will be my people, and thy God, my God."

"My shaman grandfather will be pleased to have such an obedient granddaughter." Wolfe's lips curved in his dark face. "I wonder how you'll look in buckskin, beads, and shells. How will you like chewing my meat before it comes to my mouth so that my food will be tender for me, and chewing my buckskins so they will be soft and supple against my body?"

"You're joking."

"Am I?" Wolfe smiled, showing all his white teeth and not one bit of comfort. "I'm going to walk to the stage office and buy two tickets. When I come back, I expect to see the trunks lined up and waiting to go, and you with them."

The door closed behind Wolfe's broad shoulders. Jessica looked at the ill-made wood frame and the tarnished brass hinges. As she turned away, she caught a glance of herself in the dressing glass. The odd, simple hairstyle made her look like a child playing in her mother's clothes. Each time she moved, the braid caught on the many buttons on the back of her dress. With an impatient sound, she brought the heavy braid over her shoulder and down between her breasts, where it would be less trouble.

Setting her mouth in a determined line, Jessica pulled a key ring from the pocket of her skirt, opened the padlocks on all of the trunks, and tossed the jangling ring onto the bedside table. Then she went among the wardrobes and armoires and began assessing their contents.

The first wardrobe contained shoes, boots, hat-boxes, purses, jackets, and coats. Jessica shut the doors and went on to an armoire. It contained corsets, crinolines of varying fullness, gloves, and lingerie. The third contained day dresses. The fourth held riding dresses. The fifth held the ball gown from her twentieth birthday. And so it went, until she had looked in everything.

Jessica heaved up the lid of the nearest trunk, which happened to be one that Wolfe had brought in. A sound of surprise came from her lips when she realized the trunk was already full. She had assumed both trunks were empty by the ease with which Wolfe had handled them, but this one contained her fishing and hunting gear, her favorite books, and a small sidesaddle that looked elegant despite its off-center horn.

On the top of trunk, protected by a beautifully worked leather case, lay a wedding present from Lord Robert—a matched Winchester rifle and carbine, saddle scabbards, and enough cartridges to start a war. The weapons were inlaid with intricate patterns of gold and silver. The carbine magazine held thirteen shells and the rifle held fifteen. The loading port was cleverly placed so that shells could be loaded nearly as fast as they could be shot. Wolfe had taken one look at the gift, lifted out the repeating rifle, and run his hands over it like a man touching a lover.

It's almost worth getting married to a useless aristocrat to own such a fine rifle.

Almost, but not quite.

The memory of Wolfe's sardonic words made Jessica sigh as she set aside the case and turned to an empty trunk. The top tray came free after a struggle, leaving the rest of the trunk empty. At first she tried to work as Betsy had, putting in each piece as though it were a bit of a very fragile puzzle.

Quickly, Jessica realized that she would still be

packing come sundown if she continued working with one item at a time. Besides, none of the items fit together anyway.

She began dumping armload after armload of things into the trunks. By the time she cleaned the wardrobe of shoes and purses and coats, she had filled three trunks with heaps of leather and boxes and cloth. Frowning, she tried to remember if there had been that many trunks full of accessories when Betsy had unpacked.

"I'm sure I had no more than a single trunk, and perhaps part of another that was filled with such things."

With a sound of exasperation, Jessica heaped more things into two of the already full trunks. When she went to shut them, she found that the trunk lids were stubborn and ill-fitting. The contents were stiff and oddly shaped. No matter how she pushed with her hands, the lids wouldn't close enough to fasten the hasp.

Finally, she crawled up on each lid in turn and bounced up and down to settle the contents. Only then could she force the top of the trunk to meet the bottom. The instant she climbed down to fasten the hasp, the lid popped up once more. In the end, she had to stay on the lid and struggle upside-down to close the hasps and fit the padlocks. Twice she almost locked the end of her hip-length braid in with the other contents.

"The trunks never behaved this badly for Betsy," Jessica muttered.

After packing two more trunks, she opened the gold watch that was pinned to her dress, read the time, and frowned. Wolfe would be back at any moment. She wanted to prove she wasn't a *useless aristocrat* by being packed and ready to go.

"Soonest begun, soonest ended," Jessica told herself bracingly, and blew stray wisps of hair away from her flushed face.

She piled the rest of the day dresses on top of the others and began shoving cloth down into the trunk, leaning hard on the resilient material, trying to crush everything down to the size of the trunk. Just before she jumped onto the lid in order to force it shut, she remembered the ballgown and the riding clothes. She looked at the trunk she had been jamming clothes into, then at the single remaining trunk she hadn't yet opened. The trunk beneath her hands was definitely larger.

"Oh, blazes," Jessica muttered. "The gown will have to go in this trunk."

The ballgown felt as smooth and weightless as moonlight, but it had yard after yard of material. No matter how she rolled, stuffed, bunched, and punched the dress, she couldn't get it to stay within the confines of the trunk.

Wearily, Jessica straightened. The sound of a rag picker crying his wares on the street lured her to the window. When she looked out, she saw a tall, familiar shape striding down the street toward the hotel.

Jessica rushed to the trunk, frantically smashed the ballgown down, slammed the lid and leaned her weight on it. At first the lid hung up, but it finally managed to swallow all that it had been fed. She fumbled hasp and lock into position, and slammed the padlock shut.

"One left."

As Jessica straightened and turned toward the remaining trunk, she was hauled up short by a yank on her braid. She glanced over her shoulder. The last third of her hair vanished into the locked trunk. She wrapped her hands around the braid and pulled. Nothing happened. She pulled harder. The hair remained firmly caught. She yanked and then yanked again, but stayed tethered to the trunk.

"Blast and blazes! I'll have to unlock the confounded thing and do it all over again."

Then Jessica discovered she couldn't reach the key ring she had left on the bedside table. Nor could she drag the trunk closer. Pushing seemed to have a better effect. Shoving, panting, Jessica alternated between shoulder and hands as she inched the stubborn trunk closer to the bedside table. One of the trunk's brassbound corners caught on an irregularity in the wood floor. No matter how she pushed, the trunk didn't move.

The thought of Wolfe coming in the room and finding her prisoner to one of her own surly trunks gave Jessica a desperate surge of strength. She shoved repeatedly against the top edge of the trunk, trying to jostle it free.

Without warning, the heavy trunk tipped up and rolled over, taking Jessica with it, yanking her off her feet. She gave a startled shriek as she went head over heels and landed on the floor in a tangle of soft blue cloth.

An instant later the door to the suite banged open. Wolfe stood in the doorway looking as dangerous as the long knife in his hand. The steel blade was a stark contrast to his well-cut, dark wool suit and white linen shirt.

"Jessi? Where are you?"

She grimaced but knew there was no escape. "Over here."

Wolfe stepped into the suite. He glanced in the direction of her voice, saw an upside-down trunk and a tangle of blue cloth, creamy lingerie, and dainty blue shoes. In three long strides he was next to her.

"Are you all right?"

"Just ducky," she said through her teeth.

"What are you doing on the floor?"

"Packing."

Wolfe raised black eyebrows. "It's easier if the trunk is right side up."

"Bloody hell."

Wolfe's eyes followed Jessica's long red braid to the point where it disappeared into the trunk. He started to say something, but was laughing too hard to speak.

Normally, the sound of his laughter made Jessica smile, but not this time. This time flags of anger and humiliation burned on her cheeks.

"Lord, if you could only see yourself, like a turtle in a net . . ." Laughter took Wolfe's voice again.

Jessica lay on the floor and thought longingly of the case and the weapons inside. Unfortunately, they were as out of reach as the key to the padlock.

Snickering, Wolfe sheathed his knife before he reached for Jessica. He took her braid and pulled gently, then with more force. It made no difference. She was well and truly caught.

"The key," she said distinctly, "is on the bedside table."

"Don't go away, elf. I'll be right back."

The thought of Jessica going anywhere on her short tether set off another spate of laughter in Wolfe. It seemed like a long time until he sat on his heels next to her and started fitting keys in the lock to find the right one. The fact that he kept laughing at unexpected intervals slowed down the process of freeing her quite a bit.

The third time Wolfe leaned against the trunk, all but helpless with laughter, Jessica snatched the keys from his fingers and opened the padlock herself. She still wasn't free. She couldn't open the trunk while it was upside-down. Nor could she right it. She could, however, push her laughing husband over.

And she did.

Still laughing, Wolfe caught himself with feline ease and came to his feet by the trunk. He righted the trunk, pried open the lid, and pulled out the length of red hair.

"Yours, I believe," he murmured, handing Jessica the braid.

She grabbed it with fingers that shook, wishing the braid was Wolfe's throat. The look in his eyes told her that he knew just what she was thinking.

"You're welcome," he said gravely.

Not trusting herself, Jessica turned and slammed the trunk lid down, locked it once more, and went to the sixth trunk. When she opened it, she saw that it was packed right to the top with curling irons, clothes brushes, flatirons, tissue paper, linens, toiletries . . .

"Oh, no," Jessica breathed.

Wolfe took a breath that kept dissolving into laughter. "Problems?"

"I'm missing a trunk."

He counted the trunks with a lazy, raking glance. Six. "They're all here."

"They can't be."

"Why?"

"I haven't packed my riding clothes and all the trunks are full."

Wolfe shook his head. "Somehow I'm not surprised. Hand me some of that tissue paper."

"Why?"

"I'll help you pack."

"What does tissue paper have to do with packing?" she asked.

Wolfe shot a sideways glance at Jessica. "Tissue paper keeps out the wrinkles."

"Wrinkles?"

"The things you take out of clothes with a flatiron."

She blinked. "You do?"

"No. *You* do. Ironing is a wife's duty. So is washing, drying, and folding the clothes."

"What is the husband doing all the while the wife is at work?"

"Getting things dirty again."

"A truly taxing duty," she said sardonically.

Wolfe's smile faded. "Any time you want to go back to being Lady Jessica Charteris, complete with maids and footmen to do your bidding, let me know."

"Do hold your breath waiting, my lord. It will make the time so much more pleasant—for both of us!"

2

JESSICA moved sleepily and burrowed closer to the warmth that held the cold dawn at bay.

"For God's sake," Wolfe muttered.

The weight of her against his usual morning arousal was altogether too hot. When small hands slid beneath his coat to reach the warmth of his body, his heartbeat speeded. Without waking, she tucked her face against his neck and sighed.

Wolfe closed his eyes, but it didn't help. Nothing could shut out the memory of Jessica's creamy, pink-tipped breasts rising from the ruins of her peignoir. Before that moment, he had never permitted himself to think of his redheaded elf as anything but a child.

Now Wolfe could think of little else but the womanly shape of her breasts.

He had suffered the torments of the damned every time Jessica dozed off on the endless stage ride. Invariably, the stage's erratic motions would threaten to send her to the floor. Invariably, he caught her, supported her, then finally cradled her across his lap while she slept, her breath tangling softly with his. Invariably, he found himself wanting her with an urgency that infuriated him, for he knew she didn't want him in return.

And even if she had, he would not take her. She was the wrong wife for him. No amount of desire could change that.

Yet the warmth of Jessica's breath against Wolfe's mouth as he turned his face to her went to his head like wine. The softness of her breasts begged for his hands to cup and caress them. The sweet weight of her hips against his aroused flesh was a torment he both savored and prayed would end soon.

Jessica murmured and nuzzled against Wolfe sleepily, knowing only that he was warmth and the world was cold. The brush of her lips against his skin sent a painful shaft of need through his body.

"Wake up, damn it," Wolfe said beneath his breath. "I'm not a feather bed for your ladyship's convenience."

When Jessica made a protesting sound and clung more tightly, Wolfe's arms pulled her closer despite his better judgment. He searched her face, telling himself it was the gray dawn rather than exhaustion that had drained the radiance from Jessica's skin and put shadows under her eyes.

But he knew it wasn't simply a trick of the light. Stage travel was hard on grown men. For a young woman who was used to cosseting, travel by stage was an endurance contest she couldn't hope to win.

Damn it, Jessi. Why won't you give up and go back where you belong?

Yet even as Wolfe formed the thought, he was smoothing back Jessica's hair from her face with a gentleness he was helpless to combat. She looked like fine porcelain, defenseless against a world more harshly made than she was.

With no warning, Jessica's eyes opened and looked full into Wolfe's. Even the dawn couldn't conceal her shock at finding herself held so intimately.

"W-Wolfe?"

With more speed than gentleness, Wolfe set Jessica on the bench seat opposite him, yanked his hat down over his eyes, and ignored her. Shortly, he was asleep.

Dazed by her own fitful sleep, stunned by awakening in Wolfe's arms when she had fallen asleep slumped in a hard, drafty corner of the seat, Jessica simply stared at her husband and tried to remember where she was, and why. Finally she opened the side curtain in an effort to orient herself.

Dawn was simply another, lesser shade of darkness spreading across the sky. In all directions, the land was flat, bleak, and featureless but for the icy ruts that marked the stage road. No smoke lifted into the sky, announcing man's presence. No fences marked off pastures. No roads led to distant houses or farms.

At first, the lack of trees and habitation fascinated Jessica, but after a time the unbroken monotony of the landscape numbed her as much as the cold wind pouring through gaps in the side curtains.

Jessica braced herself against the uncomfortable seat and fought to stay upright. Since they'd left St. Joseph, time had been a blur to her. She couldn't remember whether she had been traveling three days or five or fifty-five. Hours and days ran together without anything to separate them, for Wolfe had insisted that they travel constantly, sleeping upright, getting down from the stage only to use the privy when the horses were changed at one of the miserable stations that dotted the long route west.

Other passengers came and went at various stops, and ate or slept in the low, rudely built stage stations. Jessica and Wolfe did not. He brought her food to her and they ate inside the stage, where they also slept. At least the past night had been spent in privacy, for no other passengers had chosen to endure frigid hours on the stage. But the result of the relentless travel was to make Jessica feel as though she had been born into the jostling, jouncing, pounding stagecoach box and would die in the same place.

She hoped it would be soon.

Wearily, Jessica stretched and rubbed her aching neck. With cold hands, she took down her hair and attempted to brush and braid it into submission. Wolfe's stinging comments about girls who were too useless to comb their own hair had rankled deeply, as did the memory of his laughter when he had found her long braid trapped in the trunk.

By the time Jessica had managed to make two uneven braids and pin them in a coil on her head, the stagecoach began slowing. With a flurry of shouts and curses, the driver pulled the horses to a halt alongside a crude sod building that appeared, at best, uninviting. Despite that, Jessica looked forward to the stop as a break in the punishing ride.

Wolfe woke and stretched. His long, powerful arms and wide shoulders seemed to fill the interior of the stage. The necessity of completing the journey to Denver without spending a night in any of the station houses had eaten into even Wolfe's endurance. At least Jessica assumed it had. It certainly had shortened his temper to a hair's breadth.

Yet Wolfe showed no sign of discomfort. He climbed down from the stage with the muscular grace that was as much a part of him as his high cheekbones and blue-black eyes. Jessica both admired and resented the resilience of her husband's body. She felt like a carpet after a spring beating.

Nonetheless, Jessica smiled cheerfully at Wolfe when he glanced her way, for she was determined not to lose her temper with him again. No man wanted to live with a shrew, and to be fair, Wolfe hadn't even had the chance to choose his wife. It was up to Jessica to be unfailingly sweet, gentle, and pleasant to be around. Then Wolfe would be less irritable, less difficult, and more like the wonderful companion of Jessica's memories.

When Wolfe turned and held out his hand for Jessica, she leaned on his strength in a distinctly unladylike manner as she descended stiffly.

"A lovely morning, is it not?" Jessica asked, smiling into the teeth of a cold wind.

Wolfe grunted.

"I don't know when I've ever seen so many delicate shades of gray," she continued cheerfully. "Quite enough to put a dove to shame."

Wolfe shot Jessica a look of disbelief. "I've heard a cold March morning called a lot of things out here. Lovely wasn't one of them."

She sighed. Perhaps Wolfe would feel better after he had the wretched coffee Americans so admired. As far as she was concerned, there wasn't enough sugarcane in the world to sweeten that evil brew.

There was no more conversation while Wolfe strode alongside Jessica to the privy's miserable comforts. When she emerged, clutching her scent-drenched handkerchief, the cold prairie wind cut through her wool cape and dress as though they were sheerest silk. She looked longingly at the smoke streaming from the canted chimney pipe of the stage station.

The thought of being close to a fire's warmth made Jessica shiver with pleasure. Ever since Wolfe had set her so abruptly on the far side of the coach, she had been getting steadily colder. Even worse, the sound of the wind had been gnawing at her nerves, eroding her self-control.

"Wolfe, let's eat inside this time."

"No."

"But why? We're the only passengers. Sure-ly—"

"See those horses?" he interrupted curtly.

Jessica looked. There were indeed horses tied on the lee side of the rudimentary barn, which was more a lean-to attached to the station than a true barn.

"Those are saddle horses," Wolfe said.

She schooled her expression into one of cheerful interest. "Why so they are. You can tell by the number of legs."

Wolfe started to speak, gave a crack of laughter, and shook his head. How anyone who looked so worn and fragile could be so full of mischief was beyond him. He reached out and gently tugged a wisp of mahogany hair that had unraveled from Jessica's crown of coiled braids.

"That means the station is full of men who are waiting for the stage," Wolfe explained.

"Why? They have horses, after all."

"They could be borrowed. In any case, they've been hard used. A smart man wouldn't set out for a hundred-mile ride on a played-out horse." Wolfe shrugged. "But even if the station were empty, I wouldn't let you go inside. This is Cross-Eyed Joe's place."

"Do you know him?"

"Everyone between St. Joseph and Denver does. His station is the worst of a sorry lot, and he's the sorriest of all. He's a crude, blaspheming, drunken son of a bitch whose breath could back down a wolverine."

Jessica blinked. "Then how does he hold his job?"

"He cares for horses the way a mother hen cares for her chicks. Out here, being afoot can be a death sentence. You can forgive Joe's smell when he puts strong, eager horses in the traces."

"Why would being afoot be so dangerous? Lord Robert never mentioned danger when we were here before."

"Lord Robert's 'native guides' fought even better than they tracked game," Wolfe said dryly. "No Indians or outlaws were going to take on the kind of trouble twenty well-armed men could offer, no matter how tempting the prize."

Broodingly, Wolfe looked at the unusually well-bred, obviously trail-weary horses tied in the lee of the station. Perhaps those horses belonged to honest men rather than to men whose lives depended on the ability of their horses to outrun the law.

Perhaps . . . but Wolfe doubted it.

Jessica's glance followed Wolfe's to the station house, but for a different reason. A week ago she wouldn't have kenneled a dog inside something as disreputable as that sod house, but now it looked like a haven from the bleak landscape. When visiting the prairie with Lord Robert's hunting expeditions, she had thought the place beautiful with its tall grass and unexpected ponds, its melodious birds and arching blue sky, and its clean, endless vistas.

At the moment, Jessica's view of the prairie was less charitable. The landscape was in the dying grasp of winter. Mile upon mile upon mile of land lay half-frozen around her. Flat, featureless, treeless, empty of lakes or rivers, inhabited only by the long, low howl of the north wind, the prairie defined desolation; and the sound the wind made was the disbelieving cry of a soul newly damned.

Jessica had heard that sound before in her nightmares. Shuddering, she looked away from the emptiness and knew she had to be out the reach of the wind, if only for a few minutes.

"Wolfe, please."

"No. It isn't a fit place for an English lady."

"I'm Scots," she said automatically.

Wolfe smiled, but there was no humor in his expression. "I know. Scots or English or even French, that place still isn't fit for a lady."

Jessica was very tired of hearing what was and was not fit for a lady, for it seemed those rules always worked against her. On the other hand, losing her temper only caused Wolfe to bait her all the more.

"I'm an American wife," Jessica said, smiling through her teeth, "not a foreign lady."

"Then obey your husband. I'll bring breakfast, if it's fit to eat. I doubt that it will be. The food here has been passed up by skunks."

"Nothing can be that bad."

"This is. If you're hungry, we'll eat farther up the line. One of the army wives makes egg money supplying the stage stop with baked goods."

The wind's eerie cry raked over Jessica's nerves.

She trembled and looked at Wolfe with an unconscious plea in her blue eyes.

"Wolfe, just this once, just for a few minutes?"

"No."

Fear and exhaustion shook Jessica. Fiercely, she
fought the desire to cry. Her mother's experience
had taught Jessica that tears served no purpose
except that of announcing weakness, and weakness was invariably attacked.

"Get back to the stage, your ladyship," Wolfe
said curtly. "I'll bring you any food that's fit to
eat."

Jessica's spine straightened as anger swept
through her, driving out fatigue and fear for a few
blessed moments. "How kind of you. Tell me,
what did you do for entertainment before you had
me to torment, pull wings from butterflies?"

"If being an American wife instead of an English
lady—"

"*Scots.*"

"—is such a torment," he continued, ignoring
her interruption, "then you have only to say the
word and you'll be free of this rude frontier life."

"Bastard."

"Without doubt, but the word I had in mind was
annulment."

The wind moaned with a chill promise of damnation that made nightmares awaken inside Jessica. When the stagecoach was moving, there was
at least the endless rattle and clatter of the wheels
to dull the voice of the wind. But now the stage
was motionless and the traces empty while the
horses were switched. Now the stage shifted and
shivered beneath the cruel force of the wind.

Jessica knew if she sat in that fragile shell and
heard the wind screaming, she would start scream-

ing, too. Yet she didn't dare show such weakness to Wolfe. If he understood how much she feared the wind, he would use it against her, driving her back to England and a marriage with the likes of Lord Gore.

Then her nightmares would be real, rather than remaining black dreams she never quite remembered upon awakening.

Without a word, Jessica picked up her skirts and walked past Wolfe, who was staring at the weary saddle horses. As he had feared, some of them bore the marks of horses used by the South in the recent war. More than one band of outlaws had begun in the embittered rabble of a lost cause. Some had come from the North as well, men who had gotten a taste for looting and killing that hadn't gone away when the war ended.

Wish to hell Caleb or Reno was here, Wolfe thought grimly. *I could use a good man at my back right now.*

A motion at the edge of Wolfe's vision caught his eye. It was Jessica's long skirts being whipped by the wind. She was headed for the station building rather than the empty stage.

"Jessi!"

She didn't even look back.

Wolfe began running, but it was the stage he headed for, not Jessica. He knew he had no chance of reaching her before she got to the station house. He yanked open the stagecoach's door and leaped inside with the agility of a cat. The leather presentation case that held the matched rifle and carbine was on the seat.

Just as Jessica closed the station house door behind her, she looked back, expecting Wolfe to be on her heels. When she saw that he wasn't, she let out a sigh of relief. The sigh turned to a soundless gasp when she turned to face the occupants of the room.

Wolfe had been right. This wasn't a place for a lady.

It wasn't the room's dim, smoky interior, its filth, or its feral smell that put the place off limits for a lady. It was the intent masculine eyes measuring her the way a merchant measured gold dust, one soft bit at a time.

A man who had been sitting apart from the others stood up from the uneven table and swept off his battered hat.

"Something you need, ma'am?" he asked unhappily.

Even in the bad light Jessica recognized the stagecoach driver's long, bushy mustache. She smiled at him with relief, not realizing how beautiful her smile might be to men who hadn't seen a white woman for months, much less one wearing a dress that had been sewn by expert seamstresses to fit her breasts and waist like a soft blue shadow. Even wrinkled and mussed from long travel, she was like an exotic flower blooming in the midst of winter.

"I was chilled," Jessica said softly. "I saw the smoke."

"Come on in," one of the other men said, standing. He gestured toward the bench where he had been sitting. "All warmed up and ready to ride, like me."

Several of the men snickered.

The man who had spoken should have been handsome. He was tall and well-proportioned, with even teeth and regular features. His clothes were frayed but well-made. He wore a heavy split riding coat. He was the only man who was clean-

shaven. His posture was as proud as any gentleman's.

Yet there was something in the young man that
made Jessica profoundly uneasy. His eyes were like
the wind—colorless, empty, and cold. He was
watching her with a reptilian intensity that made
the skin on her arms ripple in a primitive comprehension of danger. She longed to be back in the
stagecoach with Wolfe at her side.

Jessica would have turned and fled, but she
sensed with great certainty that showing weakness
to this man would have the effect of dangling
wounded prey in front of a pack of starving
hounds.

"My name's Raleigh," the young man said, tipping his hat in a gesture that was more familiar
than polite, "but pretty gals mostly call me Lee."

"Thank you, Mr. Raleigh," Jessica said with
clipped formality, "but it's not necessary for you
to give up your seat. Just being in out of the wind
is enough for me."

"Nonsense," he said, coming toward Jessica.
"Come over here where it's warm." He kicked one
of the men's feet on the way by. "Steamer, get off
your butt and get the pretty English miss some
grub."

"Scots," she said softly, forcing herself to be calm
when every nerve in her body screamed for her to
flee.

"What?"

"I'm Scots."

Raleigh smiled thinly as he reached for Jessica's
arm. "Whatever you say, lassie. Now get your
pretty self over here and tell me what a girl like
you is doing in Cross-Eyed Joe's place."

The door behind Jessica opened, letting in a cold blast of wind.

Wolfe stepped inside. He looked out of place in his city clothes. In the muted light, the silver and gold inlay on the carbine shimmered like water. The effect was like that of a snake's scales, a warning rather than a lure.

"Morning, boys," Wolfe said.

A few surprised grunts and sidelong looks answered him. The accent and rhythm of Wolfe's speech, unlike his clothes, were Western.

With a leisurely glance that was just short of insulting, Wolfe summed up the room. Though his eyes didn't linger, each of the seven men had the feeling he had been marked for future reference. Only Raleigh didn't seem to notice the danger in Wolfe's bleak eyes.

"There's a mean wind blowing," Wolfe said casually.

Muttered agreement rippled through the room.

Raleigh dropped his hand to his side and stood relaxed and easy, watching Wolfe. Jessica saw that Raleigh's riding coat had come open. The right side was pushed out of the way behind the six-gun that he wore on his hip.

"Well, well, take a look at that," Raleigh said, whistling between his teeth. "That's some fancy carbine, suh. Never seen its equal." He held out his hand, confident the well-dressed city man wouldn't refuse him. "Mind if I try its balance?"

"Yes."

For a moment, Wolfe's refusal didn't register. When it did, a thin flush appeared on Raleigh's cheekbones.

"You're not very friendly, suh. Some would even say you're insulting."

Wolfe smiled.

Raleigh's body became less relaxed.

"Just trying to save you some grief," Wolfe said. "The trigger's real touchy. Been known to go off for no better reason than being handed from one man to another. That would be a crying shame, too. Handsome young boy like you would surely leave broken hearts all up and down the trail. Be more weeping and wailing over your grave than when Lee turned over his sword at Appomattox."

Raleigh stiffened. "Are you insulting the South?"

"No, but you are. Any man wearing a lieutenant's bars on his coat should have better manners than to grab for a lady's arm." Without looking away from Raleigh's angry face, Wolfe said, "Tom, help Cross-Eyed Joe get that fresh team in the traces."

"Yessir," the driver said.

He jammed on his hat and hurried out the door, careful not to get between Wolfe and the young man who had fought on the losing side of the War Between the States. Slowly, almost imperceptibly, Raleigh's hand began easing toward the butt of his six-gun.

Jessica's breath came in with a rush.

"I see him," Wolfe said before she could speak. He smiled at Raleigh again. "Don't let all the gold and silver fool you, boy. Repeating weapons like this one shot Southern regiments to red ribbons. If you don't believe me, go ahead and reach for that belt gun. I'll have three bullets in you before you know what happened, and I'll still have ten more left for your friends."

Behind Raleigh, the men began edging for opposite ends of the table.

"I'll shoot the next man who moves," Wolfe said.

No one doubted him. They sat very still.

Jessica forgot to breathe as the silence stretched and stretched, plucking at her nerves more savagely than the wind. Then the young man laughed and relaxed again.

"No point getting riled," Raleigh said easily. "I was just having some fun to pass the time waiting for the stage."

"Going east?" Wolfe asked.

"West."

"Next stage west will be along tomorrow about this time."

"Tomorrow?" Raleigh said, startled. "What about the one today?"

"It's full."

"But only you and the girl—"

"My *wife*," Wolfe interrupted flatly.

"You're the only ones on the damned stage!"

"Like I said. It's full."

Raleigh's body tightened again.

"It'll keep, Raleigh," said one of the other men coldly. "If the gent with the fancy rifle wants to fight the Indians up ahead all by himself, let him. One less Yankee bastard won't bother me none. I've got better game to hunt."

Raleigh glanced unhappily at the man who had spoken, but didn't argue.

"Your friend gave you excellent advice," Wolfe said to Raleigh. "Here's some more—stay inside until the stage leaves."

Jessica didn't wait for Wolfe to open the door for her. She didn't want him to have to turn his back on the men in the room. Without a word, she opened the door and hurried across the cold yard

to the stage. Not until she was inside did she begin
to relax.

Wolfe didn't. Inside the stagecoach, he kept the
carbine across his lap and watched the station with
predatory attention. No one came out.

Suddenly the driver's whip cracked like a pistol
shot, the horses jerked forward in the traces, and
the stage left the station as though the wheels were
on fire.

"Will they follow us?" Jessica asked tightly.

"I doubt it. Their horses are played out." Wolfe
looked from the window to the wife he hadn't
asked for, the young woman who set his body on
fire, the delicate aristocrat who was utterly unsuited for the Western land he loved as he had
never loved anything in his life. "You're going to
get somebody killed, your ladyship. You don't belong out here."

"Neither do you."

"The hell I don't."

"Those men took one look at you and knew you
for a stranger."

Wolfe smiled. "No one west of the Mississippi
has ever seen me dressed like this, but I was
damned if I'd look like your ladyship's roustabout.
Just as well. Jericho Slater was in that bunch at the
stage station. If he had recognized me, there would
have been hell to pay."

"Who is Jericho Slater?"

"One of the few surviving members of Jed Slater's gang."

"Why does he hate you?"

"Caleb, Reno, and I did our best to kill every
one of them." Wolfe smiled thinly. "Damn near
did. My only regret is that Jericho wasn't with them
at the time. He's as bad as Jed ever was."

Jessica frowned. "Why were you fighting a gang of men?"

"Slater made the mistake of grabbing Willow."

The change in Wolfe's voice and face when he spoke Willow's name made Jessica's breath lock in her throat. Suddenly, she had no doubt that Willow was a woman.

"Who is she?"

Jessica's stark question made Wolfe glance over at her.

"A woman."

"I gathered as much."

"A Western woman."

"Just what does that mean?" Jessica asked tightly.

"A woman strong enough to fight beside her man if it comes to that, and soft enough to set him on fire when the fighting is over. That's one hell of a woman."

Jessica forced herself to keep talking, to find out more about the woman who could make Wolfe's eyes and voice gentle when he spoke about her.

"Is that why you were so angry with me over our marriage?" Jessica asked in a strained voice. "Were you expecting to marry Willow instead?"

"Not likely. I'd have to take on Caleb Black to do that, and only a fool would take on Caleb Black," Wolfe said dryly. "He's an Old Testament kind of man. Not much forgiveness in him."

"Who is Caleb Black?"

"Willow's husband, and one of the best friends a man could have."

Wolfe watched with interest the relief that Jessica couldn't completely hide.

"I see," Jessica said. She drew a deep breath before she asked the only question that really mattered to her. "Do you love Willow?"

"Be hard not to. She's everything I ever wanted in a woman."

Jessica felt herself going pale. Until that moment she hadn't known how deeply she had been certain that Wolfe was hers, that he had been hers since he had plucked her from the haystack, that he would always be hers.

She had never expected Wolfe to love another woman. The pain of it was shocking. It took the world away, leaving only a blankness where each heartbeat shook her, making her dizzy.

The stagecoach lurched and bucked over a rough spot. The driver's shouts and cracking whip vied with the rattling of the wheels to deafen the passengers. For once, Jessica was glad of the violent motion. It made further conversation unnecessary. She braced herself as best she could, closed her eyes, and wondered how she could hurt so much and show no visible wound.

Wolfe gave Jessica a hooded glance. He knew she was only pretending to sleep, for her body was too stiff and she shivered from time to time as though standing in a cold wind. She clearly didn't have any more questions about Willow Black. It was equally clear that Jessica had no desire to hear any more on the subject of Western women.

With a rather grim smile, Wolfe tipped his hat forward over his eyes, braced his feet on the facing seat, and congratulated himself on finding a chink in the aristocratic armor surrounding Lady Jessica Charteris Lonetree. He had been beginning to wonder if she had one. Her stubbornness had surprised him. He had expected her to give up and return to England long before now. She was accustomed to being waited on, to having endless rounds of teas and balls, to being protected and comforted by everyone within reach of her bewitching smile.

None of that had happened in America. Wolfe had deliberately left her alone. When that hadn't affected her determination, he had made her go without servants, but that had been harder on him than on her. He would never forget the silky electricity of her hair clinging to him as he brushed it, or the elegant femininity of her back beneath fine lingerie as he buttoned each tiny button for her. Nor would he forget the stab of fear he had felt when he heard her scream, or the relieved laughter that had followed when he found her safe, though held prisoner by her braid.

A girl that helpless won't last long out here, Wolfe assured himself silently. *The West requires a woman with staying power. A woman like Willow.*

But it wasn't Willow's blond hair and hazel eyes that haunted Wolfe's thoughts and his fitful sleep. It was a sensuous red-haired elf weeping crystal tears.

3

THE silence between Wolfe and Jessica wasn't broken until afternoon, when a young, rather pregnant woman got on board. Her single trunk had been lashed awkwardly to the boot, for Jessica's trunks took up much of the top, even though Wolfe had decreed that only three would come on the stage with them. The rest had been put aboard a freight wagon destined for Denver.

"Thank you, sir," said the young woman, as Wolfe handed her into the stagecoach. "I'm afraid I'm more clumsy each day."

"It's a difficult time," Wolfe said, subtly eyeing the girl's waistline. In the stagecoach's dim interior light, she looked at least six months pregnant. "Are you traveling alone?"

The kindness in Wolfe's voice made the girl smile shyly at her hands. "Yes, sir. I couldn't bear being away from my husband any longer. My aunt and uncle wanted me to stay in Ohio until the baby was born, but I just couldn't wait. My husband is stationed at Bent's Fort, you see."

"Then you have an even longer trip than we do. We're going only as far as Denver."

The girl sat down thankfully and smoothed her

hands over her dress. The costume was as expensive as Jessica's, and considerably less mussed. The girl looked barely seventeen. She was plainly uneasy at the prospect of the stage ride.

"I'll sit up with the driver," Wolfe said. "It will be more comfortable for you."

"Oh, no, sir," she said quickly, looking no higher than his chest. "It's too raw out there for man or beast. Besides, it's the wilderness that makes me nervous, not you. There are rumors of Indians." She shuddered. "The thought of those murderous heathens being anywhere near me just gives me the shivers."

Wolfe concealed his amusement.

"Not all Indians are murderous," Jessica said. "Some are quite hospitable. I've spent time in their camps."

"You were a hostage?" the girl asked, horrified and fascinated at the same time.

"Hardly. Lord Robert Stewart was a friend of the Cheyenne. We were guests."

"I'd sooner befriend the Devil as a redskin, and that's a fact. You can't trust them." She smoothed her dress again and changed the subject with transparent determination. "That's a lovely dress, ma'am. Is it French?"

"Yes. My guardian preferred English styles, but I like the simplicity of the new French fashions."

The girl looked quickly at Wolfe, wondering if he was the guardian in question.

"My husband," Jessica added, stressing the word lightly, "prefers no style at all. Isn't that correct, Mr. Lonetree?"

"There's little use for silks and foolishness in the West, Lady Jessica."

"Lady?" said the girl quickly. "Then you're English?"

Jessica bit back the temptation to correct the girl. "Close enough."

"A true titled lady?" the girl persisted.

"Not here," Jessica said. "Here I am Mrs. Lonetree."

"I'm Mrs. O'Conner." The girl hesitated. "Lonetree is an unusual name."

"The true name is Tree That Stands Alone, but Lonetree is easier for most people," Wolfe said.

"It sounds Indian."

"It is."

The girl's face paled. She stared at Wolfe, noticing for the first time the man beneath the expensive city clothes.

"Dear Lord, you're a redskin!"

"Sometimes," he agreed. "Sometimes I'm an over-civilized citizen of the British Empire. Most of the time I'm just a Western man."

The young Mrs. O'Conner made a low, unhappy sound and began twisting her handkerchief between trembling fingers. She looked everywhere in the coach but at Wolfe.

Wolfe sighed, settled his hat more firmly on his head, and reached for the door of the bouncing coach. When the door was opened wide, he braced himself in the doorway and reached for the luggage railing that ran around the top of the coach.

"Wolfe, what on earth . . . ?" Jessica asked.

"Mrs. O'Conner will feel easier if I'm not inside with the civilized folks."

With that, Wolfe swung himself up onto the top of the stagecoach with feline grace and moved forward to sit next to the startled driver. The coach door banged shut.

"You're acting like a complete ninnyhammer," Jessica said, eyeing the young woman coolly. "My Wolfe is more a gentleman than anyone I've met in America."

"My family was murdered by redskins when I was twelve. I was hiding, but I saw what they did to Mother and Sissy, and Mother was seven months along." The girl's hands smoothed over the swell of her own pregnancy. "That poor little babe died before he ever lived. Savages. Murdering savages. I hope the Army sends them all back to the devil that spawned them."

Jessica closed her eyes as nightmares turned and coiled just beyond the reach of memory. She, too, had seen babies born dead. There was a horror in those tiny, still bodies that words couldn't describe.

Shivering, Jessica pulled her heavy travel cloak more tightly around her body. Wishing she could curl up against Wolfe's warmth, she did the next best thing. She curled up against the small leather travel bag Wolfe kept inside the coach with the rifle case.

Numbing miles went by. Jessica made no effort to speak to Mrs. O'Conner again. The loathing and fear in the girl's voice when she spoke of Indians were not subject to reason any more than the aristocrats who spoke of "the viscount's savage" were amenable to seeing past Wolfe's Cheyenne mother and bastardy to the man beneath.

Finally, Jessica slept, only to be brought awake by the sound of shots and a high scream of terror from Mrs. O'Conner.

"Indians!" the girl screamed, crossing herself frantically. "Jesus and Mary, save me!"

Jessica bolted upright and yanked open the side curtain while the young Mrs. O'Conner's screams pierced the interior of the coach. At first Jessica could see nothing but the flat landscape. Then she realized the terrain wasn't as flat as it seemed. The land was folded gently, providing shelter for men and animals. It also provided ambush sites for unwary travelers. Apparently, a band of Indians had waited in one of those folds for the stage to approach.

"Dear God," Jessica breathed as she heard rifle fire booming from the low hills.

Wolfe was on top of the stagecoach, exposed to every shot. He could use the driver's shotgun, but there was no accuracy with such a weapon. It was intended to deter hold-ups, not an Indian attack.

The driver's whip cracked repeatedly as he yelled at the team, demanding every bit of speed from the big horses. The coach bucked and swayed wildly each time it hit a rough spot on the road, and there were many spots. Jessica braced herself as best she could and stared out the window.

The Indians were a bit ahead and considerably to the left of the coach. They were too far away for accurate shooting. Granted, they were racing closer with every moment, and firing as they came. Even so, Jessica had hunted enough game to realize that the trap—if indeed it was a trap—had been sprung too soon.

Mrs. O'Conner's screams rose to the point of pain as she began to claw frantically at the door, as though she believed safety lay outside the coach rather than within. When Jessica grabbed the girl's hands and dragged them away from the door, Mrs. O'Conner turned on her like a wildcat. Jessica's palm smacked against the girl's cheek with a force that cut through her hysteria. Abruptly her screams gave way to sobbing. She sank to the floor and hid her face in her hands.

In the silence, Jessica suddenly heard Wolfe's rough voice and his fist pounding on the outside of the stage. Apparently, he had been trying to make himself heard over the screaming for long enough to lose his temper.

"Jessica, stop that damned screaming and hand me the rifle case!"

The frightened Mrs. O'Conner heard only a harsh male voice demanding something unknown.

"What?" she screamed, her voice so shrill it was almost unrecognizable.

"The case on the floor!" Wolfe yelled fiercely. "Pass it up to me!"

Jessica had already grabbed the presentation case and was shoving it through the window opening. Before she finished, the case was yanked from her hands. It leaped upward as though it had wings and vanished from sight. Bracing herself against the wild swaying of the coach, Jessica looked out the window. The Indians had disappeared behind a fold in the land.

Suddenly a horse burst up over a nearby rise, running flat out. A rider was bent low over the horse's neck, urging the lathered animal on. The rider was white, not Indian.

A ragged line of pursuing Indians thundered up over the rise several hundred yards behind the man. They fired sporadically, trying to bring down the fleeing rider.

On top of the stage, Wolfe braced himself and sighted down the gleaming barrel. The Indians were more than a thousand feet away and the stage swayed unpredictably. Real accuracy shouldn't have been possible under those conditions, even for someone with Wolfe's uncanny rifle skills.

Wolfe began shooting methodically, picking targets, squeezing the trigger, levering in another cartridge, shifting the barrel to a new target, squeezing the trigger again, ignoring the return fire despite his vulnerable position atop the stage. The man fleeing the Indians was in much more immediate trouble than Wolfe was.

The horse's pace fell off a few hundred yards from the stage. All that prevented the Indians from closing in for the kill was the withering fire Wolfe poured down on them from his swaying perch.

Praying through clenched teeth, her hands curled into fists, Jessica watched the man rein his horse into a long, shallow curve that brought him up to the stage. When the man was alongside, she kicked the door open and dragged Mrs. O'Conner out of the way.

The rider stood in the stirrups, grabbed the luggage railing with his right hand, and swung himself into the stage through the open door. She realized suddenly that he was a big man, bigger even than Wolfe.

Jessica yanked the door shut behind the man. A bullet ricocheted off the iron rim of a wheel with an eerie whine.

"Obliged, ma'am," the stranger said. "Might you know if the rifleman up top is getting low on cartridges?"

"Oh, Lord!" Jessica grabbed Wolfe's travel bag and rummaged quickly inside. "He has some in here. They were one of our wedding presents, like the repeating rifles."

"Sounds like my kind of wedding."

Jessica looked up into a pair of tired, yet amused gray eyes. Wordlessly, she held out her hands.

There was a full box of cartridges in each. Then her breath came in with a harsh sound as she saw the blood sliding out from beneath the cuff of the stranger's jacket.

"You're wounded!"

"I'll live, thanks to you and your husband. I can't shoot worth a damn right-handed and I'd run my horse into the ground trying to get free of those Indians."

Reflexively, Jessica and the man ducked as bullets thudded against the stage. An arrow pierced one of the side curtains and buried its lethal point in the opposite side of the stage where Mrs. O'Conner huddled. The sight of the arrow set her to screaming again.

The stranger ignored the pregnant girl. He scooped both boxes of cartridges into one big hand and turned to a front window. His shrill whistle pierced the sound of screaming. He shoved his arm out the ruined curtain and held the boxes up as close to the roof of the stage as he could. The cartridges were taken from his hands instantly.

The stage lurched and staggered, slamming the man against his wounded arm. With a stifled curse he lowered himself to the seat, reached across his body awkwardly, and drew his six-shooter with his right hand.

Mrs. O'Conner kept screaming.

Jessica leaned past the broad-shouldered stranger and shook Mrs. O'Conner. When that had no effect, Jessica slapped her just hard enough to get her attention. The screams stopped as abruptly as they had begun.

"There, there," Jessica said, hugging the terrified girl and stroking her disheveled hair. "Screaming doesn't do a bit of good. It only makes your throat raw. We'll be all right. There's no finer rifleman alive than my husband."

"I'll second that," the stranger said without looking away from the window. "He sat up there cool as a gentleman at a turkey shoot. And what he aimed at, he hit."

Mrs. O'Conner cringed when Wolfe opened fire once more, but she didn't scream again. She simply wrapped her arms protectively over her womb and trembled while the coach shook and bounced her around. Jessica smiled encouragingly before she turned back to the stranger.

"Let me help you, sir."

"It's been a long time since anyone called me sir," he said, smiling oddly. "My name is Rafe."

"Mr. Rafe," she began.

"Just Rafe."

He squeezed off a shot, then hissed through his teeth as the stagecoach lurched and banged against his wounded arm.

"Save your bullets," Jessica said as she began undoing buttons on Rafe's jacket. "Wolfe has enough for a time. Let me see to your wound."

"Wolfe? Is that your husband?"

She nodded.

"Lucky man."

Startled, Jessica looked up. Rafe was watching her with clear gray eyes. There was appreciation in his glance, but nothing impolite. She smiled uncertainly and went back to work removing Rafe's jacket.

"Luck is a matter of opinion," Jessica said. "Can you get your jacket off your right shoulder?"

Shots came from overhead. A few shots came in reply from the Indians, but they sounded distant. Rafe looked out the window, holstered his gun, and shrugged out of his heavy jacket. Jessica realized anew how big the man was. Were it not for the humor in his gray eyes, he would have been a rather fearsome presence.

"They're still coming, but not for long," Rafe said. "Your husband's pure hell with that rifle. Besides, their horses can't take much more. They ran me a good long ways before I cut the stage road."

With his good arm, Rafe braced both Jessica and himself in the wildly jolting stage while she examined his wound. Her lips tightened as she saw the amount of blood covering his gray wool shirt. Saying nothing, she ripped more of the cloth away from the wound. After a better look at Rafe's muscular arm, she let out a sigh of relief.

"It's not as bad as I feared," Jessica said as she pulled up the hem of her dress. "The bullet missed the bone. You lost a chunk of skin and some muscle, but you have plenty of both to spare. Do you have a knife?"

Rafe took a long knife from a sheath at his belt and held it out to her, haft first. "Watch out. I shave with it."

She grasped the knife carefully, glanced quickly at the golden-bronze stubble covering his face, and smiled an almost hidden smile. "Do you? When?"

He chuckled, then shook his head and said wistfully, "You remind me of my sister. She was a sassy little thing, too. At least, she used to be. I haven't seen her in years. Too many of them. Wanderlust is as bad as gold fever for keeping a man away from his family."

Jessica sliced off strips of petticoat with remarkable speed. The knife was indeed razor sharp. It made quick work of the fine, ice-blue silk petticoat whose color matched the wool of her dress. As she began binding Rafe's arm, rifle fire broke out again.

Rafe cocked his head, listening. No return fire came. "Sounds like they're giving up."

"Praise God," Jessica said fervently. "Wolfe was so exposed up there."

"You were hardly out of the line of fire, ma'am. The stagecoach isn't thick enough to stop bullets at close range."

"I hadn't thought about that," she admitted. "I was too worried about Wolfe."

"Like I said, he's a lucky man."

"Maybe one day he'll think so, too," Jessica said under her breath. She ripped the trailing end of the silk down the middle and tied off the bandage. "There. That should help the bleeding. At the next stage stop, I'll wash the wound with soap and clean water."

"That isn't necessary."

"Yes, it is," she said as she helped Rafe back into his jacket. "A man called Semmelweis discovered that the horrible infections of childbed fever could be prevented if the doctor simply washed his hands before he treated each patient. If one infection can be prevented by washing, it stands to reason that others can, too."

"Are you a nurse?" Rafe asked, easing his arm into the coat with her help. "You have very good hands, gentle and quick."

Jessica smiled. "Thank you, but I have no formal training. My guardian raised me to be able to handle the common emergencies of a country estate—broken bones, fevers, gashes, and such. I've also had experience with pregnancy and childbirth."

Enough to know that I want no part of either, Jessica added silently as she turned away to check on the girl, who was still hugging herself. *If I learned nothing else from my mother, I learned that.*

"Are you all right, Mrs. O'Conner?" Jessica asked.

Numbly, the girl nodded.

"And the babe?" Jessica said bluntly, putting her hands inside the girl's coat and pressing lightly against the womb. "Is it well, too?"

The girl stared, shaken out of her apathy by the gentle, unexpected explorations of the other woman's hands.

"Is there any pain?" Jessica asked.

Mrs. O'Conner shook her head.

A soundless sigh of relief came from Jessica. The girl's torso was supple and resilient rather than rigid with untimely contractions. Smiling reassuringly, Jessica arranged the girl's coat snugly again and sat next to her on the bench seat, giving Rafe the opposite seat all to himself.

"Tell me if that changes," Jessica said.

The girl nodded, then smiled hesitantly. "Thank you, ma'am. I'm sorry if I insulted your husband. It's just . . ." Her voice died and she crossed herself with a trembling hand. "I'm so frightened of Indians. It sh-shames me."

"Don't worry yourself about it," Jessica said. A feeling of sudden, overwhelming tiredness claimed her as the urgency of the moment passed, leaving her drained. "I understand nightmares and daytime fears better than most."

The girl looked at Jessica's hands, saw their trembling, and made a startled sound. "You're afraid, too!"

"Of course I am. I'm not too stupid to know when I might be mauled or murdered. I've simply learned how to hide my fear."

Jessica shoved her hands beneath her cloak, pulled the heavy folds tightly around her, and closed her eyes, fighting for control. It had been much easier when there had been something to do besides sit around like a chicken trussed for the spit.

Finally the sounds of gunfire faded, became sporadic, and stopped completely. The pace of the stagecoach didn't slow. One of the jolts was so great that a rear wheel lifted completely off the ground, sending Jessica and Mrs. O'Conner tumbling across the narrow aisle into Rafe. Jessica's head cracked against the side of the stage, stunning her for a moment.

Rafe caught Jessica with his right arm and braced her across his chest as the coach slammed back down onto all four wheels.

"I'm terribly sorry, sir," Mrs. O'Conner said, flushing as she righted herself and sat across the aisle once more.

"No problem," Rafe said. "Ma'am? Are you all right?"

Dazed, Jessica shook her head, trying to clear it. Sounds seemed to come at her from all sides, battering her, making it impossible to think or speak. Darkness spun around her, closer and closer.

Struggling despite the certainty that she couldn't win, Jessica fought the dark tide that was closing over her. Her last thought before she went under was a sick certainty that this was how her mother had felt each time the earl had dragged her into the marriage bed despite her screams and flailing fists, forcing her to accept the seed that one day would tear her apart.

Mrs. O'Conner made a horrified sound and went

to her knees in the narrow aisle in front of Jessica. "Mrs. Lonetree?"

Rafe didn't bother calling to Jessica. He had felt her body go utterly slack. He cradled her cheek against his chest, covered her exposed ear with his hand, and whistled shrilly enough to shatter glass, demanding the attention of the men riding on top of the stage.

"Slow down!" Rafe yelled. "One of the women is hurt!"

The words sent a chill through Wolfe. He grabbed the railing and bent down until he could look through a torn curtain into the stagecoach's interior. At first he could see nothing. Then Mrs. O'Conner moved aside and he saw Jessica cradled in the big rider's arms.

The stage was still rolling when Wolfe swung down, ran alongside, and opened the door. With catlike quickness, he leaped into the stage's interior.

"Is she shot?" Wolfe demanded, setting aside the rifle he had kept in hand.

"No," Rafe said. "The stage hit a bump and sent her flying. She hit her head so hard that it stunned her."

Wolfe grunted. "Well, that explains why the screaming stopped."

Rafe shot him a surprised look, but Wolfe didn't notice. He was too busy lifting Jessica from the stranger's big lap and onto his own. Mrs. O'Conner drew back to the far corner of the seat to make room for him. Wolfe barely noticed the girl's retreat. He was too busy controlling the irrational anger that had seized him when he saw Jessica in another man's arms.

"That was some fancy maneuver you pulled,

mister," Wolfe said as he examined the slight bruise forming on Jessica's temple. "Don't know as I've ever seen a man get on a stage like that."

"The name is Rafe, and I wouldn't have had a chance without your shooting and your wife's quick thinking. If she hadn't opened that door, I'd have had a hell of a time pulling myself up on top of the stage one-handed."

"Thank Mrs. O'Conner. I'm afraid my wife was too gently raised to be of much use in a crisis," Wolfe said curtly. He looked up at Mrs. O'Conner. "Allow me to thank you as well. If you hadn't exposed yourself to fire long enough to pass up the rifle case, we all would have had a much worse time of it."

"I . . ." The girl's voice dried up as she looked at the fierce lines of Wolfe's face, seeing the clear presence of the savage beneath. She looked away quickly. "I did nothing."

Wolfe assumed the girl was simply being modest. He smiled at her and looked back down at Jessica. His smile faded. She appeared very small and fragile. Her face was bloodless. Even lips that were normally the color of ripe cherries had gone pale.

Now will you admit what I always knew? Wolfe demanded silently of his unconscious wife. *You're not the kind of woman who can survive the West, much less raise children in it. You're a creature of lace and moonlight, an aristocrat who was never meant for hard use. You need a wealthy, titled husband who can wrap you in silk and satin and keep you from all harm.*

I'm not that man. I never will be. I can no more change what I am than you can become a woman like Willow. I can only try to keep you alive until even your stubbornness has to give way before the truth.

We are all wrong for each other.

Silently, Wolfe held Jessica's frail weight and cursed himself and her for the unholy tangle she had made of their lives; and beneath it all, he cursed the desire for her that gripped him even now, his body responding to the feel and scent of the girl he must not take, for then their marriage would be as real and final as death.

When Jessica's eyes opened, the world swung dizzily around her, and the center of that world was a nightmare with dark eyes glowering fiercely down at her. With a stifled sound, she wrenched away. Wolfe's hand came down hard across her mouth as he held her close. The ease with which he overcame her struggles would have panicked Jessica, had not her eyes finally focused enough for her to recognize Wolfe. Her struggles stilled instantly, for she knew Wolfe would never hurt her.

"Finished?" Wolfe asked.

Jessica nodded, for his hand gave her no way to speak.

"Good. We've heard quite enough of your screams of late."

"She never screamed when I was around," Rafe said evenly.

Wolfe gave the other man a look that would have frozen lightning.

Rafe gave the look right back.

"She's a good hand at bandages, too," Rafe added, opening his jacket enough to reveal his arm.

For the first time, Wolfe realized that Rafe had been wounded. Then Wolfe noticed that the bandage was made from an ice-blue silk that was the exact shade of Jessica's eyes, which at the moment were quite icy indeed. He lifted his hand from her mouth.

"Thank you, my lord," Jessica said in a voice as cold as her eyes.

"I'm not a lord."

"And I'm not a screaming ninnyhammer."

"Could have fooled me."

"It is no great trick to fool a man who is deaf, dumb, and blind."

Rafe hid his laughter behind a cough. "How is your head, ma'am?"

"Still attached." Jessica closed her eyes for a moment. "As is my tongue."

She looked up at Wolfe and remembered all her vows to be sweet, gentle, witty, and companionable. A wave of fatigue swept over her like another dark sea. It was very lonely being married to a man who looked at her with such unforgiving eyes.

"I'm sorry," Jessica said unhappily, her voice too low for anyone but Wolfe to hear. "I've done nothing but displease you. I wish we could go back to the days when you would run through a violent storm to find me. But we can't, can we? I'm sorry for that, too."

"We can end it, my Lady Jessica. Just say the word."

"Never, my lord bastard," she said softly, remembering the horror of having Lord Gore's teeth and hands raking her naked flesh. *"Never."*

Unable to bear Wolfe's eyes any longer, Jessica looked away. She had no more energy to fight him or the pain slicing through her temples with each jerk of the stage. Darkness tugged at her, a darkness it took all her strength to hold at bay. Yet it wasn't the blow to her head that drained her, it was the need to stave off the terrifying blackness of her unremembered dreams.

Somewhere deep inside her, a child screamed terror into the wind . . . and was answered by a greater terror, memories condensing where none had been before.

"Jessica?"

There was no answer.

At first Wolfe thought she had fainted again. Then he saw that her eyes were open, fixed on something only she could see.

Something terrible.

A chill touched Wolfe's spine as he realized how deep Jessica's fear must have been during the attack. Despite his vow to wear her down until she agreed to an annulment, he couldn't help but ease her closer to his body, cradling her, protecting her because at that moment she was too defenseless to protect herself.

"Jessi," Wolfe said very softly against her ear, "let me go. Don't make me hurt you any more."

Although he was certain she heard, she didn't answer him in any way.

"Is that what you want?" he asked roughly. "No quarter asked and none given?"

Jessica neither moved nor spoke. It was as though nothing had been said between them.

"So be it," Wolfe said, his voice bleak. "No quarter asked and none given."

 4

THE Rocky Mountains rose
steeply beyond Wolfe's home. Their icy peaks were
swathed in clouds, their broad shoulders streaked
by the changing season, and their feet firmly rooted
in the plains Jessica had learned to love while on
safari with Lord Stewart. She had never been to
Wolfe's home, for Lord Stewart had preferred to
hunt in Wyoming Territory. Even so, she hadn't
expected Wolfe's house to be large, for she knew
that most Americans couldn't afford such splendor
as Lord Stewart's country mansions.

However, Jessica hadn't understood what living
in a small house meant in terms of day-to-day intimacy. Wolfe had. He had been anticipating her
dismay with real pleasure, assuming that it would
bring him a quick victory in the battle for annulment.

"Your house is quite handsome, but..." Jessica's voice died.

"Yes?" Wolfe prompted, knowing very well
what was bothering Jessica.

"There is only one bedroom."

His black eyebrows lifted in silent, sardonic
amusement. "Are you certain?"

"Quite," Jessica said, slipping back into the

clipped accents she had worked so hard to shed. "And there is only one bed in that room."

He nodded.

Smiling, forcing her voice to be teasing, Jessica asked, "Are you going to make your bed in the willows with the birds?"

"Why would I do that? The bed is large enough for two."

"Wolfe, I'm serious."

"So am I. I'm not an aristocrat, your ladyship. I'm an untitled bastard. In America we have a quaint custom among the lower classes—husbands and wives share the same bed."

Jessica's heart began to beat frantically. She clasped her hands together to hide their trembling and smiled coaxingly.

"Surely you're joking."

He laughed and said distinctly, "No, I am not."

"You must be," Jessica said, her voice light despite the pleading in her eyes. "No woman would suffer a man every night."

"No *aristocrat*, surely," Wolfe retorted. "But a Western woman would. Ask Willow Black. She and Caleb share the same bed night after night after night, and both of them spend their days looking like they've swallowed the sun."

The naked longing in Wolfe's voice irritated Jessica so much that she forgot her fear of sharing not only a bedroom with Wolfe, but a bed as well.

"Willow again," Jessica said, concealing her annoyance beneath a sigh. "What a paragon she must be."

"Yes."

"Where do Western women who aren't paragons sleep?" Jessica asked mildly. "In the stable?"

"Only if they don't spook the horses."

"No stable for me, then." She took off her hat and shook down her half-unraveled braids. "The horses will take one look at my hair and think the hay is on fire."

Unwillingly, Wolfe's expression softened. In the days since the attack on the stagecoach, it had become nearly impossible to be with Jessica and not enjoy her company. She had been unfailingly cheerful, agreeable, charming, and witty. With one exception, she had enlivened the long stage ride for everyone.

The exception was the powerful blond stranger who had given them only one name: Rafe.

Wolfe and Rafe had tacitly realized they would tangle if they both stayed caged up with a laughing young woman dancing between them. Without a word spoken on the subject, Rafe had spent the remainder of the ride with the driver. At the second stage stop, Rafe had bought a horse and saddle from a homesick Easterner and ridden off toward the setting sun after expressing his appreciation of Jessica's nursing once again.

Rafe had been much too appreciative of Jessica, as far as Wolfe was concerned. Watching Jessica's glance follow the soft-spoken Rafe until he vanished into the incandescent eye of the sun had rankled Wolfe deeply. He couldn't help wondering if Jessica would have stared at Rafe in fright as she had at Wolfe when she awakened on the stage and found herself in his arms.

"You may sleep in my bed like a Western wife or you may sleep on the living room hearth like a favorite hound," Wolfe said coldly. "It's your choice, just as the marriage was your choice."

Jessica forced herself to smile. "That's very generous of you. I know how well you like hounds."

Wolfe's indigo eyes narrowed, but before he could say anything, Jessica turned away and looked at his bedroom once more. At first she didn't really see it, but gradually the lines and colors beguiled her as they had at first glance. The room was like Wolfe himself, elegant and very masculine at the same time. It was the elegance of a falcon or a cougar, a matter of balance and strength rather than delicacy.

Like the exterior of the house itself, the room's walls were composed of peeled logs. The inner face of the logs had been sanded to smoothness and polished to a fine luster, giving a warm, subtly rich feel to the room. Although the furniture had been made by a man who loved the grain and flow of wood, the stark simplicity of the design was almost startling to eyes accustomed to European luxury.

Yet the lines of bed and dresser, table and chair drew Jessica's eyes again and again, pleasing her in the same way that patterns of geese flying against an autumn sky pleased her. The beautifully colored blankets and the pale, luminous fur throw that had been folded at the foot of the bed were as rich as anything owned by a duke. A sunburst of clear crystals had been placed like a bouquet on the bedside table, but unlike a bouquet, the crystals would never fade and die.

"You have a fine sense of texture and proportion," Jessica said slowly. "The room is quite beautiful. The furniture is . . . extraordinary."

"Sarcasm, Lady Jessica?" Wolfe retorted, looking around his bedroom.

She stared at him, startled by the bite in his voice. Before she could speak, he did.

"The furniture was made by a backsliding Shaker in exchange for room and board over a long winter.

The blankets are standard trade goods from the Hudson Bay company. So are the furs."

"If I intend sarcasm," Jessica said tartly, "you won't have to inquire. You'll know."

"Will I? Then tell me what you see in this room to please a gently raised lady's eye."

"Many things," Jessica said, accepting the unspoken challenge. "The lines of the furniture are simple to the point of starkness, which emphasizes the appealing warmth of the fire, the rich colors of the blankets, and the inviting texture of the fur. The fireplace is quite clever, for it opens into two rooms at once. And is that a hipbath behind the screen?"

"Yes."

"It's quite large."

"So am I."

Wolfe watched as Jessica ran her fingertips over the straight back of a nearby chair.

"You have everything you need for comfort, and you have beauty as well," she said quietly. "Whoever made this was a fine craftsman who loved wood. See how the grain of the wood both matches and repeats the lines of the chair?"

Wolfe saw more than that. He also saw the latent sensuality in Jessica, the sheer physical pleasure she took from the feel of the smooth wood beneath her fingertips.

"And the fur," she added, walking over to the foot of the bed, "is magnificent."

"It comes from Arctic foxes. They live at the foot of glaciers whose crevasses are the exact blue of your eyes."

"Is it a beautiful color?" she asked softly.

"You know it is."

"It never seemed so to me."

Jessica's fingers speared through the thick white fur, seeking and finding its softest textures. The sound of pleasure she made as she stroked the fur brought every one of Wolfe's hungry senses to alert. The thought of those slender fingers tangling in his own hair sent a shaft of desire through his body. He turned away abruptly.

"I'll bring your trunks in here. No matter where you decide to sleep, you'll use this as your dressing room."

Jessica looked up curiously, caught by the husky note in Wolfe's voice.

"While I finish unloading the wagon," Wolfe continued, "you start fixing a cold supper and some hot coffee. The supplies are in the burlap sacks. You might as well put everything away. Then you'll know where everything is when you need it for cooking."

"Wolfe," Jessica said quickly.

He turned around.

She started to explain that she didn't know the first thing about fixing suppers, whether cold or hot. The aura of expectancy in his stance told her that he was waiting for just such an invitation to bait her again on her inadequacy as an American wife. She wasn't certain her temper was up to that at the moment.

The long, uncomfortable wagon ride from the stage terminus in Denver had tried Jessica's resilience and resolve to their limits. She was stiff, cold, bruised, and more exhausted than she had ever been in her life.

But she was expected to cheerfully conjure a meal for that most demanding of all creatures, a Western husband.

"Yes?" Wolfe asked in a silky voice.

"I was just, er, wondering where to put my clothes."

"As I didn't know I was going to acquire a wife in England, I didn't buy any dressers or armoires for your clothes." His smile was a thin white curve against the darkness of his face. "Not that it matters. You won't be here long enough to repay the trouble of unpacking even one trunk."

"Oh? Does that mean we're leaving on another trip right away?" Jessica asked in an artificially bright voice.

"We aren't. You are. Back to London."

"Ah, that trip. Well, you know how foolish it is to count unhatched chicks. I feel the same could be said of unhatched *trips*."

Wolfe looked at Jessica's bright smile and felt his temper fraying. If she had sulked or complained, he could have berated her, but her inexhaustible well of cheerfulness made that impossible.

She knew it as well as he did. Better, perhaps.

"The kitchen, your ladyship, is through that door."

"Why, so it is."

She gathered the skirts of her ruined travel outfit in her hands and eased through the doorway that was filled by her unwilling husband.

"I'll expect supper within the hour," Wolfe said as yards of soft wool brushed over his thighs, tightening every muscle in his body. "I'll expect the coffee a hell of a lot sooner."

"I'm sure you will," Jessica agreed.

But she wasn't sure Wolfe would get it.

The kitchen had a brick floor, cupboards everywhere, a pump, a sink, and a big stove. The small table in one corner obviously had been made by the Shaker craftsman who had furnished the bedroom. Sacks of supplies were lined up the length of the floor.

Now that Wolfe was no longer present to measure Jessica's mood, her smile vanished as thoroughly as though it had never existed. In the place of her determined cheer was a physical fatigue that made even standing upright an ordeal. Mentally, she was no more resilient.

Nor was there any relief in sight. No matter how hard she tried to coax some simple human warmth from Wolfe, since the Indian attack he had remained abrupt, difficult, cold, and impossible to please. If that wasn't bad enough, the wind seemed to moan without pause over the land. When she was alone, she heard the wind with terrible clarity.

She was always alone now, and never more so than when Wolfe was nearby. Automatically, her hand went to her breasts. Beneath her clothes, the locket lay concealed among soft folds of lace. The familiar contours of the necklace reassured her.

"Well," Jessica said, forcing cheerfulness into her voice, for anything was better than the unborn horror keening within the wind. "Where do you suppose Wolfe has hidden his coffeepot? And what do you suppose it will look like when I find it?"

The low ululation of the wind was more answer than Jessica wanted to hear. Hurriedly, she fumbled for the matches and lighted a lantern, for Wolfe had shuttered the windows before he left for London. She had watched various servants light various lamps all her life, but it took several tries for her to get the right combination of match, wick, and oil. The lamp smoked annoyingly, but it was better than nothing.

The wind raked over the roof and made the cap on the stovepipe rattle like distant chains, reminding Jessica of her childhood in Scotland, when she had hidden in the kitchen with the scullery maids because she could no longer bear the sounds coming from her father's suite of rooms. It had been a very long time since Jessica had thought of such things. She didn't wish to begin now.

Humming to shut out both the wind and her darkly stirring memories, Jessica set to work. The air she hummed was one of her favorites, "Bonnie Laddie, Highland Laddie." The words had always stuck her as over-simple, but the melody had a fine lilt that lifted her spirits. The more fiercely the wind blew, the more loudly Jessica sang her lively, wordless song, opening and closing cupboards as she searched for the coffeepot.

After opening every cupboard, peering in, and holding the smoky lamp aloft, Jessica still hadn't found anything that resembled the graceful sterling silver urns Lord Robert's servants had taken coffee from. Nor did she find anything like the small, plump sterling silver pots or tissue-thin china that had been used for service in the bedroom.

"Blazes," she muttered.

Jessica began the search and the song all over again. Halfway through the cupboard, she sensed that she was no longer alone in the room. She spun around.

Wolfe was leaning against the door frame, his arms crossed over his chest and an odd expression on his face.

"That song . . ." he said.

" 'Bonnie Laddie, Highland Laddie'. It's a rather silly air about a Scotsman wearing a cap."

Wolfe cleared his throat and tried not to reveal the laughter that was shaking him. "Of course. It's been so long since I heard the original words, I'd forgotten."

He made a strangled sound and looked away from a moment.

"Are you well, Wolfe?"

Silently, Wolfe struggled not to smile.

"I know my voice isn't of stage quality," Jessica said, smiling wryly, "but no one has ever laughed at it before. However, if it amuses you so, I'll sing more often."

"I doubt the verses you know would be as amusing as the ones I know." Wolfe watched Jessica tilt her head and look at him with wide aquamarine eyes. "You look like a cat when you watch me with such stillness."

The intensity of .Wolfe's eyes made Jessica's breath catch in her throat. An odd sensation trembled in the pit of her stomach, as though he were stroking her hair. But he wasn't touching her. He was simply watching her.

With an effort, she forced herself to speak. "What verses do you know that I don't?"

"Many."

"Wonderful. Teach me and we'll sing together."

Wolfe compressed his lips against the smile that threatened to overwhelm his efforts at self-control. "The verses I know would horrify you."

"Why?"

"They deal with Adam's staff, among other things," Wolfe said blandly.

Jessica looked blank. "Why would talk of Adam's staff horrify me?"

"It's also celebrated as a flea shooter, a hoe, a fishing rod, a drummer's stick, a Roman candle, a branding iron, a dagger, a sword, a dowsing rod, a ramrod, a pistol and, lately, a repeating rifle."

Wolfe's voice vibrated with suppressed laughter. "There are other names as well. Many names. And for each one, a verse to the tune you were singing."

Jessica frowned. "A tool for many purposes, is that it?"

Wolfe gave up the fight, tipped back his head, and laughed without restraint.

The rich, masculine sounds made Jessica feel as though she was standing close to a fire. Some of the tension seeped slowly from her. The feeling of relief was almost dizzying, telling her how much she had feared that she would never be able to make her husband smile again.

"As you say," Wolfe managed finally, "an all-purpose tool. Fortunately, Eve was equally well endowed."

Jessica blinked. "I beg your pardon?"

"Adam's staff had its complement in Eve."

"I don't understand."

"Eve had a fertile field for Adam to till," Wolfe said gravely, "a shadowed pool for him to fish, a deep well to be discovered by his dowsing rod, a supple sheath for his knife or sword to lie within ... ah, the sunrise of understanding shines pinkly on your face."

Blushing, Jessica covered her mouth with her hands, but couldn't prevent the sound of her giggles from escaping. Her laughter was contagious, setting off Wolfe again. Soon Jessica was laughing so hard she had to hang onto the cupboard door or fall.

Wolfe was little better off. It had been years since he had teased Jessica until they were both weak with laughter. He hadn't known how much life had lacked until this moment.

"I've missed you," he admitted before he could think better of it.

"Not as much as I missed you."

"Did you?"

"Oh, yes," she said, blotting tears of laughter from her eyes. "When you're with me, I never hear the wind."

"What an odd reason to miss someone."

"Elves are odd creatures."

Wolfe looked at the row of open cupboard doors. "Yes, they are. Why were you going through the cupboards, elf?"

"I was looking for your coffeepot."

"It's on the stove."

Jessica straightened and stared at the pot-bellied stove. She saw nothing but a battered container that looked like a tall, rather narrow pot. It was wider at the bottom than the top and had a slight flare on the rim. A wire handle stood upright above the lid.

"A coffeepot on the stove," she said neutrally.

"Umm."

The sound Wolfe made was rather like that of a very large, contented cat. Jessica glanced at him from beneath thick auburn lashes.

"How does this coffeepot work?"

"Quite simply. You fill the pot with water, put it on the stove to boil, add coffee grounds, boil for a time, and then add cold water to settle the grounds."

"Ah," she breathed, brightening. "Simple indeed."

Jessica went to the stove, took the lid off the pot, and looked around for a pitcher of water. There was none.

"Water comes from pumps," Wolfe said. "You

do know what a pump looks like, don't you?"

"You're teasing me."

"I'm not sure. Elves are unpredictable creatures. It's difficult to be certain what they know."

Jessica hadn't ever used a pump, but she certainly had seen one used. She went to the sink, set the pot down beneath the pump's spout, and picked up the long iron pump handle. She had to go up on her tiptoes to lift the handle to its fullest.

"Wait."

Jessica froze, teetered, and began to lose her balance. Before she could topple and accidently bring the pump handle down, Wolfe rushed forward and snatched her off her feet. She made a startled sound.

"You forgot something," he said calmly.

She looked into midnight blue eyes that were intriguingly close to her own, for Wolfe had lifted her until her head was on a level with his.

"What did I forget?"

"You didn't prime the pump."

The blank look Jessica gave Wolfe told him that she didn't know what he was talking about. He started to set her down, but her small, warm waist felt too good between his hands to let go of just yet.

"See that pitcher of water next to the pump?" Wolfe asked.

The deepening of his voice ruffled Jessica's nerves in a way she liked without knowing why. She nodded. He shifted her suddenly, turning her away from him. The breathless sound she made was lost in his words.

"Pick up the pitcher, elf."

She leaned across the counter, and in doing so, pressed her bottom into the cradle of Wolfe's thighs. He closed his eyes and told himself to put her down. Instead, his hands tightened around her, savoring the supple warmth of her against the ache of male hunger and need that had concentrated between his thighs.

"Now pour the water into the opening at the top of the pump," he said a low voice.

The motions Jessica made pressed her more intimately against Wolfe's hungry flesh. Water splashed and danced, shimmering in the lantern light. Belatedly, Wolfe remembered what he was supposed to be doing. He shifted Jessica again, holding her against his body with one arm while the other worked the handle of the pump. Soon water gushed out of the pump's spout and into the coffeepot until it overflowed.

"That," Wolfe said, letting Jessica slide down his body until her feet touched the floor, "is called priming a pump."

Ruefully, he acknowledged that the pump wasn't the only thing that had been primed during the lesson, but he could hardly blame Jessica for that. She hadn't known what she was doing when she pressed her backside against his groin until he could feel the very feminine flare of her hips beneath all the folds of cloth in her traveling dress.

"Why did you do that?" she asked.

For an instant, Wolfe thought Jessica was referring to the change that had taken place in his body while he held her; then he realized she was talking about the pump. He opened his mouth to answer, but the thought of explaining to a wide-eyed elf the intricacies of suction, pressure, and pumping involved in the mechanism—while at the same time his body was on fire—defeated Wolfe.

"Think of it as a religious ritual," he said finally.

Jessica tilted her head back to look up at him and realized anew just how large her husband was. Yet being held by him hadn't frightened her or made her uneasy in any way. In fact, it had been very nice, as had seeing his eyes so close to hers and feeling the warmth of his breath on her cheek. The hard strength of his arm supporting her had been even more appealing, as had been the power and motion of his body as he worked the pump. Soft sensations shimmered through her at the thought of being held that way again.

"A religious ritual," Jessica repeated in a dazed voice.

"I must have unpacked the parrot along with your sidesaddle."

Laughing softly, Jessica shook her head. "Priming the pump is a religious ritual, and you unpacked the parrot with my sidesaddle. Oh, Wolfe, do you think our wits were addled by the long trip?"

"Very likely."

For a moment she looked into the clear indigo depths of his eyes. The delicate shimmering sensation in the pit of her stomach strengthened.

"You do the most curious things to my stomach," Jessica said in a husky voice.

"Nausea, loss of appetite?" Wolfe guessed wryly.

"Far from it. You make me feel as though I've swallowed golden butterflies."

The innocent admission forced Wolfe to close his eyes, for if he kept looking at Jessica he would reach out and trace the delicate curves of her upper lip with his fingers first and then the tip of his tongue. It had been difficult enough to keep his hands off her; it would be impossible if she kept watching him with wondering, luminous eyes and talked of the first, delicate tremors of passion awakening within her untouched body.

Desire beat in harsh waves through Wolfe, but he remained motionless. He didn't trust himself to touch Jessica. If she responded to an outright caress with the laughter and honesty she had just shown, he wouldn't stop caressing her until he was sheathed within her.

Then the marriage would be all too real. She would be bound for life to a halfbreed mustang hunter, and he would be bound for life to a girl who was afraid of being a woman.

"I think," Wolfe said distinctly, opening his eyes, "it's time to get on with teaching you how to make coffee. There's too much water in the coffeepot. Pour the extra into the priming pitcher. And next time, fill the pitcher first."

"Why?"

"Because if it's dry when you go to pump the next time, you have to walk to the spring for water before you can get any water from the pump."

"I must pour water in the pump before I can pump water out." Jessica shook her head. "That hardly makes sense."

"Most rituals don't."

"What if I pump without adding water first?"

"The mechanism wasn't made to work dry. You'll ruin it."

"And your temper, too?" Jessica guessed.

"Count on it. Reno's, too. He helped me put in the pump."

"Is he a neighbor?"

"No," Wolfe said. "He hunts for Spanish treasure in the desert when he's not staying with Willow in the San Juans."

"Truly? What does Caleb think of that?"

"He approves."

"That's quite, er, exceptional of him."

"Reno is Willow's brother."

Jessica blinked and muttered beneath her breath, "Daunting prospect, being brother to a paragon."

Wolfe handed Jessica the coffeepot and gestured toward the stove. When she set the pot down, water sloshed onto the black surface of the stove. The cast iron was cold. After fumbling for a bit with the stove door, she managed to open it and peer inside. Kindling was laid out in orderly array.

"Looking for these?" Wolfe asked.

Jessica straightened. He was holding out a cup full of matches he had taken from a shelf near the stove.

"You do know which end to scrape against the iron, don't you?" he asked dryly.

"The lamp didn't light itself," she pointed out.

Wolfe glanced at the lamp smoking happily on the counter. "So I see. Were you planning on smoking fish over the chimney?"

"Don't be silly. Even I know the difference between a lantern and a fish smoker."

Jessica scraped a match over the stovetop. It broke. She took another matchstick from the tin cup.

"Besides, I'm not to blame for the smoke," she muttered, taking another swipe at the stovetop. "I did nothing but light the lamp." The match didn't catch. She pressed harder and tried again. No flame jumped to the tip. "It must be the oil you use that's causing the smoke."

"No, it's the wick *you* used. It's the wrong length," Wolfe explained. "If you trim it correctly, the lamp won't smoke."

"Then by all means, trim the wick," she retorted.

Jessica dragged the match over the stove yet again. The head of the match caught and broke off at the same time, sending a shower of burning sulphur tumbling down her skirt.

"Blast!" she said under her breath as she shook off the sparks.

When Wolfe had adjusted the wick properly, he went back to the stove. Jessica was in the process of breaking another match in half while trying to strike it on the smooth, greasy portion of the stove's metal surface. With a muttered word, she took a new match from the diminishing supply in the cup.

"Here," Wolfe said, reaching past Jessica and putting his hand over hers. "Hold onto the match. Now bring it across the spot where the fire below burned the hottest. The metal is clean there. No soot or grease is left to foul the match tip."

As Wolfe spoke, he drew Jessica's hand beneath his over the stove in a swift, firm stroke. The match blazed instantly to life.

"See?" he said.

Jessica looked over her shoulder at Wolfe. The burning match was reflected in his eyes. The contrast between the flame and the blue midnight of his irises enthralled her, as did the straight, black length of his eyelashes and the pronounced arch of his eyebrows. The intensity and intelligence in his eyes was brighter and more alluring than even the dance of flame.

The odd, shivering sensations returned to her stomach.

"Jessi?"

"Yes, I see."

"Do you? You look rather baffled."

"Just a bit shocked."

"By lighting a match?"

She smiled oddly. "No. By you. I just realized how very handsome you are."

Wolfe's eyes widened a fraction, then narrowed. The pulse at his throat speeded.

"I mean, I've always known you were handsome," Jessica continued, trying to explain. "Everyone from duchesses to maids has rattled on about your looks for years, but I never really *knew*. It's rather unsettling suddenly to see you as they must have seen you."

She laughed uncertainly. "Don't stare at me so. I feel foolish enough as it is. How could I overlook something so obvious for so many—oh!"

Jessica's hand jerked as the match burned down to her skin. She snatched her fingers to her lips and dropped the still flaming match onto the stovetop.

"Are you all right?" Wolfe asked.

Jessica blew on her fingertips before staring at them critically. "Just a trifle scorched."

"Let me see."

He looked at her fingertips, then bent his head and gently ran the tip of his tongue over them. When he lifted his head again, Jessica was watching him with an expression on her face that could have been shock or disgust.

"You needn't look so appalled," Wolfe said curtly. "It's only what a cat would do for a foolish kitten."

Jessica opened her mouth but no words came out. A visible shudder ran over her. Wolfe turned away and lit another match with a swift slash of his hand.

"Go unpack the trunks, your ladyship," he said

as he set the match to the previously laid fire. "The viscount's *savage* will fix supper tonight."

Jessica flinched. She hadn't realized how warm and affectionate Wolfe's voice had become until she measured it against the return of ice and distance.

"Wolfe? What have I done?"

"When you're finished unpacking, be sure to take some of those aristocratic bed linens you brought and make a pallet by the hearth. A nun like you wouldn't want to do something so bestial as to sleep near any man, much less a savage like your husband."

Wolfe stood up. Behind him the stove fire blossomed into orange flames.

"But—" she began.

"You said when I tired of your company you would leave me alone," Wolfe interrupted, slamming the stove door shut. "Do that, Lady Jessica. Now."

Even an aristocrat had some common sense. Jessica picked up her skirts and fled to Wolfe's bedroom. But even there, she found no peace.

The sound of the wind was very loud in the silence.

 5

WOLFE watched Jessica as she
knelt over a washtub in the lean-to at the side of
his house.

"You're supposed to be washing the shirt, not
making rags of it," he said.

"I see little difference in the process."

"Not the way you're going about it, certainly.
Tell me, your ladyship, while the servants accom-
plished all the useful work at Lord Robert's house,
what did you do?"

"I read, I played the violin, I oversaw the staff,
I embroidered—"

"My God," Wolfe interrupted. "Something useful. How did that creep into your daily regimen?
Does that mean you'll be able to repair the seams
you're pulling apart under the guise of washing
my clothes?"

"Would you prefer initials, a coat of arms, or
Jacobean-style flowers embroidered in your
seams?" Jessica asked pleasantly.

Wolfe made a sound of disgust.

She didn't bother to look up from the washtub
and the lean-to's widely spaced wooden slats. She
knew what she would see if she looked at her husband. He would be watching her with cold eyes

104

and an unforgiving line to his mouth. It had been that way for the three days since he had so startled her by running the tip of his tongue over her burned fingers.

And for those same three days, she had kept a smile pinned on her lips until her face ached.

Unfortunately, by now her face wasn't the only part of her body that ached. She was as exhausted this afternoon as she had been at the end of the stage ride. When she wasn't pumping water to wash and rinse clothes, she was carrying bucket after bucket to the stove to heat. From the stove she hauled buckets to the lean-to, poured water into the big tub, knelt, and went to work rubbing and scrubbing every piece of clothing. It usually took three or four times before the shirts pleased Wolfe's critical eye.

"That's about as much scrubbing as the poor shirt can take," Wolfe said.

"I think not, my lord. It's not perfectly clean."

"Enough, your ladyship. That's my favorite shirt. Willow made it for me last summer."

The sound of ripping cloth carried very clearly over Wolfe's last words.

"Jessica!"

"Oh, dear, look at that. One would think a paragon would choose cloth that was less frail, wouldn't one?" Jessica dragged the ruined shirt from the water and wrung it out with real pleasure. "But all isn't lost, my lord. It will make a wonderful rag for cleaning the privy."

"You little witch! I should—"

Wolfe's words ended in a curse as he leaped aside, barely avoiding the torrent of soapy water that came when Jessica upended the washtub.

"Sorry, did you say something?" she asked.

There was a simmering silence while husband and wife looked at each other. Then Wolfe smiled. Jessica smiled in return.

"I think it's time your ladyship learned to scrub something more durable than a shirt," Wolfe said.

"What's that?"

"Floors."

Jessica's smile slipped, then was resurrected. "Ah, another quaint wifely ritual. It occurs to me, my Lord Wolfe, why Americans don't have servants. Wives are ever so much cheaper."

"Too bad you dumped all that hot, soapy water," Wolfe said, turning away. "Now you'll have to get more. You do remember where the wood pile is, don't you?"

"Quite well."

"Then hop to it."

"Do I look like a rabbit?" Jessica asked beneath her breath.

Wolfe turned back. "Hurry up, my red-haired bunny. Daylight is free, but lamplight is expensive. Those of us not fortunate enough to be born into the aristocracy have to be concerned about such things."

Standing up was easier said than done for Jessica. With an effort, Wolfe restrained his instinctive move to help her. Instead, he watched impassively while she struggled to her feet.

Despite her best effort to be silent, a groan got past her lips. Wolfe took it as a sign that he was finally winning the contest of wills. At least, he hoped he was. He didn't know how much longer he could bear to twiddle his thumbs while the shadows beneath Jessica's eyes deepened more each hour. The hard physical labor of housekeeping under his critical eye was draining what strength had remained after the long, strenuous trip to his home.

Even though Jessica had trapped Wolfe into marriage, he had too many good memories of times past to enjoy grinding her down in such a manner. Yet he forced himself to watch Jessica's stiff movements without flinching. If he showed kindness, it would be mistaken for weakness, which would only prolong the process of getting Jessica to accept the futility of their marriage.

But even while he was telling himself to be strong, he was speaking.

"Just say the word and you'll never put those delicate hands into wash water again."

Jessica stretched her back and sighed. "The last time you made that offer, you objected to the word I said."

Bastard.

Unwillingly, Wolfe smiled as he remembered. Jessica caught the softening of his expression and prayed that he would relent on the matter of scrubbing floors.

Wolfe saw her hopeful expression and knew he must not give in. Silently, he picked up the bucket and held it out to her. He saw both the dismay in her eyes and the straightening of her spine as she took the bucket from his hands.

Reluctant admiration grew in Wolfe. Jessica's sheer determination was greater than that of men twice her size. But no matter how stubborn she was, her endurance was limited by her strength. In the end, he would use her own stubbornness as a weapon against her. In the end, he would win.

All he had to do was endure his own self-disgust while he wore her down.

"Jessi," Wolfe said gently, "give it up. You aren't

cut out to be a commoner's wife. You know it as well as I do."

"Better your wife than Lord Gore's."

Wolfe's temper slipped, for there was nothing he could force himself to do to Jessica that would equal Lord Gore's drunken brutality, which put Wolfe at a disadvantage when it came to convincing Jessica to give up this farce of a marriage.

"Better for you," Wolfe retorted coldly, "but not for me. There are many better wives for me than you."

"Don't count on it," Jessica said, turning away. "Paragons aren't so thick upon the ground that you can just pluck one like a daffodil in spring."

"I don't want a paragon. I want a *wife*."

"How fortunate for the paragon Willow that she is already married. Her heart would be broken if she knew that even her astonishing perfection wasn't enough to satisfy Tree That Stands Alone."

At first Wolfe didn't understand what Jessica meant. When he did, he smiled. It was the first real sign that his frequent praising of Willow's accomplishments had rankled Jessica. She had just given him a tool with which to chip away at her own monumental confidence that their marriage would work.

"Willow has passion," Wolfe said. "That's something a nun wouldn't understand, much less be able to equal."

There was no answer but that of the pump handle being worked inside the kitchen as Jessica drew more water for scrubbing the floor.

FORWARD, *back, forward, back, dip into the water, lean hard, harder, forward, back, forward, back* . . .

The silent chant had been repeated in Jessica's mind so often that she wasn't aware of it any longer. Nor was she aware of the lateness of the hour. Her world had shrunk to no larger a space than the bricks within reach of her scrub brush.

At first look, Wolfe's kitchen had struck her as small. Now it seemed the size of a ballroom.

Forward, back, forward, back.

The wind had risen with the descending sun. Now the wind moaned hungrily around the eaves and pried with transparent fingers at every crevice, searching for a way inside. Jessica began humming to shut out the horrifying, soulless cries that had disturbed even the exhausted sleep she succumbed to at night. No matter how forcefully she hummed, the sound of the wind was louder.

Lean hard, harder.

The brush moved sluggishly over brick despite Jessica's desire to finish. Despairingly, she realized that her arms had no more strength. She locked her elbows and leaned her full weight on the brush. It rolled in her soapy fingers and rattled across the floor. She barely caught herself before she went sprawling.

By the time Jessica set aside the brush and rinsed the whole floor with clean water, it was past time to be preparing supper. Not that it mattered. Whatever she prepared, Wolfe would look at it as though it had crawled from a chamber pot onto his plate.

"Ah well, I can hardly fault him for that. Even the skunk passed up the stew I made last night. Nor can I fairly be blamed. No one told me to cover the pot and keep adding water while I cooked."

The memory of the silent, nighttime visitor made Jessica laugh despite the steady aching of her body. She shook out the ruins of her once-fine traveling outfit. The skirt no longer matched the aquamarine of her eyes. Instead, the fabric more resembled a muddy pool, with dense black patches where her knees had ground the cloth against brick or the wooden slats of the lean-to where she had toiled over the washtub.

"Bother," Jessica muttered. "I should have taken the charwoman's clothes and left mine in England."

She went to the stove, flipped open the door with a metal hook, and looked inside. As always, more wood was required. The same was no doubt true for the living room hearth, which also cleverly served to heat the bedroom as well. She had been quite intrigued with the double-sided fireplace, and the artistry of the stonemason who had built it. Discovering that Wolfe had been the builder had surprised her.

In between feeding the stove and feeding the hearth fire so that it could take the chill from the buckets of water she had arrayed on either side for her bath later, Jessica barely had time to deal with preparing any food.

"Blazes!" she muttered when the paring knife slipped repeatedly in her inexperienced hands. "Tonight I'll surprise Wolfe. Tonight we'll have riced potatoes, fried pork chops from his neighbor's pig, and tinned cherries. Little enough could go wrong with that lot." Jessica sighed. "Tonight I won't have to listen while Wolfe sings the praises of that paragon of the culinary arts, Willow Black."

Jessica continued talking aloud to herself while she worked. Talking helped to hold the sound of the wind at bay, but the sustained moans still ate away at her composure. She was grateful when the vigorously boiling water added its bit to the kitchen sounds.

Soon the smell of potatoes cooking drove out the pungent lye scent that lingered after the bricks had been so thoroughly scrubbed. The clatter of a cast iron frying pan as she hauled it onto the stovetop was almost cheerful, as was the sizzle of chops when the pan warmed enough to cook the meat.

Humming despite the numbing fatigue that was creeping through her body, Jessica primed the pump and filled a huge soup pot with water. She spilled about a quart on the way to the big stove, but barely noticed. The remaining two gallons were quite enough for her to lift. She opened the stove's front gate, stuffed in several more lengths of wood and slammed the gate shut.

"What next?" Jessica asked, running through the list in her mind. "Ah, yes, the table must be readied. Another cloth to dirty, to wash, to hang out to dry, and then to put in that great pile awaiting the flatiron. Praise God, Wolfe hadn't insisted that I iron another shirt after the first one. How was I to know cloth burned so quickly?"

Jessica went to the sideboard, ran her hand admiringly across its beautifully made top, and opened a drawer. To her relief, there was another cloth left. Last night's cloth had been ruined when Wolfe had taken a swallow of coffee and then spewed it all over while swearing that she was trying to poison him.

Closing her eyes, Jessica reminded herself that someday she would find this all as amusing as Wolfe sometimes did. Until then, she must continue to smile and learn to do chores as quickly as possible.

There was no other choice. Every time her smiles

faltered or she showed how weary she was becoming, she would turn around and see Wolfe watching her, cataloging each sign of weakness, waiting for the moment she gave up on being a Western wife.

Say the word, Jessica.

Wolfe didn't even have to speak the command aloud any more. It was there in the line of his mouth, the scrutiny of his eyes, his predatory attention like a cold wind blowing through her. Yet she couldn't give up, no matter how tired she was, no matter how strange her new life was, no matter how desperately lonely it was to be in a foreign land with no friend but Wolfe.

Wolfe, who wanted her out of his life.

"Never," Jessica vowed aloud. "You will see, Wolfe. We will laugh again, sing again, read by the fire again. We will be friends once more. It will happen. It must. And if it doesn't . . ."

Jessica's throat closed. *It must happen.*

"I'll get stronger," she vowed. "I'll learn. Whatever happens to me as a Western wife can't be worse than what my mother endured being married to a Scots aristocrat who wanted nothing from her but a male heir."

The sound of the wind rose to an eerie cry, the wailing of a woman giving way to despair, screaming in agony. Jessica put her hands over her ears and began singing as loudly as she could. The wind howled unabated, for it blew only in her mind, not in the wild Western land.

With a stifled cry, Jessica hurried from the kitchen to check on the hearth fire. She added wood, then went into the bedroom and looked longingly at the big hip tub. The thought of it filled with hot water and laced with drops of fragrant rose oil made goosebumps course pleasurably over her skin. Never had she understood what an extraordinary luxury a hot bath was.

Now she did. Since they had arrived at Wolfe's home, Jessica had made do with French baths taken from the basin before she dressed. She had been too busy during daylight and too exhausted by nightfall to draw, heat, and haul bath water to the hip tub.

Tonight she would do all of that if she had to do it on her hands and knees. She simply couldn't bear going without a true bath for one more night.

Jessica looked longingly at the soft invitation of Wolfe's bed, but didn't want to soil its exquisite fur covering with her grubby clothes. Grimacing, she sat by the hearth, leaning against the fire-warmed stone. The nights of broken sleep on her hard pallet by the hearth and the days of unaccustomed work had drained her. Very quickly she fell asleep.

The sound of Wolfe shouting from the front of the house startled Jessica awake. The first thing she saw was a layer of smoke hanging just below the ceiling and curling out an open window.

"Jessi! Answer me! Where are you?"

Her first attempt to come to her feet failed because her overworked arms refused to cooperate. Her second try was more successful.

"Wolfe?" she called, her voice hoarse with sleep.

The front door banged open and Wolfe leaped inside. His dark face was grim.

"Jessi, are you all right?" he yelled, looking toward the kitchen where smoke boiled thickly.

"I'm fine," she said.

Wolfe spun and saw Jessica standing in the bedroom doorway, her hair half-unraveled and her eyes very pale against the dark lavender circles that surrounded them. He closed his eyes and let out an explosive breath as the urgency went out of him.

"Wolfe? What's wrong?"

His eyes snapped open. They were narrowed and frankly dangerous. "I thought the house was burning down, and you with it."

"Burning—oh, dear God, the chops!"

Wolfe followed Jessica's rush into the kitchen. When she reached for the frying pan, he struck her hand aside.

"No! You'll blister yourself!"

He went into the living room and returned with fire tongs. Using them, he managed to get the cheerfully burning chops outside. He placed the smoking pan in the dirt just beyond the back steps.

Behind him, Jessica sighed deeply. "Do you suppose the skunk will be any hungrier tonight than he was last night?"

Wolfe took a long time turning around, because he didn't trust himself not to laugh out loud. He, too, had wondered if the skunk's appetite would be up to the challenge of Jessica's cooking.

But sharing laughter with his irrepressible Jessi was too enjoyable, too arousing, too . . . addictive. Each time he let her get past his guard, it encouraged her to believe she would ultimately win him over. He must not do that, for it wasn't true. He would never accept the sham marriage, which meant that any kindness from him would be cruelty in disguise. Kindness would only draw out the painful process of getting Jessica to accept an annulment.

Wolfe didn't want to extend the process by so much as one second. He didn't know how much longer he could look at his frazzled aristocrat and not gather her into his arms.

When Wolfe turned around to face Jessica once more, his face was expressionless.

"What else is the skunk having for dinner tonight?" he asked in a carefully neutral voice.

Jessica smiled rather grimly. "Not a blasted thing. I put plenty of water in the potatoes and I haven't opened the tinned cherries yet."

"Canned."

"What?"

"Canned cherries in the West, tinned cherries in England."

"Oh."

Wolfe could practically see Jessica's agile mind noting the peculiarity of speech for future use. She was losing the last bits of her British accent and idioms as quickly as she had once lost her Scots speech patterns. Like Wolfe, she had learned as a child the survival value of camouflage. Being the daughter of a Scots commoner mother couldn't be changed any more than the circumstances of Wolfe's own birth could be altered. But clothing and patterns of speech could be changed, and were, depending on the people Wolfe found himself among.

Few people looked past the outward appearance, which suited Wolfe just fine. It allowed him to move freely where he pleased. He wondered if Jessica had found—and cherished—a similar personal freedom beneath the appearance of conformity. He suspected she had.

The thought didn't please him. It would only make her fight that much harder against an annulment, for her continued freedom depended on the same marriage that so badly restricted Wolfe's own freedom.

Jessica walked past her silent husband into the smoky kitchen. He followed her, noting the many gaps between the tiny buttons on her back. She hadn't been able to fasten the dress herself, or had fastened it incorrectly.

This further proof that Jessica didn't want Wolfe's hands on her at all, even to fasten her impossible dress, made anger uncurl in him. Though he knew he should be grateful she wasn't bent on seducing him into a real—and disastrous— marriage, he wasn't the least bit pleased by her aversion to being touched by him in even the most casual way.

Bloody little nun. Why did you choose me to torment with that perfect body?

Through slitted eyes, Wolfe watched while Jessica propped the kitchen door open to let out the smoke before she went to check on the potatoes. She lifted the lid and looked into the pot.

"Blazes," she said unhappily. "Where did they go?"

"Where did what go?"

"The potatoes."

Wolfe looked over Jessica's head into the pot. Nothing resembling a potato was visible in the opaque water.

"Last night the potatoes were scorched on the outside and raw in the middle. Tonight they have no middle. No top, bottom, or sides, either."

"I had no idea potatoes were such perverse vegetables," Jessica muttered.

"No wonder people leave out milk and cookies for elves. The silly bastards would starve to death otherwise." Wolfe shook his head and looked at Jessica with open curiosity. "What have you done to the canned cherries? Buried them in salt or soda?"

"It's unreasonable to expect me to learn in three days a skill chefs spend years learning on the Continent," Jessica said, keeping her voice level with an effort. "I'm doing my best to be a good wife, truly I am."

"A frightening thought. What happened to the cherries?"

She grimaced and admitted, "I couldn't open them."

"For these small things, Lord, I am damned grateful."

Wolfe grabbed a potholder, hooked his finger around the handle of the kettle of potatoes, and strode out the back door. Jessica heard a sudden hiss and explosion of steam as he poured the contents of the pot over the smoldering chops.

"Bon appetit, monsieur le skunk," Wolfe said.

The sardonic words made Jessica flinch. She doubted the wee striped beastie would be any more interested in her cooking than Wolfe was.

Jessica discovered she wasn't hungry either. Her stomach was in a knot, her throat ached, and her eyes burned with tears she would not shed. She suspected by the hard line of Wolfe's shoulders and jaw when he stepped back into the kitchen that he was waiting for a sign of weakness on her part. There would be no relenting in him, no understanding of her predicament, no comfort when she tried and failed spectacularly.

He couldn't wait to be rid of his unwanted wife.

With the last of her strength, Jessica straightened her spine, grabbed two potholders, and went to the stove. The first time she attempted to lift the big soup pot, her arms failed her before the pot was a half-inch off the stove. The pot banged back onto the black metal amid a hissing fury of spilled water. More by chance than anything else, Jessica avoided being burned by the boiling water.

Gritting her teeth, she shifted the potholders and reached for the big pot again, determined to have her hot bath no matter what. Before she had fully extended her arms, she was snatched off her feet, spun around, and found herself facing Wolfe's furious indigo eyes at a distance of bare inches.

"Are you too stupid to know that boiling water will raise blisters on your aristocratic hide?"

At Wolfe's words, Jessica's eyes narrowed until they were splinters of pale blue. For a moment she didn't answer, because she didn't trust herself not to scream like a fishwife at him.

"Even you aren't that stupid, my lord," she said finally, softly. "Or have you managed to teach a boiling pot to come to your heel like a long-tongued hound?"

"What are you talking about?"

"Getting a pot of water from the stove to the bath," she said succinctly.

"If you think you can soothe my ire over dinner by offering me a hot bath . . ."

Jessica opened her mouth to object that it was her own bath she was speaking about, not his, but Wolfe was talking again.

"You're right," he continued. "I've been looking forward to a bath much more than to eating whatever dinner you cooked. Clever of you to realize it."

"We non-paragons do our best," she said between her teeth.

"I'll remind you of that while you scrub my back." Wolfe smiled at the furious young woman suspended between his strong, dark hands.

"Tell me, husband dear, are all paragons also Amazons?"

"Willow is only an inch or two taller than you."

"But broad in the shoulders and thick in the arms?" Jessica suggested sweetly.

"She's as delicate and feminine as her namesake."

"Then how does she get hot water to her bath— one delicate demitasse at a time?"

"Paragons don't have to carry hot water to their baths. Nature does it for them."

"Ah, I knew it," Jessica purred. "She's a *witch*."

Wolfe pressed his lips together firmly, determined not to let Jessica beguile him with her quick mind and quicker tongue.

"Nothing that sinister," he said smoothly. "Caleb built their house near a hot spring. Reno put in pipes to the house."

"Lacking a husband as clever as Caleb and a brother as skilled as Reno, I'll have to manage getting hot water to my bath in the usual Western fashion—one bucket at a time."

Wolfe measured the determination in Jessica's eyes and knew she wouldn't back down on this issue. He could either carry the pot for her or stand by and watch her pour two gallons of scalding water over herself.

"I'll carry the bloody water," he snarled.

Ten minutes later, Wolfe had filled the long, narrow tub, drawn more buckets to heat, and stoked the stove. He stripped off his clothes and lowered himself into the water.

"All right, your ladyship," he called. "Come and wash your husband."

"What?"

"Wash me," Wolfe said impatiently. "That's something even you should be able to manage."

The stunned look on Jessica's face as she came to the doorway should have made Wolfe laugh; instead, it made him angry. He had been looking forward to putting Lady Victoria's advice to work: *Teach the little nun not to fear a man's touch.*

"Don't worry, Sister Jessica," Wolfe said curtly, turning his back as she edged up to the tub, "washing me won't make you pregnant."

She didn't answer. She didn't even hear Wolfe's words. The sight of him naked in his bath had taken her breath away. She had been too shaken that night in Lord Stewart's house to realize how physically magnificent Wolfe was, but now there was no wild panic or pain to distract her.

Now there was nothing but Wolfe's tawny body gleaming with water and rippling with masculine power.

A curious heat stirred in the pit of Jessica's stomach, as though she had swallowed a tiny butterfly with wings of golden flame. It reminded her of the hotel in St. Joseph, when the feel of Wolfe brushing her hair had sent heat and pleasure cascading through her.

There's passion in you, Jessi.

Fear burst in Jessica, chilling the soft heat that had come at the sight of Wolfe sitting in his bath.

I can't be passionate. I'm not some stupid lamb frisking off to slaughter. If my stomach feels odd, it's because I'm so tired I'm cross-eyed.

"I'm waiting, wife," Wolfe said.

Jessica opened her mouth. All that came out was a breathless sound. Wolfe rose from the dark, gently steaming water of the bathtub like a torso by an Italian sculptor: smoothly muscled, poised, powerful, quintessentially masculine in its elegance.

Candlelight rippled over sleek flesh like sunlight over water, heightening the play of muscle beneath skin that was as fine-grained as amber. The combination of stark male power and equally stark male beauty sent heat rushing through Jessica, shortening her breath, making her feel as though Wolfe were running his hands over her.

The thought was both frightening and fascinating. With fingers that trembled, Jessica scooped up soft, rose-scented soap and began rubbing it into Wolfe's hair. For a few moments, there was silence except for the splashing of water when Wolfe shifted in the tub and the soft, whispering sounds of Jessica's fingers as she worked rose-scented soap into Wolfe's hair.

Little of Wolfe was visible but his head, shoulders, and much of his back. The rest of him was hardly more than a golden blur beneath water that looked black but for streaks of lather and the shimmering of candlelight across the water's surface.

Despite the aching of her arms after hours of scrubbing, Jessica found that she enjoyed washing the thick, black pelt of Wolfe's hair. Working her hands through it caressed the sensitive inner surfaces of her fingers. The heat and softness of the lather sliding over her hands was another lure. When she went from his scalp to the taut skin of his neck, she found herself wanting to stroke him, testing his strength and resilience.

The golden butterfly in Jessica's stomach spread its wings again, sending heat streaking through her, making her catch her breath in pleasure.

No, not a butterfly, she told herself harshly. *It's a moth. A stupid little thing flying around a great hot flame, never knowing that the next second could be the last!*

Fear and passion warred within Jessica, making her tremble. Despite that, she couldn't help wondering what it would be like to spiral closer and closer to the flame, letting fire consume her to her very core.

Wolfe shifted abruptly, sending dark waves lapping at the sides of the tub. The slow rubbing of Jessica's fingers over his scalp was causing a heat greater than that of the bath water to gather between his legs.

"Am I doing it correctly?" Jessica asked.

The sound of her own voice alarmed her. It was much too husky, reflecting the tug-of-war between ingrained fear and blossoming desire. She enjoyed touching Wolfe far too much. Yet she was willing to risk it. Being close to him was an incredible lure.

"Yes," Wolfe answered. "You're doing very well."

His voice was deep, dark, warm. It made Jessica feel as though she had been caressed. Gentle fingertips traced the line of Wolfe's neck and shoulders. Muscles bunched and slid beneath skin that was the color of gold brushed with copper. The power in him fascinated Jessica, for he took it as much for granted as he did the air he breathed. She couldn't take him for granted in that way. Not any longer. The realization made her tremble.

"W-what did you do before I came here?" Jessica asked hurriedly.

Wolfe closed his eyes and fought the primal stirring of his body at the husky music of Jessica's voice and the magic of her fingers transforming him. Then he shrugged and let it happen, knowing there was nothing he could do to prevent it.

"I hunted, bought, sold, bred, and trained horses," he said.

Jessica's hands paused. "But there are no horses here, save for the one you purchased with the wagon in Denver."

"I sold all but my best horses when I decided to go to England for your engagement ball."

"Where are the rest of your horses?"

"At Caleb's. I spent most of the year there, helping him build his house. In return, he and Willow are taking care of the mares for me. They'll be bred by her Arabian stallion."

"Are they all mustangs?"

"Yes. One of them is an extraordinary animal, elegant and strong, fierce and intelligent. She's the color of steeldust. She'll be the foundation of my future herd."

"When will you bring your horses back here?"

"I don't think I will. This side of the Rockies is getting too settled. It's time for me to pull up stakes and move on."

"Too settled? You're joking."

"No. For the most part I get along all right with ranchers and soldiers, but townspeople take a narrow view of halfbreeds. If anything goes wrong, they come looking for the nearest Indian to blame."

Jessica's hands paused. "That's terrible."

Wolfe shrugged again. "It's simply human. If I lived here long enough, I'd get around most of the townspeople. The rest I'd fight until they changed their minds, shut their mouths, or left for more healthy climates."

"If you can make the townspeople accept you, why don't you stay?"

"My Cheyenne name is Tree That Stands Alone. It suits me."

"But you built such a cozy home here."

"I'll build another one somewhere else. Maybe up over the Great Divide, where Caleb and Willow have their ranch. Sure to God it would be easier than riding back and forth as often as I have to see them."

Jessica's hands tightened in Wolfe's hair. *Willow again. Blast that paragon. What chance do I have to persuade Wolfe of my worth as a wife when he is forever yearning after her?*

"Take a breath," Jessica muttered.

As she spoke, she pushed Wolfe's head quite forcefully under the water. He emerged instantly and shook his head like a hound, spraying water all over her.

"Again," she said sweetly.

Jessica pushed. Hard.

Smiling to himself, Wolfe slid under the water once more. This time he stayed under long enough to worry her.

"Wolfe?"

She tugged at his shoulders. He didn't budge.

"Wolfe, that's enough. Wolfe? Are you—"

Water erupted as Wolfe rose halfway out of the tub, grabbed Jessica, and held her poised over the dark water.

"Put me down!" she demanded breathlessly.

"With pleasure."

"On the floor, you devil! On the floor!"

But Jessica was laughing too hard to stand, so Wolfe had to hold her. He leaned his elbows against the tub, supporting her, smiling, calling himself every kind of idiot. He should be withdrawing from her, not teasing smiles and laughter from her beautiful mouth, and feeling as proud as a hen with a new chick because there was color in her cheeks once more.

He would never win the war if the kept siding with the enemy. Very carefully, he released her.

"I think you're well-rinsed now," Jessica said, turning to leave. "By the time the rest of the water is heated, you should be finished with your bath."

Again, her voice was alarmingly husky. At the sound of it, Wolfe narrowed his eyes. Little nun or not, she had liked washing his hair. He wondered how she would like washing the rest of him.

Abruptly he knew he was going to find out. His arm snaked out, grabbing Jessica around her hips before she could leave.

"You've forgotten something," Wolfe said.

"What?"

"The rest of me. It needs washing, too."

 6

"Y ou're joking," Jessica said.
Wolfe felt the warmth and tension of her body
and smiled. "No, I'm not. Pick up the sponge."
She bent over a bit awkwardly, for Wolfe's arm
was still around her hips. Just when her bend was
at its deepest, she felt Wolfe's hand caressing and
squeezing her hip as though testing its shape and
the resilience of her flesh. She straightened so
quickly that she almost fell over.
"Wolfe!"
He made a deep sound that could have been
stifled laughter or a muffled question.
"Your hand—that is," she stammered. "You—"
He smiled a lazy, dangerous kind of smile. "I?"
he invited.
Jessica blinked. She had never seen quite that
expression on Wolfe's face. He was remarkably
handsome, and looked every bit the devil she had
accused him of being a few minutes ago. If the
flame looked half so beautiful to the moth, it was
no wonder the poor thing ended up getting too
close.
"I, er, nothing," Jessica muttered.
Hurriedly, she started rubbing up a thick lather
on the sponge. Wolfe measured her high color and

the pulse beating rapidly in her throat. The looks she gave him as she washed his face and shoulders told him she was both nervous and intrigued by his nakedness.

Lady Victoria, my hat is off to you—along with everything else, Wolfe thought with amusement. *You're every bit as wickedly clever about human nature as I remembered. Jessica is no more a nun than I am.*

Working in a rush, Jessica rinsed Wolfe, trying not to see beneath the darkly reflective surface of the bath. It was impossible. She closed her eyes, thinking to make the bath less intimate that way.

It was a mistake. With her eyes closed, her hands seemed doubly sensitive. The sleek, hot power of his body beneath her hands made her tremble. The different textures of Wolfe was a new, pleasurable shock each time her hands moved across his chest. Heat burned softly through the pit of her stomach, making her shiver. She moved her hands across Wolfe's chest once more, telling herself that she was rinsing him and knowing that she was lying to herself. She wanted to knead his flesh like a cat, and, like a cat, she knew she would purr all the while.

Desperately, Jessica opened her eyes just in time to see one of Wolfe's long, powerful legs emerge from the water. Dark patterns of water-slicked hair began above the ankle and progressed farther up his muscular thigh than she was prepared to acknowledge.

Wolfe saw the direction of Jessica's glance and knew that the water wasn't hiding as much of him as it had before. He waited for a long, tense moment, measuring the combination of fear and desire in her. Knowing that he intrigued her as a man was violently exciting to him.

And it showed.

"W-Wolfe?"

"Surely I'm no more difficult to scrub than bricks," he said casually. "Wash me, wife."

Carefully looking no farther than Wolfe's thigh, Jessica ran the soapy sponge over his leg in a single, breathless rush.

"Rinse," she said.

The huskiness of her voice was another kind of caress on Wolfe's responsive flesh. His right leg disappeared, only to be replaced by his left. She rubbed the sponge up the flexed muscles of his calf to his knee, only to fumble and lose the sponge. Instantly it sank beneath the surface of the water between his legs.

Jessica waited for Wolfe to retrieve the sponge for her. When he made no move, she looked up. She thought she saw the gleam of his eyes beneath his black lashes, but decided she was wrong. Carefully she fished beneath the water. Her fingers met hard, smooth flesh rather than sponge. Breath hissed between Wolfe's clenched teeth.

"I'm s-sorry," she said breathlessly, snatching back her hand. "I didn't mean to . . ."

"Touch me?" Wolfe smiled without opening his eyes. "I forgive you, sweet nun."

"The sponge," she began.

"Hammer the sponge. Your fingers feel much better."

Jessica was too rattled to argue. She grabbed more of the soft soap and rubbed it into the powerful muscles of Wolfe's thigh, skimming over him in the space of seconds. Then, against her will, her own hands betrayed her and returned to enjoy the feel of his skin beneath her palms.

"Rinse," she said in a low, choked voice.

The leg vanished back into the water. Lather swirled and floated away. Before Wolfe could make any more demands in regard to being washed, Jessica surged to her feet and hurried from the room, mumbling something about checking the heat of her own bath water on the stove.

Wolfe's shuttered, hungry glance followed Jessica until she was out of sight. Reluctantly, he fished out the sponge and finished the bath, knowing he had teased her as much as he dared...at the moment.

By the time Jessica's bath water was heated and she returned cautiously to the bedroom, her heart was beating at a less frantic pace and her stomach no longer did odd little flips at every other breath. She watched from beneath lowered eyelashes as Wolfe tamped the wooden plug back in place, closing up the hole that drained the bathtub through an opening in the bricks and onto the ground below.

Jessica admired the flex and play of Wolfe's body while he emptied bucket after bucket of scalding water into the tub, then drew more water from the pump to cool the bath. It was quite easy for her to admire Wolfe's supple power, for he wore nothing but his linen towel wrapped as a loin cloth. The pale luster of the cloth against his copper-brushed skin fascinated her.

Rather quickly she began to feel the increasingly familiar sensation of having swallowed golden butterflies. As a result, her fingers were clumsy when she went to work on the buttons up the back of her dress. Even worse, her arms simply refused to flex more than a few inches. Her muscles were too tight after hours of scrubbing to have any flexibility left.

With a stifled, frustrated sound, she hooked her fingers in either side of the opening at the back of her neck and yanked. Buttons tore free and fell soundlessly onto the thick wool throw rug by the bed.

Warm, hard fingers brushed Jessica's hands aside. Wolfe began unbuttoning the dress in a silence that thickened with each jet button sliding free of its tiny hole. Finally, nothing but the long sleeves were holding the dress in place. The exquisite lace of Jessica's silk camisole revealed more than it concealed of the skin beneath.

"Thank you," Jessica said breathlessly. "I can manage now."

"Don't you want me to bathe you?"

"No, that won't be necessary thank you," she said, running the words together in her rush to have them spoken.

Wolfe's long finger traced the length of Jessica's spine. "Are you certain?"

She shivered as an odd tingling rippled through her at his touch. "Yes."

Wolfe's finger paused before retracing every bit of its journey as he asked, "Yes, you're certain you want to be bathed?"

Jessica made a small sound as curious sensations flared unnervingly in the pit of her stomach. "No, I can bathe myself."

"If you change your mind, call me."

As soon as the door closed behind Wolfe, she let out a long breath she hadn't been aware of holding and began stripping off her clothes with more haste than care. With the pot of soft, rose-scented soap in one hand and the sponge in the other, she stepped into the tub.

A delicious shivering went over her as she lowered herself into the water's hot embrace. The tremor of sheer pleasure was very much what she had felt at the long, slow stroking of Wolfe's fingertip down her spine. The realization was almost as unnerving as his touch had been. Quickly, she ducked beneath the water to wet her hair before she began rubbing soap into it.

By the time Jessica had rinsed and begun to work a second round of soap into her hair, the quivering reluctance of her arm muscles abruptly changed into something more alarming. Her arms locked in a half-raised position. No matter how hard she tried, she couldn't raise them any farther. In fact, she couldn't even hold them upright.

Soap began trickling down her face and into her eyes as her arms fell uselessly to her sides.

"Wolfe," Jessica cried out. "Something is wrong with my arms!"

Afraid to open her eyes because of the soap, Jessica didn't know Wolfe had come into the room until she felt a warm cloth moving over her face. She flinched in surprise.

"Be still, Jessi," Wolfe said. "I won't hurt you."

"I know. You just startled me. My arms, Wolfe. I can't—"

"Yes, I can see," he interrupted.

He ran his hands gently over her arms. The slender muscles were knotted and hard beneath her smooth skin.

"Do you hurt?" he asked.

Jessica shook her head. "Not really. I think the muscles have just declared a holiday. The same thing happened to my legs that day I tried to jump the creek the way you had. Remember?"

Wolfe smiled slightly. "How many times did you try?"

"I don't know. I spent most of the morning running and jumping."

"And landing in the water."

"And landing in the water," she agreed, sighing. "It made me angry that you could fly so easily over the creek time and again and I couldn't do it even once. That night I couldn't walk."

"You never told me."

"I was too proud."

"Just as you were too proud to tell me today that you couldn't work any more."

Jessica said nothing.

"I'll take care of the soap on your face, first," Wolfe said. "Your arms can wait. Tilt your head back and keep your eyes closed."

The gentleness of Wolfe's voice was matched by his fingers sliding into Jessica's soapy hair and easing her head back while he blotted up the last of the lather.

"No, don't open your eyes yet. I haven't gotten all the soap out."

Jessica heard the sound of cloth being rinsed, felt the swirling of water over her breasts, and blushed at the reminder of her own nakedness. Water ran warmly over her closed eyes, down her cheeks, down her neck.

Wolfe watched each golden trail of moisture with something approaching envy. He wanted to be that close to her, that warm on her skin, licking over her without hindrance.

And he was a fool to want any part of her at all.

"Do your eyes sting?"

"No," Jessica said hesitantly, wondering at the leashed anger in Wolfe's voice.

"Keep them closed until I rinse your hair."

"You don't have to. I can—"

"You can't do a bloody thing," he interrupted impatiently. "The muscles in your arms have cramped. Take a breath."

Jessica barely had drawn a breath before her body was shifted and her head was pushed under the warm water. Unlike Wolfe, she was almost able to stretch out in the narrow tub.

Working quickly, Wolfe stripped out lather and swirled clean water through the long mahogany strands until all the soap was gone. Only then did he prop her head above the water against the tub.

"That should do it."

Jessica tried to push a stray lock of hair from her eyes, but her arms still wouldn't cooperate. When she tried again, the struggle brought the pink tips of her breasts above the level of the water. Immediately, her nipples tightened against the cool air of the room.

When Wolfe looked down, he wished he hadn't. His body hardened in a rush that would have brought him to his knees if he had been standing. But he wasn't. He was kneeling next to an aristocratic little nun who had worked so hard at unaccustomed tasks that her arms had given out. He would have felt worse about being such a savage taskmaster, except that Jessica's revenge, while unintentional, was complete. The memory of her breasts tipped by tight coral crowns would haunt him without mercy.

"Useless blue-blooded nun," Wolfe said through gritted teeth. "Take another breath."

"I didn't mean to do this," Jessica said, stung by the tone of Wolfe's voice. "Between the clothes and the kitchen floor, I—"

The words ended in sputtering sounds as Wolfe lowered Jessica's head into the water. Moments later, he hauled her into an upright position once more. With swift, efficient movements, he lifted her long hair and squeezed water from it.

"Where is your towel?" he asked.

There was silence followed by a sigh as she admitted, "I was so eager to get into the water I forgot about getting out again."

"Hold your hair out of the water while I get—*damn*, you can't lift your arms."

Wolfe draped Jessica's hair over the edge of the tub and down onto the bricks.

"Don't move. If you slipped under the water, you'd probably drown. I'll be right back."

Moments later, Wolfe came back into the room carrying linen towels and a soft cotton flannel blanket. He dried Jessica's hair as best he could, wrapped it in the length of linen, and tucked everything on top of her head in a neat turban.

"How are your arms doing?"

"Fine, as long as I don't try to move them."

Wolfe turned aside, picked up the sponge, and began soaping it. He washed her back, shoulders, and arms, rinsed her, and began soaping the sponge once more.

"Don't panic, little nun."

"What?"

The breath stopped in Jessica's throat as she felt the sponge gliding over her collar bones, her breasts, her ribs, her belly.

"Lift one leg," he said as he soaped the sponge once more.

"Wolfe," she said faintly.

"Just brace your foot against the lip of the tub the way I did. Don't worry. I won't let you drown."

Slowly, Jessica lifted her right leg. As though it was something he did every day, Wolfe washed the delicate, high-arched foot, slender ankle, and calf. She watched him with a sense of stunned disbelief as the sponge slid beneath the water and on up the length of her leg.

"Now the other."

Dazed, Jessica obeyed, lowering one leg and raising the other. The sponge began moving over her once more. When it went from foot to calf to thigh, she shivered. But the sponge didn't stop there. It swept over the triangle of hair and then down to the soft flesh below. An odd sound squeezed from Jessica's throat. Instantly, the sponge stopped moving, remaining tucked between her thighs.

"Is something wrong?" Wolfe asked blandly, looking up.

Jessica made another small sound.

"Yes?" he asked.

She blushed brightly enough to put dawn to shame. "Wolfe, please."

"Please what?"

Putting her hands against his wrist, she tugged, but her arms didn't exert any force. His hand stayed where it was.

"Do you want me to move my hand?" he asked.

"Yes," she said, shivering.

"Then unclamp your legs."

Belatedly, Jessica realized that she had pressed her thighs together in an instinctive effort to shield herself from Wolfe's touch. The sponge, and his fingers, were caught between her legs.

"S-sorry," she whispered.

Wolfe wasn't. He had loved being pressed into the secret, silky warmth of her.

Hurriedly, she shifted, releasing him. The slow withdrawal of the sponge and the hint of a sleek, intimate caress made her feel faint. She flushed from her breasts to her forehead.

"There's no need to be embarrassed," Wolfe said in a matter-of-fact tone. "Even if a husband and wife never share a bed, a certain amount of intimacy is inevitable between them."

Jessica swallowed and watched with huge eyes as Wolfe stood and shook out the soft cotton flannel blanket.

"Can you stand up?"

Her eyes became even bigger. "No."

"Then I'll help."

"But I'm not wearing anything!" she said frantically.

Wolfe sighed and said in a very patient tone, "I know. It's the usual practice to be naked when in the bath. Can you stand or do you need help?"

"But—"

"Jessica," he interrupted, "quit dithering and get out of the bath before you take a chill."

"Close your eyes."

"This is foolish," he muttered, but he closed his eyes.

Despite her largely useless arms, Jessica thrashed around until she managed to get to her knees. She was almost to her feet when she slipped.

"Wolfe!"

He caught her, lifted her out of the tub, and stood her on the bricks. With as much disinterest as he could manage, he began drying her briskly.

"Close your eyes!" she wailed.

"I can't see what I'm doing with my eyes closed. Why don't you close yours, instead?"

Jessica blinked. "What good would that do?"

"Just a thought."

Wolfe stifled a smile and closed his eyes. Almost

immediately his hands slipped, fumbled, and ended up sliding over her hip without the towel between.

"This isn't working," she said breathlessly.

He thought it was working quite well, but said only, "Do you have a better idea?"

"Hold out the blanket tightly and I'll dry myself on it."

Within seconds, Wolfe knew it was a bad idea . . . and a good one. The feel of Jessica's small, utterly female body rubbing against the cotton in his hands inflamed him as much as bathing her had. When the blanket slipped and he felt the unmistakable texture of a nipple dragging against his palm, he had to fight to draw air into his lungs.

"There, that should do it," Jessica said finally.

Wolfe didn't know whether to be glad or sad that the lovely torment was ending. He turned his back and went to the bed. A sweeping motion of his arm opened the fur cover so that it lay flat over the bed.

"Come here and lie down," he said, carefully not looking at the naked, intensely female nun who stood trembling next to the tub. "I'll see if I can rub the knots out of your arms and back."

Uncertainly, Jessica looked at the tall man who stood by the bed. Naked but for the strip of white linen he wore wrapped carelessly around his loins, caressed by light and brushed by shadows, Wolfe's body was both beautiful and rather frightening in its obvious strength.

"Your ladyship, if I had intended to attack you like Lord Gore, it would have happened ten times over by now."

The cold anger in Wolfe's voice made Jessica flinch.

"Yes," she said faintly. "I know. It's just . . . new to me."

"It's new to me, too."

Jessica gave him a startled look. "It is?"

"I've never bathed a woman before. But then, you aren't a woman. You're a nun."

Without a word, Jessica went to the bed and lay face down. The silkiness of the fur against her nude body made her gasp.

"Now what?" Wolfe asked impatiently as he threw the cotton blanket over her.

Jessica shivered. "It feels strange to have nothing against my skin but fur."

"You'll warm to it."

She let out her breath and shifted experimentally. The fur warmed and stroked her in return. A shivering little sigh went through her.

"You're right. The fur feels quite . . . extraordinary."

Without realizing it, she moved again, stroking her body against the luxurious coverlet. The sensuality implicit in the movement went into Wolfe like a knife. It occurred to him that Lady Victoria had a point worth considering: *Teach the little nun not to fear a man's touch.*

Wolfe had been trying to ignore the passion in Jessica. At that moment, he decided it would be more intelligent of him to awaken that passion. Then the thought of a man's bed and body wouldn't be so horrifying to her. Then she would agree to end this sham marriage and find a union more suitable to her station.

Then Wolfe could find a marriage and a woman more suitable to his own desires—a strong, resilient mate who could match his passion, work by his side in the wild land, and give him children.

Next to those vital things, an amusing elf was simply that.

An amusement.

And if the thought of another man taking Jessica's untouched body made Wolfe angry at some primitive level of his being, that was too bad. Life had taught him that the hunger he felt for a female was temporary; a true marriage was not.

Until death do us part.

"First, I think some brandy is in order for you," Wolfe said thoughtfully.

"Brandy?"

"Umm."

His rumbling sound of agreement made Jessica smile. "Thank you, but I don't really enjoy spirits."

"Think of it as medicine."

"Medicine?"

"Yes. I'll bring a bit extra for the parrot, too."

"Parrot? Oh, that parrot. Indeed, it must be on the loose in here." She laughed softly and rubbed her cheek against the fur, forgetting for a moment the aches and alarming weakness of her arms. "This fur has the most heavenly texture."

Wolfe stood for an instant, transfixed by the sight of Jessica smoothing her skin against the fur as though it were a lover's body. Abruptly, he turned and walked out of the room. When he came back, he carried a small snifter of brandy in his hand.

"Sit up, Jessie."

She rolled onto her side, but when it came time for her arms to push her body upright, they weren't equal to the task.

"I don't think I can," she admitted.

Wolfe set the snifter aside and helped Jessica sit up. The cotton blanket started to slide to her waist. She made a startled sound and grabbed. Her reflexes were very slow, for her arms simply didn't want to move. The blanket fell below her breasts before she caught it.

Closing his eyes, Wolfe told himself that he was a fool to react as though he had never seen a woman naked to the waist before. Yet the image of Jessica's creamy curves and rosy nipples burned behind his eyelids, making his heartbeat deepen and increase as though he had been running uphill.

With a stifled curse, he opened his eyes, jerked the blanket up over her breasts, and pressed the snifter's rim against her soft lower lip.

"Drink."

Wolfe's voice was thick with desire, but there was no mistaking the command in it. Grimacing, Jessica opened her mouth, drank, and swallowed. An instant later, she was gasping for air and coughing. Calmly, Wolfe poured water from a carafe on the bedside table and offered the glass to her. She drank quickly. Even so, the brandy left a fiery trail from her tongue to her stomach.

"Better?"

Jessica nodded, because she couldn't speak.

"Lie down on your stomach again."

Casually Wolfe took the blanket off Jessica, shook it out, and let it flutter down over the tempting curves of her bottom and the shadow cleft between.

"Where is your rose oil?" Wolfe asked.

"In the crystal bottle on your dresser."

"There are nine such bottles."

"The one with the stopper that's the color of my cheeks," she muttered into the fur.

"Ah, that one." Wolfe looked at the fiery color of Jessica's face. "Blushing again, elf?"

She turned her head and slanted him a narrow

look. Against the intense color of her face, her eyes looked like gems.

"You're enjoying this," she accused.

Wolfe turned away before Jessica could see him smile. He retrieved the proper bottle from the dresser.

"Be careful," she said. "It's fragile."

"Don't worry. I'm not clumsy with small things."

She laughed softly and confessed into the fur, "I know. You're the only man I've ever seen who can take a handful of roses from a bush and never know the bite of thorns."

Smiling, Wolfe coaxed the fragile stopper free and poured a small amount of oil in his palm. When he sat next to Jessica on the bed, she made a startled sound. She made another sound when he began rubbing his hands up and down her body.

As he had suspected, Jessica's back was as knotted as her arms. Warmed by his hands and the friction of skin against skin, the rose oil gave its fragrance to the silent room. When his hands kneaded up her back from waist to nape, Jessica made a low sound.

"Too hard?" Wolfe asked.

"Too... wonderful." Jessica sighed. "Ah, that feels like heaven."

He smiled and continued working the stiffness out of her back. Each time he worked down her spine, he took in more of her sides, coming closer and closer to her breasts. Each time he approached her waist, he eased a bit lower. The soft flannel retreated to the small of her back, then to the beginning of the velvet cleft of her bottom. The temptation to run his finger over the intriguing shadow

was great, but Wolfe resisted it. He knew Jessica
would panic.

"Tell me where it's sore." Wolfe moved his
hands to Jessica's shoulders. "Here?"

She nodded her head without opening her eyes.
When she felt the pressure of his strong fingers
kneading out the clenched tension of the muscles,
she groaned.

"Pleasure or pain?" Wolfe asked in a low voice.

Jessica nodded her head.

"Which one?"

"Yes," she sighed, uncurling her hands along
her sides.

He laughed softly, poured more oil onto his
palm, and resumed rubbing.

"What about here?" he asked.

The gentle glide of his hands across Jessica's upper arms felt wonderful. She groaned and relaxed
even more beneath his touch. As he worked on
the knotted muscles of her left arm from shoulder
to fingertips, his hands kept brushing between her
arm and her body. The first few times it happened,
she tightened and tried to move away. Then she
forgot to be self-conscious about his touch, for it
simply felt too good to object when the back of his
fingers brushed the sides of her breast, her ribs,
the inward curve of her waist, and the smooth
swell of her hip.

The third time Wolfe's hand traced Jessica's body
without her withdrawing, he smiled and switched
his attention to her other arm. In order to reach it,
he straddled her thighs. As he worked down her
right arm, he slowly dragged the blanket lower and
lower until the full curves of her buttocks were
revealed. The breath in his throat caught as he
looked at the creamy, fine-grained skin and femi-

nine promise that lay so close at hand.

"What about here?" he asked, tracing the long muscles that ran along either side of Jessica's spine. "Stiff?"

"Yes," she sighed.

Wolfe tested, agreed, and bit back a comment about his own stiffness. The loin cloth he had wrapped around himself could not contain the change that passion had wrought on his body. The sight of Jessica's graceful hips rising from the rumpled blanket was a sweet torment. The thought of opening her legs and easing into her soft body with the fur all silky around her made him groan.

"Wolfe?"

For a moment he didn't answer. Then the talons of need eased and he could breathe once more.

"What?" he asked.

Jessica shivered with pleasure as Wolfe's hands kneaded down her back to her waist, lingered, then eased upward again with a combination of gentleness and strength that was magic on her aching body.

"That feels so good." She sighed and unconsciously arched against his touch. "It makes me dizzy."

"Must be the brandy."

"I don't think so, my lord. I think it's your hands. I didn't know anything could feel so wonderful."

"Are you sure? A moment ago you couldn't tell the difference between pleasure and pain."

"I'm sure." The sound Jessica made was more like a soft moan than a sigh. "It's like fire without pain, a pleasure that goes to the center of my bones."

Wolfe's breath caught before it came out in a soundless rush of air, for what she was describing was the essence of true passion.

"Yes," he whispered. "It's like that, fire without pain."

For long minutes, there was no sound in the room but the subtle whisper of flame and the glide of Wolfe's palms over Jessica's rose-scented skin. When his hands continued past her waist to her hips, she didn't notice for a few moments. Then her body stiffened.

"Wolfe?"

"You have sore muscles here, too," he said matter-of-factly.

"Yes, but—"

"Hush, Jessi," Wolfe interrupted firmly. "Pretend I'm still working on your shoulders."

"But you aren't!"

"That's where the pretending comes in."

For a time there was a silence that was like the flesh Wolfe was kneading—silky, taut, quivering with possibilities.

"You're not pretending."

"How do you know?" Jessica retorted.

"The parrot told me."

She giggled, then giggled some more, imagining a parrot darting brightly about the room telling secrets.

"I'm muzzled," she said after a moment.

"On that little bit of brandy? I doubt it."

"I'm a little bit myself, remember? You've said so often enough."

Not everywhere, Wolfe thought silently, sinking his fingers into Jessica's resilient flesh. *There are parts of my self that are quite lush.*

Jessica's breath broke on a ragged sigh.

"Sorry. I didn't mean to be rough," Wolfe said, smoothing his palm over the tender curve of her bottom. "Perhaps more oil . . ."

"You weren't rough," Jessica said lazily.

"Then why did you make that small sound?"

"I didn't." She smiled. "The parrot did. It's muzzled, too."

"A drunken parrot. The mind reels."

"More like the stomach."

"On a sip of brandy? Impossible."

"Then it must be the butterflies."

"What butterflies?"

"The ones in my stomach. Every time you touch me a certain way, they whirl around like leaves on the wind."

Jessica giggled again, then gasped softly when Wolfe's thumbs drew deeply beneath the curves of her buttocks, skimming the place where her thighs were pressed together.

"Like that?" he asked, his voice husky.

"Y-yes."

"Then I'll do this, instead."

Jessica's breath unraveled in broken sounds as Wolfe's lean, strong fingers kneaded down the back of her thighs to her knees. A curious, boneless feeling stole over her, a combination of brandy and the shimmering warmth of Wolfe's hands smoothing oil and pleasure into her skin. Without realizing it, she groaned softly and relaxed the tension that had kept her legs pressed together.

Wolfe took one look at the dark mahogany shadow her relaxation had revealed and locked his jaw against a sound of passionate need. Very quickly he looked away, concentrating on the slender legs that lay beneath his hands. But here, too, Jessica's femininity was obvious in each satin curve of thigh and calf, in the unblemished silk of skin never before seen by any man, and in the shivering response that rippled through her when he caressed the sensitive crease behind each knee.

"Roll over, little one."

Bemused by unexpected lassitude, Jessica responded to the gentle command. She didn't stop to think of her nudity until she felt the caress of fur from her nape to her ankles. Her eyes opened slowly, then closed once more when Wolfe dropped the soft flannel blanket over her, covering her from breasts to mid-thigh. She sighed and snuggled more deeply into the fur with slow movements of her hips.

Wolfe looked away with a soundless curse at his own foolishness in offering himself such a temptation. But his dark glance came back again, drawn inevitably by the small movements of Jessica's hips, the swell of her breasts, and the telltale rigidity of her nipples.

"Warm enough?" he asked in a husky voice.

Jessica nodded slowly.

"How do you feel?"

"Like a mitten . . . being unraveled."

Wolfe's smile was as hot as the blood surging through his veins, but Jessica didn't notice. She was adrift on a soft fur raft while strong hands kneaded her neck and shoulders, her arms and fingertips. As Wolfe soothed every knot from her aching arms, she made tiny, low sounds. Each sound was a knife sliding over the leash of his self-control, fraying it, until finally his hands slid down to her wrist and his fingers interlocked deeply with her own.

"Sore?" he asked, squeezing her hand gently.

The ragged sound Jessica made was pleasure, not pain. Her lashes stirred lazily, revealing a flash of aquamarine eyes. When he flexed his hand again, her fingers spread and laced tightly with his until their hands could not be more deeply joined.

"That feels good," she said in a husky voice.

"This?"

Wolfe's hand flexed again, caressing the sensitive skin between Jessica's fingers and sliding down until he could go no farther. He pressed palm against palm and squeezed deeply.

Sighing, Jessica nodded. "Yes, that." She smiled. "The butterflies like it, too."

Wolfe continued the seduction of Jessica's hand until she moved with him, spreading her fingers wide in silent invitation, sighing as he caressed from tip to base until her fingers closed, trapping his hand against her.

With a final squeeze, Wolfe dragged his fingers free of hers, ignoring Jessica's small murmur of protest.

"Wolfe? You're not stopping, are you?"

"No," he said as he poured more oil into his palm. "I'm just going to work on your legs some more. Let your arms relax or they'll knot up again. You're weak as a day-old kitten."

"I know." Jessica's sigh was so deep it was almost a moan. "But it was worth it."

"What was?"

"All the scrubbing. Without it, I'd never have discovered what pleasure your hands could give me."

Wolfe's eyes narrowed against a violent surge of desire. He began rubbing the length of Jessica's legs, beginning at the ankles and working slowly upward. When he reached mid-thigh, she stretched without moving her arms from her sides, arching her back and her feet, curling her toes. Her response was a knife in his loins, demanding that he take what she was so innocently offering.

"Jessi," Wolfe whispered.

Long fingers pressed between her thighs as he encircled one leg and began kneading slowly, deeply, unraveling her even more. When his hands slid up beneath the blanket, Jessica stirred. Wolfe hesitated, waiting for an objection. None came. He let out a silent breath and slowly moved his hands even higher. The delicious pressure made Jessica sigh and stretch again.

"Why have you never done this to me before?" she murmured.

"I was just wondering the same thing."

His palms slid higher. She sighed and shifted languidly.

"I'm all unraveled. 'Tis quite wonderful."

"Yes," Wolfe said huskily.

Closing his eyes, he savored the sleek resilience of Jessica's flesh, the warm shifting of her body, the languid sighs. He knew he must stop touching her soon, for the hunger of his own body was becoming unmanageable.

Yet the soft temptations of her flesh were so close to hand, so hot, that he couldn't force himself to withdraw right away. She was a heady fragrance and a hard need that was eroding his control as surely as he was unraveling her fear of a man's touch. The blanket retreated before his gently insistent hands, leaving her secrets defended only by the mahogany cloud he longed to brush with his palm.

Then Jessica shifted again and the cloud parted, and a low sound of need was dragged from Wolfe. His hand moved, brushed, lingered, burned. Then his fingers were seeking and finding and testing the softness that had been revealed.

The intimate caress sent Jessica bolt upright with a gasp of mingled pleasure and shock. When she saw Wolfe's hand between her legs, pleasure fled and shock became fear fed by a torrent of brutal memories. In her mind a stormy night descended and her mother screamed from the hallway floor as the lord ruthlessly pulled her legs apart.

"No!" Jessica cried.

"Easy, little one," Wolfe said thickly. "I won't hurt you. It's a natural part of—"

His words were lost beneath the raw scream that tore from Jessica's throat. She moved convulsively to defend herself, but her arms were too weak to push away a child, much less a man of Wolfe's strength. She drew breath to scream again, only to have a hard hand clamp over her mouth, forcing her back down upon the bed.

It was her nightmare all over again, a woman's screams cut off by the brute force of a husband intent upon rutting between his wife's legs. Jessica tossed and thrashed from side to side, but couldn't shake off the hand over her mouth or the heavy thigh pinning her own legs to the bed. Shuddering, wild with fear, she flailed against Wolfe with weak arms until he gathered her wrists in one hand and held them against her naked stomach.

"Jessi, listen to me, I won't hurt you."

If she heard, she didn't respond.

As Wolfe looked down at Jessica's struggling body, he felt a volatile combination of frank lust, shame at his loss of control, and anger at her wild fear.

"Be still, damn it," Wolfe said curtly. "I won't touch you. Do you understand me? *Jessica!*"

Wolfe had to repeat himself several times before Jessica subsided and lay still but for the involuntary tremors that shook her body, residue of her terror.

"I'm going to lift my hand from your mouth, but if you scream again, so help me God I'll slap you into sanity as I would any hysteric."

Jessica watched Wolfe with pale, glittering eyes. There was no comfort in his face—his eyes were black, his face dark and grim, his mouth a flat line. Even so, she nodded her head, for his hand was no longer invading her body. Slowly, Wolfe freed her mouth.

Jessica didn't scream, even though she was pale and trembling. When she spoke, her voice was like breaking glass and her breath was coming in bursts. Despite that, her words were all too clear.

"No wonder you were called the viscount's *savage*. Gentlemen who can't control their baser urges make use of whores, not wives. If I had thought you would ever do anything so vile to me, I would never have sought a marriage. You have no need of an heir to inherit a title or a great estate, no reason to so foul my body, yet you would rut upon me like a beast!"

Wolfe looked down into Jessica's face and felt her contempt beating at him with thick, invisible wings. Silence stretched and stretched until it was a living thing quivering between Jessica and Wolfe.

"What do you expect?" Wolfe snarled. "Ever since we got on the stagecoach together I've been breathing your air and watching you look at me when you think I won't notice."

Jessica didn't deny it, for it was true. She had always watched Wolfe. He fascinated her. And the older she became, the more the fascination had deepened.

Wolfe continued speaking, his voice harsh with frustration and anger. "You keep watching me with hungry eyes and wondering how it would be to couple with a savage, but when I—"

"Never!" Jessica interrupted wildly. "Never! I never thought of coupling with you. The thought horrifies me!"

Wolfe's eyes narrowed until they were little more than splinters of black. *"Then you will agree to an annulment."*

The words were so soft, Jessica didn't understand them at first. When she did, she closed her eyes and sought to control the fear clawing at her.

"No," Jessica said, her voice shaking. "You may be a savage, but you won't take me by force."

Deliberately, Wolfe's hand settled on the mahogany nest just above her thighs.

"Won't I?" he asked softly.

She stiffened as though he had taken a whip to her. When her eyes opened, they were so dilated with fear that there was barely any color to them. She tried to lift her hands in a silent plea, but her arms wouldn't respond. She tried to speak, but all that came from her lips was a hoarse whisper that could have been Wolfe's name.

With a barely controlled fury at himself, at her, and at the sham marriage, Wolfe surged to his feet beside the bed.

"Get out," he said flatly.

Jessica looked up at Wolfe without comprehension.

"Get out of my bed, your ladyship. You disgust me as much as I horrify you. I couldn't take you if I had to. You're not a woman, you're a spoiled, cruel child."

Jessica moved too slowly to suit Wolfe. He bent over and hauled her to her feet.

"Agree to an annulment," he demanded in a low

voice. "Damn you, let me go!"

She swallowed dryly and shook her head.

Wolfe looked at Jessica for a long moment before he spoke in a soft, cold voice that was more punishing than a blow.

"You will rue the day you forced me into marriage. There are worse things than being caressed by a savage. You shall learn each one of them."

W ITH an apprehension Jessica didn't reveal, she watched from the corner of her eye as Wolfe took a sip of the coffee she had prepared. When he did little more than grimace at the taste, she let out a soundless sigh of relief and passed him a dish of stewed fruit and a platter of ham and biscuits.

Covertly, Jessica watched while Wolfe forked ham onto his plate, ignored the biscuits, and spooned stewed fruit into his bowl. She hoped he would be less fierce after he had eaten. Perhaps then he would listen to her explanations. Perhaps then he would look at her with less contempt.

Silently, Wolfe ate, sensing Jessica's watchfulness. He said nothing to her. Nor did he look at her. It was safer that way. The rage in him was still very close to the surface. Awakening in a state of arousal that had increased at the mere sight of Jessica had done nothing to sweeten Wolfe's temper.

"More ham?" she asked in a soft voice.

"No, thank you."

Jessica took little comfort in Wolfe's politeness, for she knew it was as automatic to him as breathing and meant far less. In England his manners

153

were as impeccable as a duke's. More so, for Wolfe had no tradition of wealth and power to mitigate any social gaffe he might make. When among the English, he never forgot for one instant that he was an outsider. He had made of their customs both an armor and a subtle insult. The viscount's savage always proved better at elegant nuance than those who had been to the manor born, making them seem savages by comparison.

"Wolfe," Jessica said, "last night I was tired and frightened and—"

He interrupted curtly. "You made yourself clear last night, your ladyship. My touch horrifies you."

"No, that's not what I meant."

"The hell it isn't. It's what you said."

"Please, listen to me," she said urgently.

"I've heard all I—"

"I've never been naked with a man," she interrupted, her voice rising. "I've never touched a naked man or been touched by one and I saw how much you wanted me and I forgot you wouldn't hurt me and I—" Jessica's voice broke. "I was frightened. I felt cornered and I just . . . just panicked. Please don't be so angry with me. I—Wolfe, I liked touching you and being touched. That's why I was afraid."

"Christ," Wolfe muttered in disgust, shoving back from the breakfast table. "You liked it so you panicked? Come, your ladyship. You've had hours of pacing in which to concoct pretty excuses and that's the best you can do? I heard the truth from you last night and we both know it."

"No," she said urgently, "that's not—"

"Enough!"

Jessica opened her mouth to argue, but a look at Wolfe's icy indigo eyes made the words die in her throat. There was no indulgence in Wolfe now. Nor was there the least sign of the desire that had burned so clearly in him last night. He was looking at her like she was a stranger newly come to his home—a very unwelcome stranger.

She lowered her eyes, not wanting him to see the unhappiness and fear in her. It would take time and much work to win him back to even the uncertain companionship they had shared during the long trip to his home. It would take a miracle to regain the friendship they had known before marriage.

"After you clean the dishes," Wolfe said curtly, "let the fire go out. We're leaving."

"We're going back to England?" Jessica asked.

"No, your ladyship. If I never see England again, I'll die a happy man."

"I didn't realize you hated it so."

"There's a lot about me you don't know."

"I will learn."

"A woman never truly knows a man until they are lovers."

"Then I shall have to speak to your duchess," Jessica retorted before she could think better of it. "No doubt she'll be a font of wisdom."

Wolfe's smile made his face look harder than ever. "You have missed the point, your ladyship."

"Which is?"

"While the basics of the sexual act remain much the same no matter who performs it, the variations are still infinite. No man is the same with every woman. No woman responds equally to every man. In those differences is found much that illuminates the human experience, as well as the true measure of love."

"That's rather a lot to expect from rutting."

"Spoken like a true nun, Sister Jessica."

"I'm not a nun."

"You're more nun than wife."

"There's more to being husband and wife than the marriage bed," Jessica said with subdued desperation.

"Not for a man."

Jessica pushed back from the table without having eaten more than a bite. "I'm sorry our marriage is such a disappointment to you."

"You're not as sorry as I am, and I'm not as sorry as you're going to be." Wolfe threw his napkin on the table. "There are two leather valises beneath my bed. Use them for your clothes. We leave in two hours."

"It would help me to pack if I knew where we were going, and for how long."

"We're going over the Great Divide."

Jessica's eyes showed her surprise and relief. "Truly? Are we going hunting?"

"No," Wolfe said impatiently.

"Then why are we going?"

"To check on the horses I left with Caleb and Willow, especially the steeldust mare. And to eat real biscuits. Willow makes the best biscuits this side of Heaven."

Jessica tried to conceal her dismay at the thought of being close to the woman Wolfe loved, the paragon who could do no wrong.

And Jessica could do no right.

"For how long?" she asked tightly.

"Until you learn to make good biscuits or agree to an annulment. On the whole, my money is on the annulment."

The back door banged as Wolfe strode out to the stable. Jessica waited until he disappeared before she turned and eyed the dishes with distaste.

Half an hour later, Jessica heaved the dirty dish-water off the back step, heard metal hit a rock, and saw a spoon lying on the ground. Sighing, she walked beyond the house and retrieved the spoon that she had somehow overlooked in the bottom of the dishpan.

As Jessica straightened from picking up the spoon, she heard the trill of a hidden bird and noticed that the willows around the spring held a green promise of summer's leaves at the tips of their branches. Sunlight poured in rich, slanting fans between fluffy clouds that were so white it made her eyes water to look at them. The yellow warmth of the light was a balm and a benediction.

She tugged off the linen towel she had used as a headdress and shook out the clean coils of her hair. The untamed glory of the Western day poured down around her, lifting her heart.

Within the shadow of the small stable, Wolfe stood frozen in the instant when Jessica had shaken down a cloud of hair that burned beneath the un-bridled sun. When she lifted her hands and spread them as though to catch sunlight itself, Wolfe felt a combination of hunger and tenderness that shocked him.

Motionless, barely able to breathe, Tree That Stands Alone watched while Jessica pirouetted slowly, curtsied, then held out her arms as though to a dance partner. As she glided, dipped, and turned with the grace of flame, Strauss' latest waltz melody floated above the wild land, sung by a re-silient elf whose beauty and cruel words were a knife turning in Wolfe's heart.

No wonder you were called the viscount's savage. You are unspeakable. If I had thought you would ever do anything so vile to me, I would never have sought a marriage.

Bitterly, Wolfe turned away from the sun-drenched vision of an elf dancing; but there was nowhere he could turn away from the words echoing in his mind, cutting him in ways he couldn't comprehend, only feel. Working by habit alone, he prepared for the trip ahead. It was too soon to risk the passes, but it was safer than staying trapped in his own house with Jessica burning like a flame locked within ice, forever beckoning, forever beyond his reach.

What am I complaining about? Wolfe asked himself ruthlessly. *If she offered herself, I wouldn't take her.*

Wouldn't you? countered another part of himself.

Not on a golden platter with an apple in her mouth.

How about in bed with her softness parting for you like the petals of a rose?

No.

Like hell.

Hell is an apt description of what my life would be like afterward. No matter how hot Jessica makes my body, she isn't the wife I need.

The sardonic catechism ringing in Wolfe's mind wasn't new, but it had the desired effect. By the time he walked through the sunlight back to the house, no trace showed of the unruly desire and painful yearning that had twisted through him. His face was impassive as he went to the bedroom and found Jessica standing amid a tumult of satins and silks.

The valises were open on the bed. One was full of books, a spyglass, small boxes of fishing lures, the segments of her split bamboo fly rod, a packet of embroidery needles and floss, and other items.

Curious, Wolfe began lifting the books one after another.

"Coleridge, Burns, Blake, Donne, Shakespeare..." Wolfe set the heavy volume aside. "Leave this here. Willow has the Bard's complete works."

"I should have guessed a paragon would."

"Leave the good clergyman behind, as well."

"John Donne?" Jessica lifted dark mahogany eyebrows. "The paragon is well read."

"The paragon's husband, in this case. When you meet Cal, you'll understand. He is a dark angel of retribution. Messrs. Donne and Milton suit him quite well."

"Then 'tis fortunate Caleb married the paradigm of paragons," Jessica said dryly. "What of the rest?"

"The poets?"

"Yes."

Wolfe shrugged. "Bring them, if you must."

"I thought you liked poetry."

"I do. I happen to have a good memory." Wolfe touched the volumes with gentle fingertips. "I can visit caverns measureless to man whenever I turn my mind to it. I can see the tiger's fearful symmetry burning in the forest of the night whenever I like. And I can do it without giving my packhorse galls."

Jessica smiled almost shyly at Wolfe. "If you'll recite my favorite poems to me over the campfire, I'll leave the books behind."

He flashed her a black, sideways glance and saw the memories of other campfires in her aquamarine eyes, of the happy times when he and she had laughed together and traded lines of poetry while Indian guides and hunters alike crowded around, held by the rhythms and visions of men long dead.

"If you want poetry, you'd better take the books," Wolfe said, turning away. "My days of reciting verse are over."

Jessica's smile faded. She turned back to packing. When she hesitated between two riding outfits, Wolfe took the heavier one and put it in the valise.

"You'll need your warmest underwear," he said. "The high country will be cold."

"I looked for the trail clothes I left here years ago, but couldn't find them."

"I gave them to Willow last summer."

Jessica's mouth flattened. "Generous of you."

"I gave her the boy's saddle you used, too. Riding astride in buckskins is fine for a Western woman or a headstrong Scots child, but you're neither. You're the Lady Jessica Charteris, daughter of an earl. You will ride sidesaddle as befits your exalted station."

"I'm Jessica Lonetree."

"Then you'll ride as your husband thinks best."

"Sidesaddle? Through those vast mountains I've heard so much about?" she asked, flinging an arm out to the west, where the Rockies thrust steeply into the sky.

"Exactly."

"That's unreasonable."

"So is our marriage."

"Wolfe," she began softly.

"Say the word, lady Jessica. It has only three syllables. *Say it.*"

He waited for her to say *annulment.*

There was a pause before she said distinctly, "Sidesaddle."

"What?"

"Sidesaddle. Three syllables, I believe?"

Quickly, Wolfe turned away before Jessica could

see the reluctant flash of humor in his eyes. He sorted through the piles of finery with ruthless hands, trying not to notice the gossamer pantelets and camisoles, trying not to remember how Jessica had looked with her ruined peignoir torn away from her breasts, revealing the marks of a man's brutality on her luminous skin.

Odd that I didn't hear Jessica screaming down the house that night, Wolfe told himself sardonically. *But then, it was a bloody lord's teeth raking her rather than a halfbreed bastard's hand discovering how soft she was. All the difference in the world.*

With a vicious word, Wolfe threw the undergarments into the valise. Another riding outfit followed. Jessica added woolen stockings. The valise was full to overflowing.

"You'd better throw some stuff out of the other valise," Wolfe said, fastening straps. "You have only two changes of clothing."

"Excellent. There will be that much less to wash."

Wolfe smiled fleetingly, knowing Jessica couldn't see his face. When he looked up from the valise, no trace of the smile remained on his face. His elfin enemy was entirely too good at finding chinks in the armor of his anger.

"I'm serious about the clothes," he said, gesturing to the mounds of fine wool and silk dresses and dainty satin shoes that lay at the foot of the bed. "Wouldn't you rather have these along than a fishing rod and books?"

"My silk dresses don't know a single poem, and I doubt that I could catch even one of the fabled Rocky Mountain rainbow trout by casting a shoe at it."

At first, Wolfe thought Jessica was teasing him

again. Then he realized she meant it. She would rather take her poetry and fishing gear than one of her elegant outfits. It was the kind of choice the old Jessi would have made, but not one Wolfe had expected from the aristocratic creature who had been so perfectly coiffed and perfumed for her twentieth birthday ball.

"Change into your riding clothes while I see to the rest of the preparations," Wolfe said.

He turned away, paused, then came back and jerked the fur cover from beneath the heaped dresses. When he looked up, Jessica was watching him with curious, wary eyes.

"We might have to sleep in snow," Wolfe said curtly. "If you put this inside your sleeping bag, you should stay warm enough."

Jessica blinked, surprised by Wolfe's thoughtfulness when he was so obviously out of sorts with her. "Thank you."

"You need not look so shocked, your ladyship. I want an annulment, not a funeral."

She stared at Wolfe's broad, retreating back and let out a long breath she hadn't even been aware of holding. Frowning, she reached around behind her back to undo the infuriating buttons. There were less of them than on her travel dress, yet the fastenings were still too many and too inconveniently placed for a woman dressing alone. She thought of calling upon Wolfe for help, but discarded the idea instantly. Though she knew little about men and lust, she had gathered that the less clothes a woman had on, the hotter a man's blood ran and the more angry he became if rutting was denied him.

Memories of the past night raced through Jessica, making her tremble with more than fear. The pleasure Wolfe had given her was unique, exquisite. If rutting gave him a similar pleasure, it was no wonder he was so angry at being denied. Living with him, forcing him to breathe the very air she breathed, was unfair. She hadn't known that before, but she knew it now.

We can't spend a lifetime like this.

Then Jessica thought of what the alternative was if she agreed to an annulment and returned to England and Lady Victoria's well-meant, relentless attempts to marry off her ward to whatever minor lord was old enough, wealthy enough, and eager enough for children to overlook Jessica's common Scots mother.

The thought of enduring such a marriage brought to Jessica a chill determination to be free that no amount of reason or coercion would change. Wolfe may have preferred an annulment to a funeral, but Jessica did not.

There were worse things than death. She was as certain of that as she was of her own heartbeat. She visited those things in her sleep, where forbidden memories and horrible nightmares intertwined, and the inhuman voice of the wind promised her hell on earth.

With a small sound, Jessica put her face in her hands. "Dear God," she whispered, "let Wolfe relent, for I cannot."

 8

UNCERTAINLY, Jessica stood in front of one of the mercantile's many counters. She was accustomed to having bolts of cloth and seamstresses brought to Lord Stewart's home, or perhaps she would visit an especially popular dress designer in her shop. The idea of buying clothes already made both intrigued Jessica for its speedy practicality and baffled her as to how to go about it.

"Mrs. Lonetree? Is that you?"

The deep, gentle drawl told Jessica who the man was before she turned around. Her eyes sparkled with pleasure at the sight of the big blond man with his hat in his hands and a smile on his face.

"Rafe! What a wonderful surprise. What are you doing in Canyon City? Is your arm all right?"

He flexed his left shoulder. "It's a bit stiff and itches like the very devil, but otherwise everything is fine. I've never healed so fast. Must have been your hands and the fancy silk bandage."

"And soap."

"And soap," Rafe agreed with a wink.

"What are you doing in Canyon City?" Jessica asked again without thinking. Then she remembered. "Oh dear, I'm sorry. That was rude of me.

164

It's the one thing Betsy didn't tell me about the United States."

Rafe's sun-bleached eyebrows lifted. "Betsy?"

"My American maid. At least she was, until we got to the Mississippi. She taught me many of your customs, but not the most important Western one."

"Maybe you'd better tell me about that one. I'm new to the West."

Jessica gave a sigh of relief. "Oh, good, then I didn't insult you by asking you why you're here. Wolfe was quite clear about that. One never asks a Western man for a full name, an occupation, or a reason for coming or going as he pleases."

"Australia is like that, too," Rafe said, smiling. "so is a lot of South America."

"England isn't, except for certain people, of course."

"Criminals?" he asked blandly.

"Oh, dear, I *did* insult you."

Rafe's laughter was instant and unrestrained. "No, ma'am, but you're a delight to tease."

If another man had said it, Jessica would have withdrawn with the cool hauteur that had been taught her by Lady Victoria. It was impossible to do that with Rafe, however, and unnecessary as well. His eyes were admiring without being in the least impolite.

"I don't mind talking about what I'm doing here," Rafe said. "I was waiting for the pass to open again. I got here just before the last storm closed it."

"Then you've been here long enough to see the town. Wolfe said we wouldn't be staying long."

"Smart man, your husband. Too many drifters

are holed up here, gambling and waiting for the passes to open."

"If what Wolfe says is true, they won't have long to wait."

"Folks tell me Wolfe Lonetree knows the mountains between here and the San Juan country like the back of his hand," Rafe said.

"It wouldn't surprise me. Wolfe has always loved wild places. From what I've heard, the mountains out there are about as wild as anything on earth."

For a moment Rafe looked through the mercantile's dusty windows, but it was other mountains he saw, other wild places. Then his gray eyes focused and he turned back to the delicate girl whose light blue eyes held more shadows that they should.

"Are you here for supplies?" Rafe asked.

"After a fashion. Wolfe is buying something he calls 'Montana horses.' They're large, I gather. Big enough to stand up to the snow drifts we might find in the passes."

Rafe's gray eyes widened, then narrowed with concern. "What lies west of here has the look of hard country, Mrs. Lonetree. Too hard for a girl like you."

"Have you ever been to Scotland?" Jessica asked rather grimly.

He shook his head.

"Go there sometime in the winter," she said, "when the gale winds scream down from the Arctic Circle. Then you'll see waves higher than a mounted man break against black rock cliffs that are wrapped in ice. That's when sheep with wool thicker than your arm freeze upright in the lee of solid stone fences. Men freeze much more quickly."

"You were born there," Rafe said, for there was no mistaking the dark memories drawing Jessica's face taut.

"Yes."

"Even so, ma'am, you're looking hard used at the moment. I hope your husband's wrong about the passes opening soon. You could use a few nights of sleep."

Jessica smiled reassuringly, though she knew she would sleep no better in the coming night than she had any night since the terrible argument with Wolfe.

He had not relented one bit. No matter how hard she tried to be a good companion, he still treated her as an enemy, or worse, as a traitor who had betrayed him.

"My husband assures me the passes are open," Jessica said.

"Has he talked to one of the gold hunters?"

"No. He watched the peaks all the way from his—our—home. When the new snow melted back up the slopes so quickly, he said the pass would be open by the time we were ready to leave Canyon City."

"He's certain?"

Jessica slanted Rafe an odd glance. "You met Wolfe. Did he strike you as an indecisive sort?"

Shaking his head, Rafe laughed, remembering the uncanny precision of Wolfe's rifle work, men falling like dropped cards, one after another, with no break in the relentless rhythm of Wolfe's shots.

"No, ma'am. That's one hard man you married."

Jessica's smile thinned and turned upside down.

"Don't take me wrong," Rafe continued. "I

meant no insult. In wild country, a hard man is the best kind, whether it be for a husband, a brother, or a friend."

Rafe looked out the window again. The group of men who had been lounging in front of one of the three saloons on the main street had drifted over to the wagon, where a sidesaddle was perched on top of a sack of grain.

"Ma'am, is your husband in the saloon?"

"No. He has a rather low opinion of the local whiskey."

"Smart man. Matt had almost as many warnings about Taos lightning as he did about the Utes."

"Matt?"

"Matthew Moran." When Jessica looked thoughtful, Rafe added, "Maybe you've heard the name?"

"I'm not sure."

"How about Caleb Black? His friends call him Cal."

"Ah, yes," Jessica said with soft bitterness, "that name I've heard. The blasted paragon."

"I wouldn't know," Rafe said, amused. "I've never met the man."

"Not Caleb. His wife. She's a paragon, Wolfe assures me."

"Must be the wrong Caleb Black, then. Willy was a lot of things, but a paragon wasn't among them."

"Willy?"

"Willow Moran. At least, she used to be a Moran. Now she's Willow Black."

Jessica's mouth curved into a rueful smile. "Poor Rafe. You've had a long stage ride and a bullet wound for nothing. The paragon is already wed."

"It's not what you think." Rafe settled his battered hat onto his head with a tug. "Willy is my sister."

"Uh-oh." Jessica flushed. "I'm sorry. I meant no insult to her. That is, I—oh, blazes, when will I learn to bridle my galloping tongue?"

"Don't worry," Rafe said kindly. "Willy would laugh as hard as anyone at the thought of being a paragon. She's as sassy as they come. But, Lord, can that girl cook. I'd go halfway around the world for some of her biscuits." He grinned. "In fact, I did."

"It appears the para—er, your sister—and I have something in common."

"Biscuits?"

"In a manner of speaking. Wolfe has traveled half the earth and talked of little else but my biscuits in comparison to Willow's."

Rafe's gray eyes lit with inner laughter. "Don't feel bad about your own cooking, ma'am. Bride's biscuits are famous the world over."

"Mine are infamous. Even Messr. Skunk turned up his pointy black nose at them."

Rafe tried not to show his amusement, but the thought of a skunk passing up food was too much. He threw back his head and laughed.

Jessica smiled up at him with real pleasure. It was good to hear a man's laughter and know there was one soul in the West who enjoyed her company. Then her smile faded as she remembered how she once had been able to amuse Wolfe. Once, but no longer. Now all he wanted from her was the sight of her back as she walked out of his life.

"Don't look so down, Red—er, Mrs. Lonetree," Rafe corrected quickly.

"Please call me Red," she said, sighing, "or Jessica or Jessi or whatever suits."

"Thank you."

"No thanks are necessary. If no one out here wants his family name known, it stands to reason nicknames and Christian names would be used instead. One must, after all, call others something."

Rafe's smiled faded as he looked out the window. A familiar tension stole through his body. He had spent enough time in rough places with rougher men to know that trouble was afoot.

The men standing around the Lonetree wagon were part of the crowds of drifters, outlaws, and prospectors who had gathered in Canyon City to await the opening of the passes. Lust for gold ran through the men, but there was nothing they could do about that lust for the moment. So they talked about women waiting for them with white thighs spread, and they drank, and they bullied people less coarse than themselves.

The crowd outside had been getting rowdier with each drink from the bottle that was being passed around. When Rafe had passed them on the way to the store, he had heard their speculations on the subject of fancy foreign ladies, and if they had a special way of riding their men as well as riding their horses. Rafe doubted that the men's thoughts had become loftier with each passage of the bottle.

"Mrs. Lonetree—"

"That's too formal," she insisted softly.

Rafe looked away from the window. "All right, Red. Don't go back to the wagon unless your husband is with you."

"Why?"

"The men out there are drunk. They aren't used to decent women."

"I see." Jessica sighed. "I have a few more purchases to make, in any case."

Silently, Rafe accompanied her down the counters loaded with dry goods.

"Perhaps you could help me," she said after a few moments. "I've never bought clothes already made. Does this look the right size?"

Rafe stared in disbelief at the Levis she was holding up.

"Ma'am, I doubt that your husband could get one of his arms in those, much less a leg."

She smiled. "I was thinking of myself, not Wolfe."

Rafe made an odd sound as he measured the size of the denims and the delicate girl whose quality shone through her travel-rumpled clothes.

"That cloth is much too harsh for someone like you," he said simply.

Jessica slanted Rafe a sideways look and saw that he wasn't teasing. He truly thought she was as delicate as she looked.

"You would be amazed at how sturdy I really am," she said mildly.

After shaking out the Levis, Jessica held them against her waist. The legs fell to the floor and beyond.

"Blast."

She put back the Levis and rummaged for yet smaller ones. In time she found a pair that had been cut for a boy rather than a man. She held them up. She suspected they would be too loose in the waist and frankly snug in the hips. On the other hand, they were the smallest Levis she had yet found.

"Would you hold these for me?" she asked, handing over the Levis to Rafe.

He accepted them without a word and watched

with increasing amusement while Jessica rummaged among the shirts for one that might possibly be small enough. He was still smiling indulgently when he sensed a presence behind his back. He turned around and saw Wolfe Lonetree standing there, measuring him for a shroud.

"Rafe, what do you think of—oh, good, you're back," Jessica said, holding out a shirt to Wolfe. "What do you think of this?"

"Too small by half."

The clipped tones of Wolfe's voice brought Jessica's head up. She looked at him and sensed the anger that blazed just beneath his impassive surface.

"I rather thought it was too large," she muttered, measuring her arm against the sleeve.

Abruptly, Wolfe realized that Jessica was buying clothes for herself. "Your ladyship, we already have enough clothes for two packhorses. In any case, I won't have you parading your limbs like a saloon girl throughout the West."

He took the Levis from Rafe and tossed them onto a table before he turned back to Jessica.

"Did you manage to purchase the dry goods on the list?" he asked.

"Yes," she said.

Despite the red flags on Jessica's cheekbones, her voice was civilized. Wolfe didn't take the hint.

"Will wonders never cease." Wolfe took the shirt from Jessica and threw it after the Levis.

Her eyes narrowed into ice-blue slits as she measured the grim lines on Wolfe's face.

"I'll bring the horses from the stable," he said flatly. "By then you should have managed to get back to the wagon. The storekeeper's boy will help you carry everything."

With a black glance at Rafe, Wolfe turned and strode out of the store.

Rafe let out a long, silent breath. Seeing Jessica's husband in his dark, well-worn trail clothes instead of city fashions had convinced Rafe that Wolfe Lonetree was indeed the halfbreed who was reputed to know the mountains so well. That same halfbreed was also reputed to be the best rifle shot west of the Mississippi and a warrior to the steel marrow of his bones.

Rumor hadn't mentioned that Wolfe was fiercely possessive of his wife, but Rafe would be happy to pass the word along to the next poor fool who innocently warmed himself at the hearth of Jessica's smile.

"Ma'am," Rafe said, tipping his hat. "It's been a pleasure."

"Don't feel you must rush off. Wolfe isn't as fierce as he sometimes looks."

Rafe smiled thinly. "I believe you're right. He's easily twice as fierce. He's also damned, er, darned protective of you. Not that I blame him. If I had anything even a fraction as valuable as your smile, I'd be real careful of it, too."

Jessica's smile flashed, then faded. As Rafe turned to leave, she said softly, "God speed, Rafael Moran."

She gave the name its fluid Spanish pronunciation, lending the elegance of music to the syllables. Rafe turned back, struck by hearing his name spoken so beautifully.

"How did you know my full name was Rafael?"

"It suits you." Impulsively, Jessica touched Rafe's sleeve. "Do take care of yourself. Gentlemen are uncommon anywhere in the world."

"I'm not all that gentle, ma'am. But thank you.

You stay close to your husband. Real close. This town has an ugly feel to it right now. Reminds me of Singapore, which is to say it reminds this sinner of Hell."

Rafe tipped his hat again and withdrew to the end of the store where harness was displayed. He reached for a long, coiled bullwhip. With smooth, almost invisible motions of his left wrist, he tested the whip's balance and flexibility. Twenty-five feet of supple leather writhed as though alive beneath his skilled hand.

With a sigh at having lost a pleasant companion, Jessica turned away. She gave a longing glance to the Levis and shirt that Wolfe had discarded, but made no effort to retrieve them. She was still shocked by the primitive masculine possessiveness he had shown. She wanted to tell Wolfe that he needn't be jealous of Rafe; she would rather have a single kind look from Wolfe than a week of kindness from Rafael Moran.

On the other hand, a bit of kindness from a stranger was better than no kindness at all.

Jessica went back to the dry-goods counter, found that Wolfe had paid for the purchases, and waited for the lanky teenage boy to gather up all the packages. The task would have gone more quickly if he had been able to keep his eyes on what he was doing rather than on the single tendril of mahogany hair that had slid out from beneath Jessica's hat. The silky, subtle fire of the curl fascinated the boy, as did her light foreign accent and softly curving lips.

"Is everything all right?" Jessica asked finally.

Caught staring, the boy blushed to the roots of his badly cut hair. "Sorry, ma'am. I've never seen anything like you outside of the fairy tale books Ma used to read to me."

"That's very sweet of you," Jessica said, hiding her smile. The boy's transparent approval was like a balm after Wolfe's constant anger. "Here. Let me get the door. You have far too many packages."

Jessica opened the door, caught a package that was teetering on the edge of falling, and gathered her skirts above her ankles to avoid the mud and manure of the street. She looked both ways, having narrowly avoided disaster earlier when a rider had gone racing through the streets at a dead gallop, whooping and swinging an empty whiskey bottle overhead like a sword in one hand while firing a six-shooter with the other. The performance would have been more impressive if the pony hadn't stopped suddenly, sending the rider head over heels into the muck.

"Careful, ma'am," the boy said. "The town has gotten real lively since word of gold came out."

"Gold?"

"Somewhere up in those mountains. San Juan country."

"That's where we're going."

"Thought so."

"Why?"

"Your husband paid in raw gold," the boy said simply. "Bought horses at the stable with gold, too. Word went through here like wildfire."

When they were closer to the wagon, the boy looked hesitantly at Jessica. "Tell your husband to be careful, ma'am. Gold brings out the lowest kind of devil in men. From what I've heard, Wolfe Lonetree is a bad man in a fight, but he's only one man. I'd hate to see a delicate girl like you come to grief."

Jessica looked at the boy's pale brown eyes and saw that he was older in many ways than she had thought from his awkwardness around her. She suspected that frontier living cut short the innocence of childhood. The boy was at least six years younger than she was, but he had an adult's understanding of the harshness of life.

"Thank you," she said softly. "Wolfe will—"

"Well, what do we have here?" asked a rough voice, cutting across Jessica's reassurances. "Mighty fine clothes for a town like this. Mighty pretty gal, too. Come here, sugarplum. Old Ralph wants a good look at you."

Jessica ignored the man who was standing at the rear of the wagon, wearing a split riding coat, muddy clothes and a wide leer.

"Put the packages in the back of the wagon, please," she said to the boy.

While she spoke, she climbed into the wagon seat. Beneath the cover of her flowing skirts, her hand closed around the buggy whip.

"Ma'am," the boy said. His face was pale, his voice urgent.

"Thank you. You may go back to the store now."

Jessica smiled reassuringly, wanting only to remove the boy from the reach of the men who were gathering around the wagon.

"Please go. My husband will be along soon. Perhaps you could see what's keeping him?"

"Yes, ma'am!"

Ralph's hand shot out, but the boy twisted aside, evading capture. He sprinted for the stable, sending clots of mud flying with each step.

Jessica's fingers tightened on the stock of the whip. She sat quietly, looking at the horizon, acting as though she were alone. The comments of the men gathering around the wagon told her she wasn't alone, but they weren't saying anything she chose to overhear.

A heavy, dirty hand grabbed a fold of her hem.

"By God, I haven't felt anything this soft since Atlanta. Bet it's even softer underneath."

Several men laughed. The sound was as coarse as the muddy street.

The few townspeople brave enough to walk past Main Street's raucous saloon saw what was happening, but hesitated to interfere. The eight men around the wagon were heavily armed and drunk enough to be ugly without being incapacitated in the least. They made a formidable gang.

Nor was Jessica known to the townspeople as other than the wife of a halfbreed. It wasn't a high personal recommendation in the raw frontier town, where Indians were thought to be worth a lot less than a good coon hound.

"A sawbuck says she's wearing silk underwear," called one of the men.

Ralph's hand tightened on Jessica's skirt. "Well, sugarplum, is you is or is you ain't?"

That witticism sent one man laughing until he could barely stand without the help of the wagon.

"Come on," Ralph said. "Show a little leg to the lads."

Jessica ignored him.

"Look at me when I talk to you," he snarled. "Any slut that lies down with a halfbreed should be damn grateful that a white man will even touch her."

When Jessica felt her skirt shift, she wrenched the wagon whip free and brought its heavy stock down across the bridge of Ralph's nose with all the force of her small body. Bellowing with rage and pain, Ralph let go of the skirt and grabbed his face. Blood spurted between his fingers. Before Jessica could turn to face the rest of her attackers, Ralph grabbed her wrist, pulling her off balance.

There was a sound like a pistol shot, followed by a high scream. The grip on her arm loosened. From the corner of her eye, Jessica saw Rafe running toward her, wielding the supple bullwhip with lethal skill. As she watched, his left arm moved slightly and the long bullwhip leaped forward. The odd, pistol-like sound came again. Close to her, one of the attacker's hats seemed to leap up and fell away in two pieces. Blood poured from a gash over the man's eye.

Suddenly, the men were reaching beneath their coats.

"They have guns!" Jessica yelled.

She brought the buggy whip down as hard as she could on the closest man, but knew it wouldn't be enough. There were five men left untouched, four more were running from the saloon, and they were all armed.

"Get down!" Rafe yelled.

Jessica ignored him, for she was too busy laying about with the buggy whip.

Rafe's bullwhip sang out again, but this time it wrapped very gently around Jessica's waist. The yank Rafe gave wasn't gentle at all. It pulled her right out of the wagon and into his arms as gunfire erupted around them. Pressed between the side of the wagon and Rafe's big body, Jessica saw little of the fight.

What she did see astonished her. Wolfe was down the street in front of the stable, two hundred yards away, and he was picking off men just as fast as he could lever bullets into the firing chamber. Lead whined and crashed around the wagon. The withering hail of bullets sent the men scattering.

All that prevented every one of the attackers from being killed was the fact that Jessica was in the middle of the fracas.

"Son of a bitch, but that man can shoot," Rafe said reverently.

A lull came in the firing.

"Jessi!" yelled Wolfe.

"I'm all right!" she called back.

"If I were you, boys," Rafe said in a normal tone, "I'd see how far down into that mud I could get before Lonetree reloads."

The wisdom of Rafe's advice became apparent as Wolfe swapped rifle for carbine and opened fire again. The men who hadn't fallen already threw themselves full length onto the soggy ground.

"Hang onto the wagon, ma'am," Rafe said.

Blindly, Jessica grabbed the rough wood.

Rafe stepped back until he could see all of the men.

"Keep your heads down, boys, or you'll lose them."

It was the only thing Rafe said. It was all he had to say, for the whip in his hand was like a living thing, flicking restlessly over the fallen men, plucking at their hats and coats, nipping at fingers that crept closer to hidden guns. No sharp pistol-sounds came from the bullwhip now, simply an unnerving hissing and seething as leather licked lightly over flesh.

One of the men moaned and crossed himself.

"That's the idea," Rafe said encouragingly. "Never too late for a man to get religion."

Wolfe arrived at a dead run, carbine in hand.

Behind him came the boy from the dry-goods store, carrying the empty rifle. One by one Wolfe went to the frightened men, rolled them over with his boot, and memorized their faces. They stared back at him and knew they had never come closer to dying.

When the last man had been memorized, Wolfe stepped back. "If I see any of you near my wife again, I'll kill you."

Jessica looked at Wolfe and had no doubt of it. Even as she told herself she should be appalled, she wasn't. She sensed she would have been brutally treated by men who knew nothing of her but her name and her sex.

"I'm counting to ten," Wolfe said in a neutral tone that was more threatening than a shout. As he spoke, he began feeding cartridges into the carbine. "Anyone who is in sight when I'm finished had better be shooting. One. Two. Three. Four."

There was a frantic scrambling as men came up out of the mud and stumbled down the street. Most were limping. Several could use only one arm.

One man didn't move at all.

Somehow, Jessica wasn't surprised that it was the man called Ralph who had died. Neither was Rafe. He looked from the motionless man to Wolfe and nodded.

"Good job, Lonetree. You're everything I've heard you were. But you're still only one man and it's a long way to Cal's spread."

There was nothing friendly in Wolfe's blue-black eyes as he levered a cartridge into the firing chamber and turned on Rafe.

"What the hell business of yours is it where we're going?"

9

"RAFE is the paragon's brother," Jessica said quickly, stepping between the two men.

There was a tense silence before Wolfe spoke.

"Willow's brother?" he asked, looking over Jessica's head at the handsome blond man.

Rafe nodded.

A subtle change came over Wolfe as understanding began to sink through the adrenaline of battle. There was a visible lessening of the predatory readiness that had radiated from him when he saw Rafe standing so close to Jessica. For the space of several breaths, Wolfe looked intently at the big man who used a whip with chilling skill. Finally, Wolfe nodded slowly.

Jessica let out a slow breath and stepped aside once more.

"I should have guessed," Wolfe said. "Same honey-licking drawl, same hair, same catlike shape to the eyes." He smiled at Rafe for the first time, uncocked the carbine, and held out his right hand. "Willow's a damn sight prettier, though."

"I'd hope to shout." Rafe smiled slowly and shook Wolfe's hand. "I suppose you've heard this before, but you're one hell of a shot with a long gun."

Jessica watched the two men shake hands and felt the last of the tightness ease inside her. Having Rafe and Wolfe eyeing one another as potential enemies had been like having knives scraping over her nerves.

"You're the devil himself with that bullwhip," Wolfe said, as he helped Jessica aboard the wagon. "Never seen anything like it. Are you a teamster?"

"I'm a jackaroo, among other things. That's Australian for a cow chaser. They use stockman's whips and heeler dogs down there." Rafe paused and added, "Normally I travel alone, but I suspect we're headed the same place, and too many people know about the raw gold in that poke of yours."

Wolfe nodded slowly. "I usually travel alone, too, but with Jessica along . . ." He shrugged. "Frankly, I'd been wishing that Caleb or Reno was around. I'd be pleased to have a good man at my back."

"You've got one."

"Yes, I believe I do." Wolfe grinned. "Climb aboard, Rafe Moran, and welcome."

Wolfe gestured to the boy from the mercantile, who came running up with the gold-inlaid rifle.

"Lordy, mister, I ain't never seen no shootin' like that nowhere! And that bullwhip," he said, turning to Rafe. "Lordy, lordy. Like to make me believe in the Devil."

"Better to believe in God," Rafe said. "The Devil has enough takers."

Wolfe fished a ragged gold nugget out of his leather poke. "Thanks for coming to the stable after me. You ever need help, you put out word for Wolfe Lonetree. I'll come running. Count on it."

The boy flushed. "You don't have to pay me, mister. I just was worried about the lady."

"She's a worry to us all."

Jessica shot Wolfe a look, but smiled warmly at the boy.

"Son?" Rafe said quietly.

The boy tore his glance away from Jessica. Rafe flipped him a heavy silver coin. The boy caught it automatically.

"See that somebody reads over the corpse," Rafe said, flicking the bullwhip in the direction of the dead man. "Too late to do any good, I suppose, but I'm told an immortal soul is a resilient thing and our God is a forgiving god."

"That's not what Preacher Corman says," the boy muttered, hefting the coin.

"Get a better brand of preacher," Rafe advised dryly. "Life is hard enough without black-coated vultures croaking over you."

The boy snickered. "Yessir."

The coin glittered and spun in a rapid arc as the youth threw it, caught it, and then pocketed it with a wide grin. He trotted across the street toward the mercantile, eager to share his adventure with the people who were watching from the safety of closed doors.

The wagon seat shifted and creaked as Wolfe climbed aboard. Jessica lifted the reins and the buggy whip, obviously preparing to drive them. Wolfe raised his black eyebrows in silent question.

"There were more men in the saloon," she said simply.

Wolfe slanted a look at the building, nodded, and began reloading the rifle as he made room for Rafe on the wagon's hard seat. When Rafe climbed aboard, the seat shifted and creaked again, complaining loudly of having to carry the weight of two large men.

"If you can handle stock half as well as you handle that bullwhip, Cal will think he's died and gone to heaven," Wolfe said as Jessica turned the horse toward the livery stable. "He's got Indians and a freed slave riding herd for him when they feel like it, and Reno helps out when he's not haring after gold, but Cal is always short-handed. Come spring calving, you'll look as golden as your hair."

"Reno?" Rafe looked up from the whip he had been absently wiping clean and coiling. "Isn't that the third man who knows the San Juans like the back of his hand? You and Caleb being the other two, so I'm told."

"Reno knows the country better than I do. He's uncanny about land. But I suspect you know Reno better by another name," Wolfe said, amusement clear in his voice.

"Do I?" drawled Rafe.

"Matthew Moran," Wolfe said succinctly.

Relief went visibly through Rafe. "Matt? He's all right then? The last letter I got from him, he sounded like he had his tail in a real tight crack."

"Reno's doing fine now, except he's a damn fool for gold."

"Just like I'm a damn fool for distant horizons." Rafe grinned. "The Moran men don't housebreak worth a bucket of—" He stopped abruptly, remembering Jessica's presence. "Er, spit."

Wolfe smiled slightly. "No man does, until he finds a woman like Willow."

The buggy whip hissed and snapped well above the wagon horse's brown flank. Rafe's gray glance touched Jessica appreciatively.

"Or like your wife," Rafe said. "You handle

those reins very well, ma'am."

Wolfe's eyes narrowed and all softness vanished from his expression. Rafe felt the tension snaking through the man who sat beside him on the narrow wagon seat.

"The thing about a wanderer like me," Rafe continued matter-of-factly, giving Wolfe a level look, "is that I can appreciate beautiful things without wanting to possess them. Possessions tie a man down. And nothing, no matter how rare or beautiful, will ever be as grand to me as the sunrise I haven't seen."

With a visible effort, Wolfe brought his anger under control. He knew it was unreasonable to respond so fiercely to Rafe's simple appreciation of Jessica. Yet there it was, reasonable or not, and there it would remain until Jessica came to her senses and sought an annulment, freeing both of them from an impossible situation.

But until that moment, Wolfe fought to maintain a self-control that became more difficult every night, every day, every hour spent in the company of a girl he couldn't have, would never take, and wanted until he lived on the breaking edge of rage at having to be so close to what must be forever beyond his reach.

"You're very kind," Jessica said quickly to Rafe, for she, too, had sensed Wolfe's anger. "But no one can equal the para—er, Willow. I have a great deal of work ahead of me just to be an adequate Western wife."

Rafe frowned. "You're rather delicately made for that kind of hardship."

"You and my husband have something in common. You both equate strength with muscles."

"For good reason," Wolfe muttered.

"For bad reason," Jessica retorted. "Flowers are soft, frail, and, therefore, weak in your masculine estimation. Yet I will tell both of you fine, strong men something—the same storm that brings down a mighty oak does little more than wash the *delicate* faces of the violets living at the oak's foot."

Rafe looked away quickly, trying to conceal his amusement at Jessica's quickness. It was impossible. He gave Wolfe a rueful look and shook his head, laughing softly.

"She's got us, Wolfe."

Wolfe grunted and looked around the muddy street one last time. No one was in sight. Wolfe hoped it would stay that way.

"I take it you're going to see Willow?" Wolfe asked, turning his attention back to the big blond man who was watching him with a masculine sympathy that was laced with equally masculine amusement.

"I'm really looking for Matt, but I kept hearing about a Virginia lady who came out here last year with five fine Arabian horses. She was searching for her 'husband,' Matthew Moran." Rafe shrugged. "I figured it had to be Willy. She's the only girl I know with gumption enough to set out across wild country alone, just to find a brother she hadn't seen in years."

Wolfe's face softened into a half-smile. "That's Willow. They broke the mold when they made her."

Rafe noticed both the affection in Wolfe's voice and the shadow that drew Jessica's face into unhappy lines. He lifted his hat, smoothed his bright hair with his hand, settled his hat once more with a jerk, and wondered if Caleb Black was a jealous sort of man.

"Sounds like you know Willow real well," Rafe said to Wolfe after a moment.

"Well enough."

"And Cal?"

Belatedly, Wolfe caught the drift of Rafe's thoughts. He smiled thinly.

"Cal is the best friend I have. He's as big as you are, he has as much give in him as a granite cliff, he's greased lightning with his belt gun, and he loves Willow the way I never expected to see a man love anything, especially a man as hard as Caleb Black."

Rafe's eyebrow climbed. "How does Willow feel about it?"

"The same way Cal does, a love you can touch. Seeing them together makes you believe that God did indeed know what He was doing when He created man and woman and gave them the earth for their children."

Jessica heard both the certainty and the subtle yearning in Wolfe's voice. She didn't know whether to weep or scream at the fresh evidence of Wolfe's deep admiration for his best friend's wife.

Wolfe didn't notice Jessica's taut, unsmiling mouth. His full attention was on Rafe, who was thinking over all that Wolfe had said, and what he had not said, as well. Finally, Rafe sighed and shifted his weight, making the seat spring complain.

"Glad to hear that," Rafe said. "Willy was such a soft little thing. I was always afraid life was going to chew her up and spit her out in little pieces."

"Chew up a paragon?" Jessica said tightly as she pulled the horse to a halt in front of the livery stable. "I doubt that, Rafael. Life would choke to death on Willow's perfection. Dead life is a paradox to make the head ache. Not to mention the stomach."

At the last word, Jessica jammed the wagon whip back into its holder. When she looked up, Wolfe was watching her with veiled interest, measuring her anger. Abruptly, she knew she was simply sharpening a weapon he would turn on her at every opportunity. Yet even knowing that, she could neither stop the words nor diminish the deadly sweetness of her voice when she spoke.

"Would it be possible to stop singing the paragon's praises long enough to get on the trail?" Jessica asked. "We're making the townspeople nervous."

"THAT's the damnedest rig I ever saw," Rafe said, reining his horse alongside Jessica's, "and I've seen a few odd things in my wandering life."

Despite the bone-deep tiredness that gnawed at Jessica, she straightened in the sidesaddle and focused on Rafe, grateful to have something to take her mind off the wind.

Huge mountains rose all around the riders, their peaks invisible beneath a seething lid of slate-colored clouds. Climbing up in elevation was like riding back into winter. Wind took snow from the clouds and churned it into billowing veils of white. Wind pried at the snow on the ground, lifting particles of ice and turning them into a stinging, invisible rasp that scoured unprotected skin.

But most of all, the wind keened and moaned, prying at Jessica's self-control to get to the nightmares beneath.

"Don't they have sidesaddles in Australia?" she

asked quickly, unable to bear either the wind or her own thoughts.

"I didn't see any, but I didn't see more than a handful of white women, either." Rafe glanced sideways at her. "Is it as uncomfortable as it looks?"

With gritted teeth and a stifled moan, Jessica shifted her weight, trying to settle the voluminous skirts of her riding habit more comfortably around the sidesaddle's off-center horn.

"On a gaited horse, over level country, for a few hours at a time, it's quite comfortable."

"But old Two-Spot's only 'gait' is a trot that would shake the change out of a man's pocket," Rafe finished for Jessica, "we've been riding sixteen hours a day for three days, and you look so worn I'd swear the sun would shine right through you."

The wind flexed, twisted, and howled down from the pass ahead, carrying the icy promise of more snow.

"I don't think the presence of sunlight is going to be a problem," Jessica said, smiling briefly.

"All the same, when Wolfe comes back from scouting ahead, I'll suggest that we make camp early tonight."

"No." The naked command in her own voice made Jessica wince. "I don't want to be the cause of any delay," she added more gently. "I'm stronger than I look. Truly."

"I know."

She gave Rafe a sideways look of disbelief.

"I mean it," he said. "I wouldn't have bet you could get through the first day, much less the last two. But if you don't get more rest, you'll have to be tied to that damn fool saddle by this time to-morrow."

"Then that's just what Wolfe will do. We have to get over the Great Divide before a real storm comes."

Rafe's mouth flattened beneath the light bronze beard stubble. He knew what was driving Wolfe. They had cut sign of other men headed for the pass over the Great Divide. In the last six hours, they had skirted areas where groups of men had camped in anticipation of the coming storm. The closer they came to the pass, the more likely it became that they would stumble over other men.

"Gold fever," Rafe muttered. "Worse than cholera."

"I doubt it. I've seen cholera go through a village like a scythe through a field of grain, leaving nothing standing, no adult living to bury the dead, and only a handful of children left alive to mourn."

He stared at Jessica, surprised again. "You were one of them?"

She nodded. "I was nine."

"Sweet Jesus," he muttered. "How did you survive?"

Jessica smiled wearily. "I keep telling you. I'm not as fragile as I look."

"I hope not," Rafe said bluntly, "or you won't make it over the pass. These mountains are as rough as the ones I saw in South America, and a damn sight worse than anything Australia had to offer."

"Yet these mountains fascinate you."

Rafe hesitated, surprised by Jessica's insight. "I hadn't thought of it that way, but you're right. Of all the mountains I've seen, these are different. Taller than God and meaner than the Devil, yet there's a beauty in the basins and long valleys..."

He made a soft, puzzled sound. "It makes me

feel like somewhere ahead there's a cabin I've never seen, a woman I've never known, and both of them are waiting for me, filled with warmth."

"You're a good man, Rafael Moran," Jessica said, her voice husky with bittersweet emotion. "I hope you find them."

Rafe looked at Jessica with eyes that were the same color as the clouds. The sadness in her was almost tangible, as great as the weariness that made her lips pale and drawn.

A flicker of motion from the trail ahead distracted Rafe. Even as his hand wrapped around the butt of the shotgun he carried, the burnt toast color of the big mare Wolfe had bought in Canyon City condensed out of the black and white of the landscape.

"Wolfe's coming," Rafe said, easing his shotgun back into its saddle scabbard.

Jessica nodded and fell back into the semi-daze that gripped her whenever she let down her guard.

Silently, Rafe decided to suggest an early camp if Wolfe didn't suggest it first. But when Wolfe rode up, he had an almost tangible aura of alertness around him. Even before he spoke, Rafe sensed that there would be no early camp.

"It's snowing in the pass," Wolfe said tersely. "If we don't get through now, we'll have to make camp until the pass opens again. It could be a week or more. Even if we went without fire, it would be dangerous."

"A cold camp?" Rafe asked. "Are there more men ahead?"

Wolfe nodded curtly.

"Did they see you?"

"No." Wolfe reached into his saddle bag and withdrew a box of cartridges. "Cut to the right after you cross the stream, skirt the base of the ridge, and wait for me in the forest on the other side."

Without warning, he snapped the box of cartridges in Rafe's direction. When the other man caught it with a motion of his hand that was so swift that it blurred, Wolfe smiled.

"You're Reno's brother, all right. Fastest hands I ever saw, except maybe Cal's." Wolfe's smile faded. "How are you with a long gun?"

"Better than some and a damn sight worse than you."

"Take Jessica's carbine. Ride with it across your saddle."

Rafe leaned over, lifted the carbine from Jessica's saddle scabbard, and checked over the gun with the easy, economical motions of a man doing a familiar task.

"What about you?" Rafe asked without looking up.

"There's a knoll about a thousand feet from their camp. I can watch them and you at the same time. If they start moving, I'll start shooting. Some of them are bound to get past, though. No way I'll get all nine before they get to cover."

A blond eyebrow climbed as Rafe realized that Wolfe was prepared to kill the men from ambush, if need be.

"You know those boys?" Rafe asked.

"I had words with some of them at a stage stop."

Jessica's breath came in audibly.

Rafe looked at her, then at Wolfe. "I see. In that case, I'll be happy to pick off the stragglers."

Wolfe smiled thinly. "If anyone gets past me, watch out for a man with a brown, drooping mustache. He's wearing a gray cavalry cape and riding a black Tennessee walking horse with three white socks. He has a hideout gun behind his belt buckle, but I wouldn't recommend letting him get close enough to use it."

"Friend of yours?" Rafe asked dryly.

"Never met the man. Cal killed his twin brother, Reno got the kid brother, and I got a couple of cousins, along with some other gang members."

"Claim jumpers?" Rafe asked.

"They had it in mind. But first they took Willow. It was the last mistake those boys ever made."

Rafe's eyes narrowed.

"Don't give Jericho Slater an even break," Wolfe continued. "Those Slaters make Quantril's Raiders look like altar boys. If he finds out you're Reno's brother, he'll kill you any way he can."

"I'm an obliging sort of man," Rafe said calmly. "If a man comes to me with dying on his mind, I do my best to help him out."

The corner of Wolfe's mouth lifted. "I'll just bet you do. Give me fifteen minutes to get in position. And watch for patches of ice ahead."

As he turned his horse, Jessica said urgently, "Wolfe."

He reined in and looked over his shoulder.

"I . . ." Her voice died. She made an uncertain gesture with her hand. "Be careful."

He nodded, lifted the reins again, and sent his horse ahead on the trail at a ground-eating trot.

Fifteen minutes later, Jessica and Rafe followed. She rode tensely in the saddle, straining to hear rifle shots. All she heard was the empty, icy howl of the wind. It plucked at her already overstretched nerves until she felt as though she must scream just to shut out the wind's endless keening.

The minutes passed as though stretched upon a tanning rack. Jessica almost welcomed Two-Spot's bone-shaking trot simply as a distraction. Rafe didn't speak. Nor did she try to speak to him.

The ridge they skirted was overgrown with a combination of spruce and fir. The trees were a green so dark it looked black. Slender, white-barked aspen grew along ravines. Not even a hint of green edged the aspens' graceful, ghostly branches, for spring hadn't yet come to the high country.

In the rare pauses in the wind, the horses' breath came out in silvery plumes. The animals were working hard and the land was rising relentlessly beneath their feet. Patches of ice gleamed sullenly beneath the recent snow, making the footing tricky.

When Rafe and Jessica rounded the ridge and crossed a small clearing to the forest beyond, Wolfe was waiting for them. Jessica's heart lifted as she looked at Wolfe's dark face and easy masculine power. The renewed realization of just how handsome her husband was broke over her in a wave. The trail clothes suited him. The austere mountains suited him. In his lean hands, the heavily inlaid rifle was revealed for the streamlined, no-nonsense weapon it really was.

And Wolfe was revealed for the man he really was; he had been born for this wild land rather than for the brocade and satin of civilization. Jessica understood that as surely as she understood that she loved Wolfe for what he was, that she had always loved him, and she always would.

The realization stunned her, sinking past layers of exhaustion to the raw emotion beneath.

"They didn't see us," Wolfe said. "Too busy drinking and playing cards. Jericho will have them picked cleaner than a hound's tooth before breakfast."

"Good at cards, huh?" Rafe asked.

"He'll do until you sit down with the Devil himself."

Wolfe took the lead once more, followed by Two-Spot and the pack horses. Rafe waited until they were a hundred yards ahead before he let his horse follow. He had kept Jessica's carbine, and he rode with it across his saddle, listening for any sounds from behind.

Exhaustion reclaimed Jessica's body in a numbing gray tide. She slumped in the saddle. Staring at nothing, she endured the endless trail as it became steeper and rougher. Along the left, a snow-mantled slope dropped away a few feet from the trail. Jessica didn't notice. She was running on reflex alone, able to stay upright in the saddle but nothing more.

When Two-Step hit an icy patch and went down to his knees, she grabbed instinctively for the saddle horn, but it was too late. She was already pitching forward, beyond the reach of the curving, off-center horn. Two-Step lunged to the right, trying to regain his own balance. The sudden motion completed Jessica's undoing. She hurtled from the sidesaddle onto the snow-covered slope and began rolling down in a flurry of skirts and flailing limbs.

The startled cry Jessica had given when her horse first went to its knees was the only warning Wolfe got. He turned sharply in the saddle just in time to see Jessica thrown head first down the slope. By the time he spun his horse on its hocks and reached Two-Spot, Jessica's tumbling fall had been stopped by a thicket of alder. Recklessly, Wolfe spurred his horse down the slope to the place where Jessica lay without moving.

"Jessi!"

Wolfe's cry echoed, but there was no answer. He leaped from the saddle and ran the last few feet to Jessica, skidding to his knees beside her.

"Jessi? Are you all right?" he asked urgently.

She didn't answer.

"Talk to me, elf," Wolfe said, pushing snow away from Jessica's face with fingers that showed a fine trembling. "It wasn't that bad a fall. The snow is soft and deep, there weren't any rocks. Jessi . . ."

Gentle fingers brushed snow from eyebrows and eyelashes that were like a shadow of fire, rich mahogany. They looked very dark against skin that was almost as pale as snow.

"You can't be hurt, little one. God help me, you can't. Damn it, Jessi. *Wake up.*"

Jessica groaned and tried to sit up. She got part way, only to be yanked flat by her braids, which were wedged beneath her own body. Too dazed to understand, she tried to sit up again, only to be brought up short once more.

Wolfe caught her before she could be yanked back down by her braids for a third time.

"Slow down, Jessi. Your hair has you on a short leash again."

"Wolfe?" she asked raggedly. "Is it really you?"

Aquamarine eyes focused on Wolfe, and cool fingers caressed the dark planes of his cheek.

"Yes, elf. It's really me."

The knowledge that Jessica was truly all right went through Wolfe like a cascade of champagne, making him feel lightheaded, almost dizzy. The memory of the other time Jessica had been trapped by her own long hair made amusement shimmer in Wolfe. He smiled widely as he helped her sit up.

"Sometimes, you're like a kite with a long red tail that gets tangled in everything and hauls you up short."

As Wolfe pulled Jessica's hair free, memories and relief coursed through him. He began laughing softly and he brushed snow from her.

The sound of Wolfe's amusement cleared Jessica's mind like a brisk slap across her face. She tried to push away from him, but couldn't. Despite the laughter that kept shaking Wolfe, he hauled her to her feet as casually as he would have lifted a saddle.

For Jessica, it was the final insult. Fear, anger, hurt, exhaustion, and humiliation exploded into flaming rage. She didn't stop to think, didn't consider, didn't hesitate, didn't do one thing but grab for the hunting knife Wolfe wore sheathed at his belt. The action was so unexpected that she had the knife clear of the leather before he realized it. His hand closed around her wrist with the speed of a striking snake.

"What do you think you're doing?" Wolfe demanded.

Jessica's mouth curled into what could only be described as a snarl. She yanked and twisted her wrist but couldn't get free.

"Jessi! What the hell . . . ? Did that fall knock out what little sense you had?"

Breath shuddered through Jessica. She was exhausted, frightened, cold, and pain twisted through her right ankle with every movement; but most of all, she was violently angry at the viscount's savage, the man who took pleasure only in her failures.

"Let go of me."

The naked fury in Jessica's voice wiped all trace of laughter from Wolfe's eyes and voice.

"Not until you tell me what you're going to do with that knife," he said.

For the space of three long breaths, Jessica looked at Wolfe without answering. Finally she glanced down at the knife in her hand as though surprised to find it. When she looked back at Wolfe, there was nothing of warmth or softness in her eyes.

"My hair," she said flatly.

"What?"

"I'm going to cut my bloody hair."

Black eyebrows lifted. "I think not. At the rate you're going, you'd probably cut your own throat by mistake."

Or cut his, and not by mistake.

But neither of them said it aloud as Wolfe pried the knife from Jessica's fingers with an easy strength that heaped more fuel on the fires of her fury.

"You bastard," she hissed.

He smiled thinly. "True fact, your ladyship."

"Twice a bastard," she corrected. "Once by birth and again by choice. You work me like a scullery maid, belittle my best efforts to be a wife, and then you laugh at my pain when I'm thrown from my horse because I'm so tired I can't stay awake in the sidesaddle any longer. You are a bastard."

Wolfe's face became expressionless. "Say the word and you're free. You know the word, your ladyship. Say it!"

A stillness came over Jessica, a drawing in of strength and will that tightened her features until they looked like finely drawn wire.

"Husband."

The word was a hiss and Jessica's smile was colder than snow itself.

"That's the problem," Wolfe said in a clipped voice. "I'm your husband but you aren't my wife."

"I have a solution. Go to Hell. You'll find all the suffering there so amusing you'll split your sides laughing and die on the spot. Then you'll be free of me, husband. *And not before."*

Jessica turned away and began clawing back up the steep slope. As Wolfe watched, a faint smile that had little to do with amusement curved his mouth. Unbridled fury fairly radiated from every line of Jessica's body. He had seen her in many moods, but never like this. The delicate little aristocrat had a temper to match the glorious fire hidden in her hair.

Wolfe couldn't help wondering if she would ever come to a man's bed with a fraction of the passion she just had shown in rage. The thought of being the man to draw that primitive sensuality from Jessica brought a swift, elemental reaction from Wolfe's body that shocked him.

Cursing his masculine vulnerability to a girl who wished him in Hell, Wolfe looked away from Jessica until the hard rush of urgency subsided into an uncomfortable ache. He expected little more in the way of ease. A state of semi-arousal had become so much a part of him when Jessica was nearby that he no longer thought such discomfort unusual.

Wolfe looked back up the slope just in time to see Jessica stumble. At first he thought that her clumsiness came from anger. Then he watched her struggle to her feet, take two steps, and nearly go down again. Something was wrong with her right leg.

"Hold on, Jessi," Wolfe called. "I'll help you."

Jessica didn't even bother to look back over her shoulder. Nor did she pause in her awkward attempts to get up the steep slope.

With a muttered word, Wolfe sheathed his knife and vaulted into the saddle. He spurred the big mare up the slope. Without bothering to rein in, Wolfe bent over and scooped Jessica up on the way by, holding her firmly against his thigh. When the mare reached the top of the slope, he reined in.

"Sit astride in front of me," Wolfe said in a clipped voice.

As he spoke, he lifted Jessica over the mare's chocolate brown mane. The divided riding skirt finally sorted itself out into right and left sides allowing her to sit astride in the big saddle. The intimacy of the arrangement registered instantly on Wolfe's body, making hot talons of need sink into him. His breath thickened over the kind of words he had never in his life used in a woman's presence and didn't want to begin using now.

"Stay put," he said tightly.

Jessica didn't answer, but she didn't try to dismount, either. Wolfe slid off on the right side in a single flowing movement. His hands went to the small, booted foot that poked from the snow-clotted folds of cloth.

"Where does it hurt?"

Jessica glanced at Wolfe. She didn't have to look far. Even sitting on horseback, she had very little height on him. She hadn't his strength, either. She had nothing but the certainty that she would rather die than go back to being a bright marker on the gaming table of aristocratic marriages.

She would rather die than live as her mother had.

Memory and nightmare twisted suddenly, sending a shudder through Jessica. Before the tremor had passed, Jessica understood that she had one other certainty, as well: Wolfe would never accept this marriage; he would only become more cruel in his efforts to drive her away.

You will rue the day you forced me into marriage. There are worse things than being caressed by a savage. You shall learn each one of them.

Now, too late, Jessica believed Wolfe. Now, too late, she knew there was nothing left to stand between her and the wind.

"Where does it hurt?" Wolfe repeated impatiently.

"It doesn't."

Wolfe's head snapped up. He had never heard that tone from Jessica before, a sound as unemotional and unmusical as stone. Her eyes were the same way. Opaque.

"I saw you limping."

"It doesn't matter."

The flare of temper in Wolfe's eyes was replaced by uneasiness.

"Jessi?"

Lost in the echoes of her terrifying discovery, Jessica neither heard nor answered Wolfe's low query. He hesitated, then began probing the soft leather of Jessica's boot with fingers that were gentle and firm at the same time. He thought she flinched when he pressed deeply against her ankle, but it was difficult to be certain.

"Can you ride?" Wolfe asked, stepping back.

"I'm riding."

There was no mockery in Jessica's words, merely

a statement of fact. At the moment, she was riding a horse.

"Jessi, what's wrong?"

She looked past Wolfe, through him, seeing only the emptiness of the wind, hearing only its low, triumphant cry.

With swift, almost vicious movements, Wolfe took up the right stirrup of his saddle. He couldn't get it short enough for Jessica's slender foot to reach.

"Bloody hell," he muttered.

If Jessica heard, she said nothing.

A gust of wind brought the sound of a horse cantering closer. Wolfe glanced up, saw Rafe's big bay coming into sight, and went back to letting the stirrup down to its former length.

The trail Rafe was following told its own story. A horse going to its knees, a ragged swath cut by Jessica's body, and the deep gouges where Wolfe's big mare had plunged down the slope. Jessica's bloodless face and Wolfe's flattened mouth told more of the story, but not enough.

"Is she hurt?" Rafe asked.

"Her right ankle is sore, but it's her pride that took the worst beating."

Rafe looked at Jessica. She didn't notice him. Nor did she seem to notice anything else. There was a quality about the stillness of her body that made Rafe's eyes narrow. He had seen men who looked like that, men pushed to their limits by pain or starvation or war.

"She's finished," Rafe said. "There was a good camping spot back about a mile."

The wind twisted again, drawing a veil of snow over the cold land.

"We're going over the Great Divide." Wolfe

vaulted into the saddle behind Jessica. "See that Two-Spot doesn't get lost. The pack horses are used to following him."

A touch of Wolfe's spurs lifted the brown mare into a trot. A hard arm came around Jessica, holding her in place. Her body went rigid, but she said nothing. Nor did she fight him. She did nothing but sink farther and farther into herself, looking for a way out of the trap in which she had so brutally tangled herself and Wolfe.

She found none but to endure and then endure some more.

I can't.

And pray that Wolfe would change because she could not.

I can't.

I must be strong. Just for a bit longer. A few minutes.

The minutes passed.

A few more.

When those minutes passed, Jessica asked herself for a few more, and then a few more, until half an hour had gone by, an hour, then two. Three.

Slowly, a breath at a time, she endured, learning how to live without Wolfe as her talisman, learning how to survive in a world ruled by the soulless wind of nightmare and memory combined.

10

"**W**OLFE, I can't believe it's really you! Caleb said the high passes were buried in snow after the last storm."

Willow's husky contralto cry made Jessica's lips flatten into an unhappy line. She should have expected the bloody paragon to have a beautiful voice. Rather grimly, Jessica waited to see what the paragon looked like, but even when Willow stepped from the house, she was still concealed by the dense shadows of the porch.

"It's me, all right," Wolfe said, smiling as he dismounted and crossed the ground with long strides to give Willow a hug. "I've brought you a present."

"Seeing you is present enough," she said, laughing and holding out her arms.

The clear affection in Willow's voice and face was matched by Wolfe as he folded Willow close in a gentle bearhug. A dark combination of jealousy and despair snaked through Jessica, shaking her, for she had believed she could no longer be touched by anything but the black wind whispering to her of nightmares that had been reborn in daylight, and memories that refused to remain forgotten.

I would have had a chance with Wolfe but for the bloody paragon. She is destroying me as surely as slow poison.

Jessica stared into the shadow of the porch, but could see nothing of Willow except slender arms wrapped around Wolfe's waist.

She'll be beautiful, of course, Jessica thought bitterly. *As beautiful as this huge meadow and as perfect as those mountains crowned with ice.*

Unhappily, Jessica glanced around, measuring the glory of the mountain ranch against the darkness that was condensing relentlessly in her soul, draining color from her life as surely as the slow condensation of night would drain color from the day.

"Come and meet your present," Wolfe said, smiling down at Willow as he released her.

"Meet a present?"

"Ummm."

The purring sound of pleasure Wolfe made was a steel-tipped whip flaying Jessica's raw emotions. She had thought she could feel no greater rage, no greater despair, than she had felt the day she had ridden over the Great Divide.

She had been wrong. She seemed to make a habit of being wrong where Wolfe was concerned.

May the bloody paragon writhe in Hell.

Then Willow stepped into the bright sunlight and Jessica's breath came in with a harsh sound. The paragon wouldn't have to wait for Hell. It had already sunk its unsheathed claws deeply in her body. Willow was in the last stage of pregnancy, frankly round with the babe that would tear her apart trying to be born.

Dear God, help her in her time of need.

The silent, involuntary prayer that vibrated through Jessica was deeper and more powerful than her jealousy. She could take no pleasure in the agony that awaited Willow in childbed. Nor could she hate Willow any longer. Jessica could feel only a terrible empathy with the girl whose fate was to writhe and scream for mercy that never came, a wife's endless cycle of male rutting and childbed's torture; and over all, around all, consuming all was the black wind and the disbelieving shriek of the newly damned.

The realization of what awaited Willow made the sound of her laughter and teasing voice almost too painful for Jessica to bear. She watched with helpless agony as Willow took Wolfe's arm to steady herself across the uneven ground where small patches of snow and mud competed with the green resurgence of life.

When Willow walked past Two-Spot, she looked up at Jessica with curiosity and a quick smile that offered friendship. Jessica smiled in return, but Wolfe didn't stop or even look up.

"Wolfe?" asked Willow, tugging on his arm.

"Your present is next in line."

Grinning, Rafe kicked his right leg over his horse's mane and slid to the ground. When he took off his hat, the sun blazed in his pale gold hair, hair that was the exact color of Willow's.

Willow stared, made a sound of joyous disbelief, then began laughing and crying and saying Rafe's name over and over again. Rafe picked her up in a big hug and held her for a long time, saying things that were too soft for anyone but Willow to hear. Finally, he set her down and blotted the happy tears that were streaming down her face.

"Well, Willy, I have to say you grew up to be quite a woman. From what Wolfe told me, you've got yourself a fine man." Rafe paused, then added slyly, "Sure as hell he's a potent one."

Willow flushed, laughed, and swatted her older brother on his broad chest. "Shame on you. You're not supposed to notice."

"Be kind of like overlooking a mountain," he retorted. "When are you going to make me an uncle?"

"In a few weeks." She smiled up at her older, much bigger brother. "Dear Lord, Rafe. It's so good to see you! I can't wait until Caleb and Matt get back from checking the north meadow."

"I can't wait, period. I'll ride out as soon as we've unloaded the pack animals."

Willow slipped her arm through Rafe's and said, "I'm almost afraid to let you out of my sight. It's been years." She rubbed her cheek against his arm and took a deep breath. "Now, introduce me to your wife. She's beautiful, but I expected that. You always had an eye for beauty, whether it was women, horses, dogs, or land."

"Red is beautiful, all right," Rafe agreed, "but she's Wolfe's wife, not mine."

Open-mouthed, Willow spun and stared at Wolfe. Every question she had died unspoken when she saw his bleak, blue-black eyes.

Swallowing quickly, Willow turned to the girl who sat in her sidesaddle so elegantly. She had a delicate, elfin face, aquamarine gems for eyes, and hair whose buried fire rippled and shimmered with every motion of her body. The riding habit she wore had seen hard use, but its fashionable lines and fine fabric spoke eloquently of wealth.

Abruptly, Willow remembered. "Lady Jessica Charteris?"

"Not any longer. My name is Jessica Lonetree. Or Jessi."

"Or Red?" Willow asked innocently.

"Or Red," Jessica agreed, smiling slightly at Rafe. "It's the Western way to have nicknames, I'm told."

"Get down and come into the house. You must be exhausted. I remember my first trip over the Great Divide. If it hadn't been for Caleb, I wouldn't have made it. He ended up carrying me."

"We came the easy way," Wolfe said. "Lady Jessica has neither your strength nor your adaptability."

Willow gave Wolfe an uncertain look, wondering at the edge to his voice.

"I disagree," she said quietly. "Anyone who came through those mountains riding sidesaddle is stronger than I am."

Wolfe grunted and said nothing.

Jessica began dismounting, moving stiffly. Before she could put any weight on her right leg, Rafe caught her waist between his big hands and supported her until her left foot was able to take most of her weight.

"I could have managed," Jessica said in a low voice, "but thank you."

Only Willow saw the instant of anger before Wolfe brought it under control, just as she had been the only one to see the small, almost involuntary movement he had made toward Jessica when she began to dismount.

"No point in pushing your luck," Rafe said. "Your ankle still isn't up to snuff."

"What happened?" Willow asked.

"She fell off," Wolfe said curtly.

"It's nothing," Jessica said. "A bruise. Nothing at all."

"Nonsense," Willow said, seeing the strain on

Jessica's face. "Come in and sit down. I'll make you some tea."

"Tea?" Jessica looked stunned. "You actually have tea?"

Willow laughed. "It's left over from Wolfe's last visit. He's the only one who drinks it."

Jessica gave Wolfe a shocked look, remembering how many times she had longed for a comforting cup of tea.

"But we had only coffee," she said faintly.

"Western wives drink coffee. You wanted to be a Western wife. Remember?"

The cool taunt in Wolfe's words was unmistakable. Rafe's eyes narrowed as he winced and said something under his breath. But he said nothing aloud. He and Wolfe had reached a tacit agreement where Jessica was concerned: Jessica was Wolfe's responsibility, not Rafe's. Rafe didn't understand what was driving Wolfe, but he was certain that Wolfe wasn't a cruel man by nature.

So was Willow. With a perplexed look at Wolfe, she took Jessica's hand.

"Come with me."

"First I have to care for my horse," Jessica said.

"Let Wolfe do it."

"Western wives take care of their own horses. They curry, saddle, bridle, clean the feet of, rub down, and otherwise—"

"Go to the house," Wolfe interrupted curtly. "I'll see to your horse."

"Well, I should hope so," Willow said tartly. "Jessi has ridden just as far as you have and she hasn't a third your strength. Plus that ridiculous sidesaddle. I'd like to see how spritely you'd feel if you had to ride that way. Honestly, Wolfe, what's gotten into you?"

Jessica wondered at the dull red stain on Wolfe's cheekbones as he turned away and led horses toward the barn, but Willow tugged at her hand, distracting her.

"I've never been able to make a good cup of tea," Willow confessed, leading Jessica firmly toward the porch. "You'll have to show me how."

"A paragon who can't make tea." Jessica blinked. "Impossible. Breathtaking." She smiled slightly and shook her head. "Actually quite wonderful."

"Who said I was a paragon?"

"I did," Jessica admitted. "With a lot of encouragement from Wolfe."

"Good Lord. Why?"

"Because compared to me, you are."

Willow made a rude sound. "You've had a very long trip. It must have affected your mind. Not to mention Wolfe's. I've never seen him so edgy."

"Perhaps a cup of tea would help," Jessica suggested with an unconscious sigh.

Willow muttered something that sounded like, "A swift kick in the pants might do more good."

"Paragons don't think such things."

The hazel flash of Willow's eyes was alive with wry laughter. "Perhaps. And perhaps paragons just aren't caught thinking them."

The front door opened and closed, cutting off the sound of women's voices. The men hadn't been able to hear any real words for the last few minutes, but it hadn't been difficult to guess what the topic of conversation was—Wolfe's manners.

Or lack thereof.

After a few moments of silence, Wolfe glanced up from the pack horse he was working on and let out a long breath. Hearing it, Rafe smiled.

"Well, I can see that marriage hasn't trimmed Willy's tongue one bit," Rafe said wryly as he undid the saddle cinch. "She can still tear a mean strip when she has a mind to. Only thing she does better is make biscuits."

Wolfe grunted.

"Of course," Rafe said, lifting the saddle one-handed from the horse's back, "the fact that a man knows he has it coming tends to make it sting all the worse."

Wolfe spun around, ready to take exception to Rafe's calm words, but the other man had already turned away. Saddle balanced on one shoulder, saddle bags and bedroll slung over the other, Rafe was walking through the barn door.

Letting out another long breath, Wolfe made another stab at reining in his temper. The whole point of bringing Jessica to the ranch had been to show her how completely unsuited she was to be a Western wife. It hadn't been to point out how hard Wolfe was being on her. He knew that already.

Just as he knew his plan to make Jessica cry annulment was working. Slowly, surely, day by day, hour by hour, minute by minute, he was wearing down her certainty that she would win the contest of wills with Wolfe.

I shall not tire of being your wife.

Yes, you shall.

With each breath Jessica took, they were coming closer to the moment when she would be forced to admit her defeat and free both of them from the cruel trap of a marriage that never should have been.

Wolfe hoped Jessica would give in soon. Very soon. He didn't know how much longer he could go on grinding a graceful elf into dust. He had never felt another person's pain so clearly. It was worse than being hurt himself, for he had learned to control his own pain long ago, when he had realized that to many people his Indian mother put him beyond the pale of true humanity.

The viscount's savage.

But there was no way to control the effects of the pain Wolfe was causing Jessica. There was only the knowledge that when the pain became great enough, she would quit the sham marriage between aristocrat and halfbreed bastard.

Nothing of Wolfe's grim thoughts showed on his face as he worked over the horses, or later when he went to the house and found Jessica asleep in the extra bedroom. In the daylight filtering through the muslin curtains, she looked almost ethereal. Asleep, the fierce will that burned so surprisingly beneath her fragile surface was banked, giving no hint of what lay beneath the delicate features and fine bones.

Broodingly, Wolfe looked at the translucence of Jessica's skin and the lavender shadows beneath her eyes. Seeing her like this, he could barely believe she had the strength to sit up, much less to defy him when men far stronger than she was would have given up the game long since.

Unbidden, a memory surfaced in Wolfe . . . a cold day in spring and a creek in flood. Trapped amid the debris was a blue-eyed wolf cub whose back had been broken. The cub had snarled silently up at Wolfe, prepared to die fighting with teeth that had known nothing but a mother's milk. Wolfe had allowed the cub's needle fangs to sink all the way to the bone, for it had been the only way to get in close enough for a quick, clean kill, ending the cub's suffering.

With an effort, Wolfe banished the memory and the chill that had come in its wake. He wasn't going to harm Jessica physically, much less kill her. The trap they were caught in was less tangled than flood debris. It would spring open at a single word from her pale lips.

Annulment.

Wolfe tore his attention away from Jessica and began looking for places to put the valises and fur blanket he had brought in. The far corner looked promising, but a second look showed that it was occupied by a cradle. Stacked nearby were other tiny pieces of furniture, waiting the for next generation of Blacks to be born.

The thought of what it would be like to be awaiting the birth of his own child went through Wolfe like lightning, leaving only darkness in its wake. He set down the valises and turned to leave. His steps brought him past the bed. He stopped, held by something he could not name.

Jessica stirred and shivered with the residue of winter that still gripped the house. Despite her chill, she didn't awaken. Instead, she huddled around herself as though understanding even in sleep that she must hoard her own warmth, for there was no one to care for her.

Jessi . . . damn it, what are you doing to us? Let go of me before I do something that we'll both regret to our dying breath.

The soft fur blanket settled as lightly as a sigh over Jessica. Wolfe drew the blanket up to her chin, stared at the beauty of her hair against the lustrous fur, and then left the room in three long, silent strides.

*   *   *

"WHY am I called Reno?" he asked, repeating Jessica's question.

"Oh dear," Jessica said quickly, looking up from a plate of Willow's delicious food. "Was it rude of me to ask? I'm still not certain of your customs."

Reno smiled. The flash of his teeth against his black mustache was vivid, but not as vivid as the green of his eyes framed by thick lashes a woman would have envied. Like Willow and Rafe, Reno's eyes were slightly tilted, almost cat-like in their impact. Unlike Willow, there was nothing the least bit feminine about Reno. He was as big and hard as Rafe.

And like Rafe, Reno had been captivated by the delicate British elf whose ice-blue eyes and coolly accented English were at odds with the fire buried in her glorious hair.

"Red, you couldn't be rude if you tried."

As Reno spoke, he kept an eye on the huge basket of biscuits that was making the rounds of the dinner table. If he didn't watch closely, Rafe would make off with more than his share.

"A while back I was looking for gold over in the Sierra Nevadas," Reno said absently. "I came across an old Frenchman who had had some bad luck with a gold claim he called Reno's Revenge. Later, I found the men who had the Frenchman's gold and explained how much the old man needed it for his granddaughter. They thought it over and gave the gold back. After that, people started calling me Reno."

Wolfe made an odd sound and put his napkin to his mouth. Nearby, Caleb choked quietly on a mouthful of venison. Jessica didn't need to see the unholy laughter in Caleb's amber eyes to realize she hadn't heard the full story of how Matthew

Moran had come to be called Reno.

"Dammit, unhand those biscuits," Reno complained.

"I haven't had thirds yet," Rafe said.

"Over my dead body."

"Whatever you say."

Willow thumped her husband's broad back and at the same time buried her face in her napkin, muffling her own laughter. After a moment, Caleb turned, captured Willow's hand and brushed it against his lips. She lowered her napkin and curled her fingers through his as he returned his hand to his lap. Husband and wife resumed eating one-handed, for neither wanted to separate their closely linked fingers.

"Pass those biscuits along, boys," Caleb said dryly. "There's more in the kitchen."

A curious sensation went through Jessica as she glanced from the corner of her eyes at the slender hand that was so carefully held in Caleb's much more powerful grip. The longer Jessica watched Caleb and Willow, the more she realized that there was a genuine and quite baffling affection between husband and wife. Despite the fact that Willow was so heavy with the results of Caleb's rutting that she could barely rise unaided from a chair, Willow watched her husband as though expecting the sun to rise in him at any moment. He watched her in the same way, his love very plain in his golden eyes.

Yet at one time Caleb had cared so little for Willow that he had given free rein to his baser nature, knowing full well that the result would be her agony in childbed. Caleb didn't have the excuse or requirement of duty forcing him to put his wife at risk in such a way. There was no need for Willow's painful fate, for Caleb had neither titles nor wealth nor ancient bloodlines to pass on to another generation. Yet Willow was pregnant just the same. Even more baffling, she appeared quite happy about her state.

Frowning, Jessica tried to reconcile Willow's dangerous pregnancy with Caleb's obvious love for his wife. It was even more difficult to reconcile Willow's obvious pleasure in a man who had so little regard for her welfare. Yet there, too, Jessica had no doubt of the reality of Willow's emotions. She did not shrink from her husband's touch. Rather, she sought it in subtle ways, crossing the room just to stand close to him when he laid the evening fire.

"You sure that's how you got your moniker?" Wolfe asked neutrally.

"Close enough," Reno said.

"That's not even close enough for horseshoes," Wolfe retorted.

As Wolfe spoke, he snatched a handful of biscuits before passing the basket on down the table. A week of watching the two brothers steal Willow's biscuits had taught Wolfe to grab first and worry about manners later.

"Way I heard it," Wolfe continued, splitting a steaming biscuit, "was that old Frenchman found himself a glory hole and went to work cleaning it out. When he was finished, four men jumped him, left him for dead, and took off with the old man's gold."

Jessica looked up, caught by the thread of amusement and something else that ran through Wolfe's words. It took her a moment to identify the emotion. It was affection. The camaraderie between Wolfe and Reno was as real and, in its way, as deep as that between Reno and Rafe. The same emotion extended to Caleb. The mutual respect was striking, for it was based not on family or name or position, but on each man's assessment of the others as men worthy of friendship.

"You found that Frenchman, nursed him, then tracked the claim jumpers," Wolfe continued. "You walked into the saloon, called them thieves and cowards and some other names not fit for the dinner table, and then you demanded they return the gold they had cleaned out of Reno's Revenge. Instead, they went for their guns."

When Wolfe said no more, Jessica made an impatient sound and asked, "What happened?"

Wolfe's smile was as cool and clean as the edge of a knife. "Way I heard it, Reno waited until they got a grip on their guns and started pulling them out. Then he drew. The first two claim jumpers never even got their guns clear of their belts. The rest of them got their guns out, but never got off a shot."

Jessica gave Reno a startled look. He was pouring an intricate pattern of honey over a steaming biscuit, ignoring the conversation completely.

"After that, folks started talking about Reno's Revenge and a man who was pure hell with a six-gun," Wolfe concluded. "Pretty soon they were just talking about a man called Reno, a man who would help you if you drew short cards in a rigged game, a man who didn't look for fights but didn't back away when one found him. I liked what I heard, so I looked Reno up."

When Reno turned toward Wolfe to reply, Jessica calmly filched a biscuit from Reno's plate. Rafe saw, winked, and passed her the honey. Jessica smiled and looked sideways at Reno. She knew his quick green eyes had seen the small theft, just as she knew he could have retrieved the biscuit before she had a chance to blink. Reno had the fastest reflexes of any man she had ever met.

"Pass the biscuits," Reno said. "A certain small redhead stole one of mine."

"She's just trying to keep you from getting fat," Rafe said blandly.

"Then she better eat yours, too. Much more of Willy's cooking and the only thing that will fit around your waist is that long bullwhip you fancy."

Jessica looked from one hard, lean Moran brother to the other. She put her napkin over her mouth, but mere cloth couldn't muffle her snickers. Reno heard and turned toward her.

"Are you laughing at me?"

Peeking over the napkin, Jessica nodded her head.

Reno's face softened into a smile. "Sassy as your hair, aren't you?"

Wolfe's hand tightened around his fork as he saw Jessica's eyes sparkle with amusement. He told himself that Reno couldn't help being handsome as sin and lethal as hell. Nor could Rafe help his fallen-angel good looks and potent male charm, both of which he showed in abundance around Jessica. Neither Moran brother would have touched any man's wife, much less the wife of a friend like Wolfe Lonetree, and he knew it.

Yet day after day of watching Jessica respond to their masculine teasing like a flower soaking up warm rain had worn Wolfe raw. He couldn't remember the last time Jessica had turned toward him with light in her eyes and laughter on her lips.

And that's the way it has to stay, Wolfe reminded himself savagely. *It's been hard enough sharing a bed with her for the past week. If she looked up at me and smiled and held out her arms . . .*

A shudder of raw desire went through Wolfe. He told himself he was a fool for not sleeping with Rafe and Reno in the small cabin that had served as Caleb and Willow's home while the big house was being built. If Wolfe had been in the cabin, he wouldn't have lain awake for long hours, listening to the soft breathing of the girl who lay so close to him, yet never touched him at all. If he had been in the cabin, he wouldn't have lain rigid with a need that grew greater every moment, his body demanding what his mind would not permit him to take.

And if Wolfe had been in the cabin, he wouldn't have heard Jessica's broken whimpers and muffled cries, wouldn't have felt the erratic stirring of her body as she fought within the coils of a dark dream that came every night, waking her, waking him.

What is it, Jessi?

Nothing. I don't remember.

Damn it, what is it that frightens you so?

I'm foolish, my lord bastard, but not stupid. I'll give you no more weapons to turn against me.

So at night they lay side by side, stiff, sleepless, listening to the wind moan over the battleground between winter and spring.

"FISHING?" Jessica asked, looking up from the mending in her lap. "Did I hear trout fishing mentioned?"

Caleb and Wolfe were sitting at the dinner table, studying a map Caleb had drawn, showing the range of several nearby mustang herds. He turned away from Wolfe and looked at Jessica, who was mending one of Willow's dresses by lantern light.

"Do you like to fish?" Caleb asked.

"No," she said calmly. "I love it. I will walk through fire barefoot to get to a good trout stream."

Caleb raised black eyebrows and looked at Wolfe.

"It's the truth," Wolfe admitted. "She'll be out working a piece of water on a stormy evening when everyone else is in front of a fire talking about the one that got away."

"Why didn't you say something sooner?" Caleb asked Wolfe. "There's some good trout water nearby."

"It's too early for trout to be out of their winter torpor."

"Not along parts of the Columbine. There's enough hot-spring water mixed into the stream that certain stretches of it come alive long before anything else does."

"Truly?" Jessica asked.

Caleb grinned. "Truly."

"Wonderful!"

Jessica set aside the mending and ran into the bedroom. When she returned, her hands were full of small boxes.

"What do the streamside insects here look like?" she asked eagerly, opening boxes and setting them on the dinner table in front of the men. Tiny, carefully tied flies rested within the boxes. "Are they light or dark, big or small, colorful or drab?"

"Yes."

She gave Caleb a slanting, sidelong glance. "Yes?"

He nodded gravely. "They're light and dark, big and small, colorful and drab."

"Caleb, stop teasing Jessica," Willow called from the back of the house.

"But I'm getting so good at it."

Jessica tried not to smile, and failed. Caleb was indeed getting quite good at teasing her.

There was the sound of the wind slamming the back door, followed by footsteps as Willow walked through the kitchen into the living room. Sleet glistened in the wool shawl she had worn to the privy.

She shook the shawl and hung it on a peg near the door for the next trip, knowing it wouldn't be long before necessity overcame her reluctance to face the cold scouring of the spring wind. The more pregnant she became, the more frequently she was forced to visit the privy's drafty comforts.

"Jessi gets quite enough ribbing from my brothers," Willow continued, yawning. "Why don't you try protecting her, instead?"

"That's Wolfe's job," Caleb said, giving the other man an amused look, "and God help the man who gets in Wolfe's way."

Wolfe looked back impassively.

Caleb's grin was rather feral. No matter how hard Wolfe tried to conceal his irritation at the handsome Moran brothers' gallant attentions to Jessica, Caleb sensed the jealousy that seethed just beneath Wolfe's calm surface. Caleb would have had more sympathy for his friend, but he didn't understand why Wolfe was so hard on his young wife.

"I don't mind the way Rafe and Reno tease," Jessica said as Willow walked in from the kitchen, patting back another yawn. "I never had any brothers or sisters. I had no idea how much fun it could be."

"No siblings?" Willow asked, surprised. "You poor darling. How lonely it must have been for you."

Jessica hesitated, then shrugged. "It was all I knew. And I had the firth and forest to roam."

"I can't imagine having only one child," Willow said, shaking her head. "I want a house full of kids."

"I imagine many women feel like that before they experience childbed."

The barely muted horror in Jessica's voice created a pool of silence that expanded and deepened until she realized her mistake and changed the subject with a determined smile.

"Do you like to fish, Willow?"

"Caleb is the fisherman in the family. He's very good at it."

Caleb gave Willow a lazy, sidelong glance and a crooked smile. Though not a word was said, her cheeks turned a revealing shade of pink.

"I'm a fair fisherman," he admitted. "Don't care much for fishing rods or lures, though."

"You don't?" Jessica asked. "What do you use, then? Nets or traps? Or do you hunt like the Eskimo, with spears?"

Caleb shook his head. "Nothing that fancy."

"How do you catch fish, then?"

"Patience, stealth, and bare hands."

His smile shifted as he measured the deepening color of Willow's cheeks. His golden eyes gleamed with a frank male sensuality that surprised Jessica; up to that instant, she hadn't thought of Caleb as a particularly passionate man. She had been wrong. The hunger in his eyes as he watched his wife was barely veiled by his half-lowered lids.

"You see," Caleb explained in a slow, deep voice, "trout like to be stroked all over. That's why they hold station in the fastest currents. Isn't that right, honey? Don't they just lie there, quivering, waiting for the moment when—"

Willow's hands clapped over her husband's mouth, cutting off his words.

"Caleb Winslow Black, if you weren't too big, I'd turn you over my knee and teach you a few manners!"

Laughing, Caleb turned his head quickly aside, evading his wife's attempts to muzzle him. Believing the caress would be hidden by Willow's hands, he flicked the tip of his tongue between two of her fingers, stroking the sensitive skin.

But Jessica saw the secret caress, just as she saw the change in Willow's smile and the brief, sensual glide of her fingertip over his lower lip. For an instant, something quite primitive arced between man and wife; then Caleb smiled and pulled Willow onto his lap with gentle hands.

"I'm too big for your knees, honey. You fit real nice across mine, though."

"Caleb . . ."

Willow's voice died. She flushed and glanced toward the other two people in the room.

"Hush," Caleb said softly, pressing Willow's cheek against his shoulder. "Wolfe and Jessi are husband and wife. They won't faint if they see you sitting in my lap."

With a sigh, Willow relaxed against her husband. He shifted her more closely against his body, brushed a kiss over her hair, and leaned toward the boxes with their intriguing array of flies.

"You'll probably have some luck with this one," he said to Jessica, pointing toward something that looked like a black ant. "We have mayflies and caddis, too, so that box should fill many a frying pan."

"Is the stream you mentioned far from here?" Jessica asked.

But the question occupied only part of her mind. She was still measuring the difference between marriage as she understood it and marriage as Willow and Caleb lived it.

Is this why Wolfe can't be reconciled to our marriage? Did he expect of marriage what Caleb and Willow so obviously have—a union of lives rather than a merger of titles and wealth?

"The Columbine isn't far," Caleb said. "Wolfe knows how to get there."

"Thank you," Jessica said quickly, "but if it's close, I'll just go by myself."

"Like hell you will," Wolfe said. "If it's the stream I'm thinking of, there's a band of Utes that winters there. They like hot springs as well as white men do."

Caleb nodded. "There's a small camp. No more than three or four families. Mostly old men, women, and boys. I haven't had any trouble with them."

"Yet," Wolfe retorted. "You let down your guard and you'll be missing some horses real quick."

"Keeps a man on his toes," Caleb agreed blandly.

Wolfe laughed. "You should have been a warrior."

"He is," Willow said sleepily. She yawned and burrowed closer to her husband's strength. "If he weren't, I'd have died a year ago."

Long, amber eyelashes flickered down and Willow sighed, relaxing deeply against her husband, letting the rest of the world fade into the warm distance of sleep.

"Reno and Wolfe helped me," Caleb pointed out in a dry voice.

Willow didn't answer. She had fallen asleep. Caleb smiled and smoothed a bright lock of hair back from his wife's face.

"You're right about the camp," he said quietly to Wolfe. "It's not far from the best stretch of trout water for a hundred miles around. But as long as you keep your rifle handy, you won't have any problems. The Utes know Tree That Stands Alone. You're a legend with them."

"I'm sure Wolfe has better things to do than watch me lash a stream," Jessica said quietly.

"That's a fact," Wolfe agreed.

Caleb looked from Jessica to Wolfe and bit back impatient words. Caleb didn't know what was wrong between the two of them, but he had no doubt that something was. Normally controlled to a fault, Wolfe's temper had become as volatile as nitroglycerin. He spent the days working like a man possessed, yet from the look of him there was no rest at night, nor any peace. Jessica looked no better. When she had arrived ten days ago, she had been exhausted from the long trip. She still looked exhausted.

"Nonsense," Caleb said firmly. "It will do Wolfe good. He's been working like two men."

"Bull," Wolfe said. "Looking after our brood-mares isn't work, it's pleasure."

"And digging postholes, cleaning out springs, fencing off rockfalls and blind canyons, chopping firewood—"

"I said I don't mind," Wolfe said, cutting across the other man's words.

"Do be quiet, you'll wake Willow," Jessica said, showing both men two rows of even white teeth.

"In any case, I won't be leaving Willow while you're out working all over the countryside. The babe could decide to be born at any moment. There is enough agony and terror waiting for Willow. She shouldn't be alone in the bargain."

"Hold your tongue," Wolfe said coldly. "Not everyone feels as you do about bearing children."

"Not everyone," Jessica agreed with equal chill. "Merely every *woman*."

"That's enough!" Wolfe said.

"Jessica is right," Caleb said abruptly. "God help me, she's right about the danger. When I think of how Becky died . . ." His expression changed as he looked down at the woman who slept so trustingly in his arms. "Willow is my life."

"I didn't mean . . ." Jessica whispered, but no one was listening.

Caleb stood, lifting Willow with him. Without a word, he carried his wife into their bedroom. The door shut softly behind them.

Sleet rattled over the windows, breaking the silence Caleb had left behind. The howling voice of the wind curled through the room, filling all space, all silence, summoning all that Jessica had spent a lifetime trying to forget.

Hands clasped together until her fingers ached, Jessica fought not to show the fear she had lived with so long she couldn't remember a time without it. The need to cry out was a constant aching in her throat. Hiding her fear was becoming harder each day. The nights were becoming impossible. Soon she would hear a woman's screams mingled in awful harmony with the wind's predatory cry.

Jessica wondered whether the screams would be Willow's or her own.

 **11**

"Such a fine, delicate stitch," Willow marveled, watching Jessica embroider an ornate B on a christening gown. "I tried to learn when I was a child, but I didn't have the patience. I still don't."

"I'd rather be able to make biscuits."

"Your stew is excellent," Willow said, suppressing a smile.

"It's edible," Jessica corrected wryly, "thanks to you. Without your tutoring, I'd still be trying to interest a skunk in my cooking. You've been very patient with me."

"My pleasure. I've enjoyed having you here. I haven't really had another woman to talk to since my mother died."

Jessica hesitated. "You must have been lonely."

"Not since I found Caleb."

With a sigh, Willow settled deeper into the sofa next to Jessica.

"If there's anything else about the domestic arts you want to know, just ask," Willow said, yawning. "I'm going to be lazy and watch you embroider while the bread rises."

Jessica became very still. "Do you mean that?"

"Definitely. I feel very lazy."

"I meant about asking questions."

"Of course." Willow sighed and shifted her weight, trying to accommodate the baby's restlessness. "Fire away."

"What I need to know is very . . . personal."

"That's all right. The War Between the States made me pretty shockproof. Ask whatever you like."

Jessica took a deep breath and said quickly, "You seem to enjoy your husband."

"Oh, yes. Very much. He's a wonderful man." Willow's hazel eyes kindled with delight and her smile became incandescent.

"No, I mean you *enjoy* him. Physically. In the marriage bed."

Willow blinked. "Yes. I do."

"Do many women actually enjoy the marriage bed?"

For a moment, Willow looked thoughtful as she remembered her mother's laughter and her father's low voice murmuring through the house late at night. Willow also remembered the Widow Sorenson's eyes lighting when she talked about the pleasure of sharing her life with a man.

"I think many women do," Willow said slowly. Then she admitted, "I never truly understood it until I met Caleb. I was engaged to a boy who died in the war. When he kissed my cheek or held my hand, it was nice but it didn't make me want to be his woman. Yet when Caleb looks at me or smiles or touches me . . ."

She hesitated, searching for words.

"There's nothing else in the world for you," Jessica finished quietly, remembering how it had felt when Wolfe smiled at her, filling her world.

But he no longer smiled at her, and her world was the empty wind.

"Yes. Everything else vanishes." After a moment, Willow said simply, "I never knew babies were conceived in ecstasy, until Caleb."

The embroidery thread knotted under Jessica's tense fingers as memories spurted through her unwilling mind. "Not all babies are conceived that way. My mother's certainly weren't. She fought my father. Dear God, how she fought him."

Unhappily, Willow watched Jessica, sensing the violent tension in the other girl's slim body. She put her arm around Jessica in silent sympathy.

"Was there no love between them?" Willow asked softly.

"My father needed a male heir. His first wife was an aristocrat, who couldn't conceive. When she died, he took my mother as his wife. She was a common lady's maid. She was pregnant with me at the time. The earl had bedded her, you see."

"Then there was affection between them."

"Perhaps." Jessica set aside the embroidery and rubbed her hands together as though chilled. "But I think not. Mother was a commoner whose family was desperately poor. The earl was an aristocrat who desperately needed a male heir. I think desperation makes for a very difficult marriage bed. I know mother very much preferred to sleep alone, but she wasn't permitted to unless she was breeding."

Jessica's bleak eyes revealed much that her careful words did not.

"It isn't that way in all marriages," Willow said.

"It was in the marriages I saw. It was families and fortunes that married, not man and woman. It would have been that way in the marriage my guardian tried to arrange for me." Jessica turned and faced Willow. "But it isn't like that for you and Caleb. You come to his bed willingly. He doesn't . . . hurt you. Does he?"

Laughter and memory combined to tint Willow's cheeks a bright pink. Under normal circumstances, she wouldn't have spoken so frankly about the private side of marriage, but she sensed Jessica must have been been ill-prepared for being a wife in more important ways than her lack of skill in the kitchen.

Willow also suspected that she had stumbled on the source of the tension between Wolfe and his wife.

"I'm more than willing to bed my husband, I fear. I've been known to seduce Caleb quite shamelessly." Willow bent closer and whispered in Jessica's ear. "In fact, as soon as possible after this babe is born, I'm looking forward to becoming Caleb's woman in every way once more. I've missed it so much. I never feel so closely bound to him as I do when we share our love in that very special way."

Jessica couldn't help but smile in response to Willow's sparkling eyes and pinkened cheeks. "Caleb is lucky to have you."

"I'm the lucky one." Willow smiled at Jessica. "Any more questions? Don't be shy. Growing up as you did, I doubt you had many women with whom you could talk about such things."

"I had only one friend."

"You must miss her."

"Him, not her. Yes, I miss him terribly. Our friendship didn't survive our marriage."

"Having seen how possessive Wolfe is, I can understand it," Willow said. "Your friend must have decided that discretion is indeed the better part of valor."

"You misunderstood me. Wolfe was my friend. Now he is my husband." Jessica grimaced and changed the subject quickly. "There is another way in which you're very different from my mother."

Willow smiled encouragingly. "Yes?"

"Pregnancy was very difficult for her, yet you seem not to suffer."

"Oh, I'll be glad enough to carry the babe in my arms rather than in my womb," Willow admitted. "Just as I'll be glad not to wallow clumsily when I walk, not to visit the privy hourly, and not to require my husband's strong arm to pull me out of my favorite chair."

"But you're healthy," Jessica said seriously. "You can walk across the room without fainting, you can eat without vomiting, and you don't . . ."

Jessica's voice died as she shuddered beneath another unwanted eruption of memory.

"What?" coaxed Willow.

"You don't weep and scream and curse your fate."

"Dear Lord. Was that what your mother did?"

Another shudder wracked Jessica. Her hands became fists, as though that would prevent the gathering pressure of nightmares from erupting into memories she had forgotten long ago, because remembering was unbearable.

"And you don't curse Caleb for making you pregnant," Jessica continued urgently, determined to have it all said, all questions asked. "Do you?"

"Curse Caleb?" Willow sounded and looked appalled. Impulsively, she took Jessica's cold fists, uncurled the fingers, and placed Jessica's hands on the firm mound of her pregnancy. "Feel it. Feel the baby kick and turn and wriggle. Can you feel it?''

At first, Jessica tried to pull away, for the gesture called back more of her own childhood, when her mother had grabbed her daughter's hands and pressed them against her womb, shouting at her daughter to feel the babe, to feel it moving, proof that this one would not be stillborn. But not once had Jessica felt a babe move. Not once had the pregnancies ended in a live birth.

Willow's belly was warm and firm and resilient, and beneath the supple skin something drummed against Jessica's hands.

"It's moving," Jessica breathed, shocked. "It's alive!"

"Of course. The blessed little thing is as active as a flea."

"No, you don't understand. *It's alive.*"

Willow laughed softly, bemused by the wonder on Jessica's face.

"Yes, it's alive," Willow agreed. "Another life is growing inside me. A beautiful miracle. How could I curse the man who created this new life with me?"

Jessica said nothing, for she was too transfixed by the vigorous life in Willow's womb to think coherently.

"Here," Willow said, shifting one of Jessica's hands. "Can you feel the baby's head, all round, just fitting in your palm?"

Breathlessly, Jessica nodded.

"Now give me your other hand," Willow said. She moved it to the other side of her abdomen. "Feel it kick? A tiny little foot, but already so strong. Every week it gets bigger and stronger. Lately, it seems to grow an inch a day." She laughed. "Soon it will be strong enough to be born, and then I'll see Caleb hold his child and smile at me."

"You aren't afraid?"

"I'm strong. I'm healthy. My mother had babies without difficulty." Willow hesitated, then admitted, "Caleb wanted me to go to the fort months ago, but the weather has been too bad. Besides, I wanted our child to be born here. I didn't want to be in a strange place with strangers around me."

"When the time comes, I'll help you," Jessica said. "If you wish it. Lady Victoria saw that I had some small training, though I've never used it. She wanted me to be prepared if my future husband owned a remote country estate."

Willow said simply, "I'd like to have you nearby."

"Then you shall."

With a lifting of her heart, Jessica picked up her embroidery again and resumed working on the christening gown. For the first time, she allowed herself to hope that the gown wouldn't serve as a tiny shroud for a stillborn babe.

"Oн, do play, please," Jessica coaxed Caleb. "Reno told me you play quite beautifully. It would be wonderful to hear music again."

"That's the thing about being a Western wife," Wolfe said, giving Jessica a taunting look. "You're deprived of all kinds of civilized things."

"Not music," Caleb said. "Not unless you want to be." He put the harmonica to his lips. A beautiful chord floated through the room. "Of course, a harmonica isn't some fancy chamber music done in four-part harmony."

"Do that again," Jessica said, startled. Then she heard the blunt command in her voice and flushed.

"Please. It was very pretty."

"It wasn't Bach," Wolfe said.

"Do hush up," Jessica said sweetly. "If I had wanted Bach, I would have packed my violin over the Rockies and made all of you suffer through a nightly recital."

Rafe laughed. "You tell him, Red."

Despite himself, Wolfe smiled. "Actually, I like Bach."

"You would," Reno said. "You spent too long in civilization."

Caleb lifted the harmonica and blew gently. All conversation stopped as the first, simple notes of "Amazing Grace" filled the room. Reno and Willow began singing, falling easily into the patterns of harmony they had learned as children. Jessica's breath went out in a sigh of pleasure as brother and sister sang with voices perfectly blended.

After a moment another voice wove through the other two in a rhythmic echo that had no words. When Jessica looked at Rafe, she realized that he was humming in flawless counterpoint.

Grimly Wolfe measured the pleasure and admiration in Jessica's face as she listened to Reno's voice and Rafe's haunting music. Even as Wolfe told himself that she was every bit as admiring of Caleb and Willow, Wolfe knew it didn't matter. It was Jessica's clear appreciation of the Moran brothers that flicked like a whip over Wolfe's raw nerves.

Nor were Reno and Rafe immune to Jessica's effortless charm. Their eyes kindled with special warmth when she laughed, when she smiled, when she walked into the room. Though neither brother had given her so much as an improper look, the knowledge that Jessica took pleasure in their company—but not in her husband's—was like an acid in Wolfe's soul. The fact that he had worked relentlessly to make her uncomfortable in his presence only made the result more bitter.

I never should have brought her here. I should have guessed Reno would be wintering over with his sister. I should have known what effect Jessica's fey blue eyes and laughter would have on a lonely man. God knows the effect they have on me.

Or rather, the Devil knows. I want Jessica like Hell burning. But I can survive that. What I can't survive is watching her flit like a silken butterfly around those damned handsome Moran brothers.

I should grab Jessi and leave.

But Wolfe couldn't do that. He cared too much for Willow to deprive her of Jessica's company, especially after Willow had refused to leave the ranch in order to give birth.

When Caleb began a ballad set in waltz time Jessica began humming and keeping time with her fingertips.

"Wolfe?" she asked hopefully, wanting to dance.

He shook his head. He was tempted, but didn't trust himself. If he held her in his arms, his body would state its hunger in unmistakable terms.

"I need some water," Wolfe said, heading for the kitchen.

Jessica's eyes followed him every step of the way.

"Never let it be said that Matthew Moran sat on his hands when a beautiful woman wanted to dance," Reno said.

He went to where Jessica was sitting, bowed, and held out his hand. She put her fingers on his and stood.

"Thank you, kind sir."

Jessica smiled, curtsied, and stepped into Reno's

arms with a grace that had been learned from the finest tutors in the British Empire.

In the kitchen, Wolfe drank one cup of water, then another, cursing silently the whole time. He had wanted very much to hold Jessica, to feel her softness and warmth, to stand so close to her that he could smell her delicate rose perfume and see the intense clarity of her eyes.

Now another man was doing all those things.

The cup hit the sink with a metallic cry that was lost in the music of Caleb's harmonica. A few silent strides brought Wolfe to the kitchen door. He stood in the shadows there, leaning against the door frame, watching Jessica with a hunger he could no longer hide. Her raspberry silk dress made her skin glow like fragile porcelain lit from within. The simple chignon Willow had taught Jessica to create emphasized the delicate lines of her face. Tendrils of hair escaped to lie in soft curves at her temples, nape, and ears.

Even as Wolfe felt anger snaking through his body at the sight of his wife burning like a candle flame in another man's arms, Wolfe reminded himself there was nothing improper about the waltz. Though Reno's unusual size made an intense contrast to Jessica's fragile femininity, Reno was holding her properly, neither too close to his body nor too familiar in the placement of his hands. Nor was Jessica clinging too much. They were simply dipping and turning and skimming gracefully around the living room to the haunting melody played by Caleb.

Then the darkly handsome Reno smiled down at Jessica and began singing in his fine voice about "One morning, one morning, one morning in May . . ." when a soldier spied a Scots lass dreaming by a clear meadow stream. The soldier's manly charms quickly seduced the pretty girl, who pleaded for his arms and his name in marriage. The arms she received, and more besides, but not his name. He was already twice married—once to the army, once to a woman. Though he was a stout man, he declared he wasn't up to the demands of yet another wife.

Reno's light green eyes shimmered with suppressed humor as he watched Jessica react to the wry lyrics. Her silver laughter bubbled up contagiously, drawing smiles and more laughter from everyone in the room.

Except Wolfe. He was too angry to smile. Seeing the change wrought by Reno on Jessica's wan appearance made Wolfe feel murderous. The only thing that prevented him from going back into the other room and wrenching his wife from Reno's arms was the fact that Rafe was already there, cutting in neatly.

"My turn, little brother."

"I'm as big as you are," Reno pointed out.

"You're eleven months younger."

With an amused smile, Reno bowed to Jessica and released her to Rafe's arms.

"I'm a little rusty," Rafe admitted. "Australians ran more to fighting and drinking than fancy footwork. I haven't danced with a lady in a long, long time."

"I'm certain you'll do fine. Anyone who walks, rides, and wields a bullwhip as well as you do has a lot of natural coordination."

"Thanks, but maybe you better stand on my big feet just the same. Wildflowers aren't safe when an elephant dances."

Jessica ducked her head and tried not to giggle.

It was impossible. Rafe towered over her, his gray eyes vivid with teasing laughter. Despite his warning, he danced well, whirling her easily around the room until she was breathless with laughter.

Unnoticed, Wolfe leaned against the wall with his arms crossed over his chest, watching with an impassive face and eyes that promised Hell.

Reno helped Willow to her feet and danced her carefully around the room, moving with half the speed of Rafe and Jessica. Caleb looked over his harmonica at his wife, winked, and slowed the music even more. She smiled back at him, but still couldn't last more than twice around the room. When Reno waltzed her past Caleb's position on the couch, she let go of her brother and settled next to her husband. He pulled her closely against his body without breaking the rhythm of the dance.

Reno headed for Rafe and Jessica. Brother tapped brother firmly on the shoulder. Rafe winked at Jessica and spun her quickly, lifting her beyond Reno's reach. A moment later, Reno was back again.

"Wait," Jessica said, smiling equally at both brothers. "There's a way we can all dance at the same time."

With a few words and gentle pushes, she arranged a brother on each side of her and held out her hands expectantly. On either side, a strong, big hand closed over hers. She looked from side to side, struck by the similarity in the shape of each brother's hand. Though their hair and eye color were quite different, their blood relationship was clear in their strength and in the flat nails of their hands.

"Now, like this," Jessica said. "Step right, cross over behind, dip, straighten, step right . . ."

Both men caught on quickly. Soon they were moving as one on either side of Jessica.

Wolfe stood in the doorway, staring at the woman who looked stunningly feminine caught between the two Moran brothers. Barely five feet two inches tall, she was thirteen inches shorter than either man, yet there was nothing childlike in the proportions of her body. The curves of breast and hip, waist and ankle, showed clearly against the soft folds of her dress as the cloth swirled fluidly with her movements.

Finally the waltz wound to a slow finish. Rafe and Reno smiled over Jessica's auburn head. Both men lifted one of Jessica's hands to their lips and kissed it. She curtsied deeply, graceful as flame. Though neither man spoke the thought aloud, it was clear from their expressions that they were thoroughly enchanted by their dance partner.

"Again, Caleb," Willow murmured. "That tune is one of my favorites."

The strains of the waltz flowed through the room once more. A silent signal passed between the brothers. Smiling, Rafe released Jessica's hand and sat down.

Soon Reno and Jessica were swirling around the room again. Reno held his partner lightly, looking down at her with approving green eyes, singing in his fine voice. No one could hear Reno's words but Jessica, who flushed and then laughed with transparent pleasure. Reno spun quickly, taking Jessica with him, making her skirt billow like wind-blown flame. He stopped and dipped deeply, forcing her to depend upon his strength for her balance. When she accepted his lead without protest, his smile flashed, transforming his face, making him handsome enough to stop a woman's breath.

An icy rage gripped Wolfe.

When I touch her, she berates me as the viscount's savage, yet when Reno holds her, she looks at him as though he had just come to earth on a bolt of lightning.

I don't know who is the greater fool—me for caring, or Reno for being taken in by the conniving little aristocrat.

Wolfe crossed the living room with a predatory grace that warned Rafe and Caleb of what was coming. Reno didn't notice Wolfe's approach, for his attention was completely on Jessica's laughter, the unusual color of her eyes, and the firelight caught in her hair. The hard masculine tap on his shoulder came as a surprise.

"Patience, big brother," Reno said. "You'll get your turn."

"I will get all of the turns."

The cold anger in Wolfe's voice made Reno's head snap around. He took one look at Wolfe and released Jessica without a word. She started to smile at Wolfe, but when she saw his eyes her smile vanished. She stumbled as he spun her away from Reno.

"Sorry," she said, catching her balance by holding on to Wolfe. "You startled me."

Wolfe didn't bother to politely pretend that it had been his error in rhythm rather than Jessica's that had caused her to stumble.

"I will do more than startle you if you insist on seducing every man within reach."

Wolfe's tone was as hard as his eyes. Though his voice was too low to carry beyond Jessica, each word was distinct, making her flinch as though at a blow.

"I wasn't seducing—"

"The hell you weren't, your ladyship," Wolfe said icily, cutting across her words. "Now listen to me and listen well. You forced this marriage. Until you agree to end it, you will act in public as a married woman. This isn't Great Britain, nor are the Moran brothers members of British aristocracy. In this time and place, married women have no other man but their husband, and married men have no other woman but their wife. Do you understand me? There will be no lovers for you or for me while this farce of a marriage lasts."

Before Jessica could answer or protest, Wolfe released her and walked toward the Moran brothers. The music stopped as though cut off by a knife.

"Gentlemen," Wolfe said with deadly softness, "don't be fooled by appearances. Lady Jessica forced our marriage by claiming that I had seduced her. I did not. She is as virginal tonight as she was on the instant of her birth. *Yet we are married.* The little nun prefers it that way, for she knows I won't force her. She believes she can remain forever a spoiled child, playing at marriage, playing at keeping house, playing at being a woman."

The silence that followed Wolfe's words was so absolute that the wail of the wind outside was almost shocking in its volume. Wolfe looked from Rafe to Reno and resumed speaking in the same soft, savagely controlled voice.

"Enjoy Jessica's smile, enjoy her laughter, enjoy her lively conversation, but don't get your guts in a knot over a spoiled little tease who whimpers during storms and can't even build a fire—in or out of bed. Wait for the right woman, one like Willow, a woman, not a girl, a woman strong enough to fight by your side if she must, passionate enough to set fire to your soul as well as your body, and generous enough to give you children despite the risk to her own life. Jessica is not that woman."

Wolfe turned on his heel and stalked to the front door. The cry of the wind increased as the door opened. Without a word or a look at his wife, Tree That Stands Alone vanished into the windy night.

 12

JESSICA slept more badly than usual that night, for Wolfe's icy summation of her failures as a Western woman kept echoing in her mind, sliding past all inner barriers, cutting her in ways she couldn't name. All she could do was endure as she had endured in the past, putting pain and memories behind her, forcing them into parts of her mind she visited only in nightmares.

But tonight Jessica couldn't fight as she had fought in the past. Tonight she felt her carefully constructed defenses crumbling like a sand castle beneath a rising tide.

When Wolfe came into the room, undressed silently, and slid beneath the blankets, Jessica was more awake than asleep. The scent of him settled over her, evergreens and fresh snow. His hair radiated the cold wind that writhed over the land.

Lying absolutely still, certain that he sensed her wakefulness, Jessica waited for Wolfe to speak to her. When he simply rolled onto his side with his back to her, she closed her eyes and told herself she was grateful not to hear any more cutting words from Tree That Stands Alone.

But she wasn't grateful. She would rather have been berated than continue to lie in bed half-dazed with regret and loneliness, listening to the wind's victorious wail. Shivering with a cold that not even the fur blanket could warm, she waited for sleep to release her. In time, something close to sleep came, but there was no release in it, simply greater vulnerability.

Outside the room, a northern storm descended, fulfilling the harsh promises of the wind. A vast, ice-toothed scythe of sleet sliced horizontally across the land. Pellets of ice hammered over the roof and clawed down windowpanes while the wind screamed in a woman's voice, describing eternal damnation.

Her mother's voice.

Terror that was colder than the storm froze Jessica. Neither asleep nor yet awake, she clenched her teeth against the cries locked within her throat. She would not let Wolfe hear her.

. . . a spoiled little tease who whimpers during storms.

With a soundless cry of despair, Jessica turned her face into the pillow, fighting memories, fighting nightmares, fighting herself. Sensing weakness, the wind howled around her. Its icy fingers pried beneath her control, screaming to her in her mother's voice.

But it was Wolfe's words Jessica heard, Wolfe's words that stripped her to her naked soul.

Wait for the right woman, one like Willow, a woman not a girl . . . a woman passionate enough to set your soul on fire . . . generous enough to give you children despite the risk to her own life.

Jessica is not that woman.

The wind screamed triumphantly as memory, nightmare, and storm combined, telling Jessica that she was alone and the wind was everywhere.

The sounds she refused to make shuddered

through her tense body. Though she managed to stem her own cries, she could not stem the black tide of memories drowning her, a childhood recalled by her mother's voice screaming with the wind, incidents she had spent a lifetime hiding from except in nightmares, and those she refused to remember upon awakening.

But Jessica finally was awake now. She was remembering her mother's screams and her father's curses, two figures interlocked on the hallway floor in brutal sexual combat.

I won't remember!

Yet Jessica could not stop remembering.

Abruptly, she knew she could control her cries no longer. There was only one place where she would be free. Outside, in the center of the wind's violence, where nothing living could hear her scream.

Just as Jessica's legs slid over the edge of the bed, a powerful arm snaked around her waist and hauled her backward. The contact was unexpected, an extension of her nightmare where her father's thick arm hooked around her fleeing mother, dragging her down to the mating she had fought with every bit of strength in her small body.

Wolfe sensed the wild tension in Jessica the instant before she exploded. He put his free hand over her mouth, shutting off her scream as he bore her down beneath him on the bed. After a flurry of struggle, he overwhelmed her attempts to be free of him. Soon she was helpless, her arms stretched above her head, her wrists locked together in one of Wolfe's hands, his other hand clamped over her mouth, and his big body pinning her so completely she could barely breathe. Screaming was impossible. So was escape.

"If you think I'm going to let you tiptoe off to have your feelings soothed by one of those fine Moran brothers, you're crazy," Wolfe said in a low, savage voice.

At first the words didn't register through Jessica's panic. Finally, the simple fact that she was helpless but not being hurt penetrated her fear. It was Wolfe imprisoning her. It was Wolfe speaking to her. Wolfe, whom she had trusted from the first moment she saw him. Wolfe, who would never hurt her as her mother had been hurt. Wolfe, who had been her talisman against nightmare and waking terror. Wolfe, who might hate her, but would never rape her.

With a convulsive shudder, Jessica stopped fighting.

"That's better, your ladyship. I know my touch repulses you, but that's too damned bad. You're the one who wanted to be married, not me."

Jessica's eyes widened. She turned her head from side to side, trying to evade Wolfe's hand over her mouth. After a moment, he lifted his palm. She licked her lips and tried to speak. On the third attempt, words came.

"Being touched by you doesn't repulse me," she whispered. "Truly, Wolfe."

"You lie very sweetly, Sister Jessica, but your body tells me the truth," Wolfe said sardonically. "You would have screamed and clawed my eyes out if I had let you. Hardly the act of a girl pleased by a man's touch."

"You don't understand. I was remembering and then you grabbed me, and I didn't know what was memory or nightmare and what was real."

"Save your lies for the Moran brothers. They

believe you're half the woman you look to be. I know better."

Wolfe released Jessica and rolled aside as though repelled by the very feel of her skin.

"Wolfe," she whispered raggedly, reaching out to him. "Wolfe, you're the only one I've ever trusted. Please don't abandon me to the wind. It will steal my mind as surely as it stole hers."

The cold trembling of Jessica's hand on his arm shocked Wolfe almost as much as her words.

"It's just a storm," he said roughly.

"No," Jessica whispered. "It stole her soul. Can't you hear her screaming? *Listen.* It's the cry of a woman newly damned."

A chill moved down Wolfe's spine. The slow shudders that took Jessica's body were transmitted to him by the cold fingers clinging to his arm. Despite his anger, he could no more turn away from her naked pleas than he could walk out of his own skin. He put his hand over hers, trying to warm her fingers.

"Jessi . . . it's just the wind, no more."

She didn't hear Wolfe. She heard only the keening cry of her memories. Wide-eyed, motionless but for the trembling she couldn't control, she lay and listened to the wind, knowing that soon her mother would drag herself from her father's bed and walk the stone hallways, crying and wailing, her screams rising and falling in awful harmony with the wind.

"Jessi?"

There was no answer but her quick, shallow breaths. Slowly, Wolfe gathered Jessica against his body. Though she was so tense that she was all but rigid, she didn't fight his embrace. She simply lay against him, quivering like a bowstring drawn to the breaking point. He had felt the same shivering in her once before, when he had held her amid a fragrant haystack while a wild storm hammered all around. She had been crying with fear then.

He found himself wishing that she would weep now.

She didn't. She simply lay and shuddered at random, finally driven beyond her ability to endure. The knowledge that he had pushed Jessica to the point of breaking brought no triumph to Wolfe. Had he been able, he would have undone every hurtful word. He had never meant to bring her this low.

"It's all right, elf," Wolfe said gently. He stroked Jessica's back, trying to draw some of the tension from her. "Nothing can harm you. I'll keep you safe."

"I thought so once," she whispered. A shudder racked her body. "Nothing can hold back the wind."

"The wind can't hurt you." Wolfe's hand smoothed slowly over Jessica's soft hair. "You're safe with me."

The silence went on so long Wolfe became uneasy. He turned aside for a moment to light a candle, thinking that the warm dance of flame would comfort Jessica. When he turned back, she was watching the window with a fixed stare that made his skin cold.

"Jessi?" he whispered.

"Dinna ye hear her, laddie?" Jessica asked, her voice and accents that of the Scots child she once had been.

Ice slid down Wolfe's spine. "Who do you hear?"

Jessica blinked and her voice changed, her accents becoming clipped, English. "The earl is at mum again. First the screaming and then the bleeding and then the burying."

Wolfe looked down at Jessica. Her eyes were still wide, still focused on something only she could see, something that so horrified her that she was literally chilled by the sight.

"Tell me what you see," Wolfe commanded gently.

She closed her eyes. *"I will not remember."*

"You must. It's eating you alive. Name your devil and it can't own you. Name it, Jessi. Nothing is worse than what you now feel."

Thunder broke in an avalanche of sound that shook the house. Jessica didn't flinch, for she was caught in a far older, far more violent storm. Her eyes opened. They were sightless, fixed on a past only she could see.

"The earl wants a son," she whispered. There was no English accent, no Scots burr, nothing but the rhythms and accents of the West.

Wolfe stroked Jessica's hair, trying to reassure her.

"Go on," he said softly.

"The earl wants a son."

"Yes, I understand."

"Mother doesn't want to breed. She never wanted to breed after the first time. It near killed her."

Wolfe's hand hesitated as he remembered Jessica's certainty that women never wanted another child after bearing the first. Slowly, he continued the soothing downward motion of his hand over Jessica's tangled hair.

"Is your father angry about your mother?"

"Always. He's drunk. He's walking down the

hall to mother's room. The door is locked. He hammers on it and hammers on it. I can't hear a lot of what he yells because it's storming and she is screaming again."

Wolfe closed his eyes for an instant, hoping that the suspicions coiling coldly in his gut were wrong.

"Does your mother open the door?" he asked.

"No."

With a silent sigh of relief, Wolfe asked, "What else do you see?"

"He takes an ax to the door. Thunder and chopping and screaming. She sounds just like the wind screaming."

Wolfe closed his eyes for an instant. Very gently, he brushed his lips over Jessica's forehead. Her skin was clammy.

"He drags her into the hall," Jessica continued, "swearing he'll have a son of her if it's the last thing either one of them ever does. Some nights I thought it would be."

Wolfe's heart turned over as he sensed what was coming next. "Jessi . . ."

She didn't hear. "Mother would fight and he would beat her until she was quiet so he could rut on her. When it was over she just lay there until I came and washed off the blood and took her back to bed."

"Merciful God," Wolfe breathed, horrified. "You were just a child!"

Jessica kept talking as though Wolfe hadn't spoken. She no longer wanted to stem the floodtide of memories. She wanted only to make Wolfe understand that she hadn't withdrawn from him because he repulsed her.

"Sometimes she simply miscarried after weeks of sickness," Jessica continued relentlessly. "Sometimes she grew big despite the endless vomiting and fainting. Then she slowly turned yellow and was brought screaming to a childbed, knowing the babe within was dead. No one from the village would tend her, for they believed her cursed. I stayed with her."

"Jessi . . ." Wolfe's voice broke.

"When it was finished, I washed and dressed the tiny corpse in a christening gown. They were like wax dolls, as still and pale as the marble head-stone we placed on the grave. Six headstones all in a row."

Jessica looked through Wolfe with wide, dilated eyes. "I did what I could to keep the wind from taking them and her. The wind took them anyway, and finally it took her. I heard their voices in every storm, yet I hear hers most of all. She's calling to me, reminding me what horror awaits women in the marriage bed."

Wolfe started to touch Jessica comfortingly, then stopped, not wanting to frighten her. He finally understood all too well how a man's touch could horrify her.

A final, violent shudder went through Jessica's body. When it passed, she focused on Wolfe for the first time since memories had claimed her. She could see little more of him than his outline against the golden glow of the candle. Hesitantly, she lifted her hands to his face, needing reassurance of his reality.

"You are so warm," she breathed.

Slowly, she caressed Wolfe's cheeks, enjoying the heat of life burning beneath his skin, warming herself as though he were a fire. The simple hunger for his warmth made Wolfe understand how cold she had felt. He tried to speak, but had no words to equal the mixture of emotions tangled within him.

"I didn't mean to fight you," Jessica whispered, struggling to keep her voice from breaking. "Not my own Wolfe." Her arms went around Wolfe's neck as she pressed her face against his chest. "Please don't hate me. You're the only one I've ever trusted."

Wolfe felt the sudden heat of her tears against his neck and his own eyes burned. He made a low sound and touched her cheek with a hand that trembled.

"I don't hate you, Jessi," he said hoarsely. "Never that."

She turned to press a kiss against his palm.

"Thank you," she whispered.

"Don't turn the knife," he said, his voice fraying. "I should be the one asking you not to hate me. I thought you were just spoiled and stubborn. I didn't know you were fighting for your life."

Wolfe's lips brushed repeatedly over Jessica's eyelids and lashes, taking her tears. "Don't cry, elf. Don't cry. It tears out my heart. Please stop. I'll never be cruel like that again."

"I'm s-sorry. I know my tears d-disgust you, but I—"

Wolfe's thumb pressed gently against Jessica's lips, stilling her words. "Your tears don't disgust me."

"But you s-said—"

His thumb pressed against her lips once more. "Hush, little one. When I said that, I was furious because I thought my touch repulsed you."

"Never," Jessica said instantly, tightening her arms around Wolfe's neck. "Never never never! You were my talisman against the wind. I carried you inside my heart, but then you started hating me and there was nothing left but the wind."

Wolfe's throat closed as an agonizing combination of sorrow and self-contempt claimed him. His arms tightened, holding Jessica close enough to feel her breath against his skin.

"Where were you going when I stopped you a few minutes ago?" he asked finally.

"To the wind."

When Wolfe tried to speak, he couldn't. Then words came in a whispered rush, her name repeated with every breath as he brushed kisses over her eyelids and cheeks. He wanted to tell her how much he regretted hurting her, yet all he could think of was how he had failed to understand her.

When I'm with you, I don't hear the wind.

Then he had turned on her and driven her toward the very thing that most terrified her.

"I'm sorry, Jessi," Wolfe whispered finally. "If I had known, I never would have been so harsh. Can you believe that?"

Jessica nodded, her face pressed tightly against Wolfe's neck.

"Can you forgive me?" he asked.

Again she nodded, and held him even more tightly.

He made an odd sound. "I don't know how you can. I find I can't forgive myself."

Silently, Wolfe held Jessica until at last he felt the violent tension begin to ebb from her body. She still flinched if the wind shook the house, but she no longer trembled like an aspen leaf in a storm. Finally she let out a long, broken sigh and kissed the curve of Wolfe's neck where her face had been pressed. The skin was warm and wet with her tears.

"I seem to have cried all over you."

"I don't mind."

Jessica tilted her head back until she could see Wolfe's eyes. "Truly?"

"Truly."

She smiled with lips that still had a faint trembling. "Does that mean you've forgiven me?"

"I told you, Jessi. I didn't mean what I said about your tears disgusting me."

"No. I meant do you forgive me for trapping you into marriage?"

There was a heartbeat of silence before Wolfe sighed. "You believed you were fighting for your life. I can't blame you for that."

"I didn't know how unfair it would be to you," Jessica whispered as tears overflowed again. "I believed I would be a good wife for you, truly I did. I didn't know how lacking I was in . . . everything."

Wolfe's thumb smoothed over her lips, stilling the words she would have spoken next. "Don't belittle yourself, Jessi. It's not your fault that I'm a halfbreed bastard. You will make a fine wife for a lord."

"Stop," she said, pressing her fingers over his mouth.

Gently, he lifted her hand and continued speaking. "It's the truth. You were born and raised to grace a lord's castle."

"The truth is you're a man to turn every woman's head, and her heart as well. Surely you know that, Wolfe."

"I know that looks aren't much of a recommendation in men, horses, dogs, or women," he said dryly.

Jessica smiled despite the tears that fell slowly down her cheeks. "'Tis not just your looks, my

Lord Wolfe, and well you know it. You are so very much a man."

Wolfe bent and brushed his mouth over the silver trails of her tears. "Stay beneath the covers, Jessi. I'll be right back."

As Wolfe got out of bed, he pulled on the dark pants he had discarded earlier. When he stood, he sensed Jessica watching him. He glanced over his shoulder and saw the admiration in her eyes as she looked at his naked back. Desire coiled within him, but no anger followed. He finally understood that she wasn't teasing him just to watch him squirm. Jessica didn't realize what her look invited. She would have been frightened if she did know. Given what she had seen of sex, he expected nothing else.

When Wolfe returned, he was carrying a small glass of brandy in one hand and a pan of warm water in the other. He put the pan on the bedside table, sat on the bed, and warmed the glass in his hands. Soon the heady aroma of brandy curled upward.

"I want you to think of this as medicine," Wolfe said. "It will ease the last of the coldness inside you."

"How did you know I feel cold inside?"

He shrugged. "I've known the black ice of fear. It's not something you forget."

Startled, she watched him with wide aquamarine eyes. "You?"

Wolfe smiled at her look of disbelief. "Many times."

"When?"

"One of the worst times was when I saw a bull buffalo thundering toward Lord Robert after his horse stepped in a prairie dog hole and went down. I was the length of the herd from him, riding bareback at a dead gallop. I had seen Cheyenne hunters killed by buffalo. I knew what would happen if I missed my shot."

"You didn't miss."

"No, I didn't. But sometimes I think it would have been better if I had."

When Wolfe saw the shock in Jessica's face, the corner of his mouth turned down. Silently, he encouraged her to take a drink of brandy. She swallowed, grimaced, and swallowed again.

"I didn't mean I wished Lord Robert dead," Wolfe said finally. "But if I hadn't made such a spectacular shot, he would have left me with the Cheyenne. I was thirteen, just coming into the mysteries of being a warrior."

Jessica watched Wolfe over the rim of the brandy glass, her eyes intent, reflecting the dance of candlelight.

"Maybe it wouldn't have made any difference if I had stayed," Wolfe said, shrugging. "I was never fully Cheyenne. Part of me was always fascinated by the land across the sea where my father lived. Yet I was never fully British. Too much of me belonged to campfires and wild lands. The viscount's bloody savage."

She made a soft sound of protest.

Wolfe shrugged again. "In the end I became neither Indian nor British. I became a man who chooses his own way, his own rules, his own life."

"A Western man."

He smiled oddly. "Yes. A man with neither home nor family, and a past that was too painful to keep."

For a moment, Wolfe looked beyond Jessica. The sadness in his expression was almost tangible. Tears stung her eyes once more, for she knew what he was thinking: He was a Western man married to a woman who was all wrong for him.

"Wolfe," she said huskily.

"Finish the brandy, elf. Then I'll bathe your face and hands with rosewater. Afterward, if you like, I'll hold you so that you don't hear the wind while you fall asleep."

Jessica started to speak, only to have Wolfe's thumb press gently against her lips.

"Drink up. It will take the knots from your muscles almost as well as a rubdown."

Memories of the night Wolfe had rubbed scented oil into Jessica's aching body leaped between them like invisible lightning.

"Don't worry, Jessi," he said matter-of-factly. "I won't ever frighten you like that again. You don't have to fight for your life with me."

Eyes closed, Jessica lifted the glass and drained the last of the fragrant brandy, wondering why she felt unhappy rather than relieved.

"Wolfe?" She coughed and swallowed quickly. "Are all—that is—are most—" She coughed again.

"Slow down, elf." Wolfe eased Jessica back onto the pillows and tucked the fur blanket up over her breasts. "Let yourself relax."

He reached into the basin of warm water, retrieved a linen cloth, and wrung it out. Gently he washed her face, removing the trail of tears.

"Wolfe?"

He made a questioning sound that was rather like the purr of a very large cat.

"I thought all marriages were like my mother's," Jessica said.

"I realize that. Now."

"But they aren't, are they?"

"No."

"Even in the marriage bed?"

"Especially there," Wolfe said, wringing out the cloth. "If there is affection between husband and wife, the marriage bed is a place of pleasure for both of them. If there is love . . . if there is love, I suspect that paradise holds no greater joy."

The cloth moved gently down Jessica's arm. For long moments, the scented cloth lay over the sensitive inside of her wrist, where life pulsed softly beneath fine-grained skin.

"Most men," Wolfe continued as he smoothed the cloth over her palm and fingers, "aren't drunken or cruel. They take no pleasure in a woman's pain."

Jessica watched Wolfe with wide, intent eyes.

"Any man worthy of the name knows his own strength," Wolfe continued. "He knows that women are more delicately made, more slow to burn with passion; but once a woman burns, there is no fire to equal it, not even a man's. She will share that fire generously with a careful partner."

"Despite the pain?"

"An aroused woman feels only pleasure when she holds a man inside her body. That shared fire is the sweetest kind of burning. For both of them."

"Fire without pain," Jessica whispered, remembering.

A wave of desire went through Wolfe, but nothing of his response showed as he turned away to rinse the cloth once more.

"Yes," he said, as he bathed Jessica's other arm. "Fire without pain."

Motionless, she watched Wolfe with clear, steady eyes, loving the black angles of his eyebrows, the slightly shaggy thickness of his hair, the bottomless indigo twilight of his eyes, and the sharply defined peaks of his upper lip.

"When the fire is finally quenched," Wolfe continued, drawing the cloth down Jessica's arm, "there is the serenity of lying together in the dark and knowing you have found your true mate. There is a rightness in being joined that goes all the way to the soul. There is power as well, the power of being able to summon ecstasy at will. It's a godlike power. It's the power of creation, of life itself."

"Have you—" Jessica's voice broke as sadness overwhelmed her. When she spoke again, it was a bare whisper. "Have you known that with a woman?"

"I've had lovers. Surely that doesn't surprise you."

"I wasn't talking about your penchant for duchesses."

Wolfe looked up from the slender fingers he wanted to kiss and saw tears magnifying Jessica's eyes until they were extraordinary gems.

"What are you trying to ask me?" Wolfe said.

She closed her eyes and whispered, "Have you lain in the darkness with your true mate and felt the rightness of it all the way to your soul?"

"If I had, I would have married. Yet I know that kind of closeness can exist between a man and a woman."

Jessica started to ask how Wolfe knew if he had never experienced it, but the answer came from her own knowledge.

"Caleb and Willow."

"Yes," Wolfe agreed. "Caleb and Willow."

Sadness caught in Jessica's throat. "Is—does—that is—oh, blazes," she said despairingly, unable to order her scattering thoughts.

Wolfe's thumb pressed lightly against her lips. "Slow down, elf. You'll get yourself tied in knots again. Would you like more brandy?"

"I'll get muzzled," she muttered beneath his thumb.

He smiled gently. "I don't think so. You've had only a teaspoon or two."

When Wolfe started to get up from the bed, Jessica's hands closed around his powerful wrist.

"Wolfe? What if—that is—do only people like Willow and Caleb find pleasure in—in touching?"

A slow, very male smile was all the answer Jessica needed.

"You don't have to be a paragon, if that's what you mean," Wolfe said.

"Would you—" Jessica's voice broke. She took a deep breath and held onto Wolfe's wrist as though it were a lifeline. "Touch me. Teach me."

Wolfe's eyes widened, then narrowed in response to the elemental tightening of his body. "I won't take you, Jessi. That would make annulment impossible. I'm the wrong husband for you. You're the wrong wife for me. Lying with you would be the worst mistake of my life."

For an instant, Jessica's nails bit deeply into Wolfe's wrist. Then she released him and lay back with her eyes closed, too ashamed even to look at him any longer.

"Sorry," she said tonelessly. "For a moment I forgot what you thought of me. You should have let me go to the wind. It would have been kinder. But then, you haven't felt kindly toward me since the night I ran to your room after Lord Gore attacked me."

"Jessi, you aren't thinking at all," Wolfe said. His fingers went from Jessica's pale cheek to the soft curve of her mouth. "Or have you decided you want to be pregnant?"

Her eyes flew open. They were dark with fear, haunted by nightmare.

"Don't panic," he said calmly. "I said I wasn't going to take you. I meant it. We're just wrong for each other as man and wife."

"I can't let you go. I'm sorry, but I can't. The thought of lying beneath the likes of Lord Gore . . ." Revulsion rippled visibly through Jessica's body.

"Not all lords are brutal sots."

She simply shut her eyes and shook her head. Candlelight twisted and ran through her hair like threads of fire. Wolfe's fingertips traced one of the long locks so softly that Jessica didn't feel his touch.

"There are young, handsome, decent lords in Britain," Wolfe said, lifting his hand. "I'll see that Lady Victoria finds one for you."

"I would sooner marry the wind than suffer a man's touch."

"And a halfbreed is somehow not quite a man, is that it?" Wolfe asked harshly.

Her eyes flew open in astonishment. "I never said that or anything like it!"

"Didn't you?" Wolfe leaned over, flattening his hands on either side of Jessica's body. "First you ask me to touch you, then you say you'll never suffer a man's touch. *Am I not a man?*"

"But you are so much more than other men," she whispered. With trembling fingertips she traced the black line of Wolfe's eyebrows and the fierce brackets on either side of his mouth. "So much more . . ."

Wolfe couldn't prevent the primitive shiver of response that went through him at Jessica's words, at her touch, at the emotion in her eyes.

"Jessi," he breathed, shaken. He turned his head and kissed her fingertips, then spoke before he could think better of it. "There are ways of touching that will give you intense pleasure, yet leave you still a virgin. Do you understand me?"

Slowly, she shook her head, watching him with luminous eyes.

"I can give you ecstasy without taking your maidenhead," Wolfe said simply.

Jessica's eyes widened.

He smiled. "Oh, elf, the look on your face . . ."

"Is such a thing possible?" she asked, ignoring the heat creeping up her cheeks.

"Quite possible. There will be no pain for you, no risk of pregnancy. You will be a virgin still."

"How can that be?"

Wolfe bent down and brushed his lips against Jessica's ear. "I'll show you, but you'll have to help me."

"How?"

"I'll show you that, too."

 **13**

VERY gently, Wolfe's fingers slid into the wild, silky depths of Jessica's hair. He rubbed her scalp slowly.

"You have wonderful hands," she said, sighing. "They quite unravel me."

Smiling, Wolfe traced the rim of Jessica's ear with his tongue. She made a startled sound as sensations coursed through her, leaving a trail of goosebumps on her arms.

"Such a tiny cry," he said. "Did I frighten you?"

Jessica shook her head and watched him with heavy-lidded eyes. The scent of roses curled up from her unbound hair. Wolfe's nostrils flared as he took in the scent.

"Tell me how it made you feel," he murmured.

"Is that how you want me to help you?"

"That's one way."

"You made me feel shivery and yet very still at the same time," Jessica said, watching Wolfe. "I think a rosebud must feel that way at the first touch of the sun."

Wolfe's breath came out in a silent rush as he fought for control. "You humble me, Jessi."

She would have asked why, but the tip of Wolfe's tongue was tracing her ear once more, drawing forth another delicate tremor of sensation. Her breath caught again.

"I didn't know," she said.

"What?" he murmured against her ear.

"How sensitive my ear was." She sighed and stretched her neck, silently offering herself to his mouth. "And how good my Lord Wolfe's tongue feels."

His heartbeat paused, then deepened as sleek talons of need sank into his body. He nuzzled Jessica's soft earlobe before he caught it very gently between his teeth. He heard her breath break, then unravel in a shivering sigh.

"And your Lord Wolfe's teeth," he whispered. "How do you like them?"

Jessica's answer was to arch her neck while her hands pushed her long hair above her head, baring her neck and ear to his mouth. With a rather fierce smile, Wolfe accepted her offering. His tongue traced her ear once more, spiraling inward until she gasped at the warm penetration. He continued the rhythmic strokes until her voice broke over his name. Slowly he released her and lifted his head, enjoying the sight of her half-closed eyes and her hair fanned over the pillow.

"Is that all?" Jessica asked wistfully.

Laughing softly, Wolfe shook his head. "Where would you like to be kissed next?"

"Where else would it feel that good?"

"There are places where it will feel even better."

Jessica's eyes widened as she read the confidence in Wolfe. "Truly?"

"Oh yes." Wolfe looked from her parted lips to the curves of her body beneath the covers. "But you'll have to keep helping me."

"Does that mean I get to bite your ear?"

The combination of mischief and innocent passion in Jessica's voice made Wolfe laugh even as he felt the vital hardening of his body.

"It means I want you to keep telling me how it feels when I touch you," Wolfe said.

"I'd rather bite your ear."

He laughed, delighted by the sultry teasing in her eyes. "Not yet, Jessi. It would distract me."

"Distraction? Is that what you call those odd butterfly shivers in the pit of my stomach?"

"In a way. Those shivers are the beginning of passion, and passion is damned distracting."

Jessica hesitated, giving Wolfe a look through lowered eyelashes. "That's what I was afraid of. Being passionate."

"Are you still afraid?"

"Not with you."

Wolfe kissed her gently. "Good, because I suspect I've never known a more passionate woman, but exploring your passion will require physical intimacy. Not consummation. Just . . . intimacy. That kind of intimacy disgusted you before."

"Do you mean . . ." Jessica flushed and swallowed. "After you bathed me, when you . . . ?"

"Yes. When I put my hand between your legs."

Jessica covered her flaming cheeks with her palms. "Dear God, Wolfe. I don't know if I can speak of such things."

"Too disgusting?" he asked neutrally.

She shook her head.

"Talk to me, Jessi. The last thing I want to do is frighten or repel you."

"How about embarrassing me?" she muttered.

"I like that idea." Wolfe looked at the curves of her body beneath the fur cover. "I'll keep it in mind. Now talk to me."

"Talk?" Jessica asked in disbelief. "I can't even think at the thought of you touching me like that. I keep remembering how I accidentally caught your hand between my legs in the bath and your skin felt so much nicer than the sponge, but remembering makes me shiver and turns my heart upside down and I can't breathe for the velvet butterflies filling me and you're asking me to carry on a conversation as though we're in Lord Robert's library discussing the relative merits of Keats and Shelley!"

As soon as Wolfe untangled the torrent of words, he smiled and kissed the hands that shielded her hot cheeks.

"You felt unbelievably soft to me, both in the bath and in the bed," Wolfe said. "Touching you made me shiver and turned my heart upside down and I couldn't breathe."

Slowly Jessica lowered her hands. "Feeling like that doesn't unnerve you?"

"It should," he admitted ruefully, "but all I can think of is what a sweet delight you are to touch, and how brave you are to trust me despite your fears."

"I suspect you're saying I have no more sense than a spring rosebud."

"I suspect I'm saying I have no more brains than the sun that unwraps the rose." Wolfe bent down to Jessica's mouth, stopping only when he was so close he could feel her breath flowing over his lips. "Will you let me touch you the way sunlight touches a spring bud?"

Jessica's breath caught. "How does sunlight touch a bud?"

"Gently. Completely. Everywhere."

Her breath came out in a soft rush that Wolfe

tasted, for his mouth was covering hers. When his tongue drew a warm line over the sensitive edge of her mouth, she opened it in surprise. His tongue slid inside. Unexpected pleasure shivered through Jessica.

"I didn't mean to shock you," Wolfe said against Jessica's lips. "I warned you it would be . . . intimate."

"You didn't shock me. The butterflies did."

"Butterflies?"

"Don't look behind you, but the parrot is back."

"Hammer the parrot." Wolfe caught her lower lip tenderly between his teeth. "Tell me about the butterflies."

"I think they're made of fire, not velvet."

"Do you want to find out?"

"Yes, but please don't misunderstand if I'm startled and draw back," Jessica said softly. "You don't repulse me, Wolfe. You're the most beautifully made man I've ever seen."

"Sweet little liar. Either of Willow's brothers is more handsome than I am."

"Tree That Stands Alone, you are blind. When you walk into a room, all men are in your shade. You alone catch the light."

Jessica felt the tiny shuddering that went through Wolfe and knew that her words had moved him.

"Does that mean you'll let me kiss you intimately again?" he asked when he could trust himself to speak.

"Yes," she whispered. "Please."

The gliding heat of Wolfe's kiss sent glittering sensations from Jessica's tongue to her knees. She pressed her fingers deeply into his hair, wanting to touch more of him, wanting to be closer, wanting to feel more of the intriguing, shimmering pleasure.

The kiss deepened, strengthened. Wolfe consumed the soft warmth of Jessica's mouth until the world shrank and began to spin slowly around her. The feeling was new but not frightening, for he was still with her, as close as her breath, closer.

He was her breath.

She wound her arms tightly around Wolfe's neck, knowing he was strong enough to keep her safe in the world he had created with his kiss, a world of languid heat and butterfly wings brushed with fire. When he tried to lift his head, she protested and searched out his tongue with her own, wanting the kiss never to end.

Strong arms slid beneath Jessica as Wolfe lifted her from between the sheets. The flexing and shifting of his powerful body was another kind of fire caressing her. The bare skin of his chest and arms and back felt better to her palms than the soft fur on which she now lay. She tested the power of his torso, sinking her fingertips into resilient muscles, scoring him softly with her nails.

A deep sound vibrated through Wolfe as hunger knotted fiercely in his body, making his muscles cord up beneath Jessica's exploring hands.

"Wolfe?" Jessica whispered. "Is something wrong?"

"No. I just learned that elves have tiny golden claws, that's all."

"What?"

He laughed deep in his throat as he looked at her dazed, sultry eyes and flushed lips. "You taste of brandy," he said.

"So do you."

"I taste of you. Lick my lips, Jessi. Let me feel

that soft little tongue in my mouth again."

Surprise shivered through her. "I didn't real-ize..."

Wolfe made a questioning sound that was also a purr of anticipation.

"The kiss," she whispered. "I didn't know how intimate it had become until I heard your words. I *tasted* you."

"The brandy was all you."

"The rest of it wasn't. You're so warm and almost salty and almost sweet." Jessica shivered. "Like wine, your taste keeps changing. And like wine, you make me dizzy."

"Jessi," Wolfe said thickly, "you're going to burn me alive."

When Wolfe's arms tightened, lifting Jessica to his mouth, she went eagerly. He teased her by holding back, kissing her chastely until her arms locked around his neck in an attempt to hold him close for the kind of deep kiss he had taught her to enjoy.

But Wolfe was much too strong to be held. The tiny maddening kisses continued.

"Wolfe?"

He made a purring, questioning sound that ruf-fled her nerves, but there was nothing lazy about his eyes watching her. They smoldered behind his thick lashes.

"Kiss me the way it was before," Jessica whis-pered. "Kiss me so that I can taste you on my tongue."

Wolfe groaned and took her mouth in a seam-less, hot kiss that was more arousing and yet more satisfying than any he had ever known with a woman. His hands kneaded from her scalp to her nape to her hips, shaping her to his body. The silk of her nightgown was more of an enticement than a barrier to his fingers, for the cloth was so sheer that the heat and textures of her body weren't concealed. She was as sleek and supple as a cat beneath the silk, and like a cat she arched in response to the stroking of his hands over her back. When he finally ended the kiss, she was shivering against him as though cold; yet her skin was hot, flushed with passion.

Slowly Wolfe's intent, dark glance went from Jessica's mouth to the pulse beating quickly in her neck and then to her breasts. Her nightgown was a translucent veil too sheer to conceal her body. Her nipples were deep pink, tempting him.

"Remember the bud and the sunlight?" Wolfe asked in a husky voice. "Remember how I warned you that passion is an intimate thing?"

"I find I like that. With you."

"Good, because it begins to get intimate now."

"Begins?" Jessica's eyes widened. *"Begins?"*

"Sweet little red-headed parrot," he murmured. "Yes, it begins. Soon. It will feel good, Jessi. Even better than when I stroked your tongue with mine."

Wolfe's hand went from her neck to the fine-grained skin just below her collarbone. Her breath broke as she suddenly became aware of the sensuous weight of her own breasts. He kissed her lips slowly, deeply, until she gave her mouth to him and demanded his own in return. Only then did his hand shift, covering and cupping and caressing her breasts in the same slow rhythms of his tongue sliding over hers.

"You feel like a captive bird in my hand," Wolfe said. "Your heart is beating so violently. Do I frighten you?"

Jessica tried to speak, but all that came from her lips was a stifled sound. Nerve endings she had never known she had were responding to the slow movement of Wolfe's fingers. A net of fire licked from her breasts to her knees, making it impossible to breathe.

"Help me, Jessi. Let me hear your words. Let me hear your breath breaking if I please you."

Wolfe's fingertips closed over the velvet peak of Jessica's breast. He plucked delicately, listened to the husky breaking of her breath over his name, and felt her nipple harden in a rush that left it pressing against the sheer white silk of her gown.

"I think," he said thickly, "the bud isn't frightened of the sun."

His fingertips moved again and again. He heard the tiny cry from the back of Jessica's throat. When he finally looked away from the hungry pink bud, she was watching him with wide eyes.

"You're trembling," Wolfe said.

"I can't help it. When you look at me like that it's all I can do to breathe."

"How am I looking at you?"

"As though you want to . . ."

Jessica's voice dried up. The heat of her blush radiated beneath his hand.

"As though I want to . . . ?" he asked huskily.

"Kiss me," she whispered. "There."

"Yes. Hold onto me, Jessi. It begins now."

Frozen between disbelief and anticipation, Jessica felt Wolfe's body shift along hers, felt his mouth against the pulse beating frantically in her neck, felt his breath flow warmly over her skin, felt him smooth first one cheek and then the other over her breasts. Distantly she realized that his hands were moving down her body as well. The tiny little fastenings at the front of her gown were dissolving like snow beneath flame. The feel of silk falling away from her breasts made her shiver as her nipples drew into peaks.

Then she realized he meant to undress her completely.

"Wolfe—" her voice broke.

"This is part of intimacy. I won't hurt you, Jessi. Will you let me undress you?"

Her breath came out in a ragged rush. "Yes."

There was a shimmering silence broken only by the secret sounds of Jessica's gown being eased from her body by Wolfe's hands. She trembled visibly, but made no effort to cover herself when the cool air of the room washed over her naked breasts.

"You're perfectly formed," Wolfe said in a hushed voice. Upon the heels of that discovery came another. "And I have dreamed of seeing you like this since your fifteenth summer."

The intensity of Wolfe's voice and his indigo eyes devouring her made Jessica feel both nervous and beautiful. It was a moment before the meaning of his words sank in.

"When I was fifteen?" she asked in a low voice.

"Lady Victoria was right. I wanted you so much I didn't let myself think of you as a woman. But I couldn't control my dreams." Wolfe's voice deepened. "In my dreams I came to you, undressed you, tasted you. My dreams drove me from England."

"Not the duchess and the scandal?"

Without answering, Wolfe ran his fingertips from the pulse beating in Jessica's throat to the lush mahogany cloud at the apex of her thighs and back up again. The sound of his name shivering from her lips made him smile despite the need raking him with claws of fire.

Once Wolfe would have been afraid to continue touching Jessica, afraid to trust his own control. Once, but no longer. He had only to think of what her childhood had been like and ice condensed within him, taking the pain of unrelieved hunger from his body, giving him the strength to enjoy her without claiming her.

Yet the hunger remained, growing with each breath.

"The duchess was a convenience," Wolfe said simply, tracing a line of fire down Jessica's body again. "I thought if I took a lover, my dreams would be my own."

"Were they?"

The words were breathless, squeezed past the tension in Jessica's throat. She wanted to cover herself and hide . . . and she wanted to stretch like a cat beneath Wolfe's hand. The conflicting impulses rippled through her, tightening her nerves until she shivered.

"My dreams haven't been my own since we took shelter from a rainstorm beneath an oak. You were drenched. Your dress clung to your breasts and your nipples stood hard against the cloth."

Wolfe's dark head bent until he could kiss the wild pulse in Jessica's throat.

"I wondered if your nipples would tighten like that for me," he whispered.

The tiny sound Jessica made licked over Wolfe's senses. He set his teeth delicately where her neck curved into her shoulder.

"You haunted me," Wolfe said. "I told myself it was my age, the cold rutting with aristocratic women, my unruly body. I told myself everything but the truth. I wanted you until I couldn't look at you without being aroused."

His mouth glided lower, exploring the warm valley between Jessica's breasts. Her heartbeat shook her, but it was Wolfe's words as much as the warmth of his breath on her bare skin that made her tremble. The tip of his tongue drew a line of molten heat over her.

"You taste like a rose," he whispered.

Wolfe turned his head from side to side, savoring Jessica's warmth and her scent, enjoying her with a frank sensuality that made breath fill her throat until she ached. With a shivering sound she moved beneath him, turning slowly against his caressing mouth without understanding why.

"You're burning me," he whispered.

" 'Tis you who burn me. Your mouth is fire."

Hunger ran through Wolfe, tightening his body until he let out his pent-up breath in a long, soundless sigh.

"You've burned me for so many years," he said. "I was trying to find an excuse for leaving England when the duchess threw her very public tantrum over my absence from her bed. Finally Lord Robert agreed that he could live without the company of his bastard for a time."

Wolfe's dark cheek smoothed over the swell of Jessica's breast. Her hands lifted, but not to push him away. His words disarmed her, seducing her even as his caresses set her afire. She threaded her fingers into the midnight thickness of Wolfe's hair until she could feel the living warmth of his scalp. Sensing the response that went through him, she drew her nails lightly over his scalp once more.

"I wept when I heard you were leaving," she whispered.

"Did you? I saw only your smile and heard only the sharp edge of your tongue over my taste in duchesses."

"I was angry with you."

"You were jealous of me, Jessi. The way a woman is jealous of her man. Lady Victoria saw that. Just as she saw what I concealed even from myself."

"What was that?"

"I couldn't hear your voice, I couldn't smell a rose, I couldn't pass a room where you had recently been without becoming aroused. I was being drawn upon a rack. There was no end to it, no relief in other women, nothing I could do but leave."

Wolfe looked up at Jessica, making no effort to conceal the desire for her that had sunk so deeply into him through the years that he no more noticed it than he noticed the marrow of his bones.

"I didn't know," she whispered.

Trembling, Jessica met Wolfe's eyes. The elemental need in him rushed through her body in a glittering tide.

"I kept my need from you even more carefully than I kept it from myself," he said.

Slowly Wolfe turned his head away. His dark glance went back down her body. The contrast between pale, luminous skin and mahogany fire was new each time he saw it. So was the fullness of her breasts and hips, a lush feminine promise that was repeated in the graceful curves of her legs.

"You took the color from the sky when you left," Jessica whispered. "Oh, Wolfe, I missed you until I thought I would die. I loved you so much. I've always loved you."

His heartbeat hesitated, then resumed with a heavy pulse.

"Don't love me, Jessi. It will only hurt us both. I should have kept my need from you even now. But I can't. You are too beautiful and I have dreamed of you too long."

Wolfe bent to her breasts. His tongue traced the circle where pale satin skin became a pink temptation that he was trying to resist for a few moments longer. The edge of his teeth lightly tested her, drawing a startled sound from Jessica. Her fingers tightened in his hair.

"Don't be frightened," Wolfe breathed against her skin. "I'm not a drunken lord who will maul you until you bleed. I'm a titleless bastard who has waited a lifetime to caress you."

Before Jessica could speak, she saw Wolfe's lips part, knew the unexpected fire of his tongue licking over her nipple, felt the intimate heat of his mouth as he drew her inside. Her back arched reflexively as a thrill of pleasure and surprise shot through her. She called his name and was answered by an increase in the shifting pressure of his mouth. Heedlessly her fingers clenched his hair as sweet sensation twisted through her once more.

Wolfe stabbed sensually with his tongue at the rigid peak he had summoned from Jessica's breast. She moaned and arched against him. He sheathed the edges of his teeth in his lips and tested the hardness of her nipple. Fire splintered, drawing a ragged, passionate cry from her. Wolfe didn't lift his head until her breathing was broken and she was twisting slowly beneath his mouth. Very slowly he released her captive breast and admired the high ruby crown his mouth had created.

"You draw even tighter for my mouth than you did for the rain."

"What?" she asked, dazed.

"This." Wolfe took one of Jessica's hands and drew it lightly over her breast. "Feel your passion. Such a velvet hardness."

Her eyes opened in shock.

Laughing softly, Wolfe kissed her palm, bit the flesh at the base of her hand, and felt her body jerk with pleasure. He caught her nipples between his fingers and plucked until she forgot everything but the sensations radiating through her like sunlight through a garden.

When one of Wolfe's hands slid down the length of her body, Jessica didn't protest. The warmth of his hand stroking over her legs was simply part of the net of fire that was drawing more tightly around her with each tug of his mouth at her breasts. She didn't notice that with each sweet pressure of his palm her legs shifted and then shifted again until nothing of her softness was shielded from him.

"Remember how sunlight touches the bud?" Wolfe asked.

His voice was deep, husky, as warm and heavy as his hand resting just above the tangle of mahogany curls.

"Gently," Jessica whispered. "Completely."

"Everywhere."

Understanding came. "Dear God, Wolfe. Even there?"

"Especially there. You're going to come as sweetly unwrapped as a rosebud baring its petals to the sun for the first time."

Motionless, Jessica stared at Wolfe's dark, intensely masculine face.

"There's no need to be frightened," he said. "You want this. I can see it, even if you can't. You're already unfolding for me."

She made a sound that could have been Wolfe's name when she felt his hand ease lower.

"Don't tighten your legs," he said softly. "This is as close as I'll ever come to taking you. I want to see it."

Wolfe's hand didn't move as he lay motionless beside Jessica, waiting for her decision.

"Wolfe," she whispered, but could say no more.

"Shy little rose."

He kissed her shoulder, then drew his teeth over the place where nerves gathered. She made a soft sound of surprise and pleasure.

"I know you're aching for the sun," Wolfe said. "Let me give it to you."

The delicacy of his teeth caressing her shoulder was both sensual reassurance and sensuous promise. Slowly Jessica let out her breath and relaxed the tension in her legs. She was rewarded by the slow stroking of Wolfe's palm over her belly and hips and thighs. His mouth teased her breasts, sending pleasure licking through her once more, wrapping her in a net of loving fire.

When Wolfe's nails scored lightly inside Jessica's thighs, the fiery net tightened around her in a rush that made her moan. His hand flattened as his fingers spread wide, then curled around the curve of her inner thigh. He caressed her slowly with his palm, easing between her legs. This time she didn't resist the inevitable parting of her thighs beneath his touch.

"Jessi," Wolfe breathed, shaken by her unspoken trust.

His palm skimmed over the dark curls he longed

to comb with his fingertips, seeking the scented softness he knew ached for his caresses. Gently he pressed his hand between her legs. His fingers cupped around her softest flesh as his palm rubbed languidly over the mahogany curls that no longer concealed Jessica's sultry core.

When she felt his touch, her breath came in with a sound like silk tearing. With great care he traced her layered softness, coaxing each petal into quivering life.

"Such a beautiful flower," he said huskily. "Is there nectar within?"

Jessica didn't know what Wolfe meant until she felt herself being softly parted. The gliding penetration of his finger should have shocked her, but shock had no chance against the bubble of sensation expanding through her, bursting softly, drenching her in pleasure.

"Wolfe."

"I know," he said hoarsely. "I can feel it, hotter than my dreams."

His hand moved again, slowly, and her response spilled over, burning both of them with the softest kind of fire. She made a sound deep in her throat and lifted against his hand, needing to feel the sweet movement within her once more. He felt the frailty of her maidenhead, cursed, and began to withdraw from the satin sheath he wanted more than he wanted breath.

"Please," Jessica whispered, trying to keep him within her body. "Touch me."

"Not like that."

"Does it . . . don't you . . . do you . . . dislike it?"

Wolfe laughed deep in his throat and returned to probe lightly, hungry for the moist, clinging heat. The sound Jessica made told him that her eyes were open and what she was seeing both shocked and set fire to her.

"Yes, Jessi. Watch and think what it would be like to feel my kisses like a warm rain over every bit of you," he shuddered and whispered, "and you a warm rain over me."

Something both beautiful and faintly frightening swept through Jessica. She tried to quell the feeling, but might as well have tried to turn back the sun with a sigh.

"What is happening to me?" Jessica asked. "What are you—I can't—*Wolfe.*"

Jessica moaned his name as her body convulsed softly around him, caressing him secretly, drawing him more deeply into her while passion's sultry rain licked over his hand.

Need clenched savagely in Wolfe, making him groan as he withdrew from Jessica's body. With leashed urgency he smoothed the heat of her response over her most sensitive skin. When he caressed the nub of passion he had called from her, she cried out with surprise and violent pleasure. His fingertips circled her aroused, sensitive flesh, tugging at her, holding her captive for the hungry testing of his thumb.

Jessica arched in elemental abandon as Wolfe taught her that pleasure could be so intense it was more vivid than pain, more elemental, a sensual lightning burning her to her soul.

Wolfe's dark glance swept over Jessica, memorizing her body as it was transformed by the ecstasy he had given to her. He wanted to be within her again, to feel her release shivering around him, caressing him with sultry velvet wings. He knew he shouldn't risk tearing the fragile veil of her chastity, yet he was unable to resist.

His hand shifted as he glided very carefully into her body once more. The slow penetration drew a shivering cry of completion from her.

"Your maidenhead is so frail." Wolfe whispered. "It tells me I could take you in every way I've ever imagined and you would know only pleasure."

Wolfe's thumb moved slowly and Jessica moaned as sensuous lightning searched through her once more.

"I won't take your virginity," Wolfe said hoarsely as he bent down to her, "but I will know you in a way I've never known any woman." He shuddered and caressed her intimately, dragging his mouth over her. "Give yourself to me, Jessi. Let me taste ecstasy."

Pleasure seared through Jessica. With a rippling cry she gave herself to Wolfe, sharing ecstasy with him as his mouth moved over her with a hungry intensity, knowing her in a silence that burned, not stopping until she lay spent and shivering between his hands, her every breath his name whispered in wonder.

Then Wolfe held Jessica very hard and told himself how many kinds of fools he was. He had discovered the intense passion of an aristocratic girl who could never be his true mate. He wanted her more than ever, not less; yet he could not have her. He must not.

They were still all wrong for each other. Nothing had changed.

Bad to worse. That's a change.

It was a long, long time before Wolfe slept.

 **14**

"**I**t doesn't sound like spring out there," Willow said, rubbing her lower back absently. "First it thaws, then it freezes, then it snows, then it thaws, and now it's clear and wind is screaming down out of the north. Hear it?"

"It would be hard not to," Jessica said.

The long wild howl of the wind was as savage as anything Jessica had ever heard as a child in Scotland. Yet even as her fingers closed automatically around the locket with Wolfe's picture inside, she realized the wind no longer had the power to make her soul shiver in terror. She might never enjoy the anguished keening of a storm, but she wouldn't whimper in fear any more. She finally knew the difference between reality, nightmare, and a child's terrible memories.

I owe that to Wolfe.

Memories of the past night rippled through Jessica, leaving a breathless kind of fire in their wake. She had never dreamed that the ability to feel such pleasure existed in a woman's body. No longer did she believe all children except the first were forced upon unwilling wives by rutting husbands. The risks of pregnancy and childbirth were real, but so was the ecstasy.

She knew. Wolfe had shown it to her. Then he had held her until the last ecstatic tear was spent and the last shivering had left her.

Wolfe has given me so much, and I have given him . . . nothing.

"What an uncertain spring," Willow said, sighing as she looked out the window.

Jessica looked past Willow. Patches of grass showed through half-melted banks of snow. Bushes and trees blushed in shades of green. The creek in the ravine behind the barn was a silver rush of energy despite the wind-chilled air.

Neither the cold remaining in the ground nor the wild cry of the wind had troubled Jessica last night. She had known the burning that brings pleasure rather than pain, and then she'd fallen asleep locked in Wolfe's arms, her face pressed against the hot skin of his chest. The elemental scent and taste of him had permeated her dreams, sinking past all fears into her soul.

Intimacy. Merciful heaven. Jessica shivered with wild memories. *I never even guessed the meaning of intimacy until last night.*

"Jessi?"

She blinked and focused on Willow. "Yes?"

"Don't brood about last night."

For an instant, Jessica thought Willow had somehow guessed what had taken place in the hushed silence of the bedroom. A vivid blush colored Jessica's face before she remembered what else had happened last night—Wolfe's icy, public enumeration of her faults as a woman.

"Wolfe apologized to everyone this morning," Willow continued, "so I assume he apologized to you last night."

"Handsomely," Jessica said, knowing she was blushing.

Willow smiled despite the tension drawing her mouth into unaccustomed flatness. "That's the joy of marriage. Apologies as passionate as the arguments."

"Do you and Caleb argue?"

"Don't sound so surprised. Surely you've guessed by now that my husband can be as stubborn as a frozen boot." Willow smiled slightly. "Of course we argue."

"You, of course, aren't stubborn at all," Jessica said wryly.

"Of course not," Willow said with wide-eyed innocence. "I'm a fragile little flower of womanhood. How could I ever be so foolish as to disagree with that oversized gunfighter I married?"

Jessica laughed. "Ah, if only Caleb could hear you."

"Yes. If only."

The intensity beneath Willow's light words caught Jessica's attention.

"Is something wrong?"

"The wind. The cold. The calving could begin any moment. Caleb said last night the mares were on the edge of foaling as well."

"I know. Wolfe woke me before he left. He said something about the animals drifting in front of the storm. He was worried about the pregnant mares."

"We haven't had time to fence the horse pasture," Willow said, frowning at the untamed land. "Ishmael, my stallion, has been keeping the mares safe. But he was raised in barns and paddocks. The country just south of here is wild and broken. If the mares are pushed there by a storm, we'll have a devil of a time finding all of them. The wind is icy. If the mares begin foaling . . ."

Willow's voice died. Saying nothing more, she stood in front of the window and watched the invisible violence of the wind.

Jessica went over and put her arm comfortingly around Willow. "The men will find your mares."

"The mares, the cows, the yearling steers. We could lose everything to this damned wind. I wish I were out there working beside Caleb. We need every hand we can get. I feel so useless. I—"

Willow's voice broke as she dragged harshly at air.

At first, Jessica thought tears had taken Willow's voice; then Jessica felt the forerunners of childbirth's primal contractions ripple through Willow.

"How long has it been going on?" Jessica asked urgently.

"The storm? Since last night."

"To blazes with the storm! How long have you been having pains?"

"Off and on since midnight."

Jessica's eyes closed for an instant. When they opened, they were clear and very intent.

"Did you tell Caleb?"

"No." Willow's voice was tight, flat. "My mother told me that first babies are unpredictable. Labor can begin and fade and then begin again many times." Willow took a deep breath. "We need to save our animals more than I need Caleb to hold my hand through false labors that could go on for days."

Despite the brave words, Jessica could see the uneasiness in Willow's wide hazel eyes. She would have liked the comfort of her husband's presence.

"Is this the first time you've felt pains?"

"They've come and gone for almost two days," Willow admitted. "But that last one was different."

"May I?" asked Jessica, putting her hands on the mound of Willow's womb.

Surprised, Willow simply nodded.

For a time, there was silence broken only by the wail of the wind. The more Jessica gently probed, the more fearful she became. The baby wasn't moving. According to the books she had read, once the proper birth position had been achieved, even the healthiest of babies became quiet in the hours before labor.

So did babies that were no longer alive. Jessica had acquired that bitter knowledge watching her mother's futile labors.

"Tell me when the next one comes," Jessica said with a calmness that went no deeper than her smile. "In the meantime, you can finish hemming the receiving blankets you made."

It was half an hour before another wave of contractions swept through Willow's body. She looked up from the receiving blanket she had just folded.

"Jessi!" she called.

"Now?"

"Yes."

Jessica dropped the pump handle and ran from the kitchen into the living room where Willow was sitting. When Jessica put her hands on the mound of Willow's pregnancy, the muscles were quite hard. Frowning, Jessica probed carefully yet thoroughly. She had read enough about false labor to know that it rarely involved the woman's body to this extent. Nor had the baby changed position.

After a long count of three, Willow's muscles relaxed.

"The clenching—did it go all the way around

your body?" Jessica asked, straightening.

"It began in back and then came forward," Willow said, demonstrating with her hands.

"Can you stand?"

"Without my husband's strong arm to drag me upright?" Willow asked dryly. "We'll find out."

When Willow was standing, Jessica bent and moved her hands over the swollen abdomen. The baby was definitely riding lower than it had been, though not so low as in the drawings in Jessica's books showing women on the verge of labor. On the other hand, first babies were . . . first babies. Unpredictable.

Though Jessica waited and waited, she didn't feel the baby move with any vigor at all. When she was certain none of the fear she felt would show in her eyes, she looked up, smiled, and spoke in a teasing tone.

"As your brothers would say, 'Well, Willy, you've gone and done it again.' The baby has dropped, it's standing on its head, and it's ready to see what the world is like."

A small smile softened Willow's pale lips. She took one of Jessica's hands between her own and squeezed.

"I'm so glad you're here, Jessi."

"So am I."

It was only partially a lie. For Willow's sake, Jessica was glad to be present. No woman should have to face the dangers of childbirth alone.

Yet Jessica had hoped never again to go through the agony, terror, and wrenching futility of childbed again.

"Did you eat breakfast?" Jessica asked.

"No. I had no appetite."

"Good. Your body has more important things to

do than deal with biscuits and bacon," Jessica said briskly. "Where do you keep clean linens for the bed?"

"In the chest at the foot of—oh!"

"What is it?"

No sooner had Jessica asked when she saw the unmistakable marks of wetness spread down Willow's skirt.

"Your water has broken."

"Yes, that's it, of course." Willow smiled tremulously. "Silly of me to be frightened. I forgot that would happen. What a goose I am."

Jessica hugged Willow and stroked her golden hair as though she were a child.

"You're not a goose. 'Tis only natural to be a bit worried, especially with your first."

For a moment, Willow clung to the smaller woman, then she stepped back and straightened her spine.

"It's probably just as well Caleb isn't here," Willow said. "He's so worried that I'll suffer the same fate his sister did."

Jessica remembered the night Caleb had carried his sleeping wife from the living room. His face had been as hard as stone, yet the emotion in his eyes had made Jessica's heart turn over.

She is my life.

Jessica had wondered then what it would be like to hold a man's love so deeply. She would have moved heaven and earth and taken on Hell in order to have Wolfe look at her with such emotion.

Yet Jessica knew it wouldn't happen.

We're all wrong for each of her.

Wolfe was half right, but only half. He was the right man for her.

She just wasn't the right woman for him.

With an effort, Jessica put her own turmoil aside. Taking Willow's hand, she led her to the bedroom.

"I've been meaning to have Wolfe talk with Caleb about this," Jessica said, "but I never found the proper moment. It's been discovered that childbed fever can be prevented if the doctor washes his hands with soap and hot water between patients."

"Truly? Why would that make a difference?"

"I don't know. Yet washing is a simple enough thing to do. And while I'm at it, I'll see that the bed linens are clean, that your gown is clean, and that the rest of you is clean for good measure."

Willow smiled slightly. "If it works on hands, why not on other things, is that it?"

"Exactly," Jessica said. "Here, let me help you out of your clothes."

"I can manage."

"I can manage better." Jessica smiled at Willow and began unfastening her skirt. "There's no room for modesty at a birthing. What will happen, does, willy nilly, without so much as a by your leave. And by the time it does happen, neither one of us will have a thought in our minds but getting the job done."

Willow let out a long breath. "You're always surprising me."

"You mean I'm slightly less useless than Wolfe would have you believe?"

"What nonsense. I could have shaken Wolfe by his ears for his bad temper. You can no more help the circumstances of your birth than he can."

Jessica smiled rather grimly and said nothing.

"What surprised me," Willow said, "was that you knew nothing about, er, the physical side of marriage, so I assumed you were reticent about physical things and probably horribly embarrassed by them as well. But you're quite practical about births, aren't you?"

"I spent my first nine years on a country estate. Dogs, sheep, cats, horses, pigs, cows, rabbits, the whole lot. They all conceived and gave birth with the regularity of the sun rising."

"Particularly the rabbits?" Willow suggested with a slight smile.

Jessica laughed. "Those blessed bunnies were the only crop that never failed, rain or shine."

"I'm glad you're not a city aristocrat," Willow admitted. "I've never attended a birth, but I believe I'll need you, if only to be reassured that someone is here to care for the baby if I'm too tired at first."

Jessica's determined smile almost slipped. She had never had the luck to deal with a live birth, but that wasn't something Jessica was going to mention. At the moment, keeping Willow's spirits up was all that mattered. Talking of difficult births and dead babies was the last thing she needed.

"Now, lean on me while you step out of your skirt and petticoat," Jessica said.

Working quickly but without the appearance of haste, Jessica got Willow washed and dressed in a clean gown. The bed was prepared by stripping off the old linens, putting a tarpaulin over the mattress, and then putting on clean linens. By the time Willow crawled awkwardly into bed, another contraction had come. It, too, wrapped fully around her body.

There was no doubt that the labor was real.

"I'll be right back," Jessica said as she tucked the covers beneath Willow's chin. "If you hear the rifle, don't worry. I'm calling in the men."

"No. I'm fine. I don't need them."

"Willow, what do you think Caleb would do to the person who kept him from you when you were in need?"

Tears brightened Willow's eyes. "But the mares need him more than I do."

"Wolfe will help the mares. He loves horses as he loves nothing else on earth."

"Except you."

Jessica smiled sadly. "Tree That Stands Alone doesn't love me. He cares for me, that's all, and it's more than I deserve."

"Nonsense," Willow said.

"No. Simple truth. Everything Wolfe said about me last night was true. I forced this marriage against Wolfe's wishes. He wanted a Western wife like you. He got an aristocrat who didn't even know how to comb her own hair."

Jessica smiled at the look of shock on Willow's face. " 'Tis true, I'm afraid," Jessica said. "The hairbrush was as foreign in my hand as a gold coin in a beggar's grasp."

"Dear Lord," Willow whispered.

"But I'm learning, thanks in large part to you." Jessica smoothed her hand over Willow's hair. "Rest. You'll need your strength to bring Caleb's baby into the world."

Willow turned and looked out the window. Nothing showed but trees bent and writhing in the wind.

"They won't be able to hear the rifle," she said calmly. "They're upwind of us."

Silently, Jessica agreed, but she went to the porch anyway. The wind sucked the door handle from her grasp and sent the door slamming back upon the wall. The air was icy. Shivering, she raised the carbine that had been a present for a wedding that should never have taken place. The gold and silver inlay smoldered in the subdued light of the storm.

She fired three spaced shots, waited, then fired three more spaced shots. Shivering violently, she lowered the carbine and retreated to the house's shelter. After a brief struggle, she managed to shut the door once again, closing out the icy wind.

For a long moment Jessica stood alone in the living room, gathering herself for what was to come. Then she went to work.

Ignoring her trembling hands, she scrubbed her sharp darning scissors, wrapped them in a clean towel, and set them on top of the pristine receiving blankets Willow had prepared with such love. The thought of wrapping up one more tiny corpse sent a wave of sick despair through Jessica. She had seen the baby clothes and carefully made cradle. She had seen Caleb's love and Willow's pleasure when he held his hand on her womb and felt their baby move.

Please God, let this baby be born alive.

The wind battered the house, sending a chill through Jessica. Quickly she gathered a book and a chair and went back to Willow.

"It seemed to help Mother if I read to her," Jessica said with a calm that was wholly false. "If that doesn't appeal, I'll just sit quietly until you need me."

"Please," Willow said quickly, her voice strained, "read."

"Try not to hold your breath when the pain comes," Jessica said gently. "It only makes it worse." Jessica began reading *A Midsummer Night's Dream*.

Time went quickly, marked off by contractions

that became closer together and harder, until only a handful of minutes came between. The demands of birth took Willow's body, made it rigid, and dragged low sounds from her.

"Try not to fight it," Jessica said quietly. "Birth is stronger than any of us. We can't conquer it. We can only share it with the babe."

Very slowly, Willow relaxed despite the continued grip of pain.

"Here," Jessica said, taking a piece of leather strap from her pocket. "Put this between your teeth."

Neither woman heard the front door open. Nor did they hear Caleb's voice calling for Willow. Jessica's first realization of Caleb's presence came when a pair of riding gloves hit the floor at her feet and a large masculine hand reached past her to Willow.

"No!" Jessica said fiercely, blocking the hand with her body. "Wash yourself first. Nothing dirty must touch her or the child or you'll risk fever."

Caleb grabbed the fallen gloves and left the room in a rush. When he reappeared he was dripping water, smelling of soap and wearing nothing but a pair of clean breeches. He dressed quickly.

Willow let out a low sound as the contraction peaked. When her eyes opened, she saw Caleb fastening his pants. Almost guiltily, she let go of Jessica's hand, spat out the strip of leather, and concealed it beneath the covers.

She wasn't quick enough. Few people were when it came to hiding things from Caleb's golden eyes.

"I told Jessi not to fire the rifle," Willow said. "The mares—"

"Wolfe found them," Caleb interrupted as he

reached for a shirt. "What's this about a rifle?"

"I tried to call you in when Willow began labor," Jessica said as she wrung out a cloth to cool Willow's face.

"I didn't hear any shots."

Jessica glanced at the window. It was still light outside. The wind still howled. None of the other men had returned.

"Then how did you know to come?" she asked.

"I heard Willow calling my name."

Jessica stared at Caleb, but he had eyes only for his wife. He was kneeling next to the bed in a carelessly buttoned shirt. No one but Jessica noticed the half-unfastened clothing as Caleb bent down to Willow, talking softly, stroking her hair and smiling at her with such tenderness that Jessica felt tears catch in her throat.

When the next contraction came, it was Caleb's hands that Willow gripped. She struggled not to cry out, but couldn't stifle a rough sound.

"Go ahead," Caleb said. "Scream or curse or cry. Whatever helps."

Willow shook her head.

When the contraction passed, Jessica fished out the piece of rein Willow had hidden beneath the covers. She put the leather strip on the blanket next to Willow.

"I prepared this and kept it near because I knew you would need it," Jessica said. "If you won't cry out or use the leather, I'll tell Caleb to leave. The last thing you should be worried about is fighting yourself so as not to upset your husband. He put the babe in your body. He can share in the pain as well as the pleasure of its birth."

Willow's mouth set in a mutinous line.

Caleb kissed his wife and said something too soft for Jessica to hear.

"I didn't want to worry you," Willow said. "Love, you get upset if I burn myself cooking."

He lifted her hands and kissed them very gently. Then he picked up the leather strap. The marks of her teeth showed clearly. His fingers tightened on the dark leather.

"If I could bear it for you, I would," he said roughly.

"I know. Just having you here helps me."

It was true.

Despite the force of the contractions, Jessica saw that the lines of tension in Willow's face had eased. When Caleb bent his head and whispered to his wife, the smile she gave him was as full of love as her eyes.

Then Willow's body was claimed once more by the demands of birth. Caleb felt the tension of her muscles. Without a word, he held out the strap. She took it between her teeth just as a powerful contraction arched her whole body.

After that, there was little time for anything but easing Willow in small ways while she performed the hard work of bringing another life into the world. As the rhythmic fury of birth progressed, Jessica prayed silently, fiercely, that it would not all be in vain, all the wrenching pain and the blood, the set agony of Caleb's face speaking eloquently of his fear and love for the woman who was giving birth to his child.

Finally, the contractions came so quickly that there was no time between for Willow to recover. Panting, sweating, dazed, she tried to smile at Caleb, only to be swept up once again.

"How much longer?" Caleb asked tightly of Jessica.

"As long as the babe requires."

"She can't take much more of this."

"You would be surprised at what a woman can endure."

And Caleb was.

In the final throes of birth, Willow's hands gripped with a power that amazed Caleb, leaving bruises on his work-hardened hands, bruises that he didn't even notice until later; he had care only for Willow, for giving her what ease he could.

The sound of a baby's cries came as a shock.

"You have a son!" Jessica said, laughing and crying at the same time. "A beautiful, red-faced, crying, living son!"

Willow smiled and closed her eyes, letting everything slide away but the knowledge of her son and her husband's kiss burning in the center of her hand.

Jessica managed to cut and tie the cord despite the happy tears running down her face. She washed the baby in warm water, wrapped him in receiving blankets, and handed him to Caleb. She was stunned to see tears in Caleb's eyes as he looked at his child.

"Show Willow your son," Jessica said huskily. "Then put him to her breast. He needs to feel her heartbeat again. She needs to feel his."

Reverently, Caleb took their son to Willow. When Jessica looked up again, Willow was lying in her husband's arms and the baby was sucking eagerly, his tiny head cradled by Caleb's big hand.

"ARE you all right?" Wolfe asked urgently, pulling Jessica into his arms before she could answer.

"Willow did the work, not I."

Wolfe didn't seem to hear. He held Jessica hard against him. "When Reno told me, I kept thinking of your mother, of the horror you have of birth. I was afraid being near another childbed would terrify you."

"I was afraid, too," Jessica admitted, wrapping her arms around Wolfe's lean waist. "I was afraid it would be born dead, like all the others."

Wolfe made a hoarse sound, but the hand that stroked Jessica's disheveled hair was very gentle.

"But this baby was alive," she continued, excitement vibrating in every word. "Red-faced and crying, waving tiny fists, with black hair and long limbs. It was perfect and it was alive!"

Smiling, Wolfe bent and kissed her. When she returned the kiss rather than retreating, heat ran like leashed lightning through him. Memories of last night had come to him throughout the day, shaking him. He hungered for Jessica in ways he hadn't believed possible.

Unable to stop himself, Wolfe urged Jessica's lips apart. Despite the elemental need hardening his body, he tasted her with great gentleness, absorbing her warmth and the soft breaking of her breath when his tongue first touched hers. It was a long time before he lifted his head.

"Reno said both Willow and the boy are doing well," Wolfe said finally, looking toward the closed bedroom door.

"Yes." Jessica smiled and kissed the corner of Wolfe's mouth. "Very, very well. Oh, Wolfe, it was extraordinary. To hold a new life where none was before made me feel as though I had touched God's smile. The look on Caleb's face when he held his son told me he felt the same way."

"When will I be allowed to see this little red-faced miracle?"

"Willow can't wait to share him. As soon as you wash, you can go in."

"I'm clean as sunlight," Wolfe said wryly. "Reno ran me through the wash house personally and thoroughly. Told me he wasn't risking his one and only nephew on some dirty halfbreed."

"What?" Jessica's head snapped up. "Is he still alive?"

"Haven't you heard? He's pure greased lightning with that six-gun. I was as meek as a lamb—even washed behind my ears twice."

"I'll box *his* ears," she muttered. "Calling you names. He ought to be ashamed."

Wolfe made a smothered sound and broke into laughter as he lifted Jessica off her feet in a big hug,

"Such a fierce little elf," he said against her lips. "I was only teasing. Reno has called me some names from time to time, but none of them had anything to do with my Cheyenne mother."

The laughter in Wolfe's eyes made them a beautiful midnight blue. The strong slant of his cheekbones and his starkly defined mouth were heightened rather than blurred by his smile. Jessica realized anew how compelling Wolfe's features were to her.

Suddenly, she wondered what it would be like to look down into the face of a sleeping baby and see hints of Wolfe's beloved face.

"What an odd sound. Are you all right, Jessi?"

"Yes. No. That is ..."

Jessica's aquamarine eyes searched Wolfe's face. She slid her fingers into his black hair and found that it was still damp. The cool, sleek texture made her shiver with pleasure and say his name as she watched him with wide, wondering eyes.

"Jessi? Are you all right? You're looking at me as though you've never seen me before."

"I haven't." Before he could say anything, she lifted her mouth to his. "Kiss me, Wolfe. Kiss me hard."

The kiss Wolfe gave Jessica was deep, hot, frankly hungry. When it ended, both of them were breathing too rapidly. Just as he bent to take her mouth again, the front door closed hard.

"You keep that up and there will be one more small screamer come winter," Rafe said, trying and failing to swallow his smile.

Wolfe tucked Jessica's fiery face against his chest. "We were just getting ready to admire your nephew."

"Uh-huh. What's this I hear about a complete bath before I get to see the little mite?"

"Ask Reno."

"I did. He has a scrub brush the size of a wagon seat and pure deviltry in his eyes."

Jessica laughed into Wolfe's shirt.

"Are you strangling her?" Rafe asked politely.

Wolfe's hand slid beneath Jessica's chin. He tilted her face up and brushed a kiss over her lips.

"Are you strangling?" Wolfe asked softly.

She blushed and said something Rafe couldn't hear.

"What was that?" Rafe asked.

"She said to enjoy your bath."

"Damn. I was afraid of that. Don't wear out the little morsel before I get back."

"Which morsel?" Wolfe asked.

"Wolfe!" Jessica said, hitting his chest with her hand.

Rafe was laughing as he shut the front door behind him.

"Come on, morsel," Wolfe said, putting Jessica's feet back on the floor. "Show me the little miracle."

Willow's radiant smile belied the paleness of her skin as she welcomed Wolfe. Caleb was sitting next to the bed, holding the sleeping baby in the crook of his arm. When Wolfe walked close, Caleb gently shifted the small burden.

"Put one hand under his head and the other under his bottom," Jessica said to Wolfe.

"Jesus," Wolfe whispered, "he's tiny."

"Not for a baby," Caleb said. "He's nearly two feet long and weighs nine pounds if he weighs an ounce."

"Like I said. Tiny."

But Wolfe took the sleeping baby in his hands and looked at it with a gentleness that softened the hard lines of his face. When the baby's eyes opened sleepily, Wolfe's breath came out in a wondering sound.

"Look at those tawny eyes. He's your son, all right."

The baby studied Wolfe with unfocused eyes, yawned, blew a tiny bubble, and was asleep within seconds. Wolfe laughed very softly and touched the baby's small, perfect cheek with his thumb.

Watching Wolfe brought Jessica a feeling close to pain. She had seen the wonder in Wolfe's face when he looked from the baby's golden eyes to Caleb's. She had seen something more, too. She had seen Wolfe's hunger to someday hold a baby in his hands and know that he was part of that continuing miracle of life.

A man didn't need titles or wealth in order to want a child. The pain of the realization was so deep that Jessica barely managed not to cry out.

"Are you going to be as hard-headed and decent as your daddy?" Wolfe asked the baby softly. "I hope so. The world needs more dark angels of justice to keep the devils in line."

Wolfe looked up and smiled at Caleb. "All the same, I hope you have a daughter next time. The world needs more Western women, too."

"Have one yourself," Caleb said dryly.

Only Jessica saw the light leave Wolfe's eyes. His black lashes swept down as though he were looking at the sleeping baby once more. She knew he must be thinking of their marriage, the trap he was caught in which insured he would never have daughters or sons.

Yet when Wolfe looked up again and handed the baby to Willow, there was a smile on his face. The smile was as real as the pain had been.

"You made a beautiful baby," Wolfe said to Willow.

"I had some help."

"Damn little. A man as ugly as Caleb can't make a pretty baby."

Willow smiled and looked at Caleb. "My husband is as handsome as a god."

"To you, maybe," Wolfe said dryly. "To me? Well, I'll just say I've seen better looking things left on the ground after a buffalo herd walked past."

Caleb snickered. Wolfe turned around and gave the other man a swift, hard hug, brother to brother.

"Before this, you had the sun," Wolfe said.

"Now you have the moon and stars. Guard them well."

After a moment, Jessica looked away, for she could no longer bear the sadness she sensed beneath Wolfe's pleasure for his friend.

 **15**

*S*HE *was naked on a vast plain of ice. Nothing was alive. Nothing moved but the many-voiced wind. Far ahead of her grew a powerful, living tree that carried safety in its branches.*

She must reach the tree's shelter.

Yet the harder she tried to run, the more deeply encrusted she became in ice. She was a prisoner of cold and a plaything of the wind. Yet still she struggled toward the tree while the wind taunted her:

That woman is not Jessica.

Worst mistake of his life.

All wrong for each other.

Jessica sat bolt upright in bed just as the first light of dawn brought color to the empty sky.

"Jessi?" Wolfe's hand touched her shoulder. "Are you having nightmares about the past again?"

"No. Not the past."

"Get back under the covers," Wolfe said gently. "It's cold out there."

"It's freezing," she whispered.

Jessica lay down and turned toward Wolfe, needing his warmth to chase the chill of her own dreams.

"What is it?" he asked, stroking her hair.

"A nightmare, that's all. I was alone."

303

"You're not alone now. I'm here."

But for how long?

Wolfe felt Jessica's arms go around his neck. The softness of her breasts pressed against his naked chest. He had awakened from his own dreams already aroused. The feel of her against his skin brought his need to the point of pain. When she shifted, trying to come even closer, her hip brushed against his hardened flesh. He felt as much as heard her gasp.

"Don't be frightened," Wolfe said. "I've spent a lot of nights like this, and I haven't forced you. I never will. All I have to do is remember how terrified you are by a man's need, and why, and I have no problem at all controlling myself."

"It's not that. You just . . . startled me."

Jessica took a slow, almost secret breath, trying to banish her dream. She rubbed her cheek against Wolfe's reassuring warmth, letting it sink through the chill left by the voices of the wind repeating Wolfe's words, telling her how little she was worth as a woman. When she felt Wolfe withdrawing from her, she made a broken sound and clung to him with a strength that surprised him.

"Don't let go of me," she whispered urgently.

"I thought I was frightening you."

She shook her head. The motion sent a silky fall of hair over Wolfe's chest.

"Are you certain?" he asked.

"Very."

Slowly, Wolfe put his arms back around Jessica and pulled her close once more. She relaxed against him despite the stark evidence of his arousal. For a few minutes, there was silence but for the wind coiling through the spreading light of dawn.

"Wolfe?"

He made a questioning, rumbling sound.

"Seeing Willow..." Jessica hesitated, not knowing how to give words to what she was feeling. "The birth was..."

Wolfe kissed Jessica's forehead. "It brought back the nightmares, didn't it? Don't worry. They'll fade. Even under the best circumstances, birth is a messy process. With your memories of the past, it must have been horrifying."

"That's not what I meant. Yes, birth is messy, but so is spring. One doesn't get an omelet without breaking shells and all that."

Wolfe smiled as he nuzzled the hollow of Jessica's cheek. "Did I remember to tell you how very brave you are, Jessi?"

"I'm a ruddy little coward and no one knows it better than you."

The bleakness in Jessica's voice surprised him. Wolfe tilted her face up so that he could see her eyes.

"That's not true," Wolfe said simply. "You've endured things that would have broken most adults, much less a child."

Saying nothing, Jessica closed her eyes and shook her head.

"Jessi," Wolfe whispered, kissing her eyelids. "You had every right to run and hide on the nights your father raped your mother, but you didn't. You went to your mother and gave her what help you could."

"So little."

"So much," he countered. "You must have been terrified beyond words, yet you gave comfort to the very woman who should have been comforting you."

"There was no comfort in her. Toward the end, I think she was mad."

Wolfe closed his eyes. "It would have been a blessing."

"Yes. But it left me very much alone. I expected to die when cholera took her. I was so sick. Then he came and bathed me and fed me thin gruel and kept me warm until cholera took him, too."

"He?"

"The lord. My father. Everyone else was dead or dying. I tried to help him, but finally the wind took him, too. I think . . . I think he welcomed it."

Wolfe made a low sound. "You were so young. It tears my heart to think of you alone and frightened."

"I'd always been that way," Jessica said matter-of-factly, "until you came. I tried to keep you from seeing what a coward I was, but you knew anyway."

"Hush," he said, kissing her eyelashes. "A coward would have run from the house and left Willow to bear her child alone. You didn't. Despite your horrible memories, you stayed by Willow's side and kept your fear to yourself. Caleb said you were as calm as a doctor."

"Fear would only have made it more difficult for Willow. I couldn't do that to her." A sound came from Jessica that wasn't quite laughter nor yet tears. "You were right about her, Wolfe. She is a rare and wonderful woman. Sharing her son's birth made me . . . less fearful."

Smiling, Wolfe stroked the back of his fingers down Jessica's cheek. She turned her head slowly until she could catch his index finger between her lips. The swift intake of his breath as she tasted his skin told her that she had his full attention.

"Caleb taught me something, too," Jessica said.
"Did he?"
"Mmm."

The soft warmth of Jessica's tongue between Wolfe's fingers made him forget to breathe.

"Seeing Caleb with his son," she said, "made me realize there is more to having heirs than passing on titles and estates."

Wolfe barely registered the meaning of the words. Jessica was biting him so delicately that he might have imagined it, but even in his dreams he hadn't felt the tiny serrations of her teeth caressing him.

"You taught me something, too," Jessica continued.

"Again," he whispered.

"What?"

"Bite me again, elf."

Smiling, she dragged her teeth lightly down the sensitive edges of his finger. When she reached the base, she thrust the tip of her tongue between his fingers.

"I didn't teach you that," he said huskily.

"No, you taught me something much more important."

"Did I?"

"Yes," she whispered. "I saw the awe and the hunger in you for a child of your own. Let me give you that child."

He became utterly still.

"Love me, Wolfe. Let me love you. Let me give back to you just a part of the beauty you've given to me."

"Jessi," he whispered, stopping her words with a gentle pressure of his thumb. "It's all right. You don't have to repay me that way."

"I want to."

He smiled sadly. "You woke up terrified by old dreams."

"Not old dreams. A new one."

"Do you remember it?"

"Dear God, all too clearly. You were gone and I was alone and the wind was taunting me with my worthlessness as a wife, as a woman . . ."

Wolfe's arms tightened. "You aren't worthless."

"Then why won't you make our marriage a valid one?"

"Jessi . . . elf . . ."

She waited, watching him with hope burning in her eyes like dawn.

"Sweet girl," Wolfe whispered, kissing Jessica between words, "it has nothing to do with worth or lack of it. There is no future for a Scots aristocrat and a halfbreed bastard. You were not born for the Western wilderness. I was. I was not born for the elegant drawing rooms of London. You were. You need a husband more civilized than I am. And I . . ." His voice died. "Someday you'll admit our mismatch and ask for an annulment."

When Jessica opened her mouth to object, Wolfe took it in a deep kiss that made her moan.

"But until that day," he whispered when he finally lifted his head, "we can enjoy each other in ways that will leave your virginity intact for the lord whom you will finally accept as your husband in every sense of the word."

"I'll never accept any man but you."

"Yes, you will," Wolfe countered softly. "You have too much passion in you to live a nun's life, and you know it now. God help me, so do I. I'll die remembering your scent, your taste, the sounds you made when you burned beneath my mouth."

Before Jessica could speak, Wolfe kissed her deeply, seducing her with hot movements of his tongue. When he cupped her breasts in his hands and drew out the velvet peaks with his circling thumbs, she made a broken sound at the back of her throat. Reluctantly, Wolfe lifted his head, afraid that he had frightened Jessica with his ardor.

"Fear or pleasure?" he asked huskily.

"What?" she asked, dazed by the heat splintering through her.

His hands moved, and the heat became a sweet burning that made her arch toward him. Small sounds rippled from her lips. One of those sounds was his name.

"Wolfe?"

"Never mind," he breathed. His fingers caressed the hardened tips of Jessica's breasts, drawing her nipples into proud, hungry crowns. "Your body is telling me everything I need to know just now."

Her thoughts came unraveled as a golden incandescence splintered through her. She felt the warm wash of Wolfe's breath over her nipple and knew in another instant he would draw her into his mouth and she would be lost.

"Wait," she said breathlessly. "I want . . ."

When she tried to speak, she couldn't find the words for what she wanted to say.

"It's all right," Wolfe murmured, rubbing his lips over the velvet hardness of her nipple. "I know what you want. I want it, too."

"Do you?"

The real question in Jessica's voice stopped Wolfe. Slowly, reluctantly, he lifted his head from the sensuous temptation of her nipple.

"Didn't you know?" he whispered. "I like this as much as you do."

"Not quite."

"You sound positive," Wolfe said, amused.

Jessica's cheeks were flushed with more than dawn, but she spoke anyway, for a need greater than the pleasures of the moment was driving her.

"If you keep caressing me, you'll give me the sun," she said.

The sensual promise in Wolfe's eyes was as dark and hot as his smile. "I hope so, Jessi. I love watching you burn."

"But I don't know how to give the sun back to you."

For a moment, Wolfe said nothing. He couldn't. His heart was threatening to close his throat.

"Do you want to know how?" he asked finally.

"Is it possible? Can I give you the sun?"

"It's not only possible, it would be so damned easy. Just the thought of your hands . . ." A primal tremor of response raked through Wolfe.

"My hands? Where, Wolfe? How? Teach me."

The temptation was almost overwhelming. He had spent too much time on fire for Jessica. He didn't think he could feel her hands on him without losing control. Yet he couldn't bear the thought of repulsing her at the very instant he was feeling the greatest pleasure.

"My response might . . . disgust you," Wolfe said simply. "You don't have to, elf. Despite our complaints, no man has ever died of sexual frustration."

"Did my response disgust you?" Jessica asked curiously.

His smile was slow and lazy, yet his eyes smoldered with memories. "I've never seen anything more beautiful than you burning."

Jessica's hands slid into Wolfe's hair, pulling his head down for the kind of kiss he had taught her both to enjoy and to need. He responded with a searching hunger that aroused her as much as his hands on her breasts.

"Teach me how to make you burn," she breathed.

Wolfe drew her hands from his hair, kissed her palms, closed his teeth over the edge of her hand almost fiercely, and let out a harsh breath.

"I think we had better go slowly. That way you may stop any time you want." Wolfe looked up, pinning her with eyes that were clear and dark. "I mean it, Jessi. The thought of disgusting you is unbearable to me."

Tears burned in Jessica's eyes as she understood once again how badly she had wounded him by saying that his touch disgusted her.

"Never, Wolfe. You could never disgust me."

"I'll bet I can shock you," he said dryly.

She smiled with lips that trembled. "My dearest Wolfe, you have already shocked me to my soul."

Black eyebrows lifted in silent query.

"Every time you touch me, it gives me the most shocking pleasure," she said simply.

Wolfe's breath came in with a sharp sound. "Do I really, Jessi?"

She held out her hand so that he could see its fine trembling. "This isn't fear or disgust. This is what happens when you touch me or when I remember how you have touched me."

Gently Wolfe lifted Jessica's hand to his mouth, kissed her, then let her fingers slide away.

"Why don't you start by touching me everywhere you like being touched?" he suggested.

Jessica tilted her head to one side as she looked at Wolfe. Though the sheet covered him from the waist down, he was unmistakably and aggressively male. When she looked back up to his intent eyes, the smile she gave him was both sensual and mischievous.

"I fear I must point out a small problem." She flushed slightly and cleared her throat of its sudden huskiness. "Well, not small. Actually it's quite . . . extensive."

"What is it?"

Wolfe's teasing, lazy smile made Jessica feel as though he were stroking her. The sensation was both delicious and somewhat unnerving.

"For a man who is reputed to have the eyes of an eagle when looking over a rifle barrel," she muttered, "I fear you are somewhat blind at close range."

"How so?" he asked, measuring the heightened color in her cheeks.

"And you call *me* innocent. Have you not yet noticed, my Wolfe? We're not quite the same everywhere, which will make it difficult for me to carry out your suggestion of touching you where it pleases me to be touched."

"We both have ears," Wolfe pointed out blandly.

"Does this mean I finally get to bite yours?"

Before Wolfe could answer, he felt the warmth of Jessica's breath on his ear, the heat of her tongue, the delicate edge of her teeth. He made a low sound of pleasure as her tongue spiraled down and in, sending sweet chills over his spine. She lifted her head and saw the dark glittering of his eyes in the dawn.

"You liked that," she said.

He smiled rather fiercely. "Yes."

"Lovely," she murmured, bending to him once more. "So did I."

Jessica tested the difference between ear and lobe with her tongue, her teeth, her lips. When she had managed to draw another low sound from Wolfe, she kissed him gently behind one ear.

"We both have necks," she said against his.

"What?"

"Necks," Jessica repeated. "We both have them. I liked the feel of your mouth on my neck. Does that mean you'll—"

"Yes," he interrupted swiftly. "Please."

Smiling, she shifted, not noticing that the front of her gown had come half undone beneath Wolfe's fingers. White lace fell open, revealing her breasts just as she discovered the strong tendons and resilient muscles of Wolfe's neck. He was as hard as polished wood, yet much more supple. Life coursed through him tangibly.

"Your neck is so much stronger than mine."

"I haven't your petal softness," Wolfe agreed. "Bite me, elf. Let me feel your teeth and your warm little tongue. You won't hurt me."

An instant later he felt the edge of Jessica's teeth testing him. Her willingness to please him was as arousing as the caress itself. Knowing he shouldn't trust himself to touch her at all, Wolfe drew her gown away from one breast and looked at her. His index finger circled the creamy skin just at the point where it began to gather into the rosy velvet of her nipple.

Jessica shivered and her teeth closed a bit savagely on the corded muscles of Wolfe's neck. Heat shot through him. He caught the responsive tip of her breast in his fingers and twisted with exquisite

care. She made a ragged sound and drew her fin-
gernails down his chest. When she felt the tiny,
hard rise of his nipples, she hesitated, then circled
back to test the nubs she had drawn so unexpectedly from his muscular chest.

"Yes, we both have breasts," Wolfe said, smiling
despite the hot wires of need that were drawing
his muscles into knots. "But yours are wonderfully
soft and silky."

"I like yours better."

Slender fingers moved over Wolfe's chest,
kneading the pads of muscle, praising his strength
in silence, enjoying the midnight swirls of hair,
circling without touching the sensitive nipples.
Then her head bent, sending a wave of rose-
scented hair over him. Just before her lips touched
him, he saw the tip of her tongue. With the delicate
curiosity of a kitten, she tasted his nipple. His fingers speared through her hair, holding her close.
Her tongue flicked over him again.

"Remember how I kissed you?" he asked almost
roughly.

"Yes."

"Did you like it?"

Her laugh was as sensual as the heat of her
tongue. "Are you saying you would like to be
kissed that way?"

"Only if you want."

Jessica's answer was a change in the caress, her
lips opening over him, teasing and pleasing him
with the shifting pressures of her mouth. Her teeth
closed gently on him. The tightening of his body
was both a reward and a lure. She covered his
nipple with her mouth and sucked gently. He
made a sound that was as much felt as heard, a
breaking of breath, a speeding of his heartbeat, and

a flush of warmth spreading beneath his skin that told her she had pleased him.

An answering thrill coursed through Jessica. She would never have guessed that her touch could have such an effect on Wolfe's powerful body. Nor would she have guessed that touching him would both please and excite her. But it did. She found herself wanting to touch him everywhere, all at once, to fill her senses with him until there was nothing except Wolfe in her whole world.

Murmuring sounds that had no meaning, Jessica drew first one cheek and then the other over Wolfe's chest, caressing him, tasting him, savoring his warmth and strength, losing herself in his male textures, realizing finally that this was what she had wanted to do for so long she could not remember when the wanting had first begun.

Now he was lying beneath her hand, and she was dizzy with the power of him.

When Jessica's hand slid down the sheet to stroke Wolfe's clenched thighs, his hips moved hungrily. Remembering how she had caught fire when his hand moved between her legs, she eased her fingers beneath the sheet, wanting to give him the same intense pleasure she had known at his touch. Yet when she tried to slide her fingers from knee to thigh, his legs were too closely held to permit it.

"Don't you want me to touch you?" Jessica asked.

Wolfe didn't trust his voice. He simply shifted his legs and prayed that his self-control was as good as he had always believed it to be.

The male flesh Jessica found was utterly foreign, twin weights resting on her palm and all of him drawn tight and hard, so sensitive that Wolfe's breath was torn from his mouth when she touched him experimentally. Instantly, she tried to retreat. His hand closed over hers, tangling her in the sheet, holding her palm cupped closely against him while fire burned through his body.

Then Wolfe realized what he had done.

"Forgive me," he said raggedly. "I didn't mean to force something you didn't want."

Gently Jessica kissed the taut skin of Wolfe's waist just above the line of the sheet. "I want to touch you. I just don't know how. And from what you taught me my fifteenth summer, for all your hardness, a man is vulnerable there."

"What? Oh," Wolfe said, remembering. "That savage little gutter trick."

"That little gutter trick saved me from Lord Gore."

"What do you mean?"

"He threw me against the wall so hard I hadn't the breath to groan, much less to scream the house down around his ears as I wanted. If I hadn't used my knee as you taught, I'd have been raped on the hall floor just like my mother."

"Jessi."

Wolfe half lifted himself so that he could see her face. What he saw was creamy, half-covered breasts, hair on fire with the dawn, and a sweet mouth so close to his aching flesh that he could feel each of her breaths as a current of warmth soaking through the sheet. He stroked a strand of the long, mahogany hair that fanned across his chest.

"Your hand is trembling," she whispered.

"Yes," he said huskily. "You keep surprising me. You have little reason to trust men, yet you are more generous in your sensuality than any woman I've ever known."

"Only with you. You have never been as other men to me. You are my Lord Wolfe, Tree That Stands Alone, the man who Talks Back To Thunder on behalf of a frightened elf."

Jessica kissed him softly where sheet and skin met. The brush of his fingertips over her lips made her shiver with memories.

"You have another name, as well," she said.

"I know. The viscount's savage."

"No." She bit the taut skin of Wolfe's belly in sensuous punishment. "Never a savage. To me your true name is Takes Me To The Sun."

Wolfe wondered distantly how many more times Jessica would surprise him; and then she astonished him by drawing down the sheet and kissing the very different flesh that she had aroused.

The kiss was as delicate as the brush of a butterfly's wing and it burned as nothing Wolfe had ever felt in his life . . . until Jessica lifted her hair and let it settle over him. He felt each silky strand as a separate sliding caress, concealing and then revealing him in the same endless, searing instant.

"Teach me how to touch you," Jessica whispered, stroking Wolfe very lightly with her hands. "Tell me where you are most sensitive."

Her name shivered from Wolfe's lips. It was all he could say as he fought to control the primal pulses that were dragging him to the brink of ecstasy. For the space of several breaths he struggled, not realizing that Jessica was watching him with eyes made smoky by passion. Finally, he let out a long, shuddering sigh.

"You take the breath from me," Wolfe said.

"Then I'll give you mine."

Jessica lifted her face to his, breathing his name

into his mouth as they shared a kiss that burned with leashed hunger. Slowly, his hands closed over hers, drawing them across his aching body. With a soft, ragged sound of anticipation, she kissed the corner of his mouth, the pulse beating so strongly in his neck, the muscular swell of his chest. And all the while her hands hovered just above his fiercely aroused flesh, touching him only with her warmth.

When Wolfe finally could speak, his voice was a rasp that told Jessica how tightly drawn he was.

"Touch me here, where I ache for you," he said, pressing one small hand between his legs.

Jessica cupped and caressed him very gently, sensing the wildness quivering in him. Slowly he drew her hand higher, wrapping it around his potent flesh, urging her to measure him from base to blunt satin tip.

"There," Wolfe said hoarsely. "There I am very sensitive. It is there I would feel the shivering of your ecstasy most clearly."

Jessica made an odd sound and ran her fingers over his different textures with both curiosity and gentle care. Wolfe felt the trembling of her hands beneath his and smiled darkly.

"Is there anything else you want to know?" he asked.

"Yes," she whispered.

"What is it?"

"I want to know how it would feel to have you inside me."

"That can't be. But this . . . yes . . . I need your hands, Jessi. I've never needed like this."

Her hands moved and pleasure coursed heavily through Wolfe. She kissed the muscular curve of his thigh, the sleek warmth of his abdomen, the intriguing hollow of his navel.

Eyes glittering, half-closed, Wolfe watched her loving him in the only way he would allow. The hushed silence of the room expanded until it became as taut as the instant before lightning arced between sky and earth.

The clear pleasure Jessica took in Wolfe's body and her utter lack of fear almost undid him. It took a fierce effort of will for him not to grab her and return the intimate caresses. But he knew if he touched her, he wouldn't stop until he was buried in her, feeling her ecstasy shivering around him, hurling him into the sun.

Wolfe's fingers clenched in the ends of Jessica's long hair as he felt her warm mouth caressing his skin. Then he could watch her no longer. He could only close his eyes and fight the violent need that threatened to overpower him. Of all the sensual things he had dreamed about his elf, the possibility of her taking such open, heated pleasure in his body hadn't been one of them. Never had he been more aroused or felt more his own power as a man.

Then Jessica's tongue skimmed his blunt arousal. He made the sound of a man in torment. Her head turned swiftly toward him, sending her hair over him in silky fire. As lightly as a sigh, as hot as flame, her hair settled between his thighs. A visible shudder ripped through him.

"Wolfe? Did I hurt you?"

He smiled despite talons of need drawing his body on a rack. "Did I ever make you ache?"

She nodded. The movement sent sensual fire coursing over his erect flesh. He barely suppressed a groan.

"Sweet Jessi, it hurts only when you stop."

"But how do I touch you now? We are so different."

"I've never asked that from a woman." Wolfe looked at Jessica with eyes that were dark blue gems burning. "That kind of intimacy is too much to ask of an innocent elf."

"Is it shameful of me to admit I'd rather be wanton than innocent? I find I'm quite . . . curious."

"And I find I've never been more aroused. I wonder how much more I can take?" Wolfe drew a deep breath and let it out slowly. "We'll learn together."

"This can't be new to you."

He smiled ruefully. "But it is."

"Your duchesses—"

"Hammer the duchesses," Wolfe said roughly. "They weren't mine, nor was I theirs. I was a savage trophy for them. Not one of them gave tinker's damn for anything but cold-hearted rutting. Not one of them ever gave me half the sweet pleasure you have."

"I have?" Jessica whispered. "By touching you where you're most different?"

Wolfe smiled and stroked his thumb over her lips, the only way he would permit himself to touch her.

"That, and earlier, when you went down my body as though I were a warm spring and you were bathing in me."

"But you are." Jessica drew her cheek against the hard masculine flesh that defined Wolfe's hunger. "And I am."

"Bathing in me?"

"Yes." She turned her head and caressed him with her other cheek.

"Keep that up," he said in a thick voice, "and

there will be as much fact as metaphor in what you say."

Jessica paused, then smiled secretly as she understood. "That would be only fair."

"No."

"Yes." Her head moved again, but this time it was her mouth that caressed him rather than her cheek. "Did you not bathe in me?"

Wolfe groaned something in Cheyenne as his whole body clenched.

"You are very hard, my Wolfe."

The sound he made wasn't recognizable as a word, which was just as well. He was certain the word would have shocked her.

"You're very warm," she whispered, testing his heat with the tip of her tongue.

"You are a tease," he said in a thick voice.

"Am I? Your blood is running heavily. I can feel it." Jessica trembled with the answering rush of her own blood. "It beats more fiercely here than in your neck."

Wolfe didn't answer. He couldn't. He had never imagined how violently exciting it might be to experience his body through Jessica's eyes, her hands, her words.

Then the gentle, curious, incendiary heat of her mouth discovered him. With a murmuring sound of pleasure and surprise, she surrounded him. Wolfe's fingers clenched deeply in the covers as a wave of unspeakable pleasure exploded through him. He fought to control the wild pulses of his release, but even as he fought he knew he would quickly lose.

Wolfe barely had enough strength to drag Jessica back up his body and bury his tongue in her mouth. Then he tasted himself and her and groaned as though he were being torn apart.

The leap and shudder of his flesh beneath her hand awed Jessica. She felt the spreading, silky heat of Wolfe's fulfillment and knew that she was touching the beginning of life itself. She returned his kiss fiercely, wishing that life within her.

"I didn't mean to shock you like that," he said when he could draw a whole breath again. "When you kissed me so intimately, I all but lost control."

"You didn't shock me."

"Bloody hell I didn't. You tasted me."

"Yes," Jessica whispered. "That was the best of all. You taste like tears, only more silky and mysterious."

Her words went through Wolfe like dawn through night, transforming and renewing him in the space of a single rushing breath.

"You're going to be the death of me, elf," Wolfe said huskily, rolling over until he had Jessica caged between his body and the bed. "But first, I'm going to be the death of you."

Jessica didn't understand until she felt Wolfe's mouth on her breast and his hand sliding down her body to seek the scented petals of the flower that opened only for him. She was already sleek, sultry, hungry, for pleasuring him had aroused her. The first brush of his fingers made her gasp. The second made her cry out. The third sent a silky heat spreading between them.

The fourth sent her to the sun.

 16

A<small>LTHOUGH</small> Wolfe's expression had been rather grim when he came in from outdoors, the sight of his wife spooning chili into a big serving bowl made him pause. The slow, very male smile he gave her as he peeled off his leather work gloves told Jessica that he was remembering what had happened between them in the hushed silence of dawn three days ago—and every night since.

As Wolfe took the big bowl from Jessica, he slid the palms of his hands over the back of her fingers. Because there were other people nearby, he didn't bend to take her soft mouth in a kiss. But he wanted to, and the catch in her breathing when his palms touched her skin told Wolfe that Jessica wanted the kiss as much as he did.

"How's the little man doing?" Wolfe asked Willow, turning away from the temptation of Jessica's mouth.

Willow looked up from the shallow basin where she was carefully bathing the baby, who seemed to be enjoying the warm water and his mother's touch.

"Ethan Caleb Black is doing wonderfully well," Willow said, smiling.

"Ethan, huh? You finally decided."

"It was Caleb's father's name."

"Big shoes for the little one to fill," Wolfe said. He looked appraisingly at Willow. "Are you sure you should be up and working so soon?"

"Lying in bed is for people who are sick. I'm not."

Frowning, Jessica looked up from the pan of cornbread that was staying warm near the stove.

"In England, the women stay in confinement for several weeks after giving birth," Jessica pointed out.

"Figures," Wolfe said. His voice was rich with disgust for the aristocrats of Great Britain. "The whole lot of them is as useless as teats on a boar hog."

All Willow said was, "The longer you stay in bed, the weaker you are when you get up."

"You look tired," Jessica persisted.

"I've been a lot more tired. Ask Caleb." She picked up Ethan and wrapped his bottom in a soft cotton diaper as she continued talking. "Ethan and I had a nice long nap this morning, didn't we, button? And after lunch, we're going to have another one."

Wolfe shook his head, but it was in admiration rather than disagreement. "And here I thought that Cheyenne women were tough. Caleb must have been standing under a whole sky full of lucky stars the day he found you."

Jessica bent over the pan of cornbread, rearranging the clean cotton towel so that no warmth could escape. The fussing wasn't necessary, but it gave her an excuse to hide her face until she was certain that none of the hurt she felt at Wolfe's comments would show in her expression. Even knowing that he hadn't meant his words as a back-handed slap didn't remove the sting of them.

She had begun to hope that he was accepting their marriage. Since the night when Wolfe had discovered the source of her fear of men, marriage, and childbirth, he had been the affectionate companion of old. He had also been a restrained, generous teacher of the ancient arts of sensuality.

But now Jessica realized Wolfe hadn't accepted her as his wife. Nor was he likely to do so. His contempt for the aristocracy was as deep in him as his blood.

Jessica had been born into that aristocracy. Wolfe never forgot that, not even when in the grip of a passion for her that made him shake. It was why, after three nights of the most intense sensual explorations, Jessica was still a virgin. She was born of the aristocracy, which made her the kind of woman with whom Wolfe might play sensuous games, but not the kind of woman he thought was fit to be his true mate.

The wind flexed against the house, testing its strength and reminding the men inside of what awaited them after they had eaten. A faint scratching sound came from the windows, particles of ice or grit flung against the glass by the strengthening wind. As one, the men stopped eating and exchanged wary looks.

Without a word, Wolfe stood and went to the back door. Ignoring the ice-tipped wind, he walked away from the house until he had a clear view of the sky around the mountain peaks. The air had an odd sheen to it. The wind was alive, potent, and smelled of winter.

Although it was barely noon, the elemental harmonies of wolf packs on the prowl shivered through the forest.

Motionless, silent, Wolfe stood and absorbed all the subtle messages of sky and earth, wind, and wildlife. When he turned and came back inside, his face was impassive and his eyes were bleak.

Caleb watched Wolfe sit down. "Well?" he asked softly.

Wolfe hesitated, then shrugged. The truth would come on the wind no matter what was said or not said now.

"It's making up to snow."

Caleb muttered something Jessica chose not to overhear. Quietly she set down another pan of warm cornbread and a bowl of chili.

"How hard?" Caleb asked.

"It's going to be a real Hell-bringer." Wolfe's voice was very soft, but very certain.

"Then nobody rides but me. It's too easy to get lost in a blizzard."

"I'll start bringing in the cows and calves," Rafe said, ingoring Caleb. "My bullwhip makes the horses too skittish, but it works like a charm on those cattle."

"I'll ride shotgun for you," Reno said. "Thank God not too many calves have been born yet. They'll be a lot safer in their mother's bellies. Have the mares started foaling yet?"

"No," Wolfe said. "My steeldust will probably be the first. Once she foals, the rest won't be far behind. When they start dropping their foals in a blizzard . . ."

Caleb narrowed his eyes but said nothing. There was nothing he could say that would turn back the cold northern wind.

"Once we get a rope on my mustang," Wolfe

continued, "Ishmael will make sure the rest of the herd follows."

"Hell," Caleb said in disgust. "The last time I tried roping that steeldust of yours, she ran rings around me."

"Quick little thing, isn't she? Smart, too." Wolfe's smile faded. "If I can't talk to her—"

"Talk?" interrupted Jessica.

Caleb smiled oddly. "In Cheyenne. It's the damnedest thing I ever saw. Wolfe can go up to a mustang and 'talk' to it and half the time it will follow him like a big dog."

"That's what the Cheyenne call them, Big Dogs," Wolfe said dryly. His voice changed. "If the steeldust won't listen to reason, and we can't get close enough to rope her, I'll have to try creasing her with a bullet."

Jessica looked unhappily at Wolfe. She knew the steeldust was the core of the horse herd he hoped to build.

"I'll do what I have to," Wolfe said.

By the the third day of the blizzard, the men were exhausted from lack of sleep and long hours spent riding under the most miserable conditions imaginable. Jessica made gallons of stew, rafts of cornbread, and lakes of coffee. She kept all of it hot in the kitchen no matter what the hour, for she never knew when one of the men would walk in the back door shivering with cold and hungry as a spring bear.

"Go back to bed," Jessica said to Willow.

"You've been up cooking since dawn. It's late afternoon now. You must be exhausted."

"I'm fine. I'm stronger than I look. I always have been."

Willow looked at Jessica's drawn face and understood what was bothering her.

"The men will be all right, Jessi. They're used to riding wild country."

A tight nod was Jessica's only answer. She didn't know how much Caleb had told his wife about the problems they were having with so many wolves prowling in the storm, with the contrary cattle, and with cows calving at the worst possible time. Not to mention the wind itself, edged with thousands of icy teeth that ripped into flesh and stole the very warmth of life from livestock and man alike.

But Jessica knew all of those problems, for Wolfe had told her more than he knew with his terse answers and eloquent silences.

"If only the bloody wind would stop," Jessica said suddenly.

"Yes. If only. At least it's not snowing any more," Willow said, walking to the window. She picked up the spyglass she had put there. In the magnified circle of its view, she looked across the pasture, counting horses under her breath. It was impossible to be certain through the waisthigh curtains of snow, but she thought the count came up short.

"What is it?" Jessica asked, coming to stand by Willow.

"At least four of the mares are missing."

"Ishmael will bring them back."

"Not if they're foaling," Willow whispered. "No stallion will disturb a mare when she quits the herd to give birth." There was a tense silence before Willow added, "I saw at least one wolf. The packs are moving again."

For an instant, Jessica closed her eyes. She had seen Willow's Arabians when they were brought to the home pasture. Even heavy with their unborn foals and thick with winter coats, the mares had an elegance of form and movement that enchanted Jessica. The thought of those mares lying down in the cruel wind to give birth while wolves circled hungrily around made her feel ill. The mares would be all but helpless, captive of the need to give birth. For a time, they would be almost as vulnerable as the foals being pushed from warm wombs onto frozen ground.

"The foals . . ." Jessica whispered.

Willow looked through the spyglass, saying nothing.

"Can you see any of the men?" Jessica asked.

"No. They're probably combing the forest for cows. When the wind started coming from the northeast before dawn, the herd drifted out of Eagle Creek Basin."

With growing tension Jessica waited while Willow searched as much as she could see of the pasture through the swirling snow. When she collapsed the spyglass with barely restrained violence, Jessica knew that the mares were still missing.

"I don't see the steeldust anywhere," Willow said finally. "I think the foaling has begun."

"Dear God, no," Jessica whispered. "We can't lose the steeldust now. Wolfe was so relieved when she came to him as though she understood he would keep her safe."

Willow set aside the spyglass. "I nursed Ethan a few minutes ago. If he cries before I come back, just—"

"No."

The curt refusal startled Willow.

"Stay with your baby," Jessica said tightly. "I'll check on the mares."

"I can't let you do that. The cold is too dangerous."

"That's why you're staying with Ethan. If anything happens to you, the baby will die. If anything happens to me . . ." Jessica paused and then spoke the bitter truth with no bitterness in her voice. "No one else will die of it."

Willow clasped her hands together until the knuckles gleamed whitely. "Jessi, you mustn't go out. You don't know what this mountain wind is like, how quickly it can take the living warmth from you."

"I know about cold and wind. I've seen sheep freeze standing up in the fields and wells frozen from top to bottom like stone."

Willow's eyes widened into startled hazel pools. "I didn't know England was so cold."

"It isn't. Scotland is. Do you have winter clothing that would fit me?"

"Jessi—"

"Do you or not?"

"In the bedroom. I'll show you." Willow smiled oddly. "Some of the clothes will be familiar. Caleb got them from Wolfe. They were yours. There's a shotgun over the front door. Take it. I'll bring you extra shells."

Very quickly, Jessica was on the way out of the house, wrapped in layers of wool and buckskin that were familiar, and a hooded fur jacket that was not. She wore pants instead of a skirt and carried a borrowed shotgun. The pockets of her jacket were heavy with extra shells.

The only horse in the corral that didn't look half dead on its feet from work was a tall black gelding.

He didn't want to be bridled, saddled, or ridden. Jessica managed the first two, but was very nearly thrown before the horse gave up and left the corral with ears laid back. As she rode out into the storm, she was grateful that Wolfe had insisted that she learn to ride difficult horses and do the work of stablehands.

Before Jessica reached the pasture, she saw the first of the wolves. They were sniffing the wind eagerly and moving as though they had a destination in mind. Acting on instinct, she followed. She lost the trail partway into the sparse forest. The wind was less brutal in the trees, but not by much.

Just as Jessica was going to give up and go back to the pasture, she heard the unmistakable sound of a horse screaming in anger and fear. She spun the black gelding around and headed toward the sounds at a dead run, dodging branches and clinging to the saddle horn when the horse lunged through low spots where snow lay in powdery drifts.

At first, Jessica saw only wolves. Then she saw the steeldust mare trying to struggle to her feet in order to face the circling predators. Jessica brought the shotgun up and fired into the wolves. They scattered away, only to circle back to the mare almost instantly. Jessica fired again and again, reloading rapidly despite the clumsiness of her gloves.

After the third shot, the wolves withdrew, vanishing into swirls of wind-blown snow. Jessica dismounted and went to the steeldust. The mustang flinched and laid back her ears but was too caught up in the ultimate moments of giving birth to resist the gentle hands helping her.

As soon as the foal was born, Jessica sat down and pulled it into her lap so that the icy ground wouldn't sap the newborn's strength. Very quickly, the mustang was back on her feet and nosing curiously at the slick, wet bundle that overflowed Jessica's lap. A surprisingly long, agile pink tongue appeared and began a vigorous cleaning of the foal. When Jessica's hand or leg got in the way, it was cleaned too.

Suddenly, the mare's head went up and her nostrils flared. She shied away, but came back instantly, for the foal was a lure she couldn't refuse. She nickered urgently to her foal. In response, the foal tried to stand.

With a few strategic pushes from Jessica, the foal managed to come to its feet, but very quickly went sprawling, its stilt-like legs sticking out every which way. As Jessica reached for it, a harsh male voice cut through the storm.

"What the hell do you think you're doing out here! Southern lady, sometimes you don't have the sense God gave a goose!"

Before Jessica could say a single word she was snatched off the ground by large hands. Instants later she found herself staring eye to eye with a perfectly furious Caleb Black. There was no sign of the sensual lover, gentle father, or loving husband in him at the moment. He was a dark angel of justice with blazing gold eyes.

"Jessi!"

She smiled tentatively, but found her mouth too dry to speak. Caleb looked frankly intimidating.

"Good grief," he said, still hardly able to believe his eyes. "Riding Deuce and wearing that fur jacket, I thought you were Willow. Does Wolfe know you're out in this Hell-wind?"

The appearance of a multitude of slate-gray wraiths just at the edge of visibility saved Jessica from having to answer. Before she could take a breath, she was supported only by Caleb's left arm and there was a six-gun in his right hand. Shots came too quickly too count, their staccato thunder battering through the savage keening of the wind. Almost a hundred feet away, a wolf went down and stayed. The rest vanished as silently as they had appeared.

Jessica stared eat Caleb, astonished at his speed and accuracy. Veiled by snow, the wolves had appeared with no warning and had left in the same way. Yet if the words Caleb was saying were any indication, he wasn't much impressed by either his quickness or his skill.

"*Damnation.* How could I miss so many? Must be thirty of those sons of bitches prowling around."

Caleb didn't bother putting Jessica down. He simply tossed her onto Deuce, reloaded his gun swiftly, and went to the struggling foal. When he came close, the steeldust's ears went back.

"Take it easy, you cross-eyed cayuse. I'm going to help your baby, not eat him."

The mare's nostrils flared. Jessica had been infused with the foal's scent. Enough of it had rubbed off on Caleb to confuse the mare. Stamping her feet, lashing her tail, nickering nervously, she watched while Caleb picked up her foal and draped it over Jessica's lap.

"Take him to a stall. The steeldust won't like it, but she'll follow."

"At least three other mares are missing from the herd," Jessica said.

With a hissed word under his breath, Caleb pulled on his gloves. "Never rains but it pours.

Only a contrary female would have babies in this weather."

"Leave it to a contrary male to complain about the fruits of last summer's frolic," Jessica retorted.

Caleb gave a crack of laughter as he smacked Deuce on his muscular black haunch. "Get going, boy. Sassy little bits like your rider and that foal don't take long to freeze solid in this wind."

"I'm not little," Jessica said as the big gelding headed out.

"You know, Willow's been saying the same thing to me since I met her. Didn't believe it then. Don't believe it now. Watch Deuce. He doesn't like wind worth a damn."

"I noticed. I'll be back for the other foals."

"No. It's too dangerous with the wind and the wolves. You stay home. Reno isn't far behind me. We'll look for the missing mares."

"But what about the cattle? You need them more than you need the foals, and most of the horses are Wolfe's anyway."

Caleb didn't answer. Instead, he swung up onto his big horse with a quick motion and trotted off into the savage, waist-high swirls of snow. Beyond him, the herd of horses huddled miserably, their rumps to the icy wind.

With the steeldust in anxious attendance, Jessica rode quickly to the barn. The mustang didn't want to go inside, but she did, shying every inch of the way. Jessica put mother and foal in an empty stall, dragged in a bucket of water and an armload of hay, and hauled herself up on Caleb's tall horse once again.

Deuce didn't want to leave the barn's shelter. After a sharp contest of wills with its rider, the big gelding laid back his ears and went out into the teeth of the Hell-wind once more.

The sound of a six-gun being fired told Jessica where to find Caleb. By the time she got there, the wolves were gone. Tall, wide-shouldered, standing with his back to her, Caleb straddled a newborn foal while he rapidly reloaded his six-gun and watched the sheets of wind-driven snow for the movement of hungry wolves. When he saw none, he holstered the gun with a smooth motion and bent to pick up the foal. The mare was much more tame than Wolfe's steeldust. Other than nosing the foal insistently, she made no move to interfere.

As though understanding that the man's attention wasn't on them any more, wolves rushed in from three sides.

Before Jessica could scream Caleb's name, he straightened, drew his gun, and fired all in the same motion, emptying the revolver in a few shattering seconds. The speed of his movements shocked Jessica, even though she had seen it once before.

The wolves scattered, leaving two dark shadows behind. Instantly, he began to reload. Then he heard something behind him and spun, gun raised in his left hand. Pale green eyes glittered like gems in the man's wind-burned face.

In that instant Jessica remembered what Wolfe had said about Reno and Caleb being well-matched when it came to speed and six-guns.

"Willy, what the hell are you doing out here, and riding Deuce of all horses! Does Caleb know what damn foolishness you're up to?"

As Jessica urged her horse forward, the hood of her jacket was stripped back by the wind. Long mahogany locks whipped and leaped like flames in the late afternoon light.

"Jessi! For God's sake, does Wolfe—"

"Just give me the blasted foal before it freezes to the ground," Jessica interrupted curtly, tired of being told by tall, dangerous men that she belonged at home by the fire. "You need every hand you can get."

Impatiently, she stuffed her hair back under the hood and pulled the drawstring tight. No sooner was she finished than Reno dropped a curly-coated, ice-tipped black foal across her lap. A big rangy bay mare followed, all but stepping on Reno's heels.

"Was it you with the shotgun earlier?" Reno asked.

"Yes."

"Did you reload?"

"Wolfe taught me to hunt," she retorted. "What do you think?"

Reno's smile flashed. "I think you reloaded. I've got your carbine. Want to trade?"

"Unlike Wolfe, I can't shoot straight one-handed while riding a horse and hanging upside-down with my eyes closed," Jessica said dryly. "I'll be better off with the shotgun. All I have to do is point it in the right general direction and pull the trigger."

"You do that, Red. All the blood smell from the births and that wild wind have every wolf pack between here and the divide in a frenzy. Must be forty or fifty wolves prowling around. Damnedest thing I've ever seen. Shoot one and three more take its place." He smacked Jessica's horse on the rump. "Take her home, Deuce."

Deuce moved eagerly toward the barn once more, followed by a mare that was nearly as big as he was. The foal struggled briefly, then gave up and lay quietly while the wind keened icily around.

As soon as Deuce left the meager shelter of the pines, swirls of snow leaped up from the ground, stinging unprotected skin. The gelding tugged at the bit and humped his back as though intending to buck again.

"Don't even think of it," Jessica muttered, curbing the big horse.

Suddenly there were wolves everywhere.

With a cry of fear, Jessica dropped the reins, lifted the shotgun, and fired at a leaping black shape. Simultaneously, Deuce lashed out with his hind feet and the big bay mare charged at the closest wolf, forcing it to retreat. The mare spun back to the gelding. Instinctively, the horses protected their vulnerable hamstrings by turning their rumps to one another and facing the circling wolves. Jessica didn't urge Deuce to run for the barn; she, too, knew that the horse would be hamstrung and brought down long before it reached the barn's safety.

While Deuce pivoted and struck out at wolves that were foolhardy enough to rush forward, Jessica fought to stay upright, keep the foal across the saddle, and reload the shotgun at the same time. Yet even when she succeeded in shoving in another shell, she knew it wouldn't get the job done.

There were too many wolves.

An eerie calm came over Jessica as she raised the shotgun to fire, for she knew it would be a race to see if she got the gun reloaded again before the wolves regrouped and closed in. If she lost that race, her only hope was that one of the men had heard the shotgun's distinctive bellow and would find her in time.

She triggered the gun. Wolves scattered as buck-

shot fanned out like wind-driven hail. Some of the
wolves leaped aside, snapping and snarling, as
though besieged by bees. Fighting to hold the foal
and herself in the saddle, Jessica managed to get
another shell into the gun before the wolves re-
gained their courage.

When she brought up the shotgun again, the foal
began to slip off. Desperately, she held the foal in
place while trying to level the shotgun at the wolf
that was leading the attack—a big, slate-gray male
that had been clever enough to recognize her shotgun as dangerous and leap aside as soon as she
had pointed the barrel toward him.

The big male raced forward before Jessica could
bring the shotgun to bear again. Abruptly, he som-
ersaulted and fell. He didn't get up. Even as the
sound of rifle fire screamed down through the
wind to Jessica, another animal spun away from
the pack and lay still.

Back at the edge of the trees, Wolfe took aim and
shot again, picking off the animal that was closest
to the horses. Despite the fear hammering at him,
he shot smoothly, evenly, and accurately, using a
hail of bullets to separate the carnivores from their
intended prey.

Too damn many wolves, he thought savagely. *What
in Christ's name was Caleb thinking about, letting Willow come out when there was a Hell-wind blowing?*

Suddenly, there were no more targets. The
wolves had withdrawn again, vanishing like puffs
of smoke on the violent wind.

Reloading quickly, Wolfe rode out into the
meadow. He saw Deuce head for the barn at a fast
canter, with his rider crouched low in the saddle,
hanging onto a foal. One of Caleb's big Montana
mares followed anxiously.

Even as Wolfe admired Willow's courage in taking on the Hell-wind and wolves, he wished things weren't so desperate that they needed every hand. But they were that desperate, and they did need every hand, even the soft one of a woman who should have been rocking a cradle rather than riding shotgun over a helpless foal.

THE wind finally died at sunset, bringing relief to men and animals alike. Mares with foals were in the barn, cows with newborn calves had been herded into the corral, and the men traded off riding around the rest of the livestock. The temperature rose with each circuit Wolfe made around the cattle.

Another wind began to blow, a gentle wind from the south. By moonrise, the snow had begun to melt beneath the warm breath of the chinook. Wolfe stood in the stirrups and looked out over the glistening land. He stretched and sighed deeply, weary to his core.

"Go back to the house," Caleb called from the shadows. "The cattle can take it from here. Any creature that dies of being born in a warm wind is too weak to be worth saving. Besides, as tired as we are, we'd probably shoot ourselves instead of the wolves."

"They're gone. They won't gather like that again until another Hell-wind blows."

The certainty in Wolfe's voice made coolness condense along Caleb's spine. He cocked his head and looked at the man he thought of as a brother but didn't always understand.

"How long will it be before another Hell-wind blows?" Caleb asked, curious.

"My mother's mother saw one as a child. Your

grandchildren might see one, if they live long enough."

"Hope they have friends like you to help them."

"And wives like Willow," Wolfe said softly.

Caleb didn't hear. He had already reined his horse away and was trotting toward the horse herd that Reno and Rafe were guarding. Wolfe turned toward the house where lights were glowing in welcoming shades of gold.

Knowing how tired Willow must be, the last thing Wolfe expected when he walked into the house was to find it full of the savory scents of cooking. A pan of warm water was on the stove, along with a dry towel and soap. Smiling, he took the hint and began stripping off hat and gloves, heavy jacket and cold boots, vest and shirt and undershirt. He washed as much of himself as he could reach, enjoying the feel of the warm water and the dry towel.

The sound of a woman's skirt rustling behind Wolfe told him that he wasn't alone any longer. Even as he turned around, his blood heated at the thought of catching Jessica and holding her close to his body again. She always smelled so good, so clean. Holding her was like lying in a rose garden in the full bloom of summer.

But it was the scent of lavender rather than roses that met Wolfe. Willow smiled and held out a clean shirt to him.

"If your clothes are anything like Caleb's have been, they could stand up and shoot for themselves."

Wolfe put on the shirt, appreciating the clean softness and warmth of the flannel. He looked at the stew simmering gently on the stove and the mound of biscuits, and shook his head in silent wonder.

"They broke the mold with you, Willow. A new baby to take care of, yet you're washing clothes for four men and feeding them as well, day and night. And in between you rescue foals and shoot wolves."

Willow gave Wolfe an odd glance. "I'm with you as far as the new baby and the biscuits, but you lost me after that. Jessi did the rest, including the cooking. If any foals got rescued, it was her doing, not mine. All I did was lend her my clothes and a shotgun."

"What are you talking about?"

"Jessi. She was the one out in the storm, not me."

Wolfe's eyes widened. His hands gripped Willow's shoulders hard enough to make her wince.

"I saw you out there, riding Deuce," he said flatly. "I saw a wolf leap for you and you fired the shotgun and reloaded it while Deuce was dancing around and you were holding the foal across your lap and I didn't know if I could shoot that god-damned wolf before he took you and the foal right down into the snow!"

"Jessi," Willow said succinctly. "Jessi and Jessi and Jessi."

Wolfe released Willow and began walking quickly toward the bedroom he and Jessica shared.

"If you're looking for your fancy aristocratic lady," Willow said dryly, "try the barn."

Wolfe spun around. "What?"

"Jessi was worried that wolves might get into the barn. She knows how much store you set by that savage steeldust mustang. That's why Jessi rode out into the storm when I saw the mare was missing. That's why Jessi's in the barn now with a shotgun. She's guarding the future the same way I would have in her shoes."

Wolfe stared at Willow, unable to believe what he was hearing.

"I wanted to go," Willow continued. "Jessi wouldn't let me. She said if something happened to me, Ethan would die. But if something happened to her, nobody would die."

"The little fool."

"Is she? She may have been born and raised an aristocrat, but she's not the useless little decoration you believe she is."

Willow was talking to herself. The door slammed behind Wolfe as he headed for the barn.

 **17**

WHEN the steeldust caught Wolfe's scent, she nickered softly in welcome. He leaned over the stall door and looked inside. The breath went out of him as though at a blow.

Jessica was slumped in the far corner, asleep. The shotgun was propped against the wall within easy reach. A newborn blood-bay foal was curled against her, taking advantage of shared warmth. Silence grew while Wolfe measured the changes between the girl who had danced with him in London and the girl he was looking at now.

In London, Jessica's skin had been as fine-grained and flawless as a pearl. America hadn't been so kind. She had scratches and welts on one side of her face and her cheeks were chapped by the wind. In London, her color had been vivid, almost incandescent. Now her lips were pale, and exhaustion ringed her eyes with darkness.

It was only the beginning of the unhappy comparisons. In London, Jessica's hair had been as sleek and burnished as flame, and jewels had glinted from its intricately coiffed depths. Now her hair was wild, wind-tangled, and mixed with straw. In London, her clothes had been designed and executed in the most expensive materials available, and her skirts had billowed like clouds. In America, she wore a boy's flannel underwear, a boy's buckskin shirt and breeches, and the evidence of her assistance at several foalings was spread from her shoulders to her small, durable boots.

In London, Jessica's days were composed of teas and balls, plays and the latest books. In America, she worked like a scullery maid and stablehand combined. In London, she entertained her guests with wit and silver laughter. In America, she rarely laughed and had nearly died.

Jessi, what have I done to you?

There was no answer to Wolfe's silent, anguished question except the truth: He had almost killed the girl who trusted him when she trusted nothing else on earth.

Making no sound, Wolfe went into the stall. He picked up the shotgun, took the shell from the firing chamber, and closed the gun. The small noise woke Jessica. She sat up with a start, automatically reaching for the corner where she had propped the shotgun out of the way.

"It's all right, Jessi. The wolves are gone."

She focused on Wolfe, blinked, and smiled sleepily. "All save one, and he is my very own Lord Wolfe. I'm safe with him."

Pain went through Wolfe like black lightning, scoring his soul in ways he couldn't name. He could feel it, though, a kind of agony he had never known before. Jessica trusted him without reservation, yet he had brought nothing but unhappiness and harm to her.

"My stupidity nearly killed you, elf. When I think how close you came to being torn apart by wolves..."

"You're a fine shot," she murmured, sliding back into sleep.

"I'm a fool."

Though Wolfe's voice was harsh, he was very gentle as he lifted Jessica into his arms. When she realized he meant to carry her from the stall, she woke up in a rush.

"Wait. You haven't even looked at the steeldust's foal," she protested. "She'll be a wonderful foundation mare for our herd. I've never seen so fine a head on a foal, nor such a deep chest. It's a filly. Isn't that grand? In a few years she—"

"To hell with the steeldust and her filly both," Wolfe interrupted savagely. "Don't you understand? *You could have died.*"

Jessica blinked. "So could you."

"That's different. It ends here, Jessi."

"What?"

"I'm taking you back to London as soon as the passes are safe."

"Going to give that carriage another shot at me, is that it?"

"What are you talking about?"

Jessica smiled and nuzzled Wolfe's hard jawline. "I nearly got run down by a carriage in London, remember?"

Wolfe's mouth flattened. "I remember."

"You should. You beat that driver to within an inch of his life."

"I would rather have killed the drunken bastard."

"There are a lot more like him," Jessica pointed out.

"So?"

"So I'm no safer in London than I am here, am I?"

The tip of Jessica's tongue drew a line of sensual fire down Wolfe's jaw.

"That's not the point," he said roughly.

"Then what is?"

"I've nearly killed you trying to make you admit that you aren't cut from Western cloth. You're a British aristocrat and you deserve to have the elegant life of ease for which you were bred, born, raised, and trained."

As Wolfe spoke, he stepped out of the barn into the brilliant moonlight. The ground was cold and shiny with melting snow. The air was like warm silk.

"Nonsense," Jessica said, yawning. "You wouldn't be happy in England."

"That won't be a problem."

Jessica went very still in Wolfe's arms. All sleepiness fled before the wave of unease that swept through her.

"What are you saying?" she whispered.

"I'll leave England as soon as our marriage is annulled."

"I haven't agreed to an—"

"You don't have to," Wolfe interrupted savagely. "I'll be the one to seek the annulment."

"But why?" she whispered. "What have I done to make you hate me so?"

"I don't hate you. I never have, even when I wanted to throttle you for trapping me into marriage."

"Then why are—"

Jessica got no farther in her question, for Wolfe's mouth descended on hers. By the time he lifted his head once more, both of them were breathing quickly, hungrily.

"It's over, Jessi. It never should have begun."

"Wolfe, listen to me," she said urgently. "I want to be your wife in all ways. I want to live with you, work beside you, bear your children, care for you when you are ill, and laugh with you when the rest of the world is a hundred shades of gray."

The words were knives turning in Wolfe, tempting him unmercifully, slicing away at his self-control, making him bleed with all that could never be—an aristocratic elf and a halfbreed mustang hunter. He had known it was impossible since she was fifteen.

And since she was fifteen, he had known what Hell was: living with what he wanted forever just beyond his reach, forever calling to him across an abyss he must not cross, for if he did, he would destroy the very thing he wanted.

He had nearly done just that despite his best intentions.

"I love you," Jessica said. "I love—"

"No more," Wolfe interrupted savagely, cutting across the words that were more painful to him than any blow he had ever received. "I am Tree That Stands Alone. You are Lady Jessica Charteris. You have nothing to fear in England any longer. I'll see that you get a suitable husband or none at all."

Wolfe would have preferred none at all. The thought of another man touching Jessica added another dimension to his own personal Hell. He wasn't sure he could bear it. Yet he must. He took in a deep breath, let it out, and spoke more gently.

"I should be hung for ever bringing you to this wilderness."

"But—"

"*No more.*"

Jessica flinched at the raw pain in Wolfe's voice.

It stopped her as nothing else could have. Fear went through her in a cold wave. She closed her eyes and turned her face against Wolfe's neck, not wanting him to see her despair.

His anger she could fight, and had. His pain defeated her.

When Wolfe opened the kitchen door, Willow took one look at his dark face and breathed a wordless prayer. Wolfe walked right by her as though only he and Jessica existed.

"What is it? Is she hurt?" Willow asked anxiously, following.

"Just exhausted."

As Wolfe kicked the bedroom door shut behind him, he saw that food, brandy, and pans of warm water had been set out in the bedroom. The hearth was alive with the dance of flame.

"Can you stand?" he asked quietly.

Jessica nodded.

Wolfe set her down near the hearth he had built for Caleb's home and began undressing her with gentle hands. Jessica neither looked up nor objected. She simply stood with a docility that made Wolfe glance sharply at her from time to time. Soon she was wearing nothing but her filmy pantelets and camisole. They looked startlingly clean, fragile, and feminine after the condition of her outer clothing. He eased the undergarments from her body as delicately as though they were made of moonlight.

Jessica shivered when the last bit of lace fell to the hearth, leaving her naked before the fire and the man she loved, the man she had hurt in ways she had never intended.

Wolfe swept the fur coverlet from the bed and wrapped it around her.

"Warm enough?" he asked.

Without looking at him, she nodded.

"Are you hungry?"

She shook her head.

"When did you last eat?" he asked.

"I don't remember."

The tone of Jessica's voice went through Wolfe like an icy wind. There was no music, no laughter, none of the mischief and warmth that had danced in her voice since he had become her lover in all ways but one. The barrier of her maidenhead still lay between them, the abyss that must not be crossed.

Aristocrat and halfbreed bastard.

"Jessi . . ." Wolfe whispered.

But there was nothing more he could say. It had all been said. All that remained was to return her to the land and the life for which she had been born; a land and a life that were impossible for him to share.

In silence, Wolfe found Jessica's hairbrush and went back to the fire where she stood. Without a word, he began combing her snarled hair.

"I'm no longer so useless I can't brush my own hair."

Wolfe's eyes narrowed at the loss of color and life in Jessica's voice. It was the same for her body. Like grass flattened by a storm, she was defeated. Yet like grass, she would regain her resilience after the storm passed. He was certain of it. All she needed was rest and a return to her own place, her own people.

"I like brushing your hair," Wolfe said. "It's both cool and fiery, and it smells of roses. The feel and scent of you will always haunt me."

Jessica made no other objection, because to speak

would have been to reveal the tears aching in her throat. Wolfe was standing very close to her, yet he was withdrawing from her with every breath, every instant, and the brush was whispering his good-byes through her hair.

Eyes closed, Jessica stood with the patience of the damned while the man she loved tormented her with all she would never have of life and of him. If she could have died, she would have, but she could not. She could only endure the pain and pleasure of his touch and pray that tomorrow would never come, separating her from the only man she would ever love.

When Jessica's hair swirled about her in a shining, softly curling cloud, Wolfe reluctantly put aside the brush. Air stirred by the movements of his body disturbed her hair, weaving firelight through the silky strands.

Wolfe's breath came out in a soundless rush as he memorized the picture of Jessica standing in front of the fire. He wanted to see the aquamarine gems of her eyes, but they were hidden behind half-closed lids and thick eyelashes, as though she were too weary to bear even the sight of the man who had dragged her through Hell.

Wolfe brought the basins of warm water to the hearth. He wrung out a small, soft cloth in one of the basins, soaped it lightly, and began washing Jessica's face. The fragrance of a summer rose garden slowly expanded through the room.

"I'm not so useless that I can't wash myself," she said quietly, looking at the stone hearth rather than at the man who was so gently and so completely tearing the heart from her body.

"I know. You're tired. Let me take care of you as I should have from the beginning."

Jessica's eyelids flinched at the brush of the cloth on her cheek.

"Sore?" Wolfe whispered.

She shook her head wearily.

"Are you certain? Those welts look tender. How did you get them?"

"I don't remember," she said tonelessly.

Wolfe's fingertips caressed Jessica's cheek with great tenderness. Her breath hesitated, then frayed. When he eased the fur coverlet down to her waist, she made a tiny sound.

"Don't worry, elf. I'm not going to demand any sensual games from you. You're too tired ... and I came too close to seeing you die to trust my own control tonight."

Jessica's eyes widened, seeking Wolfe's for the first time. He didn't notice. He was looking at the picture she made with the silver fur wrapped around her hips and her hair a mahogany glory spilling over the creamy curves of her breasts.

Slowly, Wolfe rearranged Jessica's hair until it fell down her back. Even before the washcloth touched her breasts, the nipples gathered into tight velvet crowns, contrasting starkly with the pale satin of her skin.

"You're more beautiful than fire itself," Wolfe said huskily. "I'll remember you like this until I die."

And I'll want you until I die.

Yet Wolfe said nothing of that, for the knowledge had just come to him in another stroke of black lightning, another raw wound burning in the depths of his soul.

Breath trembled out of Jessica when she saw the harsh lines of Wolfe's face. She wanted to ask what was wrong, but didn't trust herself to open her mouth without crying out her need and her love for the man who didn't love her. So she stood silently, unable to speak for the sadness locked within her throat.

The fur wrap slid from Jessica's hips into Wolfe's hands and from there to the floor. He ignored the luminous beauty of the coverlet, for the curves of Jessica's legs and the dark mahogany cloud concealing her feminine core were far more compelling to him than the rare arctic fur.

Slowly, Wolfe raised the washcloth and resumed bathing Jessica in a hushed silence. The first warm touch of water made her breath unravel in a soundless rush. When Wolfe asked wordlessly for more freedom of her body, she shifted, allowing him the intimacy. For long minutes, there was only the liquid dance of water, the whispering of flame, and the glide of cloth over skin. Finally, reluctantly, Wolfe rinsed away the last bit of soap, leaving behind the mingled fragrance of rose and warm woman.

"All done," he said huskily.

He stood up in a rush and closed his eyes, unable to look at Jessica any longer without touching her in a way that had nothing to do with unspoken apologies and everything to do with the hunger whose fiery claws had long since raked him into readiness for the coupling that must never occur.

Jessica saw Wolfe's need and felt her own, both physical hunger and something far more complex. Without a word she began unbuttoning Wolfe's shirt.

His eyes snapped open.

"What are you doing?" he asked roughly.

"Undressing you."

"I can see that."

"Then you'll be able to see me bathing you as gently as you bathed me."

"No."

"Why not?"

"You're too tired."

Jessica's elegant fingers didn't so much as pause in their work. "I'm no more tired than you."

"Jessi . . ."

Her eyes met his. For a moment he didn't know if he could bear what he saw in their clear, light blue depths.

"You have done as Lady Victoria asked," Jessica said quietly. "You have taught me not to fear your touch. Now you are exiling me from your life. Will you deny me this night, too?"

Wolfe knew he should do just that, but he couldn't force the words past his lips. Jessica finally had accepted the end that he had always known must come: She would fight the annulment no longer.

He hadn't expected victory to be so painful.

You are exiling me from your life.

Silently, Wolfe removed his boots and socks, then closed his eyes and stood motionless while Jessica undressed him. With a distant sense of surprise, he realized that he had never given himself to a woman in this way, trusting her enough to surrender sensual control to her hands.

The feel of Jessica removing his shirt was exquisite. The tug and release of his belt, followed by the slow, inevitable slide of his remaining clothes down his body was extraordinary, like being naked for the first time. With a feeling of unreality, he stepped out of his clothes and brushed them aside with his foot.

The first touch of the warm washcloth against

Wolfe's face made his eyelids flinch.

"Sore?" she asked softly, echoing Wolfe's earlier question.

"You flinched the same way when I first touched you with the washcloth. Were you sore?"

"No. I wanted you so much that even the lightest touch was almost more than I could bear."

"Yes," Wolfe said simply, opening his eyes, hiding from Jessica no longer.

He felt her breath as a warm rush over his chest when she looked into his eyes.

"In this, at least, we are well matched," Jessica whispered.

Wolfe didn't answer. He couldn't. The feel of warm water against the pulse on his neck had taken his breath. The sound of the cloth being rinsed was a quicksilver music in the silence. The fragrance of a rose's softly opening petals filled his senses. The slight roughness of the washcloth brought his body to excrutiating fullness.

He closed his eyes once more, absorbing Jessica's presence into his very pores while the cloth moved slowly over his arms and shoulders, washing away fatigue with slow sweeps of warmth, dissolving everything but the certainty of Jessica's touch, her soft breathing, her scent wrapping him in a sensuality he had never known before. For an immeasurable time, he lived suspended between firelight and an elf whose touch created a new, magical world.

Water made gentle silver sounds as first the cloth and then his skin was rinsed. He sensed Jessica kneeling before him. When the cloth returned, it was to wash him without hesitation or inhibition. He couldn't hide, for wherever she touched him, she would discover his passion.

But Wolfe no longer cared about hiding, for he knew Jessica burned for him in the same way. She was touching him as if he were a dream condensing out of firelight, cherishing him in a hushed silence that was itself another kind of caress.

The washcloth slipped from her fingers and fell forgotten onto the hearth. The feel of her hands on his thighs was both relief and another turn of passion's rack. The glide of her palms over him was a pleasure so great it was pain. The gentle rush of her breath over his heavy arousal was Heaven and Hell in one.

Wolfe couldn't prevent the low sound he made when Jessica's hand cupped him. Nor could he prevent the single silver drop that condensed, speaking so deeply of the need within him.

When she kissed away the evidence of his need, she brought him to his knees.

"You're burning me alive," Wolfe said hoarsely.

"No more than you're burning me," she whispered, pulling Wolfe's hands down her body. "Touch me. Know how much I want you."

It was like sliding into fire. There was no withdrawal, no coy retreat, nothing but the sultry rose opening at his first touch, weeping for him and yielding to him at the same instant. She clung to him, watching him, seeing the shivering rush of her own passion in the expanding center of his eyes, feeling it in the silky heat gilding his hand.

Then Jessica could support her own weight no longer. With a husky moan she sank down onto the fur, drawing Wolfe with her, keeping his hand pressed deeply to her.

"You have taught me so much about a man's body," Jessica whispered. "I never would have guessed . . ."

Her voice frayed into another husky cry as Wolfe's hand cupped her and stole into her in the same sweet motion. Unable to help her response, she moved her hips in slow counterpoint to his motions, deepening his presence within her body.

Wolfe closed his eyes and tested the heart of the flower that had been given to him. He found only clinging ease and secret rain shielded by a maidenhood as fragile as flame. She wanted him as he had never been wanted by anyone, and she was telling him with each sultry drop, calling to him in a silence that was infused with hunger and the scent of roses.

"What would you never have guessed?" Wolfe asked when he could trust himself to speak.

"That you were made of honey and fire."

"It's you, not me. Honey and fire."

Wolfe breathed Jessica's name and withdrew from the satin sheath of her body, heard her cry out at the loss of him. For two seconds he endured it, for three seconds, then he could take no more of their shared pain. He slid within her again, and felt the sweet agony of her response all the way to his soul.

"Hold me," Jessica whispered. "I need to feel you pressed against me. Please, Wolfe. *I need you.*"

"I shouldn't."

"Why?"

"You're too dangerous when you burn. You make me forget . . . everything."

Yet even as Wolfe was speaking, he was moving over Jessica, crushing her gently into the fur. The feel of her along his naked body went through him in a soundless explosion of heat. When she shifted to draw him even closer, he pinned her hips with his own.

"Lie still," Wolfe breathed against Jessica's mouth. "You'll make me lose control. I don't want that yet."

"What do you want?"

"Your kiss."

"It's yours, Wolfe. Only yours."

He took what she gave, giving himself in return. It was like no other kiss he had known. He felt her as though he was in her skin, burning, and she was in his, on fire. Slowly, his body moved against hers, pleasuring both of them in the same gliding motions. She answered instinctively, opening herself, seeking him blindly, needing him until she wept.

Yet no matter how she struggled, he withheld himself.

"Wolfe," Jessica said, her voice strained. "Don't you want me? You've taught me so much about your body and my own. Teach me about the shared body of love."

"No, elf."

"Is coupling that painful? Is that what you don't want me to know? Is that what you're sending me back to England to face alone, knowing that some-day your elf will lie screaming and bleeding beneath a rutting man?"

Wolfe shuddered with a combination of rage at the thought of Jessica lying beneath another man and desire because she was lying beneath him now with her legs open and her hungry softness pressing against him, licking over him with honey and fire.

"Jessi, no," he groaned. "It must not be."

But whether he meant her coupling with another man in the future or having Wolfe buried within her now, even Wolfe couldn't say.

"Then I'm right," Jessica accused wildly. "I will be ripped apart. You have seduced me with everything but the truth!"

"Taking a man within your body won't hurt you."

"I don't believe you," she raged. "I have seen a man aroused. I have felt myself tight around no more than your finger. You are lying to me!"

Jessica's body twisted beneath Wolfe, inciting him beyond bearing. Even as he told himself to roll aside, he caught her mouth beneath his and sank down over her body, absorbing her struggles with his much greater strength. His tongue thrust heavily into her mouth and filled it as he longed to fill her body. His hips moved, dragging his hardened flesh over the softness he had called from her.

Heat pulsed through Jessica and spilled over to Wolfe, increasing the stunning sensitivity of flesh sliding across flesh. He made a throttled sound as every muscle in his body clenched with passion and a need that was destroying him.

With a low moan, Jessica arched against him, for she needed the heaviness of his body more than she needed air.

"Hold still," Wolfe said in a hoarse voice. "Don't move unless I tell you. Do you hear me, Jessi? I'm going to show you how little you will have to fear from a man. *But you must lie still.*"

She shuddered and became motionless.

Wolfe took a breath and then another, trying to get a grip on the wild, seething violence of his need for her. It was impossible. Control kept sliding away by hot increments, leaving no reality but that of the girl who lay ready beneath him, watching him with eyes that were black with passion.

"Wrap your legs around my hips. Slowly, Jessi. Very slowly."

Watching him, she shifted in slow motion until her legs circled his hips.

"Like this?" Jessi whispered.

Wolfe locked his jaw as he brushed against the sultry woman heat that lay open to him. A long shudder racked his restraint, threatening to tear it apart. He took several careful breaths.

"Yes, like that." His voice was low, almost a groan. "Just like that. Don't move, Jessi. Not one bit. I'm going to show you how easily you'll accept a man."

"Now?"

"Now. Just for a moment. Just a little bit. Just so you won't be afraid. I won't take your maidenhead, but you must lie very, very still."

Jessica's eyes widened as Wolfe's fingers caressed her, parted her very gently, eased into her so slowly that she couldn't believe it was happening at all.

And then she realized it wasn't his fingers pressing into her.

"Dear God," Jessica whispered.

"Yes. Dear God."

Another shudder racked Wolfe as he eased a bit farther into the petal softness of Jessica's body. He watched the center of her eyes expand into glittering blackness, tasted the unraveling of her breath against his lips, felt her hot, supple yielding to him, heard the small sound she made at the back of her throat as her nails scored sweetly on his arms.

"Am I hurting you?" he breathed.

The whimper that came from Jessica's throat as her eyes closed wasn't an answer, but the secret rain of her response was.

It took his breath away.

"Jessi, my sweet elf..."

Shaking, Wolfe threaded his fingers through her unbound hair until his hands were wholly tangled within the long strands. He wanted nothing more on earth than to flex his hips and bury himself in her sleek, yielding warmth.

What was making sweat break all over his body was the knowledge that Jessica wanted it as violently as he did.

"Look at me," Wolfe said heavily. "I want to see you while we're joined even in this small way. Christ knows it's not enough, not nearly enough, but it's all that can be. Look at me, Jessi. Let me see the passion in you."

Slowly, Jessica's eyes opened. She looked at the hard lines of Wolfe's face, at his body drawn with restraint and glistening with sweat. His eyes were dilated with the same passion that was sending tongues of fire licking up from between her thighs.

Then he moved slightly, retreating and returning with exquisite care.

A burst of fire drenched Jessica in golden heat. Wolfe felt it, shared it, and moved again, caressing her with his whole body. She gasped and tightened her legs around his hips, instinctively trying to deepen the tantalizing union.

Wolfe's fists clenched in Jessica's long hair as he felt his self-control dissolving in the hot, secret rain of her body. He knew he should withdraw completely from her heat, but he couldn't force himself to. She was everything he had ever wanted, and he had wanted her much too long.

Telling himself it would be the last time, he

moved again, tormenting both of them with the incomplete union.

"Does this hurt you?" he asked through his teeth.

Jessica shook her head even as she wondered at the harshness in his voice. Heat shimmered through her, making her gasp.

Breath hissed out of Wolfe as he felt passion ripple through Jessica to his own flesh just within her. Sweat gathered and ran down his spine. He knew he must draw back before the sweet violence overcame what was left of his restraint.

"You have nothing to fear from a man inside your body," Wolfe said through clenched teeth. His own need knotted and twisted within him, wrenching him until he wanted to cry out with anguish. "Do you hear me, elf? You have nothing to fear."

Jessica's breath unraveled. Her hips moved rhythmically as pleasure peaked and ebbed and peaked once more.

"Stop," Wolfe said. Tremors jerked through him at each melting of her body around him. "Jessi— stop!"

"I'm sorry. I can't. I—*Wolfe.*"

He saw her teeth sink into her lower lip as she fought the fulfillment that was taking her. He brushed his open mouth over hers as he moved very slowly within her.

"Never mind, elf," he breathed into her mouth. "It's all right. Don't fight it. Let me feel your pleasure."

Wolfe's hand moved between their bodies, capturing the silky bud. He felt the splintering, shivering heat that washed through Jessica to him. The abandon of her response took him to the breaking edge of his control, and he hung there, shaking, while she clung hotly to him, silently begging for more of him with each sultry pulse of her pleasure.

"There's such fire in you," Wolfe whispered. "You're killing me, Jessi. You could take every bit of me without pain and you must know it as well as I."

Heavy-lidded eyes opened and watched Wolfe as he teased the sensitive flower that had opened for him. Passion burned as deeply in her glance as it did in her body.

"All I know is that you are not the same as other men," Jessica said.

"In this," he moved his hips, "I am no different."

"Dear God," she whispered. "Again."

"What?"

"Do that again. Please, Wolfe. Again."

With a whispered curse that was also a prayer for strength, Wolfe moved within Jessica once more and at the same time caressed her with his fingers.

She made a low sound as a network of sensation raced through her, leaving ecstasy shimmering in its wake. She gave herself to the tender ravishment and to the man who had called passion from her depths. With each sensual peak shivering through her, she kissed him, whispering to him, telling him the only truth that mattered.

"You are . . . my Lord Wolfe."

Her words became part of the blood hammering through Wolfe's veins. Feeling and hearing the silky climax unravel Jessica was burning him so softly, so completely, that he didn't know he was wholly afire. A shudder went through him at each touch of her mouth, but her words were even more seductive, telling him what he had always known and never wanted to face.

"I will take . . . no other man . . . into my body."

Jessica's hands slid down Wolfe's hot back to the rigid muscles of his hips, seeking his very different flesh, finding it. With exquisite care, she drew her nails over him.

"Make me yours, Wolfe . . . only yours."

Jessica's name was an anguished cry against her throat as Wolfe's control broke. He drove completely into her, changing her body in a sweeping, irrevocable instant.

Her breath tore as she was filled to overflowing. He was so deeply inside her that she felt the pulses of his release as clearly as she felt her own heartbeat. She put her arms around his shaking body and held him, kissing his eyes and cheeks and the corners of his mouth until he had the breath to speak once more.

"Now you are mine, Jessi. Only mine." As Wolfe lowered his mouth to hers, he whispered, "May God have mercy on my soul."

"Wolfe?" Her arms tightened around him. "What's wrong?"

"It doesn't matter anymore. I've burned for you so long that Hell has nothing new to teach me. But I have new things to teach you, Jessi. Heaven and Hell combined."

Before Jessica could say anything more, Wolfe sealed her lips with a kiss that claimed her mouth as completely as he had claimed her body. Then his hips moved powerfully and she forgot everything but his heavy presence within her.

Pleasure coursed through Jessica with each thrusting motion Wolfe made. Her body tightened and tightened until she couldn't breathe, yet still Wolfe moved in sensual rhythms over her, against her, within her, setting fire to every bit of her, burning her alive.

She tried to speak but could think of no words, much less shape her tongue to form them. All she could say was his name, and she said it again and again as he ripped the world away, leaving her nothing to hang onto but him.

Forerunners of savage ecstasy clawed through Jessica, drawing her body into a shivering arch. She gasped at the unexpected sensations. They were more acute than anything she had ever known, almost frightening in their intensity.

"Wolfe?"

"You're feeling it now, aren't you?" Wolfe's voice was as dark as his eyes watching her. "You wanted this, Jessi. You've wanted it since you were fifteen. And since you were fifteen, I've wanted to give it to you."

Jessica gasped and her eyes widened with surprise as sensual lightning transfixed her, arching her into Wolfe's driving body. He laughed and bit her neck hard enough to leave passionate marks.

"Heaven and Hell combined, Jessi. I'm going to burn you all the way to your soul."

The restrained savagery of Wolfe's teeth against her hot skin dragged a moan from Jessica. When she made a sharp, rising sound, he sealed her mouth with his own. He took her cries into himself and dragged more of them from her, wanting all that she had to give.

Nails scored Wolfe's skin, drawing a primitive sound of need from him. The small pain simply served to focus the seething violence of pleasure. When he shifted his mouth to the pulse beating wildly in Jessica's neck, she responded to the barely veiled savagery of the caress by arching like a drawn bow.

Wolfe held her there, stretched and quivering on a rack of pleasure, and then he began moving again, driving her higher and higher with each powerful motion of his body. Her breath became as broken as his, her skin as hot, as slick, until she was wild with need for the consummation that he kept just beyond her reach.

"I can't bear it," Jessica said raggedly, dragging her teeth across Wolfe's chest in sensual punishment, twisting beneath him, seeking relief.

Wolfe laughed and bit her shoulder as he pinned her with his hips. "I've burned like this for five years. Surely you can stand five minutes?"

When Jessica's hands slid down Wolfe's body, he shuddered, caught her wrists, and held them in one hand above her head.

"None of your sweet tricks, elf."

"You are—torturing me."

"I'm torturing *me*. I'm teaching you. Wrap those beautiful legs around my waist. Yes, like that. Now lift your hips," Wolfe whispered against Jessica's mouth, biting her between each word, "and you will find what you've been seeking so hotly."

Jessica lifted toward him as he drove into her. The ecstasy was so intense, she would have screamed if she could have, but Wolfe had taken her breath even as he had claimed her mouth. He slid his arm beneath her hips, dragging her so tightly against his body that he could feel her very bones. Then he thrust into her hard and deep, wanting to find the point beyond which she would refuse him.

What he found was more sleek yielding to him, heat surrounding him, burning him, Heaven and

Hell combined as he hurtled headlong with her into the sun.

LATER, much later, Wolfe held Jessica while she slept and he counted the cost of what he had done.

 **18**

WHEN Jessica awoke the next morning, Wolfe was standing by the window, as naked and magnificent as the mountains rising to meet the dawn. He was looking out over the rugged land with an expression of loss and yearning that made her heart turn over. She wondered what he was seeing in the wild sunrise.

And why it made him so sad.

"Wolfe?"

As he walked toward Jessica, his expression changed. The gentle smile he gave her made tears burn behind her eyelids. Indigo eyes swept over her, lingering on the banked fire twisting through her hair and the crystalline perfection of her light eyes. Long, lean fingers traced her eyebrows, her cheekbones, the curves of her mouth. He sat on the bed beside her and kissed her tenderly.

"Good morning, Mrs. Lonetree."

Wolfe had not called her that before. The words pierced Jessica as deeply as the sorrow beneath her husband's smile. Trembling, she smiled up at him in return; and then her heart caught and her smile threatened to turn upside down.

She had never seen anything as poignant as Wolfe's haunted eyes and tender smile.

"Did I remember to tell you last night how beautiful you are?" Wolfe asked.

"You made me feel beautiful."

"You are." His eyes closed for an instant as though in pain. "And so fragile."

"What's wrong?" she whispered.

"Nothing. Save this . . . and this . . . and this."

As Wolfe touched each small mark he had left on Jessica's skin, he pulled down the bedcovers. The silence became thick with emotions and unspoken words.

"I'll be more careful of you next time, elf." He looked into her clear, pale blue eyes. "If you want a next time."

Jessica caught one of Wolfe's hands between hers, kissed his palm, and pressed it to her cheek.

"I loved joining with you," she said in a low voice. "I want there to be times without number."

Black eyelashes swept down, concealing the haunted indigo depths of Wolfe's eyes. "I'll try not to get you pregnant, but . . . you burn through my control."

"Don't you want a child?"

"I've caused you enough fear and hurt. I won't tear you apart bearing children who have neither titles nor estates to inherit."

"Wolfe," she said brokenly, "I want your children!"

"Hush, elf," he murmured, touching her lips with his thumb. "It's not necessary. I won't cry annulment for lack of heirs. You're safe with me. You'll never have to fear for your life again."

Jessica's hands tightened on Wolfe's. The grief in him was as real and yet as impossible to touch as night itself. It tore at her in ways she couldn't name.

"I love you, my Lord Wolfe," she said, lifting up to his lips. "I've always loved you. I always will."

"Yes. I've always known that."

Jessica waited, but Wolfe said no more. Pain twisted through her as she finally understood the source of Wolfe's unhappiness.

Tree That Stands Alone.

"You don't love me," she whispered, realizing too late what she had done to the man she loved.

"I want you, Jessi. I've always wanted you. I always will."

Wolfe fitted his mouth to Jessica's with exquisite care before he took her with a single, slow penetration if his tongue. The kiss deepened and changed until she was breathing quickly and moving hungrily against him.

"Wolfe," she said raggedly.

"Lie with me, Jessi. Let me worship your body with mine."

Jessica couldn't withhold herself from the naked hunger in Wolfe's eyes and in his body. She let him come to her, let him take her in burning silence, let him unravel her so gently that she never knew she was undone until the world turned to gold around her and she wept Wolfe's name and her love against his chest. Then he held her, letting her tears scald him in the long minutes before she took a shuddering breath and lay quietly once more.

Slowly, Wolfe eased from the bed and pulled on his clothes. The bedroom door opened and closed soundlessly behind him. Moments later, Jessica's eyes opened bright with tears. Impatiently, she wiped them away and reached for her clothes.

Wolfe found Reno in the kitchen. The empty

mugs and plates on the table showed that Caleb and Rafe had already eaten and gone out to work. From the other bedroom came the sound of Willow singing softly to her baby as she nursed him. The gentle music burned Wolfe like acid, reminding him of what he had done to the delicate girl who had always trusted him to protect her.

But he had taken her instead.

"Is Jessi all right?" Reno asked.

Wolfe gave him a slicing, sideways glance, wondering if the other man had somehow guessed that Jessica had finally become a wife in fact as well as in name.

"She's fine," Wolfe said curtly. "I told her to sleep late. Why?"

"Willow said she looked real ragged last night."

"So did I."

"That's the God's truth," Reno said.

"Three days of a Hell-wind like that would take the starch out of the Devil himself."

Reno smiled and resettled his hat on hair that was thick, black, and shiny. The light green of his eyes was like cut crystal. Looking at him, Wolfe wondered how Jessica had avoided succumbing to Reno Moran's dark charm and physical grace. Or to Rafe, who had the smile of a fallen angel and eyes that had seen Hell. Wolfe couldn't help thinking that either Moran would have been better for Jessica than a halfbreed who had nothing to speak of but an uncanny skill with mustangs and long guns.

Yet Wolfe knew he would have killed anyone who tried to take away the beautiful, sensual elf who came to him so perfectly, exploring the shimmering reaches of passion with him as no other woman had.

"That's a brave girl you have," Reno said. "Not many women would have gone out in that storm for love or money, much less for a mean steeldust mustang that most men would shoot on sight."

Wolfe's eyes narrowed against the darkness and pain streaking through him. "My fault. Jessi was trying to prove I shouldn't send her back to England."

Reno gave Wolfe a questioning look.

"Jessi told me how you stood over more than one foal, holding off wolves with your six-gun," Wolfe said, changing the subject as he poured a mug of coffee. "I owe you."

"Like Hell you do. If it hadn't been for your skill with a rifle, Jed Slater would have killed Willow, Caleb, and me."

"You get the pick of my foals," Wolfe said as though Reno hadn't spoken.

"Lonetree, sometimes you can be a bullheaded son of a bitch."

"Thank you."

Reno shot him a disbelieving look, then laughed out loud.

Wolfe smiled, but it faded quickly. The shadow of a bird flying beyond the window caught his eye. For long, aching moments, he looked past the grass and trees to the unbridled glory of the San Juans. He hadn't truly known how much a part of his soul the mountains were until he looked at them and knew he must leave their wildness behind. The pain of it drew deep brackets around his mouth.

But it had to be done.

"Remember that blue roan you fancied?" Wolfe asked quietly.

"The wild one you caught a few summers back?"

Wolfe nodded.

"I remember. Hell of a good desert horse. Best I've ever seen."

"She's yours."

"Now look here," Reno began.

"You'll earn her," Wolfe said, cutting across Reno's objections. "It will cost you most of a summer of gold hunting."

Reno's eyes narrowed as he measured the man sitting across from him.

"I want you to ride with Jessi and me as far as the Mississippi," Wolfe continued. "Between the Indians, the gold hunters, and the dregs of the soldiers on both sides of the war . . ." He shrugged.

"It gets real lively," Reno agreed.

"If it were just me, it wouldn't matter. But Jessi will be along. I'd feel better knowing you were at my back."

Reno's expression became intent as he sensed the turmoil behind Wolfe's calm words.

"I'd gladly ride to Hell with you," Reno said calmly, "and you know it."

"I'm not going to Hell. Not quite." Wolfe's smile thinned.

"England?" guessed Reno.

"It's Jessi's home."

"You'll have a hard time hunting mustangs for a living in England."

"Lord Stewart has wanted me to work for him for years. He'll get his wish."

Reno said something under his breath in Spanish about Wolfe having the heart of an ox—and the brains.

"*Gracias,*" Wolfe said sardonically.

There was silence, followed by the sound of Reno's work gloves snapping against his palm.

"When do you want to leave?" Reno asked finally.

"Soon. Jessi isn't cut out for the West."

"I haven't heard Red complain. Have you?"

The question was ignored by Wolfe. After a moment, Reno stood with the lazy grace that had fooled more than one man into thinking he was slow.

"*Amigo,* I think you're making a mistake."

"No. I'm merely paying for one."

"What mistake is that?" Jessica asked from the doorway.

"He's got some damn fool idea about—" Reno began, then broke off abruptly. The look Wolfe was giving him would have frozen lightning.

Cursing under his breath, Reno snapped his gloves against his hand again and went out the back door without another word.

Jessica looked at Wolfe curiously.

"I'm giving Reno the pick of the foals," Wolfe said.

"That's hardly a mistake. He earned it. Without him, we would have lost more than one foal."

"That's what I told him."

As though pulled against his will, Wolfe turned again and stared out the window. Jessica saw deep emotion kindle in Wolfe's eyes, then fade into the haunted shadows she had first noticed that morning when he watched the sunrise. She went and stood beside him. She saw nothing beyond the window but the beauty of the vast land.

"Wolfe? Is something wrong?"

He turned and looked at her with haunted eyes.

"Wolfe," she whispered, reaching toward him.

"Kiss me, Jessi," he said, bending down to her. "Kiss me hard and deep. When you kiss me, I don't think about what must be."

With a small sound, she went up on tiptoe even as he lifted her in his arms, letting the wildness inside him focus in the passion only Jessica had ever been able to summon from the depths of his soul.

"Does this mean you've forgiven Jessi for going out in the blizzard?" Willow asked from the doorway.

Reluctantly, Wolfe ended the kiss and tucked Jessica's scarlet face against his neck. He smiled at Willow despite the bittersweet combination of sadness and desire twisting through him.

"We're negotiating," Wolfe said.

"Her surrender or yours?" retorted Willow.

"Mine, of course. Elves are too fragile. They either win or die."

"In that case," Willow said dryly, "I'll get Ethan's bathwater and leave you to your, er, negotiations."

As Wolfe lowered Jessica's feet to the floor, a cool premonition slid down her spine, the echo of Wolfe's words.

Elves are too fragile. They either win or die.

Jessica said nothing until Willow went out of the kitchen carrying a pan of warm water in her hands. When Jessica turned to Wolfe, he was staring out the window once more. The expression of sorrow in his eyes made fear squeeze her heart.

"Love, what's wrong?" she asked.

"Nothing."

She shook her head slowly. "Your eyes are haunted."

" 'Tis your imagination." Wolfe smiled and touched her cheek gently. "Elves are noted for their imagination."

"Wolfe," she whispered. "I can't joke about what I see in your eyes. Who or what are you mourning?"

His eyes narrowed in surprise. He hadn't expected Jessica to see into him so clearly, even more clearly than he saw into himself.

Mourning.

"I'm always sad to say good-bye to Caleb and Willow," Wolfe said after a moment, the only part of the truth he would discuss.

It was Jessica's turn to be surprised. "We're leaving?"

"It's too wild here."

Wolfe's voice was resonant with finality and grief. A chill roughened Jessica's skin.

"What are you saying?" she whispered.

"We're going to England."

"I'd rather hunt mustangs," she said, "or did you want to wait until autumn, when this year's crop of foals will be weaned?"

Wolfe turned away without answering.

"Wolfe?"

"We'll be in England when the foals are weaned."

"Then we'll come back next spring."

"No." The word was soft, final.

"Why not?"

"Spring and fall are when Lord Robert's managers are most needed on his country estates."

The chill moving through Jessica congealed into ice and settled into the pit of her stomach.

"What does that have to do with us?" she asked tightly.

"I will be one of those managers."

"What are you saying?"

Wolfe looked out the window. "We will live in England."

"You hate England."

Wolfe shrugged. "Parts of the countryside are quite pretty."

"They're not a patch on this," she said, indicating the wild beauty of the mountains beyond the window.

"No. They're not."

"What of your mustangs?"

"I'm giving them to Caleb."

Jessica swayed and whispered. "You mean never to come back to the West!"

Wolfe didn't answer. He didn't have to. The shadows in his eyes said all that was necessary.

"But why? You love this land. I've seen you, Wolfe. You watch these mountains the way a man watches a woman he loves."

"Let it go, Jessi."

"No! Why can't we live here? Why must we live in England?"

"This is no place for you," Wolfe said quietly. "You have to be born for this land. You weren't."

"And you were."

He made an odd, almost helpless gesture. "Yes. But I can survive England. You can't survive the West."

"Dear God, how you must hate me."

Swiftly, Wolfe turned and touched Jessica's cheek. "I don't hate you, elf."

"You will. I've cost you the only thing you've ever truly loved. You will hate me as surely and as deeply as you love the land!"

Wolfe saw the shine of tears on Jessica's face and gathered her into his arms. "Hush, wife. You're only hurting yourself."

"I don't want to live in England," she said flatly, pushing away from him. "Do you hear me? I love the mountains. Why can't we live here?"

"You gave yourself into my care. I won't watch this wild land kill you."

Jessica's hands clenched against Wolfe's shirt, digging into the hard muscle beneath the cloth.

"Wolfe, listen to me. *I am stronger than you believe.* If I were the weak little elf you think me, I would have died as a child!"

His hand curled beneath her chin. Silently, he felt the delicate bone structure and soft skin. He smiled sadly.

"You haven't half my strength," Wolfe said. "In England, that won't matter."

"In England no one looks beyond your bastardy and Indian blood," she said harshly. "Here you have friends and a chance to build a better life for yourself. Can't you see that? Can't you see what—"

Wolfe's thumb pressed against Jessica's lips, sealing in her urgent words.

"I've always seen that," he said in a calm voice. "It's why I left England, and you. I could have you or I could have the West. I took you, knowing what the end would be. England."

"But I—"

"It's done, Jessi," he interrupted flatly. "It was done when I took your maidenhead."

"Wolfe, please believe me. I didn't mean for this to happen! Not like this. Dear God, not like this!"

Gently, Wolfe took Jessica's clenched hands from his shirt. "I know. But all your pleas and tears won't change what is. You are what you are. I am what I am. We are husband and wife and England will be our home."

Jessica closed her eyes. She would have preferred blows to Wolfe's calm summation of their marriage.

"Go begin packing," Wolfe said quietly. "I'll help Caleb for the time that is left."

The kitchen door opened and closed softly behind Wolfe.

For a long time, Jessica stared blindly at the door, seeing nothing but the tears overflowing her eyes, understanding too late what Wolfe had always known: Their marriage would destroy one of them, if not both.

Agree to an annulment. Damn you, let me go!

I'm the wrong husband for you. You're the wrong wife for me. Lying together would be the worst mistake of my life.

You were not born for the Western wilderness. I was.

Don't love me, Jessi. It will only hurt us both.

It's done, Jessi. It was done when I took your maidenhead.

You are what you are. I am what I am.

Tree That Stands Alone.

Jessica opened her eyes and wrapped her arms around herself, trying to stave off the ice radiating through her soul. With the same fierce determination she once had used to survive as a child, she searched now for a way out of the trap she had sprung around Wolfe.

When she finally found it, she washed the marks of grief from her face and went to find Caleb Black.

"DELAYING won't accomplish anything," Wolfe said, continuing the argument that had begun the moment Jessica had awakened him at dawn. "Whether we leave today or ten days after, we're still leaving."

"I said I would return to England without a fuss if you would hunt mustangs for one last time," Jessica said evenly. "I meant it."

Warily, Wolfe looked at Jessica. He had seen her in many moods, from intense fear to intense passion, but never had he seen her like this. There was nothing fey or elfin about her now, nor anything fragile. There was simply an ingathering of strength and purpose that reminded him of nothing so much as himself.

"I don't want to hunt mustangs," Wolfe said carefully.

"Then do it for Caleb. He needs more horses in order to work his ranch properly. He said so himself."

Wolfe looked uneasily at Jessica. He sensed the wild grief in her as clearly as she had sensed it in him that morning. Yet there were no tears in her eyes, no resonances of passion in her voice.

He didn't know her this way. The realization frightened him.

Wolfe's hands flashed out, pulling Jessica into his arms. "I won't take you into the wild with me," he said harshly.

"I know."

"Is that why you're so eager for me to hunt mustangs? Are you already tired of having me in your bed and body?"

The words were hardly out of Wolfe's mouth before Jessica was kissing him as though she expected to die in the next moment and wanted him never to forget what she had been like when fully alive. He kissed her in the same way until they both were breathing brokenly, consumed by passion.

"Fill me," Jessica whispered against his mouth.

"Fill me until I can't remember what it is to be separate from you. Fill me as though it were the last time."

With a hoarse sound, Wolfe swept the filmy layers of Jessica's nightgown above her waist. He whispered her name as he knelt between her legs and drew them up over his thighs. The melting ease of his penetration told him more about her love than any words could have. The sweetness of being possessed by him and possessing him in turn dragged a husky sound from the back of her throat.

"More," Jessica said urgently. "Wolfe, I must have more of you."

"You're too small. I'll hurt you."

"Please . . ."

She pulled at him, straining against him, asking for more of him, asking for all that he had to give, her words a dark fire licking over him, making him shudder with a need unlike any he had known before. With a hoarse sound, he slid his arms beneath her knees and lifted her legs, opening her without reservation. She moaned and bit her lip and arched against him, asking for more. Her silken heat spilled over him, underlining her whispered pleas.

"To think I called you a nun," Wolfe said hoarsely. "You are fire, elf. Burn for me."

Then he gave her what she was crying for, filling her, sinking into her so deeply that she felt him all through her body until she was stretched on a golden rack of ecstasy and she burned.

Wolfe felt Jessica's wild release begin and laughed with elemental triumph. He moved slowly, deeply, dragging cries from her, watching her burn, burning with her as the silky fire of her ecstasy fused their bodies together. He drove repeatedly into her, sinking more deeply into her fire, wanting it never to end. But she felt too good, she lured him too profoundly. Her words and rippling cries and sleek body demanded that he give himself to her as completely as she had given herself to him.

Even as Wolfe tried to hold back, he knew it was too late. He was too much a part of her, his body so deeply joined with hers that he didn't know where he ended and she began, two flames intertwined, burning redoubled with each breath. Fighting no more, he gave himself to her and to the ecstasy that burned ever higher, feeding on his release, renewing and consuming both of them until they burned as a single flame, inseparable.

CALEB was waiting for Jessica in the kitchen. He looked at her pale, drawn face and bleak eyes and said something savage beneath his breath.

"You really mean to go through with this damn fool idea?" he demanded.

"Yes."

"Did you tell Wolfe?"

"That wasn't part of our bargain. I agreed not to set out alone if you would agree not to tell Wolfe that I was going."

Caleb took off his hat, ran long fingers through his black hair, and said bluntly, "I think this is a piss-poor idea."

"I'm aware of that," Jessica said in a clipped voice. "I'm also aware that Wolfe would probably kill Reno or Rafe if they helped me. Wolfe won't kill you."

"You're a lot more certain of that than I am," Caleb retorted.

"Wolfe will be angry, but he knows there is no other woman for you except Willow. Reno or Rafe wouldn't touch me, either, but I'm afraid to test Wolfe's temper that far. He might shoot before he asked questions. He's frighteningly good with that rifle."

"Seems like a man as possessive as Wolfe is just might love his wife."

"Desire isn't love," Jessica said tightly.

"Jessi—" Caleb began, only to be interrupted.

"I trapped Tree That Stands Alone into marriage. I'm setting him free."

"Jessi—"

"Are the horses ready?" she asked, cutting across his attempts to speak.

There was a taut silence.

"I'm damn tempted to ride out after Wolfe," Caleb said finally.

"I can't stop you."

"And I can't stop you, either, is that it? You'll cut and run off in the wild the first chance you get, and the Devil take the hindmost."

"Of course. That's the only reason you agreed to take me to the stage in the first place."

"Blackmail."

"In a word, yes."

Caleb's mouth turned down as he looked at the darkness and determination in Jessica's eyes. It reminded him of the time Willow had set out alone on Ishmael in the middle of the night rather than go through with a marriage she believed Caleb didn't want. Willow had come very close to dying because of her determination that Caleb be set free. The memory of nearly losing her still haunted him at odd moments, making him go to Willow and hold her, reassuring himself that she was alive, safe, his.

Jessica was no less determined to do what she believed was right than Willow had been. All Caleb could do was see that Jessica stayed safe until Wolfe had a chance to sort out the mess.

Grimly, Caleb pulled out his six-gun, spun the cylinder to check the load, and holstered the gun with a smoothness that told its own deadly story.

"The horses are waiting, Mrs. Lonetree."

Tears came unbidden to her eyes. "My name is Lady Jessica Charteris."

"CALL it," Reno said.

"Heads," said Rafe.

"Tails."

Rafe flipped the coin.

Reno's hand flashed out, caught the coin, and smacked it down on the back of his hand. He pocketed the coin without bothering to look at it.

"Tails," Reno said, turning away.

As he reached for his horse's rein, the bullwhip Rafe was holding rippled and writhed as though alive. Suddenly, the tip cracked with the sound of a pistol shot.

Reno turned toward Rafe, who was coiling the whip with swift motions of his hands.

"That's your free one, Matt," Rafe said flatly. "Don't do it again. Which horses do you want?"

"Only one of us is going. Me. You're staying with Willow."

Rafe smiled thinly. "I figured that out real quick. What you haven't figured out is Wolfe was so eager to get finished hunting mustangs and get back to his wife that he left here at a dead run."

Reno hesitated, listening.

"By the time you catch up and the two of you get back to the ranch," Rafe continued, "Caleb will have a hell of a long lead on you. So which of Caleb's horses are best for making up time over rough country?"

"Willow said to be sure one of the horses we had waiting for Wolfe was Ishmael."

"All right. Who else?"

Reno's smile was as hard and brilliant as his eyes. "Doesn't matter. Everything Caleb left here is better than anything he took with him. That boy was in no hurry to put daylight between himself and Wolfe."

Rafe blinked and then laughed softly. "Tricky."

"Smart. Wolfe is going to come down off the mountain like a blue norther."

"Maybe. And maybe he'll just let Jessi go. From what I've seen, he wasn't any too pleased to be married to her."

Pale green eyes assessed Rafe before Reno showed his teeth in a wolfish smile. "And that's just what you were planning to rub Wolfe's face in, wasn't it?"

Rafe's smile was as cold as his gray eyes. "That's a fact. He was hard on her."

"He had some cause, and Jessi was the first one to say so."

"All the same, I'd like to be the one to tell Wolfe."

"Sorry, big brother. This one is mine." Reno swung into the saddle and looked down at Rafe. "Think. Why do you suppose Jessica asked Caleb to go instead of one of us?"

"I've been wondering about that," Rafe admitted, "what with a wife and new baby to look after and all."

"Stop wondering. Caleb is married to the soles

of his feet and Wolfe knows it. So does Jessi."

"Neither one of us would have touched Jessi," Rafe said instantly. "She knows that."

"Uh-huh. Now, do you want to be the one to explain it all to Wolfe while he's a half mile away, taking your measure over the barrel of a rifle?"

"If Jessi didn't love that hard-headed son of a bitch, I'd be glad to explain it to Wolfe any way I got the chance."

"So would I," Reno said flatly. "But she does love him."

Rafe's mouth tightened. He nodded and stepped out of the way.

"All right, Blackfoot," Reno said. "Let's see if you're half the running fool Jed Slater thought you were."

The tall black horse leaped forward, hitting its full stride in seconds.

THE second day on the trail, Caleb spent as much time looking over his shoulder as he did watching the route ahead.

"Stop putting a kink in your neck," Jessica said, looking up from the stream where the horses were drinking. "Wolfe isn't coming after me."

"For a bright girl, you can be stump dumb at times." Caleb checked the cinch on the pack saddle and then on his own horse. "Wolfe loves you."

"He wants me. There's a difference."

"Not for a man, honey. Not at first."

Caleb swung up on his horse and started forward again, leaving Jessica staring after him. He kept to a steady pace, not wanting her to accuse him of shirking his side of the bargain. On the other hand, he never took the shortest route around any obstacle. No point in giving Wolfe cause to be any angrier than he already would be.

It was late afternoon before Caleb reined in to study the route ahead. On either side lay a cluster of raw mountain peaks which were separated by a broad band of land that was clothed in trees, scrub, and grass. The divide was several miles wide at the bottom and less than a mile at its highest elevation. Where Caleb and Willow were, the land was green with the wild rush of spring and alive with meltwater from the nearby mountains.

"We'll camp here," Caleb said.

"It won't be dark for two hours."

Caleb slanted Jessica a cool amber glance. "It will take longer than that to get over the divide. If we don't camp here, we'll be picking our way through a half-frozen marsh in the dark with no place to sleep but sitting up in the saddle."

Jessica met Caleb's glance, sighed, and looked uneasily over her shoulder. She thought she had caught movement behind them, but Caleb didn't seemed concerned. When she looked back, he was watching her with an odd smile on his face.

"Don't fret, Red," Caleb said kindly. "I gave you enough lead on your man that he'll work off the worst of his mad before he catches us."

"Wolfe isn't coming."

"Horseshit."

Jessica gave Caleb a startled look.

He smiled as gently as though she were Willow.

"Even if you're right," Jessica said with a catch in her voice, "Wolfe couldn't get to us this quickly without riding a horse to death. He wouldn't do that."

"One horse couldn't get the job done," Caleb agreed. "Three could, though—Deuce, Trey, and Ishmael."

"What?"

Caleb looked past Jessica at the open ground they had just covered.

"If I were you," he said, "I'd spend the next few minutes thinking up ways to take the edge off Wolfe's temper."

The certainty in Caleb's voice sent a stroke of unease through Jessica. She stood in her stirrups and looked past him.

Two big black horses and one smaller sorrel had broken from the cover of the forest and were running flat out toward her up the long sweep of the grassy divide. Only one horse carried a man. As she watched, the rider leaped from the back of one of the blacks to the sorrel without slowing the pace one bit.

"Dear God," she breathed.

"Looks more like Wolfe Lonetree to me," Caleb said dryly.

With watchful amber eyes, Caleb waited while the horses thundered closer. When he saw that Wolfe's rifle was still in its scabbard, Caleb let out a silent breath of relief and gave Jessica a reassuring smile. Jessica didn't notice. She sat on Two-Spot and waited, knowing her horse had no chance to outrun the Arabian stallion.

Wolfe didn't even glance at Caleb when he galloped up and pulled Ishmael to a rearing, dancing halt. Wolfe had eyes only for the red-haired girl who was sitting astride Two-Spot with a spine as straight as a ramrod. Calmly, Wolfe dismounted, turned the hot horses over to Caleb, and then stood silently, watching Jessica.

"I'll make camp in those trees," Caleb said, gesturing toward a scattering of evergreens a mile back down the trail.

Wolfe nodded.

"You might keep in mind that she was only doing what she thought was best for you," Caleb said as he took Ishmael's reins. "The same as you were doing what you thought was best for her."

"*Adios*, Cal," Wolfe said flatly.

Without another word, Caleb reined his horse back toward the setting sun, taking with him all the horses but the one Jessica rode. Two-Spot stretched against the bit and whinnied at being left behind.

Without warning, Wolfe vaulted on behind Jessica, took the reins from her, and turned Two-Spot toward a nearby stand of aspens. Their delicate new leaves glowed an unearthly green in the slanting light. When the small breeze stirred, the leaves quivered as though alive and breathing.

Jessica felt as shaky as one of the leaves. She looked down at the dark, lean hand holding the reins, and at the arm that half-circled her without touching her. The temptation to trace the veins in the back of Wolfe's hand with her fingertips was so great that she had to close her eyes against it. An almost hidden tremor went through her as she fought not to show her hunger and yearning to touch the life that beat so strongly beneath Wolfe's controlled surface.

Wolfe dismounted and tied Two-Spot to a slender aspen. Then he stood and looked at Jessica for the longest minute of her life. She met his narrowed indigo eyes, refusing to show either the pain or the yearning that seethed beneath her outward calm.

"You looked surprised to see me when I rode up," Wolfe said.

"Caleb wasn't. He did everything but set fire to

trees so you could follow."

"I would have found you if you'd gone barefoot over solid stone."

"Why?"

The question put the match to Wolfe's temper. *"You're my wife."*

"The marriage isn't valid."

"Like Hell it isn't. I had you so deep and so hard it's a bloody wonder either one of us could walk afterward."

Scarlet flags burned on Jessica's cheekbones, but she didn't back down. "You said you would with-hold your fertility from the union despite my wishes otherwise," she said carefully. "That is grounds for annulment."

"I was trying to spare you the risk of childbed!"

"So you say." Jessica shrugged casually despite the tension that made her body feel brittle. "A mag-istrate might view your actions as less than noble."

"That's just it," Wolfe shot back. "I'm not noble. You are!"

No matter how hard Jessica fought it, she couldn't prevent a scalding tear from falling. The combination of grief and rage in her voice made it shake.

"And there it is," she said, "the one thing I can't change and you can't forgive."

"You're not making sense."

Her eyes focused on him. They were as pale and bleak as the streamside ice.

"I can learn to cook and clean and launder," Jessica said. "I can burn in your arms and you in mine . . . but it's not enough. It will never be enough. You despise the aristocracy, and my father was an earl."

"That's not—"

"You want me," she continued relentlessly, "but not as a wife. I'm not fit to be the mother of your children. I'm a spoiled, cruel child. I'm a—"

"Jessi, that's not what I—"

"—girl, not a woman, as useless as teats on a boar hog, the wrong—"

"Damn it, that's not—"

"Yes it is!" she said harshly, talking over him. "You have never lied to me, no matter how much the truth hurt. Don't begin now, when there is no more need. I trapped you, I'm setting you free. Go back to the wild land you love, the land for which you were born, the land I'm not worthy to inhabit and never will be. I am what I am and—"

"*Damnation.* Will you listen or do I have to—"

"—you are Tree That Stands Alone and lying with me was the worst mistake of your life!"

"Wrong," Wolfe said furiously. "The worst mistake of my life was promising Willow I'd try talking with you first!"

With no warning, Wolfe yanked Jessica out of the saddle and fastened his mouth over hers. She twisted and thrashed against him, but he was much too strong. He absorbed her struggles until the wild urgency of his kiss reached her on a level deeper than words.

Unable to deny Wolfe and herself any longer, Jessica yielded to him the softness he had already taken, sharing the kiss with him. It was a long time before he lifted his head.

"This is the only truth that matters," Wolfe said finally, brushing Jessica's tears away. "You are mine, only mine. And I am yours."

"You are Tree That Stands Alone."

"And you are the sun in my sky. Don't take the sun from me, Jessi."

She tried to speak, but was too moved by what she saw in his eyes to say more than his name.

"Wolfe?"

"Stay with me, Jessi Lonetree," he whispered. "Share the wild land with me. Love me as much as I love you."

Epilogue

In the following months, Wolfe showed Jessica his favorite places in the western land. Together they smelled the rain winds sweeping across the desert, wearing robes of lightning and bringing the miracle of water to a dry land. Together they stood among stone buttes anchored like great ships in a boundless sea of sand.

Together they saw a canyon so vast it could be crossed only by the sun, and at its bottom a river coiled like a silver medicine snake, untouched, untouchable. Together they stood in the sun-washed silence of cities built by men long dead. Ancient, enigmatic, set into sheer rock cliffs, nothing inhabited the stone cities but the wind. No paths led to the buildings and no paths came away, yet the cities remained, filled with mysteries and spirits of a time long past, unknown, unknowable.

Together they followed streams that had no name up the slopes of mountains that were also unnamed, climbing so high that angels sang in the ringing silence just before moonrise. Together they drank from lakes as blue as Wolfe's eyes and fell asleep in each other's arms, waking to find the aspens ablaze with winter's first kiss.

Finally they followed the sunrise back to the San

Juans. An hour's lazy ride from Willow and Caleb's home, Wolfe and Jessica built their own home along the Columbine's clear waters. There Wolfe talked to mustangs and Jessica stalked living rainbows through deep river pools. There beneath a sky as deep and wild as their love, they created new life where none had been before, boys with Wolfe's fluid strength and girls with Jessica's laughter and fire.

And through all the peace and storms of all their years, Jessica was the sun in Wolfe's sky, bringing light and life to Tree That Stands Alone.